W9-CYG-007

EMPRESS
OF
THE SPLENDID
SEASON

Also by Oscar Hijuelos

Our House in the Last World
The Mambo Kings Play Songs of Love
The Fourteen Sisters of Emilio Montez O'Brien
Mr. Ives' Christmas

EMPRESS

OF

THE SPLENDID

SEASON

Oscar Hijuelos

HarperFlamingo
An Imprint of HarperCollins*Publishers*

HarperCollins books may be purchased for educational, business, or sales promotional use. For information please write: Special Markets Department, HarperCollins Publishers, Inc., 10 East 53rd Street, New York, NY 10022.

FIRST EDITION

Designed by Robin Arzt

Library of Congress Cataloging-in-Publication Data

Hijuelos, Oscar.
   The empress of the splendid season : a novel — 1st ed.
     p. cm.
    ISBN 0-06-017570-2
    I. Title.
   PS3558.I376E56   1999
   813'.54—dc21   98-34798

99 00 01 02 03 ❖ / RRD 10 9 8 7 6 5 4 3 2 1

EMPRESS
OF
THE SPLENDID
SEASON

Memory of a Cleaning Lady in New York (1957—1962)

In 1957 when her beloved husband, Raul, had fallen ill, Lydia España went to work, cleaning the apartments of New Yorkers much better off than herself. She took up that occupation because Raul, with jobs in two restaurants, had waited on so many tables, for so many hours, and had snuck so many drinks from the bar and smoked so many cigarettes, that his taut heart had nearly burst, half killing him one night at the age of forty-one. (Lydia imagined the heart muscles all twisted like a much used table rag.) She went to work because, aside from their own children, her husband had a second little family to look after in Cuba (the devil!) and because, among other reasons involving the vicissitudes of making money, they were suddenly "poor."

She was thirty-two years old and carried herself with the imperious attitude of a young movie starlet (so she fancied). Thin but voluptuous enough to draw the attentions of men, she had fiercely intelligent eyes, a lovely and inquisitive face; her dark and curly hair falling to her shoulders. She had been living in New York for ten years by then, her family's third-floor walk-up apartment situated on a block of tenements in a working-class neighborhood not too far from the 125th Street and Broadway El. Her English was adequate but not good enough for the Woolworth's store manager to hire her, nor for the Macy's personnel department. For a few afternoons a week, she found a "part-time" in the neighborhood, at the 120th Street A&P, sweeping wood shavings off the narrow and musty floors and dusting dirt and moth wings off the tops of thirty-two-ounce-size juice cans and detergent bottles that lined the aisles, a routine that often forced her to crouch down, embarrassing Lydia when friends like Juanita Lopez or Mrs.

3

Esposito, whose husband owned a pizzeria, came along. On her way home she found herself clicking her tongue and shaking her head, as if to ask, "How did a woman of my background end up doing this?" She had such thoughts because in her other life, before she had arrived in New York, she had been the spoiled, hard-to-reach daughter of a businessman who was also the *alcalde*—or mayor—of their small town in Cuba, by the sea. She had her own maids and servants and a carriage driver/chauffeur back then, and she had never given the idea of work or the suffering of others much thought; but that was before her family, turning unfairly against her with a nearly Biblical wrath, had banished her, unprepared to contend with an indifferent world.

And now, who, looking at her putting away soup cans in a supermarket aisle, would believe her? Or care?

People in the neighborhood always found Lydia a little aloof and arrogant, for early on she had made certain conscious choices about whom her family would consort with. It had nothing to do with money—few in that part of the city had money. But she made distinctions between people without money who had class and refinement and those who did not. Like her best friend, Mireya Sanchez, a petite and beautiful public high-school teacher whom she had met at church, or Mr. Fuentes, the butcher who was also a poet—("The blood of eternity is in this steak"). Or the piano tuner, Mr. Haines, who worked at Juilliard, a few blocks away, and sometimes brought her family the odd classical recording, usually something like Liszt, which they never listened to if they could help it. (To Perez Prado, yes, to Marion Sunshine, yes, to Frank Sinatra, yes.) Or their postman, Mr. Brown, a black man with the clearest eyes on the earth and a scent of sweet lilacs about him, the most courteous of her acquaintances; or, on the floor below, that professorial fellow who was always traveling far away, Dr.

4

Merton, an archeologist or classicist of some kind with his scholarly preoccupations and eclectic tastes, the kind of gent to wear a Japanese kimono, and an ankh hanging off a chain around his neck, while throwing out his garbage; or Mr. Belky, the pharmacist, in his heavy suits even in the summer, who used to bring the family the urgent telephone messages he received in their name, as when Raul fell ill. (They did not yet have a telephone.) Then, to the contrary, there were *la gente baja*—the drunks on the street, the petty Irish gangsters who sold cartons of Virginia cigarettes out of the trunks of their Oldsmobiles down by the 125th Street pier, the drug addicts, the crazy people who shouted and threw parties all night, broke bottles in the alleys and tossed their garbage out the windows—persons whom Lydia would have been happy to live without.

Still, they were a part of her world.

With her head held high, and posture correct, Lydia had always conducted herself with a quiet dignity, dressing as well as she could afford and seeing to it that her children, Rico and Alicia, who were four and six years old, behaved genteelly. (Poor Rico, with his hair slicked to the sides and parted straight down the middle, and his shiny black shoes, high white knee socks, matador jacket, and knee pants.) Even while shopping in the crowded Klein's department store on 14th Street, where she hoped to save a few dollars—the way of the wizened poor—Lydia tried to maintain a ladylike demeanor, reluctant to push and shove and elbow her way through to the bins stacked with three-for-a-dollar boys' underwear, the seventy-nine-cents ladies' blouses, the two-dollar sneakers, or whatever else the sales help dumped from big cardboard cartons onto the "marked down" tables. Liking to think of herself as upper lower class, she moved through her days with an otherworldly detachment (shock) that sometimes put people off—"What, you think you

5

somebody better?"—and with a patience for the rudeness of others that, years later, she would say other people did not deserve. (And if she fought back, struggling over a few dollars saved on a pair of trousers or a skirt, and won, her "triumph" hardly seemed worth the trouble, at least to her children, or so they would remember, the mad scrambling for bargains always leaving them with feelings of shame.) For all that, there was always someone to express a miserable opinion about the "pretentious lady." Sometimes, as Lydia walked toward her stoop from the subway, she saw people scowling at her through their windows (or so she imagined), and on one occasion a neighborhood kid, running along the sidewalk, shouted, "Hey, Queenie," and threw a clump of lit firecrackers at Lydia and her children, the charges exploding by their feet. Alicia, in her lemon-yellow raincoat, began to cry as if the world was going to end, asking her, "Why was that man so mean?" in the same way she asked about why her Poppy was sick. To that, as to many other questions, Lydia had no answer.

She'd sigh, move on.

Livelihoods

She had tried, as well, to master the cash register at the pharmacy, thanks to Mr. Belky, without much success, and for a time also worked at Jimmy's Steak House on Lexington Avenue, where her husband had fallen ill, but she was not too fond of Jimmy and, in any event, he did not pay her much and she disliked hanging around all day in that kitchen, with its hamburgers and sizzling vats of shortening and fries. (The smell stuck to her the way it stuck to her husband, Raul, who could never shake it.)

In any event, her days found her fretfully, diligently trying a number of things—jobs of the poor—before entering into the occupation that would be her own for the next thirty-three years, a cleaning lady.

With a widowed Cuban friend named Concha Alonso she had gone door to door trying to sell Korean-made toys; she had cut hair, ever so briefly, for the pretty Cortez sisters on Amsterdam Avenue (it did not work out); had hawked, in her own aristocratic way, candy on street corners; and, with another friend, Virginia, whose husband was also sick, attempted to peddle homemade shampoos to the big department stores, a few of their products taken by some kindly East Harlem merchants.

There had been another enterprise with her friend Concha, to make and sell their own cloth dolls for Christmas. These they'd fashioned after the famous American Raggedy Anne doll, but with black and cinnamon faces, sewing five dozen of them in Concha's apartment on West 111th Street. On those days these ladies, the widow and the near widow, with good-natured fervor, cut, measured, and sewed, skills that, incidentally, they had acquired in New York, years ago, as new arrivals, the two having met in a sewing factory downtown. As they worked, Concha's elderly grandmother paced in the hallway, perturbed because they had taken over her bedroom. Tormenting them, she carried on about their "idiotic stupidities." "If you were birds," she warned them, "you two would be swimming in the ocean."

Every now and then Concha, thinking about her husband and how he'd left her alone to fend for her family, would begin to cry. When that happened Lydia's practical—or impractical—side came out. She would get some cold cuts from the corner, the cheap kind, like baloney, and a ten-cent loaf of Wonder Bread and a big bottle of Ballantyne Ale and they would sit in the kitchen with their modest feast, laughing and telling dirty stories, even as the grandmother's voice echoed in the halls: "Next thing you two will be on relief. May God pity your souls."

The dolls turned out nicely, but failed to sell, so that they ended up donating most of them to an orphanage and giving the rest away to the kids of the neighborhood. They had a better success setting up a last-minute Christmas-tree stand in front of Freddy's Bodega on 122nd Street; these two attractive *latina* women, in their thirties and dressed like lumberjacks, put out a sign that said "Lovely X-Mas trees for sale," but the trees, of questionable origin, were often dry and brittle, the needles dropping off, even as their buyers, happy with the bargain prices, dragged them through the snow. Then there were the homemade cakes for Three Kings Day, or the Epiphany celebration, which went well. But even that little success dried up after the holidays, and Lydia, faced with the responsibility of supporting her husband and kids, without a family in the States to help her, and with friends who were as poor as herself, passed some difficult nights, trembling in her husband's arms.

Raul
Despite her troubles, the Christmas that followed Raul's illness was good, thanks to the generosity of local merchants and friends, and Rico's dapper Cuban godfather, *su padrino,* Mario, a singer who worked for the Transit Authority and who always showed up at the apartment with shopping bags of pastries and candies and gifts for the children. His were welcome visits—no chicken neck stews for dinner when he came over— but even so, Lydia's apprehensions grew daily because lurking behind every positive thought and hope for the future was the suspect health and behavior of her husband. Within three months after his attack, Raul began sneaking smokes on the street (she saw him once from the bus coming uptown on Broadway) and drinking booze again, amber pint and half-pint bottles collected at the bottom of the garbage cans in the kitchen. For all her distress, she couldn't blame the poor man.

What happened to him had put an official end to his youth and any illusions of immortality, and that weighed heavily upon him, though he, with slouched shoulders, and lost in thought, did not, in those days, mention a word about it.

In fact, at first, from a certain angle, Raul seemed nearly optimistic, dressing in a suit a few days a week, setting out to make social calls and, if the weather was fine, taking the kids to the park or the zoo. On Sundays he accompanied Lydia and the children to church. During those Masses, he sat through the service with what the children would remember as a "look of curious expectation" upon his face, as if he were awaiting the sudden appearance of Jesus or the Holy Ghost over the altar, the ritual and music inspiring him, his brow gnarled with thought and contemplation—of death? of afterlife?—though he did not give the responses and rarely sang along with the hymns. He always threw a dollar into the collection basket, even if, in Lydia's opinion, they could not afford to, and she would say, "But Raul, God is already rich!" Afterwards, as they would file out into the street, he made a point of telling the Irish priest, Father Malloy, "Good service, *Padre*," and punctuated the compliment by rapping the priest on the back. Then, with Lydia walking silently beside him, he would say things like, "Wouldn't it be nice if we really knew that God exists." And, "But of course, He does," for the sake of Rico and Alicia, who were sometimes confounded by the doubt or disappointment in his eyes.

Raul did not go back to work for a year, until the late spring of 1958, and after a while, the tedium of staying home got to him. Sleeping badly, he had dreams of his own flower-covered coffin appearing in their living room, awakening with a start, and pacing, exhausted and tense, in the mornings. When someone mentioned that he might be better off with a hobby, Raul, a man of simple tastes, seemed at a loss, as he was one of those

9

fellows who'd known only work from early childhood. Aside from fishing upstate or off the Hudson pier for polluted bass, and watching television, he was hard-pressed to engage in an outside interest, even when Lydia bought him a Chinese checkers game, which he played with the children, and a piece of balsa wood that she hoped would inspire him to take up carving. He did practice on the Hohner concert harmonica that Lydia bought him, learning the melody to "Moon River," and sometimes he sat in the living room strumming on his old beat-up guitar, a true love of his life, but just as often, feeling perplexed by his enforced indolence, he stashed his instruments in the closet, to gather dust.

At night, he would stand by the window, watching the moon rise over the projects, Harlem bursting with life, receding into the distance, to the east and north.

The Kind of Cuban Who Lived Mainly for Work

The poor man should have seen his illness coming: by the time the pains had started creeping up his arms, they'd been married for six years and he, never saying a word about what he was feeling, used to gasp for breath as he slept. Some days he barely made it out of bed, but he always dressed for work, no matter how he felt. When Lydia would tell him, "Stay home today," he refused, for that was not part of his manly duty. Even though the pains had been going on for months, Raul just imagined that they were muscular, from arthritis, as he was always lifting heavy trays and hoisting chairs onto table tops at the end of the last shift. The kind of Cuban who lived mainly to work, he ignored his symptoms. When his chest felt sore and his arm sometimes went numb, he used hot compresses and Vick's Eucalyptus ointment, tried short naps between shifts, whenever possible, took a lot of aspirins, but never found the time to see a doctor, despite Lydia's occasional entreaties, as "destiny was destiny."

And why waste the money on a doctor or drag his tired bones down to the public clinic, when he could spend it on other things, like candies for his children, or on gambling with his pals from Brooklyn, or on Arsenio Rodriguez records to play on the hi-fi; why bother? he would say, even as things hurt inside.

A Long Night

One afternoon during the autumn of 1957, Mr. Belky, the pharmacist, climbed the three flights up to the apartment and, hat in hand, stood breathless and sweaty before their door, saying, "Mrs. España, I haff sometink for you."

With four-year-old Rico by her side, and in the half-light of the foyer, Lydia read the note in her careful and deliberate manner, her lips moving with every penciled word. Manny from the restaurant had called to say that Raul had been taken to Knickerbocker Hospital after falling ill while waiting tables. She read it over a few times before reaching into her skirt pocket to give Mr. Belky a dime (he refused it), and then she put on a different pair of shoes and dress. Leaving her children with her upstairs neighbor, Mrs. Lopez, she got someone from the building to take her by car to the hospital.

She passed the night in an emergency ward filled with unfortunates, and pacing impatiently outside the room where the doctors were doing something—what she did not know—to her dear husband, Raul. Part of that night she prayed, though she was not especially prayerful—or brimming with gratitude or hope—because her husband was still a young man and did not deserve "all this." Trying to think positive thoughts, she nevertheless kept worrying about finding the money for his funeral, if it came to that, and wished to God that she had not, earlier in the day, been so aloof with him, when he, surprising her from behind, had started to caress her breasts through her

11

cotton nightgown as she stood before their bedroom mirror, brushing out her long dark hair.

"Raul, *por favor*," she had said.

During that long night, with sirens sounding through the hive-wired gray windows, she missed her family. She had not seen them since she left Cuba, hearing little save from one of her sisters, who'd had a kind heart and felt sorry for her. (Thank God for friends like Mireya, for she would have been desolately lonely without her.) Because her mood worsened she found herself shouting at the nurses to do something more for her husband (Lord, how she worried about his dying alone). A social worker, who spoke some Spanish, managed to calm her down, giving her a couple of "relaxation" tablets. But the next morning, when she had to stand over his bed in the ward, surrounded by machines and with wires and beeping instruments attached to him, the strangeness—and difficulty—of her situation saddened her.

What had happened was this: he was working his day shift at Jimmy's Steak House in midtown, a joint whose good specials were popular with the middle-rung executives and office workers who lunched there. Balanced on one of his shoulders was a large metal tray, heavy with four Tuesday specials—each platter holding a nicely grilled twelve-ounce porterhouse steak, smothered in butter, salt, and a few sprigs of parsley, an aluminum-wrapped baked potato with sour cream and chives inside, and a rubbery-tasting salad (the kind that was delivered in big plastic bags once or twice a week). Moving through the crowded room, weaving between the press of chairs, he had the sudden impression of being whacked in the chest with a baseball. Turning around he had expected to see shattered glass flying about from the front window on Lexington Avenue, as that would have explained why people were so startled, and then he realized that they were interested in him and that he was falling and that the heavy tray was dropping from his hands. Then, he found himself resting on the restaurant's tile floor, the mess of food all around him, the back of his head aching. Even though he could barely breath, he was worried about making a bad impression on his boss, Jimmy, who had come out from behind the cash register to take a look at him. There were others—the maître d', Luigi, and one of the kitchen girls, Maria, and one of the cooks, José, and several other waiters, Maurizio the Neapolitan and that other Cuban fellow with whom he worked, Manny—looming over him, all concerned. When they kept repeating his name, "Raul? Raul?" he heard their voices through a room filled with cotton, though the ambient background sound of the restaurant itself was annoyingly loud, plates and utensils clacking like seashells (perhaps he was thinking about the seaside towns of his youth in Cuba).

Through all of that what Raul really cared about was keeping his job. He had tried to get up, and although kindly hands were touching him, and Maria had undone his collar and loosened his bow tie, and someone else had thought to take off his bright red jacket (which he'd never liked anyway), he somehow felt that he was being punished—for what he did not know. As an overhead fan turned slowly, he noticed the nice, slightly gritty art deco molding of the tin ceiling above him. And then, as someone lifted his head onto a pillow, with the smell of potatoes and bloody grilled meat strong in his nostrils, he descended into a kind of sleep.

So it was that on certain mornings, when she would sit in the kitchen trying to figure out the week's budget, Lydia nearly came to tears, feeling underqualified and undeserving of those challenges and responsibilities suddenly imposed upon her. Nothing in her youth, nothing in her loveliness, or her sexual ardor, or a husband who had never wanted her to work and promised that he would labor like an animal for the family, had prepared her for this. Just trying to add the numbers up right, or fretting that something terrible would happen if she did not pay the electric bills or rent on time, sometimes put a broodish scowl on her pretty face, made her quick to judgment, and quick to unfairly punish her kids. Gradually her children began to see in her a certain severity that was never really intended for them, the fitfulness of a once spoiled child, used to having things come easily, now having to count pennies and resew old clothes and look around for bargains and work and work and work.

Sometimes, on her most heartsick days, Lydia, feeling hard-edged about reality, would attempt to recapture the hopeful-ness of her youth, and yet, asking God to look out for Raul and her children, she felt that no one was there.

Still she was greatly comforted by the crucifixes and images of the Virgin she kept in the apartment; and when, in Raul's company, she attended Mass, a nice feeling of wealth and grandeur came over her, for churches were the mansions of the poor.

The Angel

Once, in the days when Raul was in the hospital, she half-fainted while standing by the edge of a subway platform, from fatigue or sadness, nearly falling in front of an approaching train, as if the platform had suddenly tilted. Aware of what was happen-ing and carrying a bag of groceries to bring home to the family, she had felt more worried about the breakfast rolls (ten for fifty cents!), which she had found in a bakery near the hospital, spilling out of her bag onto the track, than about herself. Just then, as she was toppling forward, her eyes closing, a man in an epauletted London Fog trench coat (all the rage in that epoch) who had noticed her unsteadiness caught her by the arm and pulled her back toward the turnstiles. He made no big deal about it, telling her, "You should take more care, lady." Thanking him, she collected herself and made her way home safely, preparing sandwiches for the children, and that evening, when mentioning this incident to Mireya, she told her: "I don't know what to think. Maybe that man was standing there for a particular reason."

Years later, she would change that to: "Once, in the days when Raul first became sick, and I was coming back from the hospital, I nearly fell from a train platform but an angel saved me. *Te juro. Un angel de Dios.*"

Lydia, the Cuban Cleaning Woman (1958)

In the early spring, the year after Raul had fallen ill, it was the butcher, Mr. Fuentes, who sold her several pounds of chicken legs and said, "The soul of the sun kissed the flesh of this bird, as delicious as life itself." And with that, knowing her troubles, Mr. Fuentes came up with the name of an acquaintance who cleaned apartments for a living. This "little bird," another Cuban woman, spoke with Lydia and put her onto a forlorn college professor whose apartment on West 110th Street was a horror. She had told Lydia, "Listen, it may sometimes feel bad cleaning up after others, but you are left alone and can choose your hours. . . . Sometimes these people can be very nice."

She called the professor, who sounded like a lonely old man, and first stood before his door on a rainy April afternoon, the scent of pissy kitty-litter boxes, disintegrating books, bachelorhood, and rotting linoleum hitting her instantly; and though she smiled and nodded at him respectfully—to her mind he resembled the genius Albert Einstein—she set woefully about

15

doing something which, in her youth, she could never have imagined, being someone else's servant. In Cuba she had never washed her own clothes or ironed, cleaned the floor, or even made her own bed, and when she had daydreamed of a future, she had not seen herself on her knees scrubbing the mildewed tile walls of a bathroom in the seventh-floor apartment of a retired and not altogether tidy university professor.

Now she passed those days telling herself that such labors were "temporary," for such work did not come easily to her. In those circumstances she learned that there was a difference between cleaning up after someone else's shit and cleaning up after your own and that there was very little she would not do for her family, no matter how unhappy she sometimes felt.

And there was something else: she almost began to enjoy her access to other people's homes and the *cositas* that defined their lives.

The Spanish Cleaning Lady

At first, it took her a while to get used to the idea, but soon Lydia, willfully attending to her duties, was cleaning for other college professors who lived near Columbia University; and these jobs led to even more jobs. In time, she got her own kit of rags and scrub brushes, and two light-blue cotton maid's outfits hung in her closet, bargain-priced dresses that she bought from a Hasidic fellow on Delancey Street in downtown Manhattan. ("Look here, Mireya," she once said to her friend. "*Qué barato son.*") She began to enjoy the odd solitude of the profession (at least people were not watching you all the time), learned to laugh at things, and to greet employers with a smile.

This back before she grew tired of it all.

Riding the bus or train to work she would make the acquaintance of many other cleaning ladies and housemaids and delight in their company. She'd say. "*Oyeme, chica,* where'd you get

16

those shoes?" to strike up a conversation. Or, "It's almost the weekend. What are you going to do?" And in those days, just before the event of the Cuban revolution, she would launch into harmless nostalgia about her *pueblo* and how she often missed it. She knew the look—the tennis shoes, the shopping bag filled with wax-paper-wrapped sandwiches, the thin twelve-carat neck chains with a crucifix or Virgin medallion; the slightly distracted, heartbroken, and daydreamy expression on the ladies' faces, wistful mascaraed eyes, shoulders primly back, raincoats in the spring and autumn, heavy coats and woolen hats in the winter, and high rain boots, especially in the snow (from fear of losing a job over sick days). She knew where they shopped—Klein's on 14th Street, John's Bargain Stores throughout the city, Annie's on 125th, Alexander's downtown or in the Bronx. She knew their watery eyes in the flu season, the early morning depressions in January and February when everybody, even the rich bosses, were melancholic, when the ladies only wanted to go home to their kids. ("*Ay, how I wanted to stay in bed.*") She could practically read their thoughts as they looked up admiringly at the Miss Subways ads in the overhead racks, knew how they played the numbers and daydreamed about winning new washing machines on the *Queen for a Day* television show. She knew the magazines in their coat pockets (Spanish-language *Look, Vanidades,* or *La Bohemia*), the occasional letter from San Juan or Mayaguez, Santiago or Havana, reread in the jostle and crowds of the subways, again and again ever so slowly, to help pass the early morning loneliness. Or a New Testament or some book opened on their lap— on dreams or an aspect of the supernatural (*Living Your Days by Numbers, The Meanings of Your Dream Last Night, Why the Spirits Have Reason to Care*). There were the aching hips, the slightly bent backs, the thick nylons with runs in them, bandaged knees and fingers, cracked nails, the lavender perfume, the oversized purses, the change bags—hands held out carefully monitoring the change and counting out the two tokens' fare— the way the cleaning ladies nervously pressed their purses to their breasts whenever some rough-looking kids came along, those few dollars a significant part of their futures.

Sometimes, despite all her boundless "dignity"—that wondrous pride-saving province of the poor and working class— she got up in the morning and vomited, not from morning sickness or from something she'd eaten, but out of a kind of despair, the "bad nerves" that come from getting down on one's knees to wipe clean a stranger's toilet; from swallowing one's pride, out of necessity.

Quite simply, she had turned around to find that Lydia España, from Cuba, the Empress of the Splendid Season as her husband once thought of her, had somehow become Lydia the Spanish cleaning lady.

And she went to work because she didn't want her kids to feel poor or disadvantaged. She wanted to make sure that even if neither she nor Raul knew how to read or write English in any educated way, Alicia and Rico would learn what they had not. There would be no shortages of pencils or notebooks or school books if they needed them. She embraced her profession for the family's sake, for the future; so that when the handsome young Cuban salesman came to their door selling a 1959 edition of the *World Book Encyclopedia*, and spoke of the future ("*Señora*, you look as intelligent as you are beautiful, and the *nenes* obviously deserve the best. Believe me, *Señora*, they will all go to college reading these books. *Eso yo le juro.* I promise you . . . "), she had the money to buy that set for them.

(. . . *And if the truth be told, she would tell herself one day, she bought that encyclopedia not only to help her kids with*

18

their education but because the salesman was tall and well groomed and smelled sweetly of Old Spice, and because his hands were well manicured and his alert eyes nearly melted her heart: she would have bought a dead whale from him that night, because as he, showing her an example, flipped through its fresh ink-smelling pages and acetate transparencies—of the human body and the planets of the solar system—she nearly shook and had to contain her desires, to kiss him or to cry in his arms over Raul, or from a kind of bodily loneliness—she did not know. ...)

Empress of the Splendid Season (1949)

The whole business left Lydia on edge, but her worries only strengthened her resolve and, as well, deepened her nostalgia for that "other" Raul, the man she had fallen in love with. They'd met at a Valentine's Day party in a social club in the Bronx intended for Spanish-speaking lonely hearts. It was 1949 and Lydia, working in the sewing factory at the time, had been dragged to the party by friends. Raul had gone there to work, waiting tables, and as he poured some of the "table rum" into her glass of Coca-Cola, a conversation had started up between them: about Cuba. He was thirty-four at the time. He wore a white uniform that had brass buttons and smelled like freshly bleached laundry. With a long and angular face and overly brilliantined dark hair, combed back, with its receding lines by the temples, a thin, barely prominent mustache, a terseness about his features gave his face the quality of a mask. Or of a matador. He was not quite handsome, but nevertheless attractive, not so much for his deeply set *gallego* features, or his sharp nose, his wide creased brow—that came from a poor man's worries—but for his general dress and manner, and for the compassion and longing (or suffering) that she saw in his

19

eyes. Although there were better-looking men in the world, to be sure, like the polished fellows circulating around the chiffon-covered tables eyeing all the unattached *pollitas,* there seemed to be something infinitely more refined about this waiter, who had a quiet and nearly reverent manner when it came to his job.

In that hot and crowded social club, she read something else in his eyes, *work ethic* and *decency,* and in his manner she saw someone who would show her respect, in the way that others might not. And she saw the possibility of salvation.

During the course of the evening he asked her out, and their courtship, which began the next weekend with a date on a Circle Line cruise around the island of Manhattan, flourished in the social clubs and dance halls of the city. For six months Raul diligently appeared before the door of the rooming house where she lived, on Lenox Avenue and 116th Street, at exactly seven-thirty every Saturday night (if you were peering out of her window you might have seen him pacing about the sidewalk below, checking his watch, and waiting for the proper moment to ring her *timbre,* as he always arrived early). He brought her flowers, picked stem by stem at the local Italian florist (now that was work he would have liked, he used to think), and a box of Schrafft's chocolates that Lydia saved for the movies.

He usually took her to the Roseland Ballroom or to one of the more famous dance halls on 110th Street, a ten-minute walk away. Ever formal and attentive to Lydia, he remained the gentleman, at first preferring the slow dances, the boleros and ballads, over the mambos and cha-cha-chás, and, though he was not a romantic sort, the right piece of music, say *"Dulce Engaño"* ("Sweet Deception"), could bring out the poet hiding in his soul; a few drinks helped too—he liked no-nonsense whiskey. On one of those Saturday nights during a slow dance, with his face pressed against hers, his nostrils reveling in the scent of her long and wavy hair, which she'd earlier washed with some special rosewater concoction, he recited a poem. He had made the words up, during his many trips carrying trays from kitchen to table in one of the joints he worked in. Reveling in the scent of her hair, he began:

Lydia, I am to you, as a sparrow adoring the sky;
Lydia, you are as the moon reflecting upon the water,
which is my soul;
Lydia, you are the queen of queens of beauty,
the Empress of my love,
and you preside over the splendidness
of my feelings for you,
like the morning sun on the most glorious day
of the most beautiful and splendid season,
which is love . . .

Swallowing, unable to keep his head from shaking, and dabbing his face with a handkerchief, he then asked her to become "the wife of an ordinary worker, a humble waiter. . . ."

And she had answered: "Yes."

Later, as he always did, he brought her home. Usually they would quietly kiss for a few moments—not wanting the landlady next door to hear them—and he would head back to Brooklyn, but that night, in a celebratory mood, she took his hand and, throwing self-restraint out the window, pulled him into her narrow room with its narrow bed, where she exhibited, in an unrestrained manner, the kind of foolhardy proclivity that had gotten her into trouble with her family in Cuba, years before. (For reasons she did not always understand, as a young proper girl from a good family, she had a propensity for giving of herself to others.)

21

On that evening, long before she, the Empress of the Splendid Season, became Lydia the Spanish cleaning lady, her scent of *eau de roses* shampoo and Chiclets mixed with the sweat of bodily ardor; a kind of intoxication overwhelmed her, as she, for the first time, beheld, kissed, fondled, and holified the body of that man, even as he spread and touched the thighs and breasts of his woman. . . . They stayed in that bed until she'd bitten her right hand raw to keep from screaming out; until her neck ached from so many writhing turns, until a dampness made their skins stick whenever they moved. They stayed in bed until the early morning, when the *Señora* in the apartment next door began to click on lights and move pots and pans and flushed the toilet; until they heard the milkman's truck on the street below, and the other seamstresses and factory workers who shared the same kinds of rooms she had began to stir, perhaps daydreaming about love.

Quietly Raul had gotten dressed and, as she dozed in bed, with his two-tone cordovans in hand, he made his way out and tiptoed down the stairs. Seeing him by the door, and the pure affection in his gaze, she had stretched her body and slipped into a delicious sleep.

It was that state of intoxication, a moment of mutual glory, that Lydia remembered in the hard days.

A Few of Her Jobs
Some jobs took her over to sunny apartments on Riverside Drive, others as far east as First Avenue. In many of the buildings there were doormen and porters, to hold open the doors and to keep the marble fixtures sparkling. Often as not, in crowded lobbies or elevators she'd stand off to the side, as unobtrusively as possible, her gaze fixed upon her shoelaces; more often than not, she entered the building through a service entrance and got the apartment keys from the superintendent or doorman, who kept them hanging on a board.

She worked for a lot of Jewish people, mainly over on the West Side—some of them old ladies whose heavily accented English she could barely understand; often they would hang around her as she worked, following her from room to room, or she would find herself accompanying them on walks in the park. Kindhearted and glad for the companionship, some of these ladies would hold her tightly by the arm as if she were in the family—and sometimes, her heart teeming with both affection and resentment, she would feel like tearing away from them, her head busy with thoughts about the way her own family in Cuba had once rejected her.

Other bosses had last names like Perkins, Spencer, and Monroe and hardly ever spoke to her, outside of telling her what to do. If they were bachelors, their apartments tended toward a lingering scent of pipe tobacco, of a cherry blend; the younger ones played golf or tennis and often kept pictures of themselves in yachtsmen caps posed atop the prow of a boat. Their vacations were spent in places like Newport, Martha's Vineyard, Cape Cod, and Nantucket, names that meant nothing to her, though the photographs she saw while dusting the piano top and mantels seemed pleasant enough, proof of life far beyond the world she knew.

Mostly Americans, her employers were largely unaware of her past. Few knew that she was born in Cuba and, if they reflected about this at all, they generally thought of her as Spanish, as in "the Spanish cleaning lady"—as someone tirelessly and, perhaps, ever-happily dedicated to the well-being and orderliness of their lives.

There was a certain Mr. Bernhardt of West End Avenue, an actor, whose career had long since gone into decline; Mrs. Levine, whose husband, the poor man, had thrown himself in front of a Lexington Avenue train; Miss Jenkins, a young actress, in a wheelchair; blind Mr. Canterbury. And many others, over the years, among them the occasional perennial "bachelor" who she suspected of enjoying the intimate company of other perennial bachelors.

A Brownstone Off Central Park West

One fellow, a certain attorney of about thirty-five, lived on West 83rd Street, his home a brownstone, with big hanging pots of ferns and potted trees, and with Tiffany windows, all kinds of antiques, and a fireplace. Prosperous and dapper, he seemed the orderly type, whose worst mess might be a few dishes left over from a frozen TV dinner or Chinese food eaten on the run and left in the sink. She liked him because he was impeccable in his dress. Sweet smelling with cedar wood and seasoned leather, his closet was filled with Parisian shoes and three-piece suits from a store called Brixton's of Savile Row in London, the labels of which she read with fascination— Europe? England? France? Who in her recent acquaintance had ever been to Europe, that elegant place? And she liked him because he tried to speak Spanish with her, when many others would not—could not. He gave her carfare and sandwich money and always treated her with respect.

She would generally go there on Wednesday afternoons, just after a weekly job on West End, but on one occasion, when mixing up her schedule, Lydia arrived to find the general tidiness of his place turned upside down: cushions were thrown about, curtains pulled to the floor, wine bottles and pieces of shredded clothing everywhere. Having cleaned the kitchen and bathroom, she eventually made her way to his bedroom, where strewn about the bed and floor were countless photographs of handsome and muscular naked young men in various states of arousal. Her face heated up and she blushed, and although one

24

part of her wanted to leave that room instantly, she found herself sitting at the edge of the bed examining these shots of men performing certain acts. They made her feel *queasy* at first, then *ashamed*—was it a reflection on her to be so taken with those photographs?—then *nostalgic*, for she had been with some magnificently proportioned men in her past—and finally *giddy*—it all seemed so funny.

Then she came across certain devices for the giving of erotic pleasure, and she supposed, erotic pain; and with them she noticed the condition of the bed sheets, which frightened her.

He had a cat, a darling fluff ball of a kitten with a delicate bell collar, who cowered under his bed (as she would have), his claws sinking deeper and deeper into the carpet the harder Lydia tried to move him.

"*Gato,*" she said, "you poor, poor thing."

Worried about losing this work, should he find out that she knew his secrets, she decided to hide the fact that she had been to the apartment (another part of her wanted to chide and lecture him about the cardinal sins). Dutifully, she went back into the kitchen and pulled from all the cabinets those plates and jars and utensils that she had put away, and she spread some water around in the bathroom, replaced the towels and the dampened bath mat, his laundry that she had planned to wash. She found herself reaching into the garbage for handfuls of ash and butts to refill the pipe and cigarette ashtrays that she'd emptied out; in time, after putting things back into serene disarray, she'd left the place more or less as she'd found it; she did not know what else to do.

Returning the next day she found that this employer had hidden everything away. When she next saw him, a couple of weeks later, coming home just as she was leaving, he was carrying some flowers and looked somewhat cross, she hoped from work, but he smiled at the sight of her and said, "Mrs. España, you always leave my home looking so clean."

25

"And you always look so handsome."

"You're too kind."

Altogether, he seemed prim and proper as always, handsome in a blue serge suit. He was courteous, holding the door for her, as she sidled out past him, in her tennis shoes, raincoat, and shopping bag filled with this and thats, *cositas,* and such.

Out onto the street of brownstones between Central Park West and Columbus she'd felt a tremendous relief. It all went well between them from then on, the gentleman pleased with her work, and Lydia to remain in his employ on and off for another twelve years.

Noticing the Pentagram
on Mr. Malone's Bedroom Wall

In those years when she had first started her long lesson in humility and the separation of the classes, she happened to go to work for a gentleman whose involvements with the arcane arts and the supernatural were such that going inside his apartment always made her anxious, as if she were being followed by a ghost. The pay was fair, the street and building pleasant enough. But she had wondered why one of her colleagues, Miriam Flores, a Dominican woman with a possessive attitude about her clientele, who resided on Lydia's "two-faced" list, had so eagerly passed on this gentleman's name in the first place: Noel Malone (or Moran or Mulhany—the name, which she never wrote down, fell oddly on her ear).

"I appreciate it very much, Miriam, but why are you giving me this work?"

"My daughter just had another baby," she told Lydia. "And coming down from the Bronx wears me out. Besides, I know that the *señor* will like you very much."

"Okay," said Lydia. "Give me his address."

Arriving at Mr. Malone's apartment one morning she came across certain decorative flourishes that were not commonly found, even in the apartments of the eccentric rich. Books were everywhere on high shelves and framed prints covered the walls—for he was an art collector—and he owned numerous statues, namely of angels, cupids, and winged creatures that were set out on tables and pedestals. He had a fondness for the tangled nature of plants and vinery. His occupation? He seemed to work in a profession that required a lot of thinking for he had a formal study. (Perhaps he was a "shrink," or *psicólogo*, as her son Rico would one day be, but she could not say for sure.) He had numerous diplomas on one wall and many many books, in various languages.

But that was not what she found unusual. Dusting in the master bedroom she noticed on the wall above Mr. Malone's bed a *pentagram* faintly painted in blue, and in his bathroom, the wall above the commode was covered with crucifixes hung upside down. (He kept stacks of *Playboy* magazines there, too.)

Though she was tempted to set the crucifixes right, she knew enough to mind her own business, one of the cleaning lady's most important rules.

Still, there was something generally "irregular," as she would tell Raul, about the atmosphere of the apartment. Though on a high floor and filled with light, the apartment seemed, in some way, perpetually dark. Perhaps it was due to the abundance of animal-footed cabinets and chairs, the heavy pleated window drapes somehow funerary. (What of bright and cheerful colors?) When she would peek out the window, to admire the wide street and handsome buildings, like a Persian boulevard in the setting sun, she would have the momentary apprehension that someone had entered the room behind her, though no one had.

Once she looked out and heard whispers and reasoned that the pipes, in heating up, had made the noise, but then, in the kitchen she heard a voice say to her in Spanish, "Where are you going?"

She grew uneasy working there. Where she had once viewed the inventory of his apartment with the same degree of detachment she felt for others—dusting a room filled with low- and high-class *tarecos* or *chucherías*, bric-a-brac and apartment nonsense—the contents of Mr. Malone's apartment began to play upon her superstitious side, that part of her that had absorbed the magic of *santería* while growing up in Cuba, the things she used to hear about the resurrection of the dead and spells she half believed to that day, even if she had been raised a traditional Catholic.

In his hallways there were cabinets in which he kept certain clay images of ancient Assyrian ritual figures, demonic—*sí, demoníaco!*—beings with bird-beaked heads and broken-wing arms (what archeologists would identify as post-animistic deities), crude, primitive, and barely gods but, undeniably, giving off, in Lydia's uninformed opinion, emanations that made the dark hairs on her arms rise. Among them was a figure, made of rotting wood and painted nearly entirely black, of the Egyptian jackal god, Anubis, also exerting an odd influence on her, for in the evenings when Lydia—done with her day's work and with the small of her back aching and her hands scaly from her ministrations—went home and eventually, after cooking dinner and watching TV, fell asleep, it was a certainty that she would have nightmares. These were not the kind of nightmares to which she was accustomed.

In her nightmares the apartment was on fire, or she would find herself running naked down a crowded street in an unnamed city, or someone would climb in through a window and carry her children away, or she would have to use a toilet on a downtown street during rush hour without finding one, or the El train would fly off its trestle and slam into the apartment building, walls collapsing and people crying out from pain everywhere, or there would be an explosion. Or she'd have a dream in which she would see a version of herself as a child going through the apartment with a sledgehammer smashing up the things she loved, like the lamp that Raul had gotten her one anniversary, with its Chinese style decorations and fantastic porcelain flowers, or Raul's Brazilian catgut guitar on which he, in a relaxed mood, strummed simple chorded versions of old Cuban songs in the evenings. Or the nightmare in which she found herself, inexplicably, kneeling before a stranger sucking him, the man's prolific issuance not sperm but blood. And there were more, like a dream of seeing her husband breaking into pieces like brittle glass. And these made her sit up, heart palpitating in the middle of the night.

Worse was the impression that mysterious beings were appearing in her bedroom at night and plotting to take her away to the lightless world of death: all that from cleaning in Mr. Malone's apartment.

After a while, she decided that the nightmares were not worth the one dollar an hour that she was getting, and on the advice of a clairvoyant friend, Esmeralda, she gave notice. That had not been easy, because Lydia liked her employer. He had a soft and priestly face, sandy hair, and deep blue, innocent eyes. Like many a normal fellow in those days, he favored pinstriped suits, ties, and shirts with button-down collars and seemed like a nice man, but she told him: "I'm pregnant again and the doctor told me I have to stay home. You understand, don't you?"

"Yes, and if you know someone, I'd appreciate it."

She found him a nice Mexican girl, Juanita Perez, whom she knew from "around," but forewarned her: "He's a peculiar sort and his apartment needs a different kind of cleaning."

As for that employer, Mr. Malone? Some years later, while riding the subway, Lydia, fascinated, saw something in the newspapers about him. He had married a much younger woman who, as it turned out, belonged, in the parlance of the newspapers, to his "religious cult." In the religion-crazed 1960s Malone (a devotee of Aleister Crowley, the anti-Christist) became famous among New Yorkers who sought his guidance and the benefit of his powers. Though Malone was considerably older than his wife, she had become ill with an inoperable cancer and had come home from the hospital to die. Despondent, he held nightly rituals over her dying body to restore her health, but she died anyway and the body, left in his living room, surrounded by bowls of rotting fruit and candles and incense, began to give off a strong odor. A maid working next door—not Lydia or Juanita, thank God, but someone else—called the police.

The cops and emergency services people came and removed the corpse, and poor Mr. Malone, head bowed and in a thunderstorm of photographers' cameras, was handcuffed and taken to Rikers Island. And this was what finally happened: released on bail he returned to his apartment and jumped out of his tenth-story window, the most remarkable detail being that, even on impact, with his head crushed on the sidewalk, and body bruised and limp, not a bone had broken through his skin, nor had this gentleman shed a single drop of blood.

"Dios mio, Miriam," she had cried.

Her Life When She Went to Work for Mr. Osprey

Looking back she would always say that she had enjoyed the company of her fellow cleaning ladies but disapproved of the long hours, the lack of benefits, and the cavalier attitudes that some employers had regarding salary ("One dollar an hour is all we *with our grand apartment and trips to Europe and lunches at the Waldorf* can afford to pay you"). The lack of respect and the tightfistedness some employers had about even the smallest raises baffled her; many people penny-pinched when it came to their "help," haggling (*quejando*) over a ten- or fifteen-cent-an-hour increase in pay, why she did not know.

The hardest part of being a cleaning woman had to do with the way people looked at her; often as if she were "nothing." It hurt her most when men did not notice her. The nature of the work itself, the outfit, the end-of-the-day fatigue, the messiness of that labor were not glamorous, so what could she expect? She was not a movie star, not a fashion model on the cover of magazines, not a radio or television glamour girl, not a nightclub singer, not a Miss Subways. Nor was she married to a millionaire or a doctor or a ten-thousand-dollar-a-year advertising man. What could she do? She'd go walking along the street on her way home from work, with her bag and her change of clothes and several other items (lipstick, powder, pack of Kleenex, chewing gum, rosary, a mirror), and recount how dizzily the past had run away from her and how the world, with all its sundry events, had been turned upside down. On some days, while riding the subway, she would sit wishing that some man would pay her a compliment. She'd sigh, catching her reflection in a dirty subway window, her features hollowed out and distorted by the strange yellow light, a feeling of exhaustion with her "new life" sometimes coming over her.

Other Days
She sometimes felt happy. At holidays the porters and doormen would offer her a drink of brandy in their back rooms. She would work on her birthday, March 20, and find herself telling someone that it was her happy day.

Quejando
Through all this, Lydia had maintained an almost mandarin serenity, not always with success, and she tried to impress her children, especially her son, Rico, with a sense of self-worth. Even though she was raising her ever-American children with the notion that they had come from good stock, *gente refinada*, that they were "somebodies," that their maternal grandfather had been the mayor of a small town in Cuba and that she had once been a member of local society—to which they would say, as trains rumbled past their windows, "Yeah, yeah, yeah"—she began to notice an air of resentment about them.

Was it the fact that they saved every penny, walking five extra blocks to save five cents on a quart of milk, or that outside of Coney Island or the occasional trip to Lake Sebago with "Uncle" Mario in his rusty-fendered Pontiac, they never went anywhere? Was it the way that Lydia, whatever the shortcomings of their financial situation, gave the appearance of living well, dressing, or trying to, like a rich lady, when, in reality, she was always worried about money? Or the way she scavenged through Goodwill shops in Upper East Side neighborhoods, or the Salvation Army stores, searching for bargains for herself and for her kids—a habit that distressed them as they got older. (Ask Alicia or Rico about the hand-me-downs that dogged every step of their childhood and adolescence. Or about buying a First Communion dress or suit off one of the racks set up in the living room of a stranger's apartment on 108th Street off Amsterdam, or the kind of sidewalk sales that took place when one of the neighbors died, the widow—usually it was a widow—hawking her late husband's shoes, shirts, and neckties, such items hanging off the railings or displayed folded neatly on the stoop.) There was something the kids could not get out of their minds—that they were of the "lower" class. Was she not a cleaning lady who had to get on her knees? Hadn't Alicia and Rico accompanied her to work and seen the way she could be treated, learning to look at the world through amazed and envious eyes? Hadn't they seen what the "good neighborhoods" were like and how people of means (or what seemed like means) lived? And wasn't her husband "only" a waiter, who nearly dropped dead from being on his feet too long, and drank and smoked too much because he was always worried about money and who, in acts of desperation, threw a lot of it away on the trotters at Belmont and with the hoody gamblers he met at his job? What were they in the end, anyway, but some poor little family, tucked away in an uptown tenement, whose fate, in all likelihood, would turn out like all the others?

With Mr. and Mrs. Osprey (1964)

There had been a Cuban cook, a friend of the family's, who moonlighted in the Ospreys' kitchen when they had special social events, grand dinners to entertain world diplomats and businessmen, and he heard that Mr. Osprey was looking for a new woman to help clean, and he passed this bit of information to Raul.

Before she knew it, Lydia found herself making the first of what would become routine journeys. That day, as on countless others, she'd walk down the hill to the 125th Street El, and catch the number 1 south to Times Square, switch to the shuttle, and follow the stairways to the uptown Lexington Avenue train, getting off at the 68th Street station; the stairway rose up into what might well have been a different city in another country, an avenue of elegant shops and white-and-yellow-tulip-filled traffic islands, and though part of her was arrogant enough to feel the equal of the wealthy people who lived there (if the truth be told, *better*), another part of her was intimidated by the imposing surroundings, as if, while crossing the street, she might come across an immigration official who would demand to see her documents—and send her back to Cuba.

She must have checked the address on Park Avenue, written on a piece of grocery bag, a half-dozen times before coming to Mr. Osprey's majestic dwelling. The building took up a square city block—no matter how many times she laid eyes on its immense ornate facade, its spires like Buckingham Palace, astragaled gates and fountained inner courtyard, its magnificence overwhelmed her. White-gloved doormen, elevator men with sparkling buttons and uniforms and shoes and reverent manner, the gleam and polish of the marble floors, the gold-leafed ornamentations along the high walls, and the pink and blue clouds of trompe l'oeil heaven above the lobby, with its French travertine table and vase of luminous, cream-skinned orchids, the resonant echoes of her every step as she made her way to the elevator—taken together, they struck her as evidence that the good Lord rewarded some, like Mr. Osprey, and castigated others, like herself, with a less easy route in this life.

At the interview, held in his study, Lydia, fragrant with Coco Chanel perfume, comported herself with quiet dignity, even as she was suppressing a great nervousness—she had yet to work for anyone of such means and demeanor; a kind of anxiety about making a good impression on him overwhelmed her. The trappings of his worldly success worked on her psyche like a nearly supernatural emanation. She did not feel bitter, or particularly entitled or "owed" (though at times she would think that were it not for destiny she would be sitting in his lofty club chair). That is, she was nervous because of desire; a desire to *feel* wealthier, if only in a momentary way, and to become a better person, of higher status, simply by association.

A refined and aristocratic attorney in the practice of international business law, Mr. Osprey knew the former president of the United States, Eisenhower, with whom, in his ruddy baldness, he shared a resemblance. Or so she imagined because on top of his Steinway in his living room there indeed was a picture of Mr. Osprey and Eisenhower playing golf together. He was tall, blue-eyed, and nattily dressed in a dark serge suit, white crisp-collared Arrow shirt, red bow tie. He had one of those nice close-to-the-scalp haircuts, the kind one got at the Waldorf Astoria or another fancy hotel (so she imagined), and though his long and gnarly hands had been manicured (this was the kind of fellow you would never see clipping his own nails on a subway or a bus, a practice she considered "low-class"), he suffered the curse of bristly ears and hairy nostrils, which drove her to distraction. During their conversations, she'd break into a little smile and find something else in the room to look at—his nineteenth-century globe of the world, his Explorers Club certificate, another photograph of himself with several important-looking people (among them, as she would later learn, the German rocket scientist Wernher von Braun)—her maternal side wondering how such an otherwise well-put-together man could be so careless about his grooming.

Tremendously cordial and courtly, Mr. Osprey further surprised Lydia by conducting part of the interview in Spanish. One of those New York gents with an intimate knowledge of Latin America, he told her that his father used to have something to do with cattle in Argentina, and he had spent several summers there in his youth. *"Bueno, Señora España, mire aquí"* (Look here), and he made a point of showing her the "Spanish corner" of his bookshelf, where he kept copies of Cervantes, Quevedo, Galdós, and other authors of reknown that neither she nor her children ever had the opportunity to read. He told her that the family had once owned a "little" apartment in Buenos Aires and a "little" retreat in Mexico and that he had picked up a "little" Spanish at Yale where he made the language his minor. Over time she'd learn that he owned an apartment in Florence, an island in Greece, a boat, an airplane, among other things; and that he also spoke French and German.

He had a wife, an elegant blond-haired woman, whose nickname was Mimsy, or *Meemsie,* as Lydia would pronounce it, and three children, two boys and a girl.

He asked her, in English, about herself; and though she had conveyed only the essential details, and had been careful to seem precise and impressive—"My father was the *major* of my town in Cuba" and "My husband is a waiter and I have two children"—she left his erudite presence with the feeling that she had ruined her chances for the job. Why hire her when he probably would prefer a pretty young housemaid from Switzerland?

As it turned out, Mr. Osprey, having a great fondness for the housemaids who had helped rear him in Argentina, decided to hire her. The afternoon she telephoned him from the corner and got the good news, she experienced a momentary elation, the overcast street seeming to swell with light, as if she had somehow risen in the world. To celebrate she bought a bottle of fizzy Asti Spumante from O'Brien's Liquors, then purchased a spicy undergarment from a lingerie shop in Harlem. Back in the apartment, she gave the kids some pizza money and sent them upstairs to a friend, Paula Cortez, took a shower, and, waiting for Raul to get home, stood naked before their bedroom mirror checking out her figure—"*Ay*"—then put on her most seductive negligee, saved for a rainy day, her breasts peeking out through a cluster of embroidered blossoms, striking naughty un-cleaning-lady-like poses. Lost in a reverie, she fantasized about Raul, that they would fall upon the couch making love in the shadow of the El, her husband covering her body with kisses and telling her something that she did not often hear lately, "You're so beautiful."

She, the cleaning lady, would climax like the queen of China.

The Mornings

In the mornings, on those days when she was going over to Osprey's, she was extra careful about the way she looked. Nicely coifed, her shoes sparkling, her manner of dress elegant, she would wear a discreet pair of earrings, a string of pearls, and a light-shaded lipstick, put a carnation (from the flowers that Raul had brought her) in her coat collar, and much good perfume (too much) on her face and neck. She looked so fine that if she were younger, she could have been going out on a Saturday night date. Her children ate their breakfasts of cereal or fried eggs and good chorizo (what Raul loved), Lydia running back and forth between the stove and table in the effort to please her man. Then she would get the children out the door to school, and shortly find herself cutting through the crowds on her way to Osprey's.

On some days when the weather uptown was "gray and jive," as the street kids would put it, she left the subway a few blocks from Osprey's and seemed to enter a jubilant spring sunlight. The air over there seemed to smell good, the hot stench of the sewers did not come up like it did in West Harlem, and the animal life that crept through the wall cracks or scurried up dumbwaiter shafts out of the basement had magically turned into pompadoured French poodles with dainty bell collars and Lhasa apsos and other noble breeds of dog. Nor did she hear the pop, pop, pop coming from the menacing projects, of mischievous kiddies at night, or of husbands threatening to throw their wives out into the street.

"Over there," the future, with its infinite promise, loomed like the first spring of youth.

She felt glorious at times.

"Over there," it all seemed beautiful, and to think that she was part of it now, even if she had other situations, like Cuba and her husband's occasional descent into torpor and suffering, to distract her.

In that neighborhood, she was honored to be in the presence of the great. On different occasions she saw Mr. Osprey in the company of Nelson Rockefeller, and John Lindsay, then mayor of New York, and, as well, many important-seeming men. Wernher von Braun himself came to Mr. Osprey's one afternoon just as Lydia was leaving. She saw these important people from afar like she saw movie stars from afar, the actors Paul Newman and Joanne Woodward, whom she admired very much, making their way past the entranceway of his building, arguing, laughing, talking.

Glamour and money, cleanliness and good manners everywhere she looked.

The Magnificent Apartment

Osprey's apartment consisted of five bedrooms, a dining room, several long halls, a sitting room, a formal living room, a den, several servant's rooms, a billiard room, three full and two half bathrooms. A single room of the apartment was dedicated wholly to the storage of trunks and suitcases. In her rounds through the apartment, long as the shuttle train, wide as her parish church, she dusted Mr. Osprey's second-century Roman copy of a Greek statue of Hercules, after the school of Praxiteles of Athens, which he kept in a corner of the living room, and each time she dusted around this being, she asked herself, "What would I do with this *tareco* if I had it uptown?" He owned modern paintings, weird knobby bronze Italianate furnishings, German art deco couches and chairs, brown leather club chairs, numerous pipe and cigar trays, a parlor grand piano and several antique violins and music stands, ceramic trays from the Far East and the Philippines, walls and walls of curlicue-framed Romanesque style mirrors, dozens of beautiful (for she found them breathtaking and envied him these possessions) sixteenth-century Dutch paintings of sea scenes and still lifes by Jan Davidsz de Heem, and several small Florentine portraits from the school of Piero di Lorenzo, which seemed to have come from Heaven. Cleaning his carpets (Chinese, art deco, Persian Kirmans), she fantasized about the history of mankind, the curvy rug weaves reminding her of epic desert flicks and ancient palaces in Hollywood movies. She would mutter to herself, "Hmmm," because these were rugs that they had most likely purchased in their spectacular travels, commemorated in pictures everywhere.

Mr. Chang

Navigating the deep rooms of Osprey's apartment, Lydia became the ever-polite silhouette at the far end of the hallway near the high pantry cabinets, efficiently moving a vacuum cleaner into the nooks and corners, or bending over a mop and pail.

She worked mainly in silence, daydreaming, but every so often she chatted with Mr. Chang, Osprey's cook. Dressed in white and smelling of vanilla, he always seemed to be chopping up vegetables in the kitchen or drawing meat from the huge freezers: steaks, pork loins, a half-dozen chickens, their heads to be lopped off on a chopping block for formal dinners. Facing the freezer with its large doors and old-fashioned metal handles, elegant with engravature, he once told Lydia: "This

41

came from a mortuary in Kansas City of the 1920s. Mr. Osprey bought it years ago at a very good price from an old mortician," and he'd laughed, splitting a leg of lamb with a cleaver. "Climb in and cool off."

She would keep him company while he prepared certain foods, the cleaver coming down over clumps of scallions, parsley, ginger, and all kinds of ingredients. No matter what her mood she found his artistry uplifting. Every so often he would pull Lydia aside, sit her by the table, and make her a sandwich and a bowl of soup. (She especially liked his good lentil soup, made with small chunks of salted pork, and hard-crusted French bread and salad.)

And she liked the way he stepped aside or waited for her as she'd leave a room, manners she was trying to impose upon her children. Finding something noble and assuring in Mr. Chang's gentility, it was her idea that his essential elegance would rub off on her, like a scent, and that she would bring it home to her family, lifting those spirits that needed to be lifted: up with the veil to the future.

Often as she worked she would see Mr. Chang in the kitchen sitting on a stool either reading a Chinese newspaper with its indecipherable script, or working with a pad over a folded-up *New York Times* or *Herald Tribune*, newspapers whose vocabulary, for all her intelligence, was beyond her. She observed Mr. Chang as he read articles aloud to himself, and thinking that she might embarrass him if she caught him in the act, always cleared her throat or whistled as she approached, to give him warning.

"I keep a little pad, with new words," he told her one morning. "I put a new word in every day. See, Tuesday was *thermal,* which means 'something with heat.'" And that impressed her—her own patience, for all her desires and ability to undertake such studies, weakened by the mounting responsibilities of her life. What impressed her the most about Mr. Chang was the way he wrote in a meticulous script: notes to various delivery men, notes that he left for Mrs. Osprey, that perfumy emanation of pinkness at the other end of the apartment, and notes he left in Chinese, recipes perhaps, on a cork board.

"Saves memory," he told her.

Gradually he became one of the more impressive people of her professional acquaintance, for he could do something well that she could not, for all her airs: read and write proficiently in English.

Words

By the time she went to work for the Ospreys she had been in the United States for more than fifteen years, and while she had gotten used to life in New York, and some things had gotten easier—especially her lilting spoken English—when it came to reading and writing she sometimes froze, doubting herself and her own intelligence. At many things she was adept—sewing her own dresses, copying the fashion magazines or what she saw in department store windows (she bought the cloth on Delancey, the buttons over on Canal), or dancing the conga. She could chitchat a mile a minute in Spanish if a subject appealed to her, but when it came to English, she was blocked up, *tupida*; no matter how much she tried to improve that aspect of herself, she somehow could not. She could not understand her difficulties; the simplest notices from the landlord threw her into a state of confusion, and she always had to depend upon a dictionary, sounding out the words as she read—that is, moving her lips.

Raul left such chores as letter writing to her. It would take her hours to compose a letter to the immigration department pertaining to their relatives in Cuba, but even then she had a hard time letting these letters go. Such were her limitations that whenever the family received any legal documents in the mail,

43

say insurance papers or leases, they showed these to Mireya or one of the Cuban professors they had gotten to know from the university. The English language made her jumpy—as if the words could explode like glass from the paper.

When it came to reading, she never had the nerve to let her children know the scale of her limitations (even though they did). For a time she had helped them with their own reading and writing—she'd cook dinner, and afterwards she would do her best to read to them, from newspapers and golden-spined children's books that she bought at the five-and-dime store—but soon they had surpassed her. (If she were a school kid she would have been in the fourth grade.) Both she and Raul had kept up with them to a certain point, but when the children began to move on in Catholic school (the five-dollars-a-month school) and were passing into the fifth and sixth grades, Lydia could no longer contribute to their learning. Not having the vocabulary, she nodded whenever they read aloud by the kitchen table, even if she felt helpless when it came to explaining what certain words meant.

She got into the habit of bringing home stray books that she found discarded on the sidewalks near the university or left out in the hall by students. And there were a number of bookstores on Broadway, stores whose high stacks of books on chemistry, mathematics, world literature, and history she and Raul had found daunting, but every so often, with the astute Mireya by her side, Lydia would pick through the discounted used-book bins on the chance they might find something to help her children. And then there were the books that the Ospreys had thrown out, antiquated law books, biographies of great English barristers, business textbooks, this odd assortment, along with a host of fashion magazines (courtesy of Mrs. Osprey), coming into the household, her children, in the midst of dealing with entangled feelings, rarely sorting through them;

these books to survive into the future, gathering dust in four-shelf bookcases (also scavenged) in the hall.

Her own tastes extended to simple pulp fiction in English, with those covers of cheap women in torn garments, *Readers Digest* magazine, and the Sunday comics. These were what she attempted to read on the subway while going to work. Otherwise she kept to the Spanish language potboilers that she'd buy in certain Harlem shops, to religious pamphlets, newspapers like *El Diario*, and letters from Cuba.

And sometimes, secretly, she would read from a Spanish language New Testament, the gentle compelling language reminding Lydia of her mother.

During the Days of Her Glorious Past

Often while scrubbing floors she remembered the days of her once glorious past. Aside from being the mayor of her small town, her father, *Don* Antonio Colón, had been the owner of several businesses—among them a bakery and general store, *La Bodega Colón,* which took up a popular street corner near the church plaza. As she told her children until it made them sick (*if she had been so rich why were they poor now?*), they lived on a shady and verdant street, and there was a time when she had a dozen fancy bisque dolls, a closet of fine dresses, a bed with nicely embroidered cushions and a canopy of French lace. Seamstresses gathered in the parlor with their baskets of fabric spread out over the tile floors. Ever precocious, she had learned to make drawings of the flowers in their patio garden and to sing in a voice that echoed, both lovely and shrill, through the house, and she used to take piano lessons, imperiously scolding her teacher when he tried to teach her how to count time properly or to correct her on the fingering of her scales. She had never tried hard in school, rarely studying, for she thought herself smarter than the rest and she felt so entitled to things that

45

when she went to Mass and looked up at the altar, she imagined herself in a high circle of angels near God, a trail of fluttering silk a mile long under her. When she was very young her father had thought her the most delicate and high-strung of his daughters, as if she were a porcelain doll, and doted upon her. For a long time she could do no wrong, and he tolerated her when she behaved like the devil, playing jokes on her family and neighbors and writing dirty songs, for she had a precocious "Catalunian" imagination.

He would call her "my flower," "my life," "my precious."

He was a serious man—among the photographs of him that survived her travels and her fits of rage, there was one that would sit framed on the dresser, in the cluttered bedroom of their uptown apartment. What Rico and Alicia saw was a formally posed studio shot (circa 1945) of a thin man in a dark suit, his thoughtful, teacherly face, in wire-rim glasses, with white hair, prematurely aged, even though he was only in his forties then. Long after he died, in 1963, a few years after Castro came to power, Alicia and Rico would sometimes hear Lydia, home in the early evening from one of her jobs, sigh, repeating, "The poor man, how I made him crazy." And sometimes they would see her, for all her strength and her hard demeanor, quietly weeping by his portrait and that of their maternal grandmother, neither of whom they had ever known, Lydia occasionally going into a trance—or nearly so—as if those photographs were much more than photographs of the dead.

Each day passing happily, as if her very life was the cause of special celebration, she had lived in the spectacular sunniness of youth, beauty, and prosperity in a town where mirth was more common than sorrow. There was a time when she and her sisters took special joy in visiting the bakery in the morning; her father would step out of the doorway, with its flour mists and smell of sugar and lard, the air dense with that holiest of scents—not of incense or of candle wax but of baking bread. Without a word, he would take them for a walk along the peaceful cobblestone street, flower pots and jasmine plants aglow, everyone along the way greeting them with respect and, she had always thought, the grandest affection; people calling out, "Good morning to you, *Don* Antonio! And hello to your beautiful daughters!"

In a time when most Cuban children were shoeless, she was hardly aware that others suffered in this life. Although she saw the poor in their pathetic huts by the roads and in the fields, and prayed for them in church, she never thought about giving them something out of her own pocket. Her father, after all, contributed to the church and paid his servants well and treated the local poor people with respect and charity, leaving out loaves of his bread and soda crackers for them to take in the late afternoons. When it came to justifying the existence of the poor, it was her opinion that God, in His infinite wisdom, knew what He was doing in setting the destinies of people apart in such a way, for if everyone in the world were the same, where would human compassion be? How else would one know whom God favored in this world? And was not the existence of suffering in this life one of the great mysteries of His ways?

In short, Lydia was spoiled and could not, in those days, look much further than the shuttered windows of their stucco-walled house, or feel compassion for the suffering of others.

Reading movie magazines when she was a teenager in the late 1930s, she preened before mirrors, her vanity getting the best of her. In a household that saw frequent salons—poets, singers, fellow politicians, and business people passed through to pay their respects—she grew accustomed to the attentions of men. In a matter of five or six years, the reticent, moody, but delightfully pretty girl who wore sun hats and favored blossom-colored dresses became brooding and "sultry"—a slight pout that she'd picked up from some film dominating her expression. By the time she was sixteen, she had begun to notice the way that men stared at her, with great desire, happy that they wanted her attention and, perhaps, to please her sexually.

Better looking than her sisters, she made heads turn when she walked down the street, for liking to show off her nice hips and derriere, she exaggerated her stride. All the shopkeepers knew Lydia and had their nicknames for her—"Angel," "*Reina*" (Queen), "Dorothy Lamour" (as in "*Mire, Señorita Lamour, por favor, diga 'Hello' a Bob Hope!*"). Men followed her progress with their eyes and they imagined the body under the tight, brightly patterned dresses that she wore, to the consternation of her parents.

Something had made her, as a young woman, hungry for such attentions, but in her father's opinion, her appetites went too far. Or went too far for a man who began to experience his own difficulties, for late at night she would hear her father's voice, as he sat up going over his financial troubles with her mother, his voice sometimes raised in a shout, as he took out his anxieties on her. Of that ilk of man who thought women sometimes frivolous, he watched her growing into young womanhood and raised a lightning bolt eyebrow at her superficial tendencies. Whenever he caught her making eyes back at one of the handsome fellows who called to her from the street, he would stop in his tracks and, no matter what they had been planning, whether they were on their way to the movie house on a Sunday afternoon to watch American gangster films or to one of the local *Sociedades* for an afternoon dance, he would send the others ahead, and holding her tightly by the wrist, take her back to their house where he administered with a belt the punishment he believed she heartily deserved. Demanding that she remember she was not just anybody but the daughter of Antonio Colón, that he would not stand by and watch one of his daughters walk the road of whores (even though he frequented the bordellos himself), he sometimes beat her until his arm tired and she could not sit for several days without a stinging pain.

Of course, that didn't work, and she began to daydream more and more about men.

She passed the first years of her budding maturity pining away for magnificent love. She could have married when she was eighteen, courted by a local politician's son, a banker in Cienfuegos, in whose eyes rolled numbers. Decent in character, ever polite and gentlemanly, he did not seem to have a carefree bone in his body and his lack of caprice bored Lydia, for whom life—that life she would miss so much—was already too peaceful and dull. Her days spent largely in idleness, she lived for the weekend dances at the Gallego Society and for the house parties that she heard about through her maids, raucous all-night affairs held out in the *campo*, the musicians playing the old style rumbas: old women, *mambises*, taught her how to dance, her hips on those nights the center of the universe. Under the spell of the Yoruban gods and Ginger Rogers, she turned every male head toward her.

In the autumn of 1947, on a moonless starlit night, when she was twenty-two years old, she went to a dance at the Gallego Society and there, rumbaing happily (and if the truth be told, a little tipsily), caught the eye of the orchestra leader, a thin and elegant dark man of early middle age. In a hall festooned with Chinese lanterns, she passed the evening with abandon, twirling about the dance floor with different partners, laughing and shaking her body to the rhythms of the cornet-led rumbas, the duennas watching her with envy for her youth and disapproving of her lack of respect.

Later, after the dance ended, the orchestra leader, having dedicated a song to her, invited her to "take a little walk." There was
a veranda behind the club: bamboo poles and a grand awning,
more lanterns and a wall of mosquito netting, ruffling ever so
softly in the breeze; behind that, a little walkway and steps, then
a lower patio with a bench where they sat and talked and
laughed. They had been drinking rum from a flask when she
began to tell this man about herself, that she lived in a too strict
household, that her father, whom she loved very much, was
unable to understand her free-spirited ways; that he, with his
dulcet-toned voice and his thick trumpet player's hands holding
her tenderly, was the kindest man in the world, for whom, under
the wistful, watching stars and the towering palms, she felt
tremendous gratitude. And when he asked her, "But what have I
done for you, girl?" she told him, "You're kind to me."

Then, even if he was twenty years older, she kissed him and
he, blissfully unaware of her father's importance in that town,
began to fondle her through her dress and she responded; then
they began to kiss some more, her plump tongue finding his,
and even though she confused the insect cries with the cry of
her sister calling her, and her stomach was as taut as stone, as
the night screamed cacophonously around her, she did not care
about anything and let him move her off the bench, to the back
of the garden, where he leaned her against a wall; lifting up her
skirt and pulling down on her undergarment, she took his
hand and pushed it into the dampness of her pubic glory, the
heat from her sex pulling him further and further in, and she
told him, "Show me what you can do for a woman like me."
And because she was tired of her father's severity, she opened
her legs and, watching the starry sky above, allowed this man
to "take advantage."

*... with a slow and delicious burning inside of her, she
screamed at heaven, long ago ...*

At five in the morning, having nervously made her way back along a route of narrow cobblestone streets, and with barking hounds rousing everyone in her house, she found her father waiting for her with a strap. Later, with several other men, he set out after the musician. She spent the next day weeping and protesting his harshness, and although both her mother and her sisters had interceded on her behalf, her father remained inconsolable about the nature of her character and her proclivity for men. Because it was 1947 in Cuba and not sixteenth-century Spain, instead of killing her or sending her for life into a nunnery, her father decided to kick his daughter out of their house and the good life she had known.

She never saw him again.

The Princess of Cuba in New York

That she ended up in New York City later the same year involved a small inheritance left her by her great aunt, on whose lap she wished she could have wept, and some money that her mother, distressed by recent events, had given her. When she arrived in the city she had the expectations of a small-town Cuban woman whose impressions of America had first come through the exaggerated fantasies of Hollywood films, where life was all pearl necklaces, fancy mansions, speakeasies, gangsters, cowboys, and unbelievably glamorous women or drop-dead handsome men like Tyrone Power and Errol Flynn (*ay, Errol!*), or from the kinds of often straitlaced and not always altogether lovable business executives who ran some of the larger concerns in her province—like General Electric and United Fruit Company—fellows in their chauffeured Bentleys she saw from the side of the road from time to time when they visited her father, some of these men—not

51

all—communicating, in her opinion, a rather condescending attitude toward the Cubans in their employ.

She did not look back, but felt sad when thinking about her sisters and mother, and the sweetness of her former life; it had been particularly hard to say farewell to her mother, who, loving Lydia, had prayed to God that her daughter could somehow remain at home with the family, that her husband's anger would fade, that nothing bad would befall her. Just the same, in the absence of a miraculous intercession Lydia found herself in Manhattan.

It had not been easy to discover, in such a complicated city, where she had a few names to call upon, how life really works for people without money and connections. For within a matter of months, the grand princess of Cuba was reduced to the rank of an apprentice seamstress in one of those nonunion shops where wages were low and conditions bad. (The kind of shops that her kids would one day study in college sociology courses and read about in sophisticated newspapers like the *New York Times*, with detachment, as if finding oneself in that kind of situation could never happen to people of intelligence and ability, such as themselves.) Her job was to sew fake pearls onto fabrics on Delancey Street for ten hours a day in exchange for a bed, a handful of tokens, and ten dollars a week. She had been hooked up with that job by a Puerto Rican woman she met while walking disconcertedly through Times Square during rush hour, trying to read the indecipherable subway maps for a route to an address near Coney Island where some Cubans lived. In those days, confusing maps and labyrinthine subway lines loomed large in her mind as being what a lot of life in America was about. Laughing, the nice Puerto Rican woman had given her directions. Then, just as she was walking away, the woman added: "If you're looking for work I know somebody who knows somebody. Are you interested?"

"Oh yes, if I don't work, I won't eat," Lydia told her.

And she took down a phone number and went off in a rocking train, with old lacquered cane seats and Irish train conductors, to Brooklyn.

Riding the subways for the first time had shocked her: it would have seemed inconceivable to her a few months before. Like a kind of death, particularly in the hot months of August and July, the subway cars were thick with sweat and malodorous vapors; clouds of agitated air, burnt ashes, spittle, piss, and all kinds of things she had never smelled before, odors from a kind of Hades, exhausted her. But that was her life. Often when she got home she retired to her small room in Harlem with its little cot and took very long baths, her body soaking in the tepid water, pipes clanking. Afterwards, as she stood by the window, watching Lenox Avenue, the darkness of the city seemed like a wall that had come down sadly around her.

At the sewing factory she at first felt out of place, work being something new to her. One morning, as Lydia and her new friend Concha made their way into the main work room, Lydia told her, "*Chica*, now I know how Marie Antoinette felt before going to the guillotine. The poor thing." No guillotine but long wooden tables, small windows, narrow doors, bins and bins of cloth scraps, spools of fabric, and a constant noise of rows and rows of sewing machines churning; the encroaching shadows, sharp as blades on the psyches of the sun-accustomed workers, the fine-looking girls, hoping for some kind of romance to save them, some of them sleeping with one of the bosses, if that would lead to some improvement in pay or job.

She and Concha shared a lot of laughs together, but sometimes the others mistook, as many would, Lydia's intense and intelligent expression for snobbery or her descents into melancholia for indifference. But she also had a bawdy side to her that tended to come out on Fridays, when the workers made plans to relax a little, if possible, since most of the women, if they had families, went home to take care of them. No easy life. (Years later the same faces would be on the subways, sad Mexicans with their shopping carts of flowers and forlorn airs, 1948 and 1996, one and the same, new generations of struggling workers trying to find one measly way to make a little money, earning in a week of peddling their wilting bouquets on the sidewalks or the subway platforms what a chichi Soho artist will piss away on a lunch with friends at the Four Seasons or the 21 Club, *that '89 Bordeaux and a bottle of Pellegrino please. . . .*) Now and then she and her friends went out together, and after a few beers the bawdy tales flowed, the ladies loving them, and then, afterwards, back in Brooklyn—or later in Harlem—Lydia would feel alarmed by the state of her life: it would come to her that her future lacked promise; that the respect she lived for was not forthcoming.

As she would tell (lecture) her own daughter years later, she made a few mistakes, involving men: like the fellow named Ramón who bedded her on a rooftop in the Bronx (a mattress, a rooftop picnic, after a festive birthday party) and she had confused his tremendous passion with love. They met every now and then when he would call her at the factory, or leave a message at the boarding house. Their sex life was spectacular, undisciplined, and "modern." Professing love for her, he did as he pleased with her and often left her standing alone by her door at two in the morning. Still, she was happy enough, until, as such things go, she found out he was married. Then there was a sweet fellow named Fulgencio (yes, as in the Cuban dictator) whom she met as he held a door open for her on the way into Macy's department store, a doorman who took her out for several months and treated her well, a perfect candidate for a husband. A man of culture, which she liked, he did not take her to the dance halls and supper clubs like some fellows (not that he could afford to) but to classical music recitals and museums, places that appealed to her aristocratic side; but in the end, he was too formal, too timid around her physically, his lack of amorous behavior leading her to decide that he was not worth the trouble.

There were others, mainly Cuban and Puerto Rican fellows, not an American among them, even if there were American men around to tip their hats and smile at her when she walked by. (She did not trust or understand them.) On occasion, she "gave herself" to a man, one could suppose, as some kind of distant vengeance against her father. But sex was something she considered a salvation in those days, an escape from some inward terror, or loneliness, which she never liked having to bear for long.

... Then she met Raul, and as the years passed, she cleaned apartments, and while performing the most mundane of tasks, like beating a stranger's doormat to death outside his courtyard window, she daydreamed about sex and her earlier life of privilege. ...

Her Own Apartment (Circa 1960)

Walking into Lydia's apartment the first thing one saw was a picture of Jesus Christ with his sacred heart ablaze, in a thirty-nine-cent frame; further along the narrow hallway walls were framed photographs of Raul and Lydia in the days of their courtship and later, after their marriage ceremony, the couple posed on the steps of City Hall. There was a shot of Raul, dapper, in a purple felt-buttoned uniform, with several of his fellow waiters in front of Jimmy's, and a picture of Lydia and Raul seated by a back table at the Havana-Madrid nightclub, celebrating their marriage with friends, among them Rico's *padrino*, Mario, with his date, a girl remembered simply as Lola. The Louis Perez Orchestra was performing that night, and the wedding party's table was covered with champagne bottles, daiquiri glasses, platters of food and pastries—that meal the costliest of their lives—and the partyers, including the pretty brunette with the sultry, if wistful, expression, Lydia, decked out in their best finery. Her hair in a Betty Grable coiffure, she was wearing a pink dress with puff sleeves, something that she, having once worked in the sewing factory, put together herself. A string of Mallorcan pearls, hot off the docks, her new husband's birthday gift to her, lay low against the delicacy of her breasts. On her hand, her three-hundred dollar wedding ring, with its dotting of minuscule diamonds. . . . That night they spent hours at a time out on the dance floor, Raul lifting out of the languor of his ways, eyebrows raised high, a cigarette dangling from his mouth, and Lydia shaking her hips and laughing, her pretty face jubilant, as she and Raul danced, in love, basking in the remaining glories of their youth.

Baby pictures, in oval frames, little Rico and Alicia, sucking their fingers and staring into the camera with their moist dark eyes, expressions sweet, guileless—photographs that Raul and Lydia cherished. Then their "all-American" children pictured sitting on Santa Claus's lap at Macy's (during their one-gift-each Christmases), the trip downtown with the children one of those rituals that Raul carried out without fail; another shot of the kids at the Thanksgiving Day Parade (Alicia propped on her father's shoulders) reaching out to the grand Popeye balloon, and, one mist-ridden Sunday, on the Staten Island ferry, gathered with their mother by the railing, the Statue of Liberty, beacon of freedom, in the distance behind them. . . . Raul and Mario with the kids in Riverside Park on a snowy day; a shot of the family on the boardwalk of Coney Island. . . . They had a picture of Alicia sitting beside Rico at his seventh birthday party, when Lydia had invited some of the neighborhood kids into the kitchen to drink Coca-Colas; half a cake, with tart lemon frosting, left over from an office party held in Jimmy's restaurant, the treat that the kids devoured in the half-light of the kitchen ("We have to save money on electricity").

Their furniture was second hand, or third hand, with the exception of their RCA black-and-white TV set, purchased on credit, in a place of honor in the corner of the living room, miniature American and Cuban flags thrust into a holder on top alongside a pair of crooked rabbit-ears antennae. A large wall clock, with pinched metal sun rays extending outward, "made in occupied Japan," was on the wall above the red plastic-covered couch; somehow that clock, in conjunction with several Chinese style vases, which she had filled with cloth flowers—chrysanthemums and roses—and with a pair of red upholstered chairs, acquired at a church sale, suggested to Lydia the court of Louis XIV and endowed the apartment with tropical nobility. Between the windows was a hi-fi console that Raul and a friend had rescued from the sidewalk of East 61st Street, and inside it were stored a stack of dance and romantic tunes, as performed by the orchestras of Percy Faith, Enrique Madriguera, Xavier Cugat, and, direct from Cuba (the gift of a friend), the boleros of the great torch singer Susanah Morales. They also owned Perry Como and Bing Crosby records and many old-fashioned classical 78s, which Lydia had found under the ground-floor staircase, where tenants stashed their discards. Hence, scratchy versions of Rachmaninoff and Brahms made it into that apartment, as well as a slightly chipped plaster bust of a brooding Beethoven.

On a Good Day

On a good day, when Rico's godfather, handsome Mario, the singer, used to flirt with her, or when she was nicely dressed and caught a man looking lasciviously at her, she felt pleased by her own beauty; in her thirties, she'd say, looking at herself in a mirror, "Not bad for an old bag." Capable of mocking women her own age whom she saw on the streets and in shops, if they were overweight, badly made up, or wore too-tight slacks over too-plump figures, she took pride in her natural grace and tastefulness.

She liked those people in the neighborhood, like the Puerto Rican barber Mr. Ortíz and his wife, Estelle, because they were sociable and quiet, their house parties genteel affairs. She and Raul sometimes went over for dinner with the kids and afterwards retired to the living room to watch color TV and to play canasta, Lydia España launching into what she considered genteel conversations, mainly about church activities and the good sales at good stores, like Bloomingdale's, which she wished she could afford—none of the raucous gossip that would consume her in her later years. Or on their mutual days off, Lydia and Mireya would practice the rudiments of ladylike behavior, holding informal salons in the living room of the España apartment, where ladies of similar refined manner (*latinas* mainly, although there was also the Italian lady, Mrs. Esposito) gathered to discuss their problems and at times to practice, under Mireya's guidance, their English and some French (the subjects Mireya taught at the George Washington High School).

There were enough good times for the family to enjoy, despite Raul's shifting states of mind, for she, if not Raul, had maintained a sense of some kind of hope for the future. Feeling flush enough, they'd have friends over to the apartment, like Mario, or Mr. Fuentes, the butcher, who brought them steaks and *pasteles* as special treats, and big jugs of wine—the butcher reciting an impromptu verse in Spanish once for his hosts and once in English for the kids, Rico and Alicia, as if they might not understand the eloquence of his *poesía*:

> *What was once splendid when God made*
> *the world is splendid again because of*
> *our mutual company; who needs*
> *the magnificent sun when we have this beautiful*
> *woman's smile? Or the morning light when we*
> *have Lydia, pretty in a blue dress?*

And whether it was good verse or not did not matter, for the butcher, elegant in his suits and well mannered at the table, loved to make toasts and to forget, as workers do, the week's little humiliations and failures. On those days, Mario, in a crisp tan suit, with a new young wife, and a job with the MTA as a token clerk down on 59th Street, and his life moonlighting as a pretty-boy singer (holding forth on plans for a new recording—"Something I'm thinking of calling 'Love Songs for Tropic Nights'") would borrow Raul's battered guitar and concertize for the benefit of all. Elegant, intelligent friends from here and there stopped by—important people, like Dr. Ruíz, a physician with a practice in Queens, or Armando Jiménez, an attorney, whose office was on Broadway and 128th Street—but also waiters, cooks, and dishwashers, dancers and singers, subway clerks and superintendents, bodega owners and doormen, dime-store clerks, cops, transit workers, printers, garbage men and boxers, even raucous commie-leaning union organizers—their conversations flying with prejudices about politics and Cuba and the way society worked lasting long into those pleasant nights.

When the music came on, these were the kinds of men to dance ever so closely with their wives, without once looking over at another woman, to gaze deeply into their eyes, without wavering or doubt, the kinds of men to stand before a door to let a woman pass, to drink just enough to enjoy themselves, but not to get drunk, the kinds of men, she told her children, she'd known growing up in a beautiful house in Cuba.

"You're full of it" was something often said. And "Are not we Cubans crazy and beautiful at the same time?" And *Salud! Cheers! To your health! To long life!"*

And conversely there were bad nights that got out of hand, when Raul, with undiscriminating friendliness, invited over the kinds of men and women whom Lydia did not care for; on

59

those nights he delegated her to the kitchen and to the service of these strangers, some of whom he barely knew. Shady acquaintances from the rougher side of the union came along with their wives, the women wobbling and bouncing shamelessly in tight ruffle-skirted cha-cha-chá dresses; some of the men taking liberties with her in ways that she found disturbing. . . . She often passed those evenings without saying as much as a single word to anyone, thinking these kinds of revelers beneath her. As the party unfolded she kept her alert eyes on her husband, counting his drinks and the number of times he smiled too fondly at one of the women, her expression becoming more and more severe; until her soft and lovely features became stony, her eyes narrowed, her mouth tightened, until she surprised herself by how much she resembled her father.

The next day she would have to deal with the mess—cigarettes dashed out on the window sills and floating in drink glasses, paper cups and plates left everywhere (the roaches scampering about), the cleaning of the pots and pans. . . . Then she'd have to look after Raul, who suffered breathlessly in bed with the worst kinds of hangovers. Later, she gathered the garbage into bags, the bottles clinking, repeating, "Mierda," as she emptied the ashtrays or found a piece of shattered cheap china, or a cigarette burn in one of the chairs, or a butt ground into the shredding linoleum floor.

You see, even though she was a cleaning lady in her private life, she also worked hard, without getting very much credit for it. . . .

Letters

Since first coming to the States Lydia had kept her family informed about her progress in New York, never letting on that she had her occasional pangs of homesickness, or confessing that she even missed her father. She had written them letters that spoke of her wish to visit the family in Cuba with the kids or of the sisters coming to New York. Somehow, the visit never happened and with the revolution became an impossibility.

During those years, her mother had written Lydia regularly, gentle letters ("*We love and miss you so very much . . . and pray to God that you are happy, that the saints will watch over you*"). In them, she always brought up the subject of Lydia's father and urged Lydia to forgive him for his bad temper; to reconcile with him before it was "too late" (her mother always calling her "*Mi vida*," "*Mi hijita linda*," "*Mi corazón*"). For her part, Lydia, after a prolonged period of silence—seven years—finally began to write her father, but he never answered. At first this had not bothered her, but as more time passed, his stubbornness embittered and saddened her. On the other hand, as much as she hoped to hear from him, memories of the way he had treated her—of a hard palm, a reddened face, a strap rising in an arch over her, in flashing blue and red streaks of light (the emotions of fear and anger) around her— made his continued silence tolerable.

Still she had always ended her letters to her mother and sisters with this salutation, ". . . and tell Papa that his bad daughter still loves him." She kept her hopes up until a letter from her sister Elena mentioned that *Señor* Colón was suffering from the kind of circulatory fatigue that seemed to overwhelm certain high-strung Cuban men, who went from early manhood, to middle age, to old age within the breadth of fifty years; that he, like so many other older Cubans, had not been happy with the revolution, for his businesses had been taken from him, and the family forced to live in much reduced circumstances.

One night in 1963, without knowing why, Lydia fell into a restless sleep, her head filled with memories of the Cuba of her childhood. She was walking in a garden with her mother . . . a man in white riding by on the cobblestone road on a bicycle, tipping his hat, the sun flamboyant through the trees . . . when, in the middle of the night, she felt two hands pressing against her side and pushing her off the bed.

"For crying out loud, Raul, leave me alone," she cried, but he was sound asleep. She tried to doze, but shortly after she felt herself being pushed again. "*Carajo!*" This time, she got out of bed and went into the kitchen for a glass of water and upon her return saw her father standing by the foot of their bed, looking just as she had always remembered him, from years before: ever serious, in a linen pinstriped suit, his expression bewildered, imploring. . . . "Poppy?" she said. And then he was gone.

That next afternoon, as it happened, on her thirty-eighth birthday, which she had planned to spend with Raul and friends, she received a telegram informing her that her father had passed away the night before. Uncommonly quiet all that day, she had been tempted to cry several times, but could not bring herself to do it, especially when the children were around. But she quivered and shook, and drank several beers in the early afternoon, then wrote her mother and sisters a letter. Later, she and Raul went out to meet with Mireya and Mr. Fuentes and his wife, heading over to one of the movie houses on 96th Street and Broadway, but on the way, they stopped off in church, where, in honor of her father, Lydia knelt before the altar and prayed for him, asking God to fill her with loving feelings for the man so that his soul, if watching her, would not be offended.

And Raul's Situation?

His juicy ex-wife, Olivia, had arrived in Miami (back in '62, the darling *puta*) and from the beginning she had put more demands on Raul for money, now that her kid, whom she had started to call Rocky because it sounded so American, was getting older and in need of many things. Miami was expensive, much more so than Cuba, she claimed. Where Raul used to send her fifty or sixty dollars a month (what he earned before taxes each week), mainly because she'd made him feel like a piece of shit with guilt over their failed marriage, she now demanded twice that amount. He had once told Lydia, on a boozy night, that his life with Olivia had begun to fall apart because she had a hunger for other men; when he left her she had indignantly claimed abandonment, accused him of cowardice—no wonder he got the hell out of Cuba. Divorcing her from afar, he nevertheless suffered because of her continuing influence upon him: any contact with his ex-wife left his stomach in knots ("My love," Lydia would say when he came into the apartment looking particularly ashen, "what does she want now?"). Every month he and Lydia had screaming arguments about the payments, but he diligently sent his ex-wife whatever he could afford (and at the expense of his own family!). Every so often, he spoke on the telephone with her, mainly so that he could have a word with his first son; conversations that often left Raul sad, and sometimes caused his hands to shake, the man calming himself with a hearty, ever-healthful drink and a smoke by the window.

The Other Man (1965)

On some days, away from Raul, she found herself thinking about Mr. Osprey. There had been the odd compliment—Osprey sticking his head into a room where she was cleaning and remarking, *"Qué bonita estás"* (How nice you look today")—or giving her a bouquet of flowers that he'd picked out on the way home. He surprised her the first Christmas in his employ with a gift of twenty-five dollars, and this he had since increased to forty. His generosity touched her and yet it was the way he handed her the envelope and then placed one hand below and another on top of her left hand, holding her for a moment and looking, so she thought, with affection into her eyes, that had delighted—or frightened—her.

He often spoke to her in English, throwing in Spanish fragments; sometimes he attempted to speak only in Spanish, but the truth was that they had little to say to one another, in any language, so their exchanges, well intended as they were, often seemed awkward—*she was only a cleaning lady and he was the boss*—and yet, unless Lydia was imagining things, there were moments when a sexual tension rose between them. Once he had looked at her in a way that forced her attention back to the floor she had been sweeping (she imagined that he was erect inside his trousers) and she experienced a general weakening of her limbs. And on occasion, while saying, "Good day, *Señor* Osprey," or while sorting through his laundry, she had conjured the image of his large bony hands caressing her breasts and touching her under her dress, that thought lasting only fleetingly. Her other imaginings had to do with the plots of the dime-store plantation novels she sometimes read, books about master-slave love.

Nothing ever happened between them, but she often laughed to herself, amused by the capriciousness of her thoughts, as if they had come to her from the soap operas, the cleaning woman's staple, that she watched in the midafternoons. Often, as she dallied with her dust cloth in hand and paused in the window light as if she were the *dueña* of Osprey's *casa*, she daydreamed about having her own large walk-in closets and art deco vanity, or of traveling with Osprey on a transatlantic ocean liner to Europe. That she, like a Cuban Cinderella, could ring a bell and that Mr. Chang would wait on her, that her friends like Mireya and Concha would visit and eat lunch in her well-appointed living room, that her own children, whom she would call "my darlings," would be sent off to the best schools, to learn to read French books with pretty covers.

In time, she began to have a certain repetitive dream. In the middle of the night she often found herself flying naked over the rooftops of the city, the wind languid and moist over her skin— her whole body delicious with sensations so extreme she would awaken wondering if she had been taken aloft by an angel.

She was still young then.

Dulzura

One afternoon when Mr. Osprey came home early from the office he called her into his study. Prowling in his closet he had found an album of faded yellow-rimmed Brownie photographs and this he opened on his desk. In pencil, barely legible against the dark carbon paper were names: "Buenos Aires: Avenida de la Independencia," "Boulevard del Prado," "Uncle Peter's House."

In one of its pages he found a shot of himself as a boy of about twelve or so, a lanky fellow with a full head of hair, dressed in khaki trousers and a white shirt, posed in front of a patio wall, with plants and potted palms, and beside him a lovely-looking *mulata* woman of about thirty, in a maid's outfit: while he leans devilishly forward, hands in pockets with a cocky smile and a self-satisfied, successful glint in his eyes, she stands stiffly at attention trying hard to smile for the camera.

"Maria-Luisa was my favorite in my Uncle Peter's house in Buenos Aires. She was Bolivian and dear to us all."

"She was your maid?"

"Yes, I'd known her since I was a child, from the moment *que estuvimos en Argentina*. It was quite wonderful and marvelous, as Mr. Ira Gershwin would say," a reference she did not get. "And this Maria-Luisa," he said with great fondness, "was pure *dulzura*."

She began daydreaming about Mr. Osprey as a teenager, startled by this housemaid in his bedroom in Argentina, the shutters closed, the rain and wind slapping at the roof, Maria-Luisa undoing her dress and seducing him; clouds bursting above, and lightning, a frantic bout of lovemaking—something she found herself fantasizing: the housemaid's grinding body, her knees pinning his forearms to the bed, Osprey's lanky frame beneath her—why was she dwelling upon such things?

"*Dulzura,*" she would remember him saying, again and again.

And speaking of Osprey, there had been the year of an afternoon solar eclipse, during the Johnson presidency, '64 or '65, when all of Manhattan went dark for about an hour. It was the summer, and Mr. and Mrs. Osprey and their children had gathered in the hallway for the special occasion; all were in a state of exhilaration for they were heading over to the Sheep Meadow in Central Park to watch, along with hundreds of others, that solar event. Vaguely aware that "something with the sky" was going to happen—Raul had mentioned reading about the eclipse in the Daily News—*Lydia could not understand the excitement. That the sun's light would be blocked by the moon seemed sad. Still, she was feeling unhappy about being stuck inside with Mr. Chang to work, when, as if reading her mind, Mr. Osprey called out to them, "Come along to the park." Then: "And don't worry about work!"*

... Shortly, they were out in the heat of the day. While Osprey's boys ran off to be with some of their friends, Mr. Osprey directed Lydia and the others into a circle; with clouds floating over the Central Park West skyline, Lydia identified, as a game, the buildings in which she had upon occasion worked—the Colorado and the Nebraska. Then Osprey bought Coca-Colas for everybody from a vendor; bees, flying free in the meadow, hovering about them, Lydia slapping the abejas from her head. Osprey, with a handkerchief pressed to his fair-skinned brow, laughed. Someone from the New York Amateur

Astronomical Society was handing out cautionary pamphlets about what and what not to do during the eclipse; suddenly, a short and stout fellow, also of the Astronomical Society, blew a whistle like an athletic coach, and announced through a bull horn, "Ladies and gentlemen . . . it's time."

In the sky, the sun, a glaring white disc like a god, acquired a barely perceptible shadow at its edge.

As the eclipse began, Osprey handed Lydia a piece of dark acetate and said to her, "Whatever you do, Lydia, don't look at the sun directly."

He did so with great authority, gravely, as her father might have; she nodded, ever so tempted to just take one long look with her naked eye. She had the fantasy that Osprey would take care of her if she went blind, that all responsibilities would be lifted off her shoulders, that Osprey would lead her along the street of his fine neighborhood, that she would never have to clean a floor again. . . . But she obeyed, for he was the boss and knew everything. Besides, he had grasped her by the elbow, in a reassuring way, and Mrs. Osprey had winked at Lydia, and Mr. Chang had raised the dark acetate to his eyes, an air of reverence about him. She watched the sky, observing as the moon entered more deeply the face of the sun.

"Lydia, what do you think?" Mr. Osprey asked her. "Have you ever seen an eclipse before?"

"Once, when I was little," she said.

What she remembered was being about four years old and huddled in her house in Cuba with her sisters, Elena and Anna-Maria, and with her mother, who, when the sky had darkened, told them: "The world is coming to an end." And: "Pray my children, that God restores the light."

"It's miraculous and beautiful," Osprey had said to Lydia.

She nodded, even if the eclipse's natural splendor escaped her. In the same way she missed the point of grandeur of the sea, the moon rushing through the blossoms of a tree. She was there, but, at the same time, absent. Nevertheless, for Osprey's benefit, she had cried out, "It's so wonderful!" And, "Qué interesante!"

When the burning C shape of the sun's outline began to emerge from the lunar shadow, the greatest darkness passing, Lydia thought that observing an eclipse was like witnessing the intersection of opposites, the poor and the rich, the sad and the happy, the lost and the glorious.

With Mr. Chang

Now, in the course of her first years of employment with the Ospreys, Mr. Chang had taught her, in their time together, a few things about the diversity of cuisines. Outside of frying morning eggs with bacon, and plantains at night, most of her meals were haphazard operations, even something as basic to Cuban food as *habichuelas negras* always seemed to have a powdery consistency, for she had never learned to cook, and besides, had no natural talent for it. But through Mr. Chang, the humble bay leaf took on importance in her cooking life, as did certain combinations of spices and herbs, which Chang swore improved both taste and mental agility: nettles good for sleep, or ground cayenne pepper for tranquillity, that kind of thing. No, she would not eat squid in its own ink, but in time, before she knew it, she had not only become something of a health food *aficionada* but had learned about soy and oyster sauces, pureed squashes and carrot juices, the curative properties of ginger and garlic, and how to make, among other stews and broths, a passable and surprisingly pleasant vegetable soup (its magic ingredients: Nine Spices).

Hanging around the kitchen, taking in Mr. Chang's cooking techniques, Lydia marveled at all the elaborate drinks he made for Mrs. Osprey: not of alcohol but of various vegetables, tubers and carrots and long-stalked greens, liquefied in a blender and thickened with a handful of vitamins and "life enhancers." Sometimes, if Lydia seemed a little low or worn down, Mr. Chang would make her a health drink, too.

Mrs. Osprey

The good life, with money and the knowledge of things, made a difference. Mrs. Osprey was living proof of this. Madame, as Mr. Chang referred to her, was an elegant blond, somewhere in her forties, and yet she looked, in Lydia's opinion, thirty or thirty-five; she had a perpetual blush about her cheeks and so much clarity in her eyes as to suggest a mystical connection between herself and the world.

A tallish woman—that is, taller than Lydia—Mrs. Osprey possessed the kind of uncurvaceous figure that held no interest for a certain kind of man. She did not look like a butcher's wife, or like Mario's big-hipped, large-bosomed flame, his wife. Still there was something graceful and noble about Mrs. Osprey: having once fleetingly spied her in the late afternoon applying powder to her face after a shower, her pale white body visible through her French doors, Lydia had an inkling of how the royal courtesans had comported themselves—or so she thought. Mrs. Osprey was friendly enough with her cleaning lady, but it took her five years to go from calling her "Mrs. España" to "Lydia dear."

She liked silk dresses, favoring pink and saffron yellow as colors, and upon occasion wore Chinese or Japanese style slippers, affecting an exotic style, which was reinforced by the antique Asian cabinets and chairs that she kept in her private room. Occasionally Lydia saw her going through a black lacquered jewelry box with the enthusiasm and happiness of a child looking at her toys. Lydia observed this impartially, and though a part of her could not resist thinking that such trappings were meaningless in the end—in death—she could not help coveting, if only passingly, certain of Mrs. Osprey's possessions, mainly jewelry, diamond earrings and brooches, and, especially, an antique pearl necklace that she often wore.

"They belonged to my grandmother. They're from Vienna before the First World War."

Although they would never become good friends, Mrs. Osprey made a point of talking with Lydia, however fleetingly, in the course of the day. Usually the subject was health and health food, about which Mrs. Osprey, seeing a nutritionist and reading every book on that subject, seemed to know everything. "Not that one can live forever," she once told Lydia, "but I have learned that with the proper diet and with the occasional fast, a person can live to be a hundred, if you put your mind to it!"

"Oh yes, *señora*, to live that long would be very good."

(If you have the money.)

She was always giving Lydia advice and, as well, dark brown bottles of different vitamins and nutritional supplements like tingly niacin to take home for herself and Raul. ("What, are you crazy?" Raul would tell her. "I'm not gonna start with that shit!") And she gave Lydia jars of facial cream and different marmalades, left over from the Ospreys' European vacations. Every now and then Mrs. Osprey, when she wanted to thin out her closet, might offer Lydia a garment, a ripped velvet dress, a Christian Dior that had begun to bore her, or a pair of elegant elbow-length white suede gloves with a torn finger or a few of its buttons missing, easy to repair. The dresses were small for Lydia—Mrs. Osprey being much thinner (too thin for the men who went to dance halls)—but she brought them home for her friends or, just in case a God sat in judgment in Heaven, to give to church charities.

Mrs. Osprey would sometimes appear in Lydia's dreams as a mannequin peering out from a fancy store window.

Her feet a size six like Mrs. Osprey's, Lydia sometimes took her shoes, usually of a French make, which madame would leave out in the hallway near the servant's entrance; high-heeled shoes of swirling jet black or cardinal red leather, or with cloth flowers and instep straps of fortified silk. These Lydia brought to the Puerto Rican shoe repair man on 129th Street and wore them with great joy, because, as she walked along the street, she knew they would be surely noticed.

From what Lydia could tell, Mrs. Osprey really loved her children, as much as any mother, for every so often Lydia would see them together as the children came home from school, or as she took them to Central Park or the toy stores of Madison Avenue. She'd call them "My darlings," and if one typical pose remained in Lydia's memory it was this: Mrs. Osprey leaning over them, or on bent knees, brushing out her daughter's hair, or adjusting the collar of one of her sons' coats, tightening his scarf, or buttoning a shirt—what any mother would do for a child.

Lydia was always telling Raul and her own children at dinner what a nice family she worked for, how Mrs. Osprey, in particular, was such a wonderful person. For all of that, what struck Lydia the most was that Mrs. Osprey, for all her personal generosity to Lydia and her love for her children, did not seem particularly affectionate to her husband. The few times she had seen them together, Mr. Osprey seemed nearly somber around her, coming home from his office and quickly disappearing with a drink into his study. Mrs. Osprey would never kiss her husband in front of Lydia, and always greeted him in a restrained manner. It seemed one of those marriages that cleaning ladies talked about, when the couples stayed together for the children or because it would be too expensive for the man to divorce.

Such ideas or imaginings would do nothing to change the world, but on those days when she saw Mr. Osprey looking a little low, and her presence made him smile, she went off into a reverie of speculations and regrets about the past, among them that she, as a young woman, had not somehow met up with Mr. Osprey when he was a young man. She imagined a scenario in which Osprey, on a sightseeing tour of Cuba, came to her town, and they met in the *placita* on a Sunday afternoon, where, once upon a time, she used to go for walks. As in a fairy tale, they would have fallen instantly in love. . . . Her strict father would have liked him and taken him under his wing. They would have attended certain high society functions, galas at the Gallego Club or at the Sugar Growers Association, watching the men smoking cigars out on the veranda. She would have been the lovely daughter, alluring in the garden, waiting for the approval of her father and the attentions of the ambitious and serious American man. And, just like that, because he was honorable and in love with her, they would have been married—in two ceremonies, one in her Cuban town by the sea and the other in a place like Newport—the finest families deboarding their yachts to shower the young couple with gifts—that beautiful and vivacious Cuban girl, who, the life of the party, had taught all the high society people how to dance the conga and that lucky *son of the future,* big as Hemingway, as handsome and dashing in white as Errol Flynn. . . . She took such thoughts, on the most dreary of days, home with her as she rode the subway, bought her milk and two-day-old bread at the store, as she climbed the stairs to her family.

She would be with the Ospreys for nearly twenty years, time that passed quickly into the air. She'd work for them one or two days a week, depending on the season, her services earning Lydia between two and five-fifty an hour (her rate when she left him). With the passage of years, she would come to say *"Señor"* or *"Señora"* Osprey with the reverence a good subject or lord would give to a king or queen. How the very name, when she first heard it, struck her as something odd,

nearly ugly, like the name of an obscure bird!—and yet, enraptured by the patterns of good fortune that characterized their
lives, there was a part of her that fell in love with the family;
Lydia, the Empress who conspired to return in some way to a
lost glory; for the Ospreys, with their love for the refinements
of life and lordly good manners, were among the blessed, the
inheritors of the earth.

The
Glorious World

Thinking about the days before Raul's heart attack when she had the time to take care of her kids like a normal mother, when she was convinced that her children completely loved her, always threw her into a nostalgic reverie. There had been a kind of serenity about her life then, whatever its limitations. Because Raul had not wanted her to work ("never again" is what he promised her), her days were spent in the service of the children and the household (and in imperious musings before her mirrors). She had often thought that she would always be a housewife, and, her dreams of future romances out the window, she resigned herself to the simple joys of that existence, finding her greatest pleasures in her children. As she watched her daughter and son playing with their *juguetes* on the living room floor, her heart always went out the most to her youngest, Rico.

With his perpetually running nose, bad sinuses, chronic coughs, puffy eyes, he was the frailer-seeming of the two, a kid, just like his father, laid low by too little self-confidence, who in his manner seemed as if he would never attempt to branch out into the world. He had always been the quiet one, like *pan con ojos,* or "a piece of bread with eyes" ("fly on the wall" if you like). He was a kid whose friends from the local Catholic school were, even as children, already falling apart—a diabetic boy named Louie, a chronic asthmatic named Joey; kids whose presence in the apartment vaguely depressed Lydia, as if they might further bring him down. She wondered if he could hear properly because on many occasion, as he got older, when she would call out to him, he rarely acknowledged her, especially if she spoke to him in Spanish. Was he stupid? She could not say, but compared to Alicia, who had been a curious, more outgoing child, he seemed like a mute, prone to solemnity and withdrawal.

Naturally she had always felt protective of her attractive daughter, but in some part of her psyche, she tenaciously clung to the idea that her boy Rico would remain her baby forever. Her happiest image of Rico? On a spring afternoon in the park, the boy at three, tottering after her, arms wide open, mad and anxious to plant a kiss upon her face, the day so serene, the meadow filled with dandelions and daisies, the sky and the river the same brilliant blue, birds circling the treetops, a hum—of distant insect song and the miasmic wind—the clang-clang of a Good Humor truck approaching; her son tumbling into her arms, his face and hair smelling of lemon shampoo and Ivory soap, pressing against her, Lydia telling him, *"Mi hijo,"* and kissing him, in a manner she had since forgotten. . . .

At Osprey's When Rico Was Eleven

And yet . . . Lydia would remember with sweetness how he had been a good companion to her, how he always found a small corner to play in while she went about her jobs. She remembered taking him over to Mr. Osprey's three or four times, when he was home sick from school and she could do with company, and, on each occasion, despite the fact that one of the doormen patted him on the head and Mr. Chang made him certain nice treats, he was always shy when it came to having the run of that apartment. He was careful, even if she encouraged him, about looking around ("Work hard and this will be yours one day. . . ."). He was so well behaved that the black lady who came in to bake special desserts for the family used to say, "Wish I could take this one home."

The first time he had gone there, when he was about eleven years old—in 1964, the year when Lydia started to work for Osprey—his eyes nearly burst forth from his head at the fantastic elegances everywhere in sight. The fact that the Osprey family had three bathrooms, and one with a bidet, whose function he found baffling, had given him something to think about, a vision of a sparkling clean heavenly life on earth. Thanks to the labors of his mother, every pipe, tile, and glowing fixture seemed beautiful and suited for angels rather than humans. And the way Mrs. Osprey had decorated one of the bathrooms with several large potted trees made for grandeur on a scale that heretofore he could not have imagined.

On other occasions he helped his mother in her work, wiping down counters and dusting here and there, particularly enjoying Osprey's library. Founts of knowledge, the books with their old-fashioned bindings emanated so much silent life—or wisdom—they seemed like nearly sentient beings. The brass ashtrays and a sextant that Osprey kept there gave Rico the impression that he had boarded an ocean liner. But there had also been the children's bedrooms, each with a dresser and closet, bookcases filled with old children's classics, which Rico had never read, like the Wizard of Oz series and the Hardy Boys adventures and the fantasies of C. S. Lewis.

The oldest son had his own record player and television. And the beautiful daughter had a closet filled with a dozen fancy coats and as many dresses.

Beholding his surroundings, Rico would think, "If we had such things then Poppy would not feel so bad, and the subways wouldn't shake the apartment so much, and there would not be so much shouting at night."

What was most fantastic were their toys; in the corner of one room, facing the courtyard, there was a four-foot-high French puppet theater, with stage, backdrops, and half a dozen mannequins, featuring the characters of the wolf, the fool, the prince, the beauty, the witch, the angel. There were souvenirs, here and there, presumably of European vacations: a model of a gondolier, a Phrygian cap, a cricket bat. Photographs: of the pretty blond daughter, then about Rico's age, in a striped bathing suit on the deck of a schooner somewhere beautiful; of Mr. Osprey and his children taken with the comedian Danny Kaye and his red-haired nephew who attended their same prep school on the Upper East Side of Manhattan.

Most agonizingly, in a hallway cabinet between the boys' rooms were an array of lead soldiers in crimson frocks and busby hats, hoisting sabers and British flags, marching in row after row; and a marching band with drummers and trumpeters; then forty dashingly posed Hussars wielding lances that in their fine detail were something that Rico had rarely seen except through Fifth Avenue store windows. (Who had seen a set of the Knights of Agincourt in anybody's apartment in the South Bronx or in a Harlem pawn shop, circa 1963–64?) It was as if (he fantasized) the King of England had bestowed his approval and blessing upon each of the soldiers, these beings evidence of a world where there were no hardships in life, where men did not suffer, toys far beyond anything Rico or his friends knew.

(But there was the .38-caliber pistol that "Poppo," one of the local kids, carried around in a paper bag, and used for shooting out car windows from the rooftop; and there was the piece of roof coping that Johnny James beat a schoolteacher half to death with; and the beer and soda bottles collected for the two and five cents returns, the money going for more cigarettes and more bottles of beer, and small, serious explosives, so-called ash cans, which were—it was said but never seen—tied to the necks of alley cats or to the wings of pigeons and exploded, cruelly, coldly, and in the best spirit of street fun. And there were the hitting games in which the participants could pound, punch, kick, bite, push down, and, in general, beat the life out of someone, a broken wrist, cracked cheekbone, splintered ankle, torn kneecaps, and any other number of painful effects not at all unusual.)

Lydia was always mindful of the way he would look at things, especially at that cabinet, examining its contents with great envy or curiosity or hope. Observing him, Lydia had the impression that he was truly moved by the opulence of Osprey's apartment. She hoped that the evidence of so much worldly success would serve as a future motivation, that it would free him from the small thinking of the lower classes, that he, and hopefully Alicia, would never have to endure their humiliations. . . . Hard work, she told him, again and again, was at the root of all that was good in the world.

On the other hand, the immigrant's life, no matter what you do, her children had to be reminded, was never easy. Look: Poor Raul never learned to relax after his illness, and instead of taking better care of himself, he became more careless, not carefree. His heart woke him in the middle of the night with odd eruptions of pain—he'd have three more heart attacks over the coming years—*and he had acquired so fatalistic a view of his own life and future that he kept talking about making a will, lamenting that he did not have more by way of property and money to leave his kids when the inevitable happened. . . . If, while half-dozing by the table, he noticed Rico slinking by him, Raul, gladdened by the sight of his son, would call him over, so that they could sit together and Rico could pour him out a glass of beer or whiskey and listen to Raul and his stories about the waiter's life, or, if his friends were around, about the ups and downs of their jobs. . . . And that had been tolerable when Rico was just six or seven, when he could not quite "see" what was going on, but as he got older and entered a preco- cious, streety adolescence, he began to feel that things were not right: nearly every evening, at about nine o'clock, Raul, under- taking a nightly ritual—"man to man"—would grab his son's hand and wrap it around his wrist, asking, "And do you hear my heart?"—the heartbeat heavy and ponderous—repeating*

*"I'm tired" and "Help me" and "Give me your youth. . . ." For
a long time, he'd accepted this placidly. He'd sit with Raul until
he couldn't take it, or until his father, sorely tired from his
week's exertions, fell asleep at the table, Rico slipping off into
his cluttered room, to find refuge in one odd volume or other of
the encyclopedia that his mother had bought from the handsome Cuban salesman. His mind drifting, his eyes scrutinized
the unbelievable and distant places of some other world.*

(As an older version of himself, in graduate school, he would
think of these visits to Osprey's and write, in the pretentious
manner of the young who believe they have invented all the
original thoughts of life: *"The poor crave wealth, and the
wealthy crave immortality."*)

Beauty

She would recall Rico's fascination with Osprey's handsome
children, whom he saw one afternoon, when he was hanging
around the pantry with Mr. Chang, the two boys and the beautiful daughter, as they were coming home from school. And
how Rico, skulking in the shadows, glimpsed Osprey's daughter in the hall, as she was making her way into the living room.
Something of the lights may have caught her hair because it
glowed angelically, and although she was a teenager, and in pigtails and in a plaid skirt and long woolen stockings and penny
loafer shoes, she was so self-assured that Rico would not have
been surprised if she had started floating across the room. By
the piano she sat, practicing Bach, and he stood by that doorway spellbound at the serenity of it all. (And because she
exuded a precocious femininity, the sweet scent of her youth
and sexuality emanating through her skirt, and all around him.)
He had remained there until Lydia, with her coat in hand, saw
him and, laughing, told him it was time to go home.

His Early and Happy Life (1966)

A pensive-looking teenager, Rico especially suffered because of Lydia's insistence at turning him out like a young gentleman. In that neighborhood, where one had to conform with the streety ways or else find a way of becoming *invisible,* Rico had it the hardest because as a teenager he was saddled with the label of foppish *maricón,* especially because of those *"fucking"* white brass-buckled shoes that Lydia used to make him wear. She always dressed him in a certain way, in high knee socks, freshly ironed shirts and bow ties, neatly pressed shorts or white *pantalones,* and a blue blazer that she had purchased at a Gimbel's sale. She taught him to iron his own shirts, to meticulously fold his trousers, to darn his stockings, to pare his nails, part his hair, damp with Vitalis, in a way that pleased her ("My gentleman!"), to keep his shoes shined. Having enforced a code of behavior on Rico, Lydia would not let him leave the apartment without her consent, even to buy his father a pack of cigarettes (Winstons) or bottles of beer at the corner, and when he did leave, she made sure, if she could help it, that he went out properly attired and groomed.

With the Ospreys (1967)

As a family, they had met the Ospreys only once, on a New Year's Day, Mr. Osprey having invited Lydia with her loved ones to come by, *"para tomar una copa."* Raul and Rico in suits and winter overcoats, Lydia and Alicia in their finest dresses, fresh from visiting other friends in Manhattan, arrived at Osprey's in the late afternoon. To Raul, who stood in the doorway with his hat in hand, docilely waiting as if on a station platform for a train to arrive, the experience was daunting, a favor he was doing for Lydia, and, after all she had told him, he wanted to meet the man himself. (The man with the powerful heart, the finely fed stomach, a mind close to the wonders of nature and the wonders of God.)

Decorated for the holidays in a way that would not be found in an apartment, say, on 122nd Street and Amsterdam Avenue, Osprey's place came straight out of a magazine or movie, with candlesticks, holly and ivy and bowls of fruit, a wreath of paper flowers, a vase of fresh flowers, and, marching across one side of their dining room table, a line of crimson-jacketed toy soldiers, which Osprey would bring out at that time of year. Twelve feet high, a floor to ceiling balsam fir, aglow with lights and fussy European ornaments. And there was Mr. Osprey himself, in a bright red sweater before the fireplace, smiling at them. No doubt about it, Osprey was courtly and cordial, a cut above the kind of man that Raul, dealing with half-drunk business executives, had grown accustomed to. Fidgeting with his hat, Raul was even more surprised by Lydia's complete demureness in Osprey's presence, for prior to meeting with Osprey, as they were walking over from Fifth Avenue, she had been carrying on about Raul's drinking, her voice, sharp as a stiletto, cutting the air, begging him to lay off the booze at her employer's residence.

In any event, what would later be recalled was how Osprey made the family feel at home: perched on the edge of the couch, where Lydia and Alicia were sitting side by side, Raul grabbed handfuls of nuts off the coffee table, cautiously appreciating the beautiful things around him: the French glassware displayed on specially lit shelves, the grand piano, the gothic wood carving of a kneeling saint about to be beheaded atop the mantel, the art deco bar that rattled with bottles, as Osprey poured sodas for Alicia and Rico, a glass of port for Lydia, and for himself a brandy, offering Raul one as well, which he happily accepted. Within a very short time, Osprey poured a second for himself and Raul, as if the two were old friends, so that

Lydia had a sudden insight into something she had long suspected: Mr. Osprey had a weakness for drink.

Shortly, Mrs. Osprey, smoking a Lucky Strike in an ebony holder and transcendent in a long white gown, swept into the room with her two sons, her wrists jangly with bracelets as she offered her hand. Her sons, Thomas and William, tall and blond and cleft chinned, or *"Tomás"* and *"Guillermo,"* were wearing blue blazers that bore the insignia of a prep school and crisp white shirts, without ties, however. When they quite politely leaned forward, in their spectacular handsomeness, to shake hands with the family, the older brother, Thomas, said, in an impeccable Castillian accent, *"Es un placer conocerles,"* and his facility impressed everyone very much.

Neither Rico nor Alicia, feeling shy and uncertain about their own Spanish and what everybody might think, responded in kind.

(Hadn't that been one of the things Lydia had driven her kids crazy about at the table? About how refinados y bien educados eran—*so smart that one of those very handsome boys spoke a Spanish that was almost better than her own, and certainly better than her own children's. Alicia's Spanish, sprinkled as it was, not by literary allusions or aphorisms but by errors of syntax and meaning, as in the instance of taking the word* embarazada, *which meant "pregnant," to mean "embarrassed," as in the sentence* "Me siento muy embarazada cuando no hablo buen español" *("I feel very pregnant when I don't speak Spanish well"). But at least she got some things right, whereas Rico's Spanish was spotty at best, mainly because he put most of his effort into English, which was what Lydia had wanted for them, even if she sometimes forgot that she had insisted upon it.)*

When the boys sat on the couch, Mr. Chang appeared with a tray of crustless sandwiches—cucumber with butter and dill and deviled egg—and more drinks were poured: then Perry Como's voice came out of the stereo console, Raul commenting, "That's nice, very nice music." Moved by the comfort of drink and love surrounding him, Raul raised his glass and said to Osprey: "You're a lucky man," to which Osprey responded with his own toast, "To family."

The children, for all the niceties, were bored, and worried, for their Poppy had started to slouch forward and his eyes were wide open with happiness (which could easily turn into sadness). And Lydia was staring crossly at him. Then a voice, Mrs. Osprey calling out into the hallway to her daughter, "Marie, are you coming?"

Rico, who had expected to see a ten- or eleven-year-old girl in pigtails and plaid skirt, was startled by the teenager, whom Lydia had described as *"muy muy bonita y lista,"* striding briskly into the room, her sudden presence cutting quickly through Rico's torpor. In a black knee-length coat, collar and cuffs of white fur, a white fur cap, a pair of ice skates slung over her shoulder, and with her blond hair cascading down her back, her lovely features, sullenly refined—oh, with the pert, slightly upturned nose, the high cheekbones, the Jean Shrimpton eyes, long lashed and mascaraed—she cheerfully said, "Hi, everybody, Happy New Year." Then she gave Lydia a hug, and, introductions made, everybody else a handshake.

As she approached Rico, he said, scrambling for something to say, "Hey, how's your piano lessons going?" Then: "I can remember being here with my *moms* and hearing you. It was beautiful."

"Thanks, but I haven't touched the piano in years. . . ."

"Well, I wish I could," he said looking "humbly" down into his cupped hands.

"Besides, I hate being kept indoors," she added. Then to everyone else, "I'm really sorry I can't stay long to chat with you all, but I have a skating party to go to in the park."

"So soon?" inquired her mother.

"Yes, everybody's waiting for me over at Wollman's."

"You do whatever you have to do, my dear," said Lydia. Then everything went in reverse, and now they were saying good-byes to the daughter. Soon enough she had gone to the door, briefly turning back to cry out, in a friendly way, *"Ciao!"*—a holdover from the Ospreys' grand Italian tour of the year before.

The Españas remained for an hour more. It should be mentioned that Lydia, for all her familiarity with the Ospreys, had felt uncomfortable during this visit. Worried that something would go wrong, particularly with Raul, she had noted how many brandies he'd consumed, and once when he began to take his pulse in front of the Ospreys, she had nearly slapped him on the wrists, but they seemed oblivious that he was doing anything out of the ordinary—or they ignored it. And when his eyes began to water, from joy and happiness and release, and he got up to use the bathroom, she had been terrified that he might bump into and break something expensive, like the blue Lalique lamp on the hallway table, or slam into the newly installed tropical fish aquarium beside it (how wonderful life would be floating angel pink through the crystal serenity of the water, Lydia had thought). No disasters befell Raul: Osprey showed him the way, and she was pleased by how kindly her employer treated Raul. At one point she saw them standing before an ornate French cabinet on the other side of the living room, Mr. Osprey explaining to Raul how he had found the cabinet in Antwerp, "antique capital of Europe," during his honeymoon with Mrs. Osprey, and the two of them laughing about something. . . . As she looked at the tall man standing next to the short man, she suddenly felt sad, for she wondered what their lives would have been like if they were rich like the Ospreys—would, for example, Raul have fallen so ill? And would the children be more happy around her?

Then Osprey and Raul rejoined the group, drinks in hand. There had been a discussion between Osprey and Lydia about Cuba, for he was interested in Caribbean politics, but it was not a good subject with Lydia, who, after all was said and done, missed her family in Cuba and disliked Castro. Plans for the coming days were mentioned: the Ospreys would fly up to their house in a place called Martha's Vineyard—the first time Rico or Alicia had ever heard of it—where they were to remain for a week, while the children were still home from school.

"Then it's back to the office for this slave," Osprey joked.

"I know what you mean," said Raul.

"Another drink, then, to the holidays?" suggested Osprey.

Later, Osprey presented the family with a number of small, elegant gifts, gloves and wallets, and, in an envelope, fifty dollars in cash, for he was not a cheap man.

Sitting as upright as he could, Raul did not particularly feel like leaving when the time came; in fact he wanted to take Osprey uptown to meet some of his pals like Mario and to that bar on 108th Street with the sexy young girls dancing in cages, or to a little restaurant run by a Dominican man, which was a joyful place to be. But shortly Osprey's wife told her husband, "Don't forget we have dinner tonight at the Johnsons'."

On the way out, Raul, carried away by the excitement, told Mr. Osprey, "You are beautiful, and your wife and family is beautiful, and I love you, all of you." Then: "Happy New Year!"

As they made their way down in the elevator and Lydia España did not say a word, Rico and Alicia, knowing their mother's silence did not augur well for Raul, gave each other sidelong glances and prepared themselves for the coming tribulations of that holiday evening.

A Kind of Love Story (1967)

After that visit with the Ospreys, Rico thought about Marie nearly every day, her presence haunting his dreams, his adolescent sexual fantasies, and, in fact, his speculations about the workings of the "outside world." The problem was that he did not know how to broach the subject with his mother, for they never spoke about personal matters. He went about his normal business, attending high school, working part time as a messenger, and in the evenings restlessly waiting for a way of mentioning his interest in Marie to his mother.

In the course of weighing his options he thought about calling the Ospreys and speaking to the daughter, but he somehow felt that he was not "good" enough, or did not have the right to do this, or that by doing so he would endanger his mother's job. He'd hoped after some time to forget about her, and even though there were a few girls in the neighborhood who liked this careful dandy, Marie became the focus of his escapist fantasies. On three different weekends he had gone to Wollman Rink in Central Park on the chance he might encounter her again. Renting skates, despite his inexperience, he caught a glimpse of her in the midst of an accomplished group of handsome and pretty skaters and, trying to pursue the graceful Marie, he floundered. On many a night when he sat in the kitchen with Raul after dinner, or on the living room couch with the family watching television (the television with the two small flags, one Cuban, one American, mounted on a stand on top), he imagined himself as a great skater, and Marie Osprey, spiraling in circles on the ice, pirouetting, her face happy and impressed at the sight of him.

He saw her floating in a snow-globe, the city silhouetted behind, the snow falling noiselessly down around her: an all-American, New Yorkish tableau.

When he finally approached Lydia, as she was preparing a pot of chicken and rice for dinner one evening, Rico said, "Hey, Mama, can you tell me something?"

"Yes?"

"You know when we went over to visit the family on Park Avenue?"

"*Sí, los Osprey.*"

"Well, I wanted to know if you could tell me where the daughter goes to school?"

With that Lydia's eyes widened.

"You want to know where the daughter goes? You?" And that made her laugh. "*Pero hijo,*" she told him. "You should know better."

He was about to head into his room, to hide himself away with some books and fantasies, when her manner changed, and she told him, "If you want to know, the daughter goes to a fancy school called Dalton," which she pronounced *Dowl-e-ton.* "Okay? . . . But don't do anything stupid, *hijo.*"

A few days after this conversation, about three-thirty on a February afternoon, Rico was waiting outside the Dalton School, on East 89th Street. He was wearing a suit and coat, had slicked back his hair, and carried a bouquet of flowers. In an envelope, a note that he had agonized over, stating his romantic intentions toward Marie. He waited, hatless, the cold stinging his ears. Girls, passing by, saw his goofy, uncertain manner and the way he was eating Twizzlers and either smiled (hopeful for him) or laughed among themselves. A few times he stopped one of the students. "You know a girl named Marie Osprey?" But they rushed past him: He went into the door-

90

way, where a security guard told him to wait outside; he smoked two cigarettes; paced to the corner and back and, losing patience (freezing), he nearly said to hell with this, when Marie, in the company of two friends, walked out of the school doorway and headed toward Park Avenue. She was wearing a fluff-brimmed hooded cape, a long scarf, and leather boots. Crossing the street, he approached her, calling out, "Marie, you remember me? Rico . . . Rico España?"

"Oh, hi."

"I got something for you." He handed her the flowers and envelope. She opened the note, blushed—from sentiment or embarrassment he did not know—and then took a few steps back.

"Anyway, I just wanted to ask if you'd like to hang out sometime? I mean, can I call you at home?"

"I'll let you know, maybe next week?" Then: "We're going to a dance class in the Village. Would you like to walk with us to the taxi?"

She didn't say anything further. On the corner of Park, Rico, feeling like a doorman, hailed them a taxi, and then, as they were getting in, he said to her, "Now don't forget what I asked you, okay?"

But as the taxi pulled away, she gave Rico a brief wave and then turned to talk with her friends.

Walking over to the West Side, he caught the subway home and thought about the price of the flowers, four dollars, and that he had lost the afternoon's wages, three dollars and seventy-five cents, for he had taken off from his dollar-twenty-five-an-hour job to see Marie. Slipping in and out of his psyche, this phrase, *"cleaning woman's son."*

* * *

Getting off at 116th Street, he walked across the Columbia campus to visit his friend Joey on Amsterdam; when he got to his apartment there was some kind of party going on inside: Joey's older brother was home from basic training in the army, and, with Joey's parents out, their living room was jammed with well-wishers and friends. Among the visitors, there was a flamboyant hoodlum, named Mike Díaz, holding court in the kitchen. He was a sturdy and good-looking mulatto with reddish hair, whose pastime was, it seemed, the imbibing and sale of heroin. A Kool cigarette in his mouth, he was sitting in the kitchen, holding a lit safety match under a spoon in which he was cooking a white powder; shortly it turned into a liquid. Now it happened that each time Rico had previously found himself in the company of such friends, he had shown no interest in partaking. And when someone offered him the chance to "skin-pop" (for five dollars) he always refused. But Rico had often seen the euphoric effects of the drug, which various friends had described as "something like coming in every part of your body," or as "a slow creamy heat rising inside you," and that had always seemed tantalizing. On this night, while luxuriating in the physical pleasure of the drug, Mike made the offer, and Rico, all of fourteen years old, deliberated and put his five dollars down on the table. From a wallet Mike pulled out a small wax-paper envelope, large enough for one postage stamp, and told Rico, "Knock yourself out."

In the living room, a jazz recording, "Manteca Suite" by Charlie Parker and Dizzy Gillespie, was playing on the phonograph, and the older neighborhood kids were drinking and smoking and laughing. Private in his way, Rico, having gone into the bathroom to snort, not shoot, the drug, slunk back into the living room on rubber legs, his body in a quandary of contradictory physical sensations, for while he had experienced a mild physical elation, he also was nauseated;

there was something unsettling or disorienting about the sensation—the heroin had probably been cut with too much strychnine.

Aside from all that, he could not, for the life of him, eliminate from his thoughts the image of his father and mother waiting for him by his door; somehow the prospect of their torment and disappointment with him—for he wanted to be "good"—sank him low. One thing had not necessarily led to another, but his naive and well-intended encounter with Marie Osprey in front of her school had somehow contributed to that evening's capitulation and guilt.

At forty, looking in the mirror at "the beginning of the end," as Concha put it, Lydia remembered the events of a single afternoon when her woman's body was as new and startling as that of her own daughter. She recalled how she had once gone to visit her great-aunt, on her mother's side, who lived in Havana, a conservative, quite religious woman. This great aunt was a childless widow who had surrounded herself with crucifixes and religious statuary, in preparation for the kingdom come, and her house, a roomy nineteenth-century villa, with whispering walls and doors that seemed to open on their own (or so Lydia pretended), had the atmosphere of a haunted nunnery. Of pious manner and with a propensity for dark dresses, the old woman had taken Lydia shopping along Obispo Street in Havana. She, a crow in a plumed hat and orthopedic shoes, and Lydia, shapely in a florid summer dress, were making their way along the crowded sidewalk, with its throngs of sailors, straw boaters, vendors, tourists, and spies, when they decided to stop for a drink in the La Florida bar. Famous to both locals and tourists, and best known for its mojitas, it was a grand saloon of the old-fashioned type with swinging doors, like those of cowboy movies, overhead fans, tile floors, curlicue-backed iron chairs, and a serving bar from the turn of the century, its shelves cluttered with bottles of rum and aguardiente *and exotic Cuban beers that left many a customer reeling.*

It happened that as they were having their refreshments, while this great aunt was lecturing Lydia about the pitfalls of being a beautiful young woman in a dangerous world, and singing the praises of Our Lord Jesus Christ and the true comforts of life—or afterlife—reminding her young grand niece that lust and vanity were the devil's own and that she had spent the last twenty years remembering her dead husband, to whom she would be forever wed—just then, as this aunt was making the sign of the cross, there appeared, among the milling tourists and bar habitués, a tall and broad-shouldered, well-tailored man.

Dressed in white from head to toe, he crossed the room, and at the sight of him, her dear great-aunt's pious hands began to tremble: he was an American movie star, most famous in his time ("Mire es Robin Hood," a few voices had said) and he not only radiated health and virility, his tanned face nobly aglow, but the promise of pure and ecstatic sex in the blueness of his eyes. When he glanced over at them, giving Lydia and her great very Catholic aunt a quick wink and a smile that said, "My what a pretty young woman," it was her great-aunt who gasped, let out a sigh, and fainted dead away.

Later, as she helped her great-aunt to her feet and they sat by a table, sipping batidas, *Lydia looked over at the actor. He had watched all this with both amusement and concern—it must have happened often—and just then, giving her a look that stiffened her virgin's nipples, he said something in English, which she could not understand. But she smiled at him and said, "Yes." And that made several of his American friends laugh.*

Nothing more came of it. The actor settled into a corner table to play cards and get drunk with his cronies. Lydia and her aunt left the bar, and as they made their way along the streets, Lydia, her mind penetrated by the pure lust of that man's gaze, found that she could not get rid of him; she imagined him as a lover, his hands touching every part of her body, his beautiful mouth covering her with kisses, her great-aunt's voice—"I've never seen any man like that before, God forgive me!"—becoming fainter, as the most delicious sensations concentrated in the center of her body. . . .

As she stood on the corner of Calle 26 waiting for the light to change, she pressed her legs together and felt a bud of pleasurable dampness there. She could not wait to get back to her great-aunt's house, where she threw shut the door to her little nun's room and, resting on the bed, probed inside her undergarments, daydreaming about the promises of certain kinds of gazes, carrying on until she doubled over into herself and nearly awakened her great-aunt from a nap, after kicking over a potted plant with the curled tips of her toes.

That happened long ago, when she was sixteen, in 1941. . . .

The World As She Knew It

By the mid-1960s many of the Irish in that neighborhood had left, though several large families remained on 123rd, on the hill around the corner from where Lydia and Raul lived. A new Chinese restaurant went into business near the El train entrance, and over on Amsterdam Avenue a Japanese joint had opened on the first floor of an apartment building near an old Civil War–era stone water house. Students abounded because of the universities, City College to the north, and to the south Columbia and Barnard ("Barnyard"). In those days they still mainly stayed in campus housing, the males, for the most part, crew-cutted and wholesome seeming, the females, teacherly. Gradually there had appeared scruffy young people, who sometimes stood in front of the subway kiosks, handing out mimeographed sheets of poetry or asking for money.

Watching the world from her window, Lydia did not miss much and had a good memory for things that had vanished. She was aware of how the strolling Italian troubadours, who sang and played Neapolitan airs for dimes and quarters under people's windows, had stopped coming to their street. She recalled how for years she had seen, for reasons she could never comprehend, a great number of *enanos,* or dwarves, professional circus performers, walking on Broadway—to a hotel on 125th Street most hospitable to them—who abruptly, or seemingly so, were gone. She remembered when a certain kind of extremely flamboyant black homosexual—with earrings, high heels, lipstick, slick straightened hair, and silk turbans— strutted along the avenue, sometimes in the company of a blond-haired young man, defying the tougher fellows on the street—and often getting beaten up for it: they seemed to have vanished, displaced by a crowd of hoods, who cased apartments and sold drugs out of the projects.

Winters were quiet, summers chaotic, the building trembling whenever the uptown or downtown number 1 IRT zoomed by on the tracks, and there was street ash on the sills, and traffic and blaring TVs, and people breaking things and shouting at the top of their lungs, and little kids running wild, sometimes playing games like Ringolevio on the rooftops, every so often some poor kid flying off—and you heard engines and ambulances and cop cars and sometimes (though it would happen much more frequently in the future) gun shots from the projects and east along 125th Street, with its broken traffic lights.

Now and then there still came up the street certain throw-backs to the turn of the century: a junk man in his horse-drawn wagon, a rag man picking through people's garbage, an ice man in his truck, a dapper-looking man in shirt and jacket selling fruit from a cart, and another selling and repairing umbrellas. Coal men came along every few weeks to dump a river's worth of coal into the building basement down chutes. The hardest job of all, as it seemed to Lydia? The seltzer delivery man's, for the fellow was always climbing many flights of stairs with heavy cases on his shoulders. She always saw him stopping by the stoop to rub his aching sides, his walk pained, back bent.

Neighborhood deaths moved her, and even if she had not been the best of friends with the deceased, she would go to the funeral and sit in the last pew; sometimes she tried to make a "day" of it, particularly if the funeral fell on the weekend when everybody had off. Something about the pageantry thrilled her, the solemnity of the procession, the beautiful choir singing in Latin, the incense, the dead body itself carried aloft by pallbearers the farthest thing from her mind. She usually hauled poor Mireya along, at first sitting in the pew as she would at dance parties, stiffly, her hands held rigidly over her lap, but once the processional started, she began to nod, as if watching a stage play, later offering a small critical appraisal, as they'd made their way with the crowd down the church steps—"The priest's voice was a little weak, but he had a lot of feeling." Or: "What handsome pallbearers!" Or: "Did you see how the widow kept looking at a certain man?"

In those days, she had kept her eyes open to what seemed, at the time, a sudden influx of Cubans: after Castro's revolution more Cubans—like the Cruz, Torres, Díaz families—had started to move into the neighborhood, their respectability and ambition impressing her. Lydia, in fact, had been among the first to make their acquaintance, to offer what she could by way of help, some clothing, towels, tableware, some money and much, much, much advice. In a low admonitory voice, she warned them to be wary of certain "types" from the projects who would conk you in the head and take all your money, or worse (these things did happen, now and then—though the thieves could come from anywhere).

She noticed that in her own building the front door was always broken, and for the first time, in 1966 or so, that the plaster walls had begun to crack, water leakage corroding the hallway ceilings and a hairlike fiber sprouting out from the walls in the dampest places. Her children sometimes reported seeing rats, which she attributed to their active imaginations, even when whole loaves of Wonder bread had been mysteriously eaten through in the kitchen, and droppings were found under the sinks. (The dark sink interior where the plaster was rotting and the vermin perhaps lived.) There were roaches, too, proliferating everywhere, as if God had sent them from Heaven. Home from work in a lousy mood Lydia hunted them down, killing them with bug spray and the heels of her sturdy black shoes, sighing, as she had terrorized her children to keep the apartment clean. "Raul, it's those new people across the courtyard," she was always saying.

The Kids Slipped Away

Bad enough that she had become the head of the family, paying the bills (fretfully walking down to the Con Ed office on 125th Street with the cash payments) and taking care of just about everything, but she suffered the most, in a way that surprised her, when the kids abruptly, it seemed, began to slip away from her despite all the things she had tried to do for them. In the course of her preoccupations and worries, Lydia had forgotten how to simply pass the time with them in the unagitated, affectionate quietude of a sweet Cuban mother. Everything she told them had to do with the lousiness and roughness of the world, the dishonesty and lack of refinement of people and their schemes. Even when the occasional cousin, finally leaving Cuba, popped up to stay with the family for a month (like cousin Ramon), the kids, ever polite and helpful, were by no means elated by the sudden discovery of family. Part of it was that Rico and Alicia were from different worlds, and part of it was that Lydia, raising them, had told them again and again to beware of others, even relatives, because people will take long before they will give.

Despite the oddness and solemnity of his ways, their Poppy somehow commanded more of their children's respect and affection. Even though Lydia brought them gifts from outside, the items he brought home, usually trivialities, somehow struck them as more enchanting. On some days he'd disappear for long periods—sitting in the park with a newspaper and talking to the dogs, which he seemed to like more than people. A few times he lobbied Lydia about acquiring a pet hound, and when the kids were little they wept and cried, too, about having pets, but Lydia, thinking about the unfastidious nature of animals and how they sometimes pissed and did their business in the house and prowled about on filthy ground, refused to have the creatures tracking such muck home. Once she allowed Rico a small turtle, which she summarily flushed down the toilet when she thought the sleeping creature dead (so she would tell her boy), and on another occasion, for several months, they baby-sat a cheery parakeet, the property of Mrs. Mulroony, a neighbor, that they kept in a white cage in the living room, its song in a language that Raul liked and seemed, in some odd way, to understand, for whatever it said sometimes made him smile and caused him to spend a lot of time speaking animatedly to the little creature. It disturbed Lydia to think that Raul was going a little "wrong" in his thinking, but his own children found him simply more "human."

Sometimes Lydia, her children by her side, would head off into the expensive stores on Madison avenue with their pallid clerks, pretending that she had, in fact, much more than a few dollars and a handful of tokens in her purse. Once, they had gone into an antique shop on Madison Avenue where, Rico remembered, his mother had become fixated on a cumbersome and gaudy "antique" coat of arms, manufactured in nineteenth-century Madrid, as the salesman said; she inquired as to its price—"Nine hundred dollars, madame"—and then opened her largely empty purse—for they were walking part of the way home to save the carfare, a lousy forty-five cents—and pretended to be counting out a wad of bills, her lips mouthing, "five . . . six . . . seven . . ." so convincingly that the salesman told her, "If you don't have enough cash, we can take a check for the balance, madame."

She had then told him, "I must think about it. My husband sometimes gets angry when I buy such things."

"You may take your time, madame," the clerk had said.

Later, Rico and Alicia looked at each other, as they followed her out, each showing the other a shrug or a roll of the eyes, having understood little of why she was now laughing and saying, "What a fool! He thought we were rich! The fool!" (What else had she said? "This was almost as good as buying that ridiculous piece of junk!" And: "Did you hear him calling your mother 'madam'? Did you?")

Until her children had, to her mind, begun to go bad, all Lydia ever wanted was for them to have as much refinement as did the children she saw coming in and out of the majestic lobby of Mr. Osprey's building: crowds of boys and girls in blue blazer school outfits and tartan skirts; children with their au pairs and governesses on their way to the French Lycée or to piano, ballet, or singing lessons, or to learn the essentials of etiquette at a special school. She wanted her children to be like Osprey's own children, quite aware of their place in the world—their wealth of knowledge, their good clothing, the books they owned, the *many possibilities of their lives* (where to vacation, what to eat, what to learn, how much to spend). Only thing was she did not know quite how to do it.

Over the years she would often speak about Osprey's children at dinner, saying things like, "He's sent his boys off to *Sevilla* to study Spanish for the spring holiday," "They are so well-educated, you should hear the Spanish they speak." And, her eyes tenderly aglow, "*El Señor* Osprey and his family are *very important and special people.*" Since they'd hardly had contact with Mr. Osprey, Rico and Alicia had to take their mother's word for it, his image like that of a Santa Claus, or a president (poor Kennedy whose limousine had winged its way to heaven). In a way it was an honor to know that their mother worked for so fine a man, and over the years they had been delighted when she came home from Osprey's with odds and ends that, to their eyes, were fit for the best: discarded board games that they, in their neighborhood, would never have encountered: Tri-tactics, Dover Patrol, Risk, and, on one occasion, a box worth of boys' clothes and girls' dresses. She would come home with special treats for Christmas, a box of freshly baked cookies, or a cake, a used pair of roller skates or a box of discarded *Punch* magazines or books like *Tales of Tarzan* and *Pellucidar* by Edgar Rice Burroughs.

Still they sometimes tired of hearing so much about Osprey, for while she spoke so highly of him and his family, she, being as strict with them as her father had been with her, had little good to say on their behalf; as if they were nothing, and Osprey and his kids were everything.

The Cleaning Woman's Beautiful Daughter (1965)

For years, as she looked at her daughter, Lydia España would think that Alicia had inherited the homelier attributes of the family. As a girl, she had the natural charms of any child—a curiosity about the world and an enthusiasm about whatever affections were shown to her. Her smile was lovely and there was so much liveliness in her dark eyes that just about every adult she encountered seemed delighted by her: on numerous occasions she walked away from the Jewish candy store with free peppermint sticks, from Fuentes' butcher shop with slices of ham and bologna, and from the Cortez sisters' beauty salon with sample bottles of strawberry-scented shampoo and girls' comics. Until the age of nine it seemed as if she would take after her mother in looks, but within a few months her face changed; her features filled out, her nose blossomed, and her eyes suddenly seemed small. A dark mole appeared on her right cheek and flourished, growing larger; a thin line of facial hair crossed her brow: by ten, Alicia was in a state of distress.

Even though Raul doted on her and there were always wondrous beings in the apartment to sing her praises (like Mireya, who always called her "*bonita*," or the butcher Fuentes with his name for her, "my walking ode to beauty," and "Uncle" Mario, who whistled like a wolf whenever he saw her, and often declared, "You're going to be a real killer-diller one day"), she had to contend with the neighborhood children, who insulted her on the street ("skank" was something she often heard).

But there was also Lydia's disapproval: she never said a negative word to her daughter about her appearance, but her pitying expressions, the way she furrowed her brows, sighing, left her daughter in a disconsolate state of mind; and there were the days when Lydia, nostalgic for her youth, spoke of how the men in Cuba used to whistle and call her Dorothy Lamour, how a famous movie star had once admired her in Havana, and that men still talked to her on the street, even if she had nearly ruined her figure bringing her children into the world—on those days Alicia could not stand to be in the apartment.

At the same time she could not bear to go out.

When Alicia was a girl, Lydia dressed her for church as a vision of 1930s Cuban propriety, in a lace-trimmed sea-blue dress, white knee stockings, black patent leather shoes, and a blue straw hat with a swirly yellow ribbon around the brim, like one of the dolls Lydia had owned in Cuba. When she sat with her daughter at night, Lydia held forth about the very grand and lovely Catholic mythologies with which she herself had been raised: the Savior should always be at the tip of one's thoughts, for He was a friend, watching one's acts. She taught Alicia (and Rico) to cross herself whenever passing by a church, to light candles whenever possible, and to be aware—greatly aware—that lurking everywhere was evil. Alicia took everything in, circumspectly, and in the manner expected of young Cuban-American girls, quietly.

She was not a particularly good student, but because the nuns treated her well, she volunteered to work for them after school. In their convent apartments, on 121st Street, she helped to straighten up, or to peel vegetables or scrub pots in the kitchen. She liked the nuns' tidiness (she was a cleaning woman's daughter, after all), the way the tiny rooms were so neat, the simple decorations of wooden crucifixes or plaster virgins on their walls, and how the nuns seemed serenely content with their isolation from the "real" world. She worked for them without pay. If they paid her at all, these nuns did so with food: peanut butter and jelly or roast beef sandwiches, which the Españas never ate at home. These Alicia devoured happily. Mainly she took refuge in their kindness.

It was on one of those afternoons when Alicia was cleaning for the nuns, with the kitchen radio on, that she first heard the Beatles; she had yet to have a period, but the bell clarity of the guitars and the cherubic pretty-boy intimations of their voices pierced through her in a way that might be described as sexual: sitting in a chair in the kitchen, so that she could put her ear to the radio (for some of the nuns did not like that kind of music) she left a wet spot in the shape of a leaf. She became obsessed—not with the situation in Cuba, or with the civil rights movement in the South, or with the disenchantments of her family—but with the "Fab Four," the walls of her room filling with Beatles fan magazine posters, and the needle of the pink five-dollar record player Raul had bought her as a present the year before coming down, over and over again, on her precious copies of the latest famous Beatles 45 rpm recordings. She sat a few inches away from the television screen watching them on the *Ed Sullivan Show*, Lydia and Mireya on the couch beside her, amused by her interest. (And Raul? He was working a party in his restaurant that night.) Rico, still very much a little kid, did not quite understand his sister's exhilaration. But on that night—in fact every time she listened to the music—a layer of herself was peeled away; the simple melodies of those songs and the excitement of her emotions (for she was not sad when she listened to them) creating in her the notion of a new self, as if the music had induced the growth of a rejuvenated and beautiful skin.

On the Cusp of Physical Change
at a Party at Mario's (1964)

One Summer day Mario threw a birthday party in his new place off Amsterdam and 118th Street. He had been in that apartment for about five months, having moved there when the university had bought up the block where he lived and, in the name of institutional expansion, evicted many long-time tenants. While sitting around with his wife and some musician friends, watching a Saturday afternoon ball game, there had been a pounding on his door: two large men in trench coats had come to hand him his eviction papers. While most tenants left docilely, holdouts were harassed; doors were kicked in, octogenarians threatened with lawsuits, heat and other services withheld—the things one read about in the newspapers that went on all the time all over the city. Mario had immediately gotten his own shifty lawyer, refusing to move even after almost everyone else in his building had capitulated, and held out until he was given five thousand dollars as a kind of compensation for his troubles and a different apartment across the street, where the partyers were now gathered.

(As Dr. Merton, one of Lydia's learned neighbors, would put it, "Victory goes to the bold.")

Once he'd moved out, they'd started to raze the buildings across the way: cranes with wrecking balls, bulldozers, and demolition teams were put to work: the shrill of a whistle followed shortly by a blast, an explosion going off every half-hour or so for months, as the entire block was leveled—much to Mario's exasperation, for he sometimes worked night shifts for the MTA or played at all-night mambo parties and looked forward to his rest during the day. The other side of Mario's street was a fortress of scaffolding, construction trailers, pneumatic drills and pulverizers, refuse carts, and, behind wire fences, clusters of compressed oxygen tanks for welding.

The afternoon of his party, neighborhood friends, Mario's coworkers at the MTA, and fellow musical moonlighters from all over the city turned up with their shapely and unshapely wives and girlfriends, bringing instruments, boxes of pastries and pots of cooked food, birthday gifts with silky ribbons, and shopping bags of popular recordings. He had invited old friends like the first man with whom he had ever worked, as a fresh arrival in New York from Cuba, a Jewish furrier named Mr. Greene, who, in a plaid leisure suit and curly toupee, had the air of someone about to go off on a golfing holiday. He passed the time beaming a gold-toothed smile at the partyers and letting toddlers bend and twist his dense, sun-spotted, many-ringed hands, as he sat immobile in a chair. Ortíz, the barber, and his wife, a dapper couple, came in formal dress with their young children, as if attending a wedding. And, among others, Mireya had come along—Lydia encouraging a hopeless romance with a postal worker named Daniel who was in love with her. (Erudite Mireya did not want to get married and have a man stick his vicious thing inside of her, for she preferred her books, which, in her opinion, were quieter and better companions than men. During their long walks together, Mireya and Lydia enjoyed wondrous speculations about a world without men, and how, God willing, if they lived long enough, on savings and pensions, they would share an apartment, and enjoy the fruit of their years without the burdens of female responsibility.)

But for more successful courtships, happy news: there was Mr. Fuentes, the butcher, still unmarried but suddenly stricken in middle age with love. He arrived with a large box of cold cuts, a case of beer, and a saintly looking younger woman named Flora. In a bell-shaped white dress and with a silver crucifix down her chaste front, she seemed in some way to epitomize the principles of Mr. Fuentes' aesthetic view of the world: she was pretty and lyrical, conservative and a little corny at the same time. He spent the evening, dressed formally in a blue suit with a tightly knotted polka-dot tie (high blood pressure or the tension of his neckpiece or his poetic love bringing a tinge of red to his ears), doting on her, his attention such that anyone looking at him expected a major declaration of his devotion, or a marriage proposal, as if at any moment the man would drop to his knees with a ring and bouquet of flowers in hand.

The story went like this: working behind the cashier's counter in Woolworth's, Flora would leave her job and spend her free evenings handing out religious pamphlets in front of the porno movie house on Broadway. In a blue straw schoolgirl's hat trimmed with a red ribbon and a blue white-belted dress that reached her ankles, she was a member of the Pentecostal church on Columbus Avenue. (You want to know something the rich can never buy? All the money in the world could not buy the sensation of standing out on the pissy pavement of 106th Street on a sunny Sunday morning and hearing the services from behind the sheet metal door into the church: bongos and organ and cheap electric guitar, tambourines and maracas, and a chorus of singers, exuberant and joyous, as if that place of worship were a nightclub in some fancy strip, but emanating a pure music of the heart and soul. The big-limousine people who attended Riverside Church wouldn't have a clue about it because they would never find themselves walking down a trash-littered street on a Sunday morning if it killed them, unless it was in an exotic place like India.) Flora and Mr. Fuentes met when she came into his butcher shop to buy some cold cuts for a lunch at her apartment. She looked at him with her pretty green eyes and serene expression and asked for two pounds of bologna, two pounds of salami, and a pound of American cheese, which Mr. Fuentes wrapped in wax paper with trembling hands. From that day forward he had kept his eyes open for her, nearly lopping off his left hand while trimming a sirloin steak for a customer, as she caught him looking out the window, a backwards "Fuentes" stenciled in flecked gold letters on the window. When Flora smiled sweetly at him, Mr. Fuentes, a lifelong bachelor whose favorite movie was Marty, *began to fall in love. . . . Now, at the party, that was Flora, his Florita forever until the heavens turned into ether and vapors, sitting sweetly beside him on the red plastic-covered couch, laughing and covering her mouth with her dainty white gloved hands.*

(Or as Fuentes, who had once coached the unpoetic Raul about poetry, would put it: "Her flesh, her form, her being is not of earthly matter.")

107

Lydia noticed how they whispered carefully into each other's ears, that every whisper led to a kiss and then a sigh, and though she approved—"*Qué mona,*" she would say to chain-smoking Raul—another part of her sat across the crowded living room with her hands folded on her lap, wistfully remembering, perhaps, the days when Raul could not keep his hands off of her ... the Empress, in her mounting bodily longing, her thoughts taking her far away.

Having worked all day, Lydia was hungry enough to go straight to the plantains platter, a plate of which she doused with salt and vinegar, and she ate a plate of rice and chicken and then she drank several cups of rum punch. She had been sinking like stone into the cushions, her mind busy with all kinds of speculations about the direction of her life. Looking about the room at the happy dancers, at the joyous, untroubled (for all their troubles) couples on the dance floor, at the jam of men in the kitchen and the kids playing and running through the rooms of the apartment, she wondered, among other things, about the curious nature of her daughter, for whom she had only good wishes and, as well, a small measure of sorrow.

Alicia had practically begged Lydia to let her stay at home. She just wanted to sit by her open window with a fan blowing on her, listening to her music. She paced in the hallway swearing that she was too sick to leave, for in truth she did not feel well. Holding Alicia by the wrists and repeating, "*Mírame!*"— "Look at me!"—Lydia told her, "Whatever you may think about your mother and father, we are a family; and that's all you have to know. *Me entiendes?*" And although Lydia had been very cross (and full of her own rages that day) coming home from work on the hot, soot-aired subway (thinking "*Coño,* this is what I will be doing for the rest of my life!")—

Raul, in a calm, good-natured way, had taken Alicia aside, saying, "My precious, just remember that your mother has to work hard," and "What the hell, you'll have a good time over there, you know."

As they were walking over together, Alicia had been as stonily silent and temperamental as her mother, never smiling, even as Raul, who still doted on her as if she were a pretty six-year-old girl again, offered to buy her some Milky Way candy bars and stopped to point out a big stuffed animal in Mr. Grable's window. *What ailed her was her realization that looks, in this world, were a kind of currency, good as money, and in those days, she felt as if her pockets were empty.* Her mood was not helped by Lydia's comments: "She's so spoiled—maybe we should just let her clean apartments or wait on tables for a week, just to see how easy that is, huh, Raul?" ("Whatever you say, my love.")

Still, Mario, who never wavered in his flattery of her, made Alicia smile: "My God, young lady, but you're looking good!" And his enthusiasm was such that Alicia blushed. Then he told Rico and Alicia, "You can hang around in my back room with the air conditioner watching TV or listening to music, or go up to the roof—whatever you want." She and Rico had settled for the chilly room, taking in, with a half-dozen other children, a monster movie on television.

For that party Lydia wore a tasteful Dior knockoff that she'd sewn herself and based on something that belonged to Mrs. Osprey, a peach-colored, rich-looking bit of business that with her costume jewelry gave Lydia the air of a grand dame. . . . She had been sitting imperiously on the couch with Mireya when Mario, bowing in the manner of a Havana Yacht Club concierge, took her gallantly by the hand and said, "Come along, beautiful." She was not one for dancing in those days, but Mario, *el padrino,* had a way about him, so when he gave her a killer look and pulled her out of her seat, she allowed herself to get carried away by the music. In his living room, raucous with friends and music, she sang and danced, turning in circles, Raul nursing a drink, staring at her with admiration: by then many of the other ladies had joined in, that conga music of the 1930s and 1940s something they'd never forgotten, couples of Lydia's age enjoying the raucousness of passing youth, and Mario, elated, bowing before her, as if she were royalty. . . .

What Had Happened Earlier That Day

That very morning, when Alicia awakened, the sheets under her had been damp from sweat, the air heavy, her limbs and head weighed down from the plentitude teeming through her body. She had been barely able to get out of bed, and moved through the confines of her room—in the back of the apartment, with its view of the courtyard and the laundry lines, where the poor besotted overly plump alley cats picked cautiously through the piles of trash—as if through water. Wobbling as she made her way into the bathroom, a neuralgia pain seemed to be emanating from her hip joints and through her pelvis. Her breasts, which had just a few days before been humbly small, were ever so bloated and her brown nipples suddenly swollen like the tips of a Coney Island balloon, a kind of nightmare of bodily affliction coming over her so that, in the late afternoon, in that other room, as she watched television, Alicia related not to the beautiful young heroine of the movie but to the gargantuan monster towering over the rooftops of some distant city.

Later, the partygoers gathered around Mario's piano in the living room and, in the heat of the day, à la the Cuban salons of the nineteenth century, trumpet players, guitarists, and singers performed an informal, slightly tipsy concert, old hands, children paying their respects to the notion of congeniality—even the most tone-deaf couples, strengthened by love and booze, sang a duet in honor of the birthday man himself. That afternoon some wonderful, well-known musicians and song writers took their place before the keyboard, offering renditions of their hits (mostly from the 1950s), a few torch singers whom Mario knew from the clubs of the city holding forth, as if in the Copacabana or Ciro's of Hollywood, people coming in and out of the living room with paper plates of food and beer to watch and applaud. . . . Mario himself lingered over the piano, snazzy in a tan suit, smoking a cigar and winking and applauding the performances, his wife going around with a Brownie camera, flashing blue lights everywhere. Expected to show off a talent, no matter how minimal, one by one each of the guests performed before the agreeable crowd; beside Lydia on the couch, Raul, on the verge of docility, surprised everyone by getting up; strumming a guitar he sang an old Benny Moré tune, from the days when "Cuba was Cuba." Then suddenly it was Lydia's turn, and while, in years past, she would have sung in a voice she had trouble keeping in pitch, or told a little *chiste*, a naughty rhyme from her youth, this year she played the piano. A few drinks had helped (of course) and memory—for as she listened to a version of Ernesto Lecuona's "*Noche Azul*" ("Blue Night") on the record player, she drifted back, ever so briefly, to her childhood when, among other things, she was a troublesome and difficult piano student. Just then, as she lay her hands on the keyboard (her calloused, rough, moisturized fingers) they were possessed by their memory of a piece by Schumann, "Fantasia in G," a simple study, which she had not played in over twenty-five years. But somehow the notes came to her. Back straight, shoulders firm, head held high, her eyes left that room, and Lydia, transported by the music, and by the joy of competence, performed ably before that gathering of mystified, and then delighted, onlookers.

Now at about six in the evening, just as Lydia was washing her face in the bathroom, and just as Raul slipped back into the kitchen to get another beer, just as Mario trilled his fingers on some high piano keys, during a spirited rendition of "*Quizás, Quizás, Quizás,*" just as Fuentes, the butcher, sighed after a kiss to the neck of his beloved, and as Mireya abruptly blushed because her escort had whispered, "If you knew how I feel," just as the kids on the street below began to kick a volley ball back and forth, and as her own children, Alicia and Rico, sipped Coca-Colas from the can and played Monopoly (for the thrill of becoming temporarily wealthy) with two other children, a man in a trench coat came walking up the hill and, pausing to watch some teenagers on the street, took a last drag of a cigarette and flicked the lit end of the butt into a paper-filled trash can; soon the paper began to smolder and then burn, the box bursting into flame and spreading: first to a pile of wood scraps and then to a shed, next to a wire pen in which a dozen compressed oxygen cylinders were stored. Abruptly, the top of one of these cylinders blew off, and a hissing river of bluish-white flame gushed five stories high, the other canisters soon shaking as if about to explode.

Boom!

A few of Mario's friends had been sitting by the fire escape smoking when the blast had occurred; there was a second loud blast, then a third, more of the flames shooting into the sky: the sun, moving in a summer haze, was scorched further white, and somebody screamed, "*Dios mío!*" for it quickly began to dawn on people what would happen if one of those canisters tipped over in their direction. A kind of panic ensued—people jamming the narrow hallway out of Mario's apartment, but there were enough calm souls at hand: Mario, standing outside his own door, drink in hand, repeating "*Tranquilo, tranquilo,*" Fuentes, who escorted Flora gallantly along, their arms hooked, their expressions saying, "If this is the moment, we

112

will be in paradise together." Even Raul had the composure to call the fire department. Emerging from the bathroom, Lydia herself had been caught in the crowd; some women were crying, others were making the sign of the cross.

... And in that moment, when they put their Monopoly game aside just when Rico's prospects were looking good, Alicia felt a ball of damp cloth, of a warm and viscous texture, unfurling inside of her; with a sting of embarrassment and shame, she realized (as she heard the second blast) what was happening. Her mother had warned Alicia about the physical changes that come to a female at a certain age ("It's something you'll have to get used to, whether you want to or not," Lydia had said), and so she knew that the sensations, of her bottom dropping out, were natural and God given. Even so, her feelings of shame and fear were so strong that she was barely aware of what had been happening on the street: even when Mario roused the children out of the room, she had wanted to hide and examine herself, to see if she were bleeding to death. She would have been content to lock herself in the bathroom—any bathroom—until this scourge in her body passed. It was Rico, however, who told her, "Alicia, we gotta go," and so she found herself descending the stairways, beside him, heading not into a smoke-filled street, but into an atmosphere filled with her own apprehensions.

Most everybody was out of the building when one of the cylinders finally tipped onto its side, setting ablaze a construction trailer and several parked cars: a Cadillac, a Citroën, a 1968 Pontiac. Shortly after, another cylinder exploded and the crowd scattered to the top of the hill, taking shelter behind some cars and watching the flames from a distance. A great column of smoke rose. Black cinders and acrid smoke darkened the windows. Fire trucks arrived, the firemen carried hooks and pikes and hoses and approached the hissing blaze with caution and fear; abruptly running back whenever they heard another metal canister hissing, as if about to explode. A sixth cylinder toppled onto its side and began to spin in a circle like a Chinese pinwheel firework, then shot about fifty feet into the air before dropping into the rubble. The crowd cheered and whistled as if watching a circus.

The Dangerous Time (1965)

That same summer Alicia began to ripen into a local attraction. Her body filled out in all the right places, her face redefined itself, despite her lingering acne, becoming a mask of loveliness. In a Brighton Beach bathhouse, as they changed garments, Lydia found herself admiring her daughter's firm and beautiful body; it struck Lydia that the full-breasted beauty who had nearly burst out of her black one-piece bathing suit was her daughter . . . and it made her feel suddenly old. Out on the sand the same kind of working-class Romeos who would have been indifferent to her just a few months before were suddenly congregating near the family's blanket, showing off with body builder's tricks and tumbling on the sand to impress her. Everywhere she walked there was a man to ask her if she wanted a soda or an ice cream. In its first bloom, her body was so attractive that a hissing sound (like that of the burning canisters) followed her about, men sucking air in through their teeth like serpents. (Hers was the kind of fine young teenage body that had surged past the unsexy prettiness of girlhood into unavoidable nubility—paging Nabokov!) Lydia watched her closely, telling Alicia, straight out, "You don't want men like that in your life—you want someone decent, like your father." (The one with the drink in his hand, over there.) She saw to it that Alicia wore a chain and crucifix around her neck, and as she scampered across the sand, her wondrous body in motion, the crucifix flipped against her bosom. Rico, laying the umbrella beside his father, noted that no less than twelve dif-

114

ferent men, from young to middle-aged, had come to their blanket to talk to Alicia that one afternoon.

From that time on it seemed that whenever Alicia walked down the street toward the subway, to school, to her part-time job at a bakery on Broadway, to "downtown" and the other world, menace flourished in the eyes of men. She now attracted as much attention as Lydia had in Cuba, these latest versions of macho whistling and calling out—"Hey, Mommy"—what sexy women heard.

The Word She Had Never Used

Theft was not an English word that Lydia had ever used, but there eventually came a day when a lady who worked in Mr. Belky's pharmacy, Brenda Myers, knocked on the door, and that word came up in a quite disturbing sentence. Just home from work, with moisturizing cream on her face and hands, Lydia thought it might be Mireya or Concha so they might all go out for a walk in the park (just before dark when the river was beautiful like mica or shale with light, but ever cautiously and wary of strangers, keeping their eyes open, even if just to sit on a bench and watch the boats go by, share a bottle of beer) and she had happily intoned, "*Ya voy.*" Before her in the hallway stood Miss Myers and her own daughter, Alicia, then fifteen years old and sullen, head bowed, her eyes unable to make contact with her mother's. A long-limbed woman of about forty in a flower-patterned wash-and-wear dress, with a beehive hairdo, heavily shadowed eyes, earrings and oversized bracelets, Brenda Meyers, winded from smoking cigarettes and having just run down the street after Alicia, had to rest for a moment before speaking.

"Mrs. España, I don't enjoy telling ya' this, but I'm here because I've just caught your daughter in the act of a theft."

"Don't tell me!"

115

"I was in the back when your daughter grabbed a package of cigarettes, a box of chocolates, and a Ronson lighter, not a cheap item, from behind my counter."

"My little girl? I can't believe it."

"She thought she was pulling a fast one, but what she didn't know is that we have little mirrors. We have one at an angle on the ceiling above the counter, and then a second one that catches that mirror, and that's how—"

"I don't understand, she's always been such a good and honest daughter. . . . I swear this to God."

"I didn't call the police, because I've known your family for ten years, and I didn't want to give you that kind of trouble. But I'm telling you to do something about her because if she does it with me, she'll do it with someone else, and the next time she gets caught, somebody else might not be so nice."

"Yes, you are very kind to let me know this."

Lydia had begun to wipe off the face cream with a towel, and in a low sad voice added: "You know who we are, Miss Meyers, decent people. You know how me and Raul have tried to raise the children properly. How this happened, I don't know." Then: "Believe it when I tell you that we would never never offend you. And as everybody knows we have been very good friends with Mr. Belky for many years." Taking hold of Brenda's arm, she added: "You know her father, my husband, he is not always feeling so well, because he had *un ataque de corazón* when the children were small, and I think maybe this has been hard on them. But I promise you, she will never take anything from you again."

She turned to her daughter and gently raised her daughter's head by the chin, so that she could see her eyes.

"*Mírame hija,* tell your mother who gives of her life blood to put clothes on your back, who has given you everything, why you would do this to such a nice woman like Miss Meyers. *Por qué?*"

But her daughter, dressed in a Columbia University sweatshirt that she'd found in the laundry room and a pair of tight jeans, shrugged and turned away, her face half-covered by thick strands of hair.

Lydia tried again.

"I don't know why you should do such a thing," she said to her daughter. "I don't understand this at all." And to Miss Meyers: "She goes to a good school, Sacred Heart of Mary. If she wants to play the piano, we arrange for lessons at the church. If she wants a dress she just has to ask for it, and we do what we can. . . . Not the best but one that is close. You know how the public school children dress? The ones who live in the projects? They are poor, poor, poor little things, who don't know nothing about manners or education, not even God. We teach her religion. We take her to the church." She thought for a moment. "We even take her to the dances at the good school."

She was referring to the square dances at the Horace Mann School, her hope being that Alicia would meet boys and girls of good breeding of her own age.

"Okay so we don't have so much money, but if God can tell me what we haven't done for this girl—" Just then, grasping at her own throat, she added with great resolve, "But now she is going to promise us both that she will never do anything like this again."

"It would be for her own good."

"Now Alicia, say after me these words: 'I promise the world that I will never never take something from Mr. Belky's pharmacy or from anybody else ever again.' Now say it."

But Alicia turned away, repeating in the most exasperated tone, "Mommmmeee, please."

"I want you to take this woman's hand, this very nice woman who could have made so much trouble for you, and crossing your heart before God—"

"It was only a stupid pack of cigarettes."

"—you will promise that this will never happen again, for as long as you live. No more *robos, sí?*"

"Mom . . ."

"Say it."

Just at that moment Alicia was given an out by Miss Meyers, who said, sighing, "Sweetheart, I just want to make sure you don't make a mess of things. Just tell me it won't happen again and that'll be that, okay?" Then in an even quieter voice, "Can you do that for me?"

It was that quietude that won Alicia over, and although she could barely look up from the floor, covered in stained octagonal tiles, she managed this: "I'm sorry, Miss Meyers, it won't happen again."

"That's the right attitude. You understand, I wouldn't be here except for your own good." Alicia nodded. "Anyways I got to get back to the store."

Lydia and her daughter waited by the doorway as Miss Meyers made her way down the stairs.

"Be careful with the stairs. *Ten cuidao,*" Lydia told her. "And thank you, thank you. You're very kind." To her daughter: "Say good-bye!"

Pausing on the stairwell to light a cigarette, Miss Myers looked back upon Lydia's grateful and smiling countenance and savored the satisfaction of having done something right for a change (her romantic life was a disaster, that's why she was so overweight and wore too much makeup and cheap jewelry, the ladies would say). The instant she was out of sight, Lydia's attitude abruptly changed: she slapped her daughter in the face and shoved her into the apartment, shouting, "For cigarettes, you did this to me! For *basura,* a pack of cigarettes and candy!"

The door slammed shut, and neighbors like the gentle professor Merton, carrying groceries and climbing the stairs to his second-floor apartment, a copy of *The Annals of Tacitus* tucked inside his coat pocket, could hear shouts and weeping and the crashing of things being knocked over—all that coming from the apartment on the third floor.

Indeed, that little run-in with the pharmacy lady unnerved Lydia, for lately, in the past year or so, since becoming beautiful, Alicia had grown increasingly more difficult. No matter how Lydia had tried to impose rules upon her—"Only to protect you!"—she had gravitated toward a pattern of undesirable behavior. She seemed to become half deaf whenever Lydia called out orders to her, or asked Alicia to accompany her down the street. In the late afternoons, when she came home from school or work, she tended to lock herself up in her room, listening to *los Beatle* for hours at a time. She did not have much patience when it came to family excursions—"I don't like the bickering," she once said to Lydia, and Lydia had taken offense, even if she had to ask, *"Qué es* bickering?" Something untoward was going on in the España household—*how Lydia loved to get out of there on some days over to a wonderful place filled with culture and gentility like the Ospreys'*—why this was going on, Lydia, for the life of her, could not say.

One evening, bored by the midsummer heat, Alicia stayed out on the rooftop with a boy until two in the morning. Earlier that night, she had played some volleyball on the side street with friends and when one of the boys suggested that they go up to the rooftop to catch the river breezes, she had liked the idea because then she could look out toward the projects, at all the lights in those windows and their intimations of different lives, and at the airliners on their way to La Guardia or Idlewild airports (what was later called JFK) as they passed overhead, saying, as if in a game, "I wonder where they came from?" The boy was so nice that she let him put his hand inside her blouse and they kissed for a long time, but nothing more happened. Nevertheless, when she snuck into the apartment (at two in the morning) she was caught by Lydia, just in time to receive the second worst beating of her life (broomstick, shoe, hand-slaps, belt). After all her attempts to give her children glimpses of a better world, after all her and Raul's *sacrificios* on their behalf— after all that she was forced to call her own daughter "*una desgraciada*," a malcontented ingrate, and to wash her mouth out with a concoction of Lavoris and baking soda. The punishment did not work. Tell her to walk east and she walked west; Lydia's position—"I am your mother and I am to be obeyed"—countered by "And what is this, Cuba 1942?"

"If you don't respect me, Alicia, then you cannot be a daughter of a Cuban."

And to this, Alicia, already deep into another world, had answered, "And if to be a Cuban's daughter is to be put down for no reason, then you can keep your Cuban this-and-that."

So said the girl who once used to sit on her lap and, cuddling, ask, with sweetness in her eyes: "Mommy, tell me, what was Cuba like?"

In the Days of James Bond (1967)
If the kids wanted to know about their mother's disposition, and why something soft and beautiful and young had changed inside of her, they might have looked to their father. Living with a man who'd nearly died at so young an age made Lydia only more aware of the fleeting nature of existence (something that Cubans were never supposed to think about). For months, beginning one late fall, after she'd been with Osprey for several years, in 1967 or so, it seemed that she lost the daylight. That is to say, in the mornings she would leave for work in the dark and return at night in the dark. Shadows (she swore) seemed to multiply, the asphalt streets and the bumpy cobblestones that

spread out from under the El glowed eerily in the moonlight, if there was any moonlight. Packs of mangy dogs roamed the streets, poking through the garbage, eyes yellow and souls forlorn. Trying to sleep she seemed to hear only the little nails of rats or mice skittering through the rotting inner walls, and the steam heat rising and clacking the pipes. One month when she was starved for light, she went to see *Lawrence of Arabia* five times. The sun, the blue desert sky, O'Toole's whimsical expression soothed her. Chills erupted frequently in her bones.

At night she sat in bed, thinking about her kids and their future, and listened to late night radio talk shows, a palm-sized Japanese transistor radio (John's Bargain Stores, $3.99) held curled against her ear. As Raul tossed and turned, snoring, she heard discourses on Vietnam, kids and drug use, free love, civil rights, the Soviet Union, and the cold war.

She often pondered the questions brought up on those shows: "Should JFK have dropped the atomic bomb on Cuba to get rid of Castro, leaving cities devastated and millions dead, in the name of freedom?" (*"No!"*) Or, "Where were you on the day JFK was assassinated?" (Lydia had come home from work in time to see her two American children just after they'd heard the news, the priest of their school having told them, "Let us pray that his soul be commended unto God," her two American children moved enough to cry.) And she tried to comprehend other pressing American issues of the day, enjoying the simple company of the late night voices, until her eyes closed and she dropped the radio, the case splitting open and the Eveready batteries rolling across the linoleum floor.

On those nights, she'd think about Raul; in 1965 he'd endured a second heart attack, a *cardiac episode* it was called. This took place at five-thirty one morning, after Raul had stayed up all night drinking and smoking and playing whist with some friends. Smoking a cigarette at the kitchen table after his friends had left, he felt a pain rising out of his gut toward his heart, put the cigarette out, and then, forlorn as a sickly child, climbed into bed beside Lydia, curling himself around her and saying to her, meekly, "Lydia, please, I think I better go to the hospital."

He ended up staying in the hospital for two weeks, a doctor telling him, "You are a lucky man."

It must have been so, because after his hospital stay he kept on tempting fate. The medicine cabinet was filled with drugs that he did not care to take. Finding it impossible to reform his ways, he would come home from work, have a few drinks, and declare happily, "What the hell, if you gotta go, you gotta go." Two hours later he would say, "What does any of this matter, anyway?" An hour later, he would call his children into the kitchen to tell them, "You should know that your Poppy's not going to be around all that long, so be good to him." And by midnight, sometimes, his voice carried into the hallway, asking, "Doesn't anybody here care about what's going to happen to me?"

With that, he took on the air of someone waiting on a desolate subway platform at three o'clock in the morning.

Now that he was older, with mortality staring him in the face, what made Raul happy were the attentions of his family. He lived to come home, and although he had his bad nights, contentment often visited him, despite himself. Lydia's presence, her strength and occasional affection, gave him great joy, though she was the worse for wear. The two of them were something to see, as they sat after work in the kitchen, Raul with his special padded shoes, soaking his feet in a *palangana* of tepid water and Epsom salts, Lydia drinking a beer while her kids rubbed her aching shoulders. On those evenings Raul felt so grateful to Lydia that he would find himself following her

around. Sitting on the pink furry toilet-seat cover in the bathroom, he would hold forth about the day's events while she
undressed and took her shower. He'd hang around her as she
cooked dinner and then sit at the table waiting to be waited on.
(Raul's favorite meal, incidentally, was fried steak with lemon
and onions, the rind, or *pellejo*, bad as hell for your health but
ever so tasty, sweet plantains, and rice and beans, with a side dish
of garlic and olive oil and salt-smothered yucca.)

At first, Lydia was so fond of him that none of this behavior
exasperated her, even on those nights when she wanted to just sit
down and read a book or talk with one of her friends. Usually the
hours passed pleasantly, but at night, when he suffered in bed,
especially in the months after his hospital stay, when he was
haunted by bad dreams that often made him shout, she herself
felt like weeping. Yet she refused to let anyone know what was
going on inside her: she was, above all, *fuerte y dura*. They
shouted at each other, but she had no doubt of her love for him.
Often she found him asleep in the living room, where he loved to
watch old black-and-white movies on the television. She would
remove his eyeglasses, his shoes, covering him with a blanket,
and trying to make the man as comfortable as possible, give him
a kiss. Sometimes his eyes would flash open, and Raul, taking her
by the hand, would tell her, "You're my woman."

Of course, living in the good old USA for so long, he had
acquired a number of New York-isms. The term *ticker* for his
heart he'd either gotten from "Irish Al," the dishwasher from
Killarney, or from an MGM film—who knew?

("The ticker's not what it used to be," he'd say to company.
Then he would feel his pulse and add, "But what are you
gonna do?" Then in Spanish, "*Carajo.*")

Generally speaking, Raul had *New York* written all over him: years in the restaurant business around all types of citizens had not only given him a grasp of Italian, a little French, Greek, and German, as well as Yiddish, but he had, like Mario, picked up a "mid-New Yawky" accent, half out of Brooklyn, as it were, with Spanish inflections. Baseball, pizza, Sen-Sens, cigarettes—first Chesterfields, then "Luckies," then Winstons—and, as with everybody else in the world, movies became part of his life. Looking at this slight and frail-seeming man, one would not have guessed his taste in films—Tarzan, John Wayne and Randolph Scott westerns, and, beginning in the early 1960s, James Bond movies, starring Sean Connery—the scenery, the weaponry, the absurd, exhilarating plots, the beautiful women in bikinis helping Raul forget his troubles: the back and forth between the kitchen and the dining room at Jimmy's, the accounting at the end of the day, the occasional hard feelings between himself and the younger waiters, who had no sympathy for the fact that he had been ill, and considered him a slacker if he took, with the bosses' approval, "five" to rest every so often, the fatiguing side effects of his heart medications, disruptive letters or telephone calls from his angry ex-wife if he was as much as a few days late with the money. ("*If you are a decent man you will do the right thing and continue to put food in the mouths of your own flesh and kin. And if you aren't decent about it, believe me, I know people in New York who would do me a very nice favor taking care of you, my love.*") And, beyond these things, a fantasy that his gravestone would say something like "Raul España, 1920—19—, Cuban waiter who never complained a day and got nothing for it," a sense that he was not everything he should be in the eyes of his beloved wife, nothing like the heroic Bond himself.

In a Better Life

Of that generation that still wore ties and jackets and hats when they went out in public, he bought a fresh flower every other day for a quarter from a flower seller on Lexington Avenue, near Jimmy's. He was often seen on subway platforms, street corners, or by bus stops with a carnation pressed to his nose, his eyes closed during his respectful appreciation of what he considered one of God's good wonders. Flower shops enchanted him because, aside from the rosemary and oregano of the kitchen, the leafy salads drowned in oil and the plastic flower centerpieces that sometimes graced the tables, he lived largely in a world of grilled steaks, baked potatoes, meat loaf, and fried chicken, foods that, while delicious and necessary, lacked the soulfulness of a single rose.

In a better life, Raul used to think he would have been a florist, passing his days in a sunny window among orchids and forsythias, but it was a hard way to make a living, and despite his fantastic respect for flowers and nature, Raul lacked a horticultural education. When he was a young man fresh from Cuba, in the mid-1940s, knowing little of the English language, work in a kitchen as a dishwasher was about all he could find; for all its shortcomings, his last fifteen years of waiting tables was a grand step up from washing dishes, and, short of being a cook or owning a restaurant himself, he had done well enough.

At whatever hour he came home, he was always the image of grandeur, no matter how lousy his wages. In the cooler season he wore a secondhand overcoat with black velvet collars, a silk scarf (gift from Lydia), and a black-brimmed Homburg. People who did not know him took him for some kind of professional, and when someone, like the new fruit seller on the street, asked, "You ain't a lawyer, are you?" he would feel flattered enough to say, "No, but if you have some troubles and want to talk about them, let's go have a drink."

In the habit of finding much contentment in watching action and cowboy programs on TV after he came home from work, Raul wanted to put enough money away to buy a color set. Sometimes when he took the kids out for a walk they would stand in front of the Zenith television shop on 121st Street and Amsterdam and watch different shows—*Bonanza* or *Gunsmoke*—silently through the window, the big 25-inch screen glowing like a god, or as enchanting as a beautiful woman or a trunk filled with jewels. Someone would say, "Maybe one day, huh, Pop?" and Raul, rustling his hands in his pockets and blinking, a little sadly, always told the children, "We'll see."

But no matter how many extra blocks they walked to pay a few cents less for a quart of milk or how, at the end of the day's work, they waited in the long lines at the co-op supermarket on 124th Street to save a few dollars on their grocery shopping, money flew out of their pockets. Yes, his children would have crawled on their knees from 125th Street to the Bowery to change the look of disappointment they saw on his face.

Years later, when his son, Rico, charging his patients one hundred and fifty dollars per forty-five-minute session, would have a bank account big enough to choke a horse, and more than enough money to buy a dozen color TV sets if he liked, it would kill him to think that it had all come too late for him to take care of his father.

In time Raul began to dream about his heart. Doctors at the hospital, in giving him their recommendations as to his home care, inspired him to ask around the 125th Street library for books, and reading about the heart and the human circulatory system, he suddenly acquired a new take on the quivery pans of internal organs that he saw in the glass cases inside Mr. Fuentes' butcher shop. (One day when Raul was contemplating the bulky and sanguinated heart of a calf, the butcher proffered this: "*What was once chewing the grass of a meadow becomes that nourishment on the ceramic fields of our table.*") He claimed that he was aware of the "abused" weight inside his chest. There was talk of some kind of operation but he refused on the grounds that he was in "God's hands," and because the French stationery shop owner on Broadway had gotten one and died on the operating table. And yet, the longer he kept after his own pulse, the more he began to feel amazed that the little machine kept on going, like a Timex, day in and day out. There was the night when he dreamed that the calf's heart was sitting on the end table by his bed, that it began ringing like an alarm clock at three in the morning. In a panic Raul sat up, sweating, his real heart beating frantically. Swinging his arms he knocked over the table lamp, a glass of water, and a stack of Lydia's romance novels, imagining that it was the heart falling and rolling under the bed, a commotion that woke everyone in the apartment.

And in the middle of one night he had his "religious dream." Having been feeling anxious about his health, he awoke to see a great tongue of light floating before him; this light "told" him—and this is what he reported to Lydia in the morning— "*Aquí te encontrarás la verdad,*" or "Here you will find the truth." Hearing this, he sat stunned in his pajamas at the edge of the bed, and then he knelt on the floor, his head tilted toward the ceiling, hands folded in prayer.

In the morning, when he told Lydia about his "vision," she told him, "What a pretty dream." But it changed something inside of him, for aside from certain other affectations like the white carnation in his lapel, he began to wear something that he had not worn before, an expression of utter sanctity. Shortly thereafter, he got in the habit of greeting friends and passersby with the words, "God bless you."

Lydia did not always know what to do with him.

Other Jobs

Substituting for her friend Carlita on the East Side, she cleaned a two-bedroom apartment on 84th Street off Second Avenue (too far over, but money was money) where a large number of stewardesses shared the rent and stayed on different days of the month. Laundry lines full of lady's hosiery and underwear were strung out over the courtyard and the bathroom was cluttered with travel bags and curlers and more medicines than she had ever seen outside a hospital. Cleaning those rooms, she discovered hotel ashtrays and towels, lipstick-rimmed airline coffee mugs and plates and pens, silk airline scarves in evidence everywhere—souvenirs and the little amenities of their jobs. (How she envied those who could travel the world, the extent of her own excursions, the Bronx and Brooklyn dance halls or beaches, thank you.)

She would clean there in the morning, leave in the midafternoon. The doorman and building staff were professional enough and she had gotten into a slight flirtation with the handsome Puerto Rican superintendent. In a good delicatessen around the corner she would spend thirty-five cents on a roast beef sandwich and looked forward to walking over, if the day was nice, toward Gracie Mansion park and eating a late lunch. But one morning, in the third week, as soon as she had arrived and opened the door, she distinctly heard a man and a woman talking in the bedroom, then the intermittent sound of kissing. She wanted to leave. But it was pouring outside and she didn't feel like going down to the lobby, and she didn't want to hang around in the hallway or in the stinking garbage room (as she had once before while a man and wife were having a terrible fight, and she sat on the stairs reading a newspaper until she heard the door slamming and could not bear it when the wife came to the door bruised and in tears). So she decided "To hell with this" and slammed the door behind her and went into the kitchen, clanking pots so there would be no mistake that someone else was in the apartment. Thinking that she would begin in the kitchen, which would give the people a chance to clear out, she heard them as they started to make love: bed noises, the man crying out in pleasure, a radio or glasses knocked off a table, then the woman moaning "Oh God," over and over again.

As Lydia remained in the kitchen, cleaning out the oven for nearly half an hour, she felt like lecturing them: "You should not be fornicating when you know your cleaning woman is coming to the apartment. Especially in the morning!" It was about ten-thirty when that bedroom door finally opened: a clicking of bottles, and the smell of booze. A black man in a naval uniform came out into the living room; when Lydia cleared her throat, he turned, saying, "Hey, how ya doing?" Drunk, drunk, drunk, was what Lydia thought. Then the woman came out after him. She was a plumpish blond with milky white skin, about thirty. She wore a light-blue night-gown and fluffy slippers, and she was drunk, too: "Be careful, and don't forget me when you get to San Diego, promise?" she said, but as if her mouth were stuffed with feathers. Then, "I'll let you know when my husband's away."

"Right by me. . . ."

Then she gave him a long and lingering kiss by the door, and when he'd left she went into the bathroom to take a shower.

The pleasures of life and youth reverberated in her voice as the stewardess sang ("Downtown"). Lydia, murmuring to herself, continued to work, nodding ever so briefly when the stewardess, in a robe and with a towel wrapped around her head, came out and went into her bedroom. Later, she approached Lydia as she was arranging some magazines on a coffee table. The stewardess was well dressed—pillbox hat, jacket and trousers, white high-heel shoes, as if she were going out to a fancy luncheon, like the kind that Mrs. Osprey attended. She wore too much rouge, in Lydia's opinion. She said, in a Southern-sounding accent, "I assume you speak English, yes?"

"Yes, *señorita*."

"Good—I'm just going to say one thing to you, which is don't breathe a word to anyone about what you saw here this morning, understand?"

"Who do I know who would care?" And she stepped back demurely, bowing her head. She was wearing a little golden crucifix that Raul had given her for Christmas, and this she touched as if to "swear" on the cross.

The stewardess smiled.

"And when you do the bedroom I want you to know that I left the sheets rolled up in the corner; there's fresh linen in the closet."

"No problem."

"I guess you know your pay is in an envelope in the kitchen drawer."

"Yes."

Then: "Now don't forget what I said to you."

"I promise you."

When the young woman left, Lydia headed straight into the bedroom; on the floor, a stewardess's uniform, a light-blue brassiere, a pair of torn black panties. On a dresser, a picture of the young woman with a man, somewhere in Europe, an inscription saying, "For Linda, Happy Birthday, Mike." There was a scent of sex in the air, despite the fact that they'd splashed cologne everywhere; the sheets themselves were still warm to the touch. She thought, "Young people have no judgment and they're crazy."

Earlier, when the stewardess cried out in pleasure, Lydia, reeling with the memory of how much she used to scream sometimes, remembered what a good sex life was like, and for a fleeting instant, her ears burned with jealousy. Up to that moment, she had not given much thought to stewardesses, but suddenly her head was rife with speculations—it occurred to her that being a stewardess would be exciting; to fly around the world and have love affairs with handsome men. . . .

Pissed off to no end, she collected the sheets and sat on the bed. Then she opened the window and the rain-cooled air, rushing into the room, seemed like the freshest air she had ever breathed: To see the world.

The Good Dr. K—— (1967)

There had been an elderly psychiatrist in the West 90s, "a woman who studied with the very famous Sigmund Freud," a friend of Lydia's confided as they were walking along West End Avenue. "Do you know who Freud is?"

"I never heard of him."

"He is someone very important to people who are sick in the head," and her friend made a crazy sign with her index finger. "He invented a way for people to come and share their dreams with him, so that if they had a problem or certain kinds of worries he could help them."

"Like the witches of our childhood?"

"Yes," her cleaning lady friend said. "People come at a certain time of the day and they sit or lie on a couch and confess their innermost thoughts; sometimes their sins. People go to seek out the deepest causes of their troubles. Couples go when their marriages are falling apart, single people when they are lonely." Then she added: "These doctors are called psychiatrists," which she pronounced *see-key-a-treast*.

"So they're like priests?"

"It is almost the same as when people go to confession, but different, because they don't believe in God," her friend said nodding. "This one, she is very nice lady, very old, and not always careful in her habits. Every time you go there she will tell you that she studied with Freud. And she will show you a picture of them together."

Lydia's temporary employer lived on an upper floor, in a large apartment with a view of a street of brownstones, that was decorated in an old world fashion: what met the eye were the multitude of books, many, written in German and smelling of dust and paper rot, left in stacks on the front hallway floor; others overflowed immense floor-to-ceiling bookcases—and there was a wall of photographs, which her friend pointed out, as they stood in the musty hall. "You see that baldy with the beard? That is Freud."

"How serious he looks." Lydia looked around and asked: "Is there a lot to do here?"

"The kitchen, the bathrooms, and the room in which she sees her patients. But otherwise she doesn't want anything touched." She whispered: "She has a room filled with old newspapers, another of old clothes that she never wears anymore." Then: "But she is very nice."

Shortly the doctor arrived: an older white-haired woman, on crutches, dressed entirely in black, her presence reminding Lydia of a saggy-skinned and wrinkled witch who terrified her in a recurring childhood dream.

"Dr. K——, this is my friend Lydia, who will be taking care of things here while I am away."

Lydia shook the doctor's hand and looking around cheerfully told her, "It's a nice apartment you have, doctor."

"You think so? For me it is my hell and prison on earth." And she stomped one of her crutches against the floor. "My heaven was the clinic." Then, in a heavy European accent: "Did Luisa tell you that I once studied with Sigmund Freud in Europe?"

"Oh yes."

"That was many years ago, before the war, before I came to this country." And she walked over to a window and looked

132

off into the distance. "I can pay you twenty-five dollars for the day, which I think is very fair, yes?"

"Yes." It was more than what Mr. Osprey paid her at the time.

"Good, then you will come on Fridays for this month. Luisa will show you what to do."

The apartment was gloomy, even more gloomy than the apartment of the supernaturally inclined man who had leapt from his window: there was little air, for the windows had been nailed shut and had not been cleaned for a very long time. Many of the rooms were dependent upon the sun, as the doctor did not like leaving the lights on, but even then light broke through the curtains intermittently, in solemn shafts. Only a sweet, natty-haired tomcat, whose front teeth had been broken (the doctor, a kindly person, had taken him in from the street) helped to relieve the monastic atmosphere, creeping out of nowhere and purring and rubbing itself against Lydia's legs, at the most unexpected times. . . .

"The only thing you must never do when the doctor is here is to make noise," her friend then confided. "You can't vacuum when she is seeing her patients. And no music. Once I was playing the radio really softly at the other end of the apartment, but she somehow heard it. . . . Most importantly, if you see any of her patients, pretend you don't notice them; even if they are crying or look crazy, do nothing, even if they smile or say hello. Understand, Lydia?"

"Yes."

The doctor was the kind of person who took endless comfort in having many possessions and the dustier the better, as if dust were a kind of armor. Lydia never felt particularly comfortable working in that apartment, half-suffocating and experiencing allergic symptoms. (How she would have loved to polish the doctor's bronze lamps and candlesticks, with their patina of time, elegant to collectors, filthy to a cleaning woman.) But she found herself thinking that the many photographs of this Sigmund Freud and Dr. K——, as a pretty young woman, were interesting. One photograph of them standing on a street corner somewhere in Europe—Vienna?—she liked very much: the woman was wearing a long-skirted dress that reached her ankles, a big-buttoned blouse and vest, a broad buckled belt, and a large sun hat with a silken scarf around its brim. In one of her hands, a parasol, on which she leaned—what she heard Dr. K—— refer to as *"umbrello."* Freud, who was dressed in a black suit and derby, held her by the elbow. Standing in front of a spired zoo or park fence, they were looking at each other in an affectionate manner, Lydia thought.

She would not, however, trade her life for that of the doctor's.

Indeed, she had seen the troubled people hurrying from her consultation room, some of them in tears, and had grown accustomed to hearing their low murmuring voices through the door while she went about her work, trying to mind her own business. Seeing some of the patients with their sad and troubled expressions, she counted her own blessings. She had hardly any contact with the doctor, but on the third Friday of her temporary employment, when the doctor came out to take a tea break, she invited Lydia into her kitchen to talk.

Lydia did not want to, but the doctor was insistent, sitting her down and pouring her a cup of tea. For reasons she did not understand, Lydia said, "My father never drank tea. We only drank coffee, and very strong coffee at that. He died a few years ago."

The doctor, her eyes sympathetic, looked at her and nodded. "Were things good between you? Were you at peace with him?"

"I wish I had been."

"And?"

"I wish I had been taught more about life."

"The thing with life," the doctor began, "is that only so many opportunities come along, in love, in a profession, in matters of

travel and adventure. When I was young I fell in love with someone who did not love me; and because I was naive and ready to
wait forever I did not allow myself to look for others. I was stupid, because, when that ended, and badly, I believed that there
would be others, but, you see, I was already too old and set in my
ways. Then there was the war. I had many friends and colleagues
who were sent to the concentration camps, but, on the advice of
a mentor, I had escaped to Switzerland, where I lived for ten
years. There I found a position at a research institute, where we
worked to develop drug treatments for the mentally ill . . . but I
was blamed for some things that went wrong there—it was not
my fault, but some of my patients, to whom I was administering
injections, fell into paralysis and died." And she pounded on the
table. "That's how I ended up here in New York."

"*Ay*, that's a sad story," Lydia said.

"We all have some sadness in our life, don't we?" Then,
changing her tone, and smiling: "You have a very nice face, and
you are such a good person I would like to give you a present."

Extending her hand, so that Lydia could assist her, she got to
her feet and opened a cabinet. From this she removed a lovely
cookie tin, which she laid down on the table. Removing the
lid—a Swiss winterland scene of a young couple driving a
sleigh through the snow—she said: "This is a kind of nut brittle I have made. I don't cook very much, but I had an uncle
who was a confectioner and I have never forgotten the recipe.
Would you like one?"

The hand offering the brittle was shaking, and the doctor's
face was weary: "Really, my dear, it's very very good."

"I can't," Lydia told her. "I'm on a diet."

"You on a diet? Bosh . . . Please, you must try one; I made
them just the other day. They are delicious, with caramel and
pecans and other secret ingredients."

"I really can't."

"But please, just try this little piece."

The doctor broke off a piece of brittle and Lydia opened her mouth in the way she did in church while taking communion, accepting the candy as if it were a wafer. While doing so, she had the look of someone about to eat poison.

"It's not so bad, is it?" the doctor asked, watching Lydia.

The candy was reminiscent in its richness of the way candy used to taste to Lydia when she was a little girl; as rich as the earth and the sugar that grew out of it. What was it that she used to especially enjoy, long ago, when she was still on good terms with her father? A piece of guava jelly on a simple cracker from his bakery, its tastiness, to that day, never surpassed. And that taste of candy did something else, for as she chewed, the doctor's eyes seemed to take on a happy cast, and Lydia could imagine her as a little girl in her uncle's bakery, enjoying herself in the way that Lydia used to enjoy her father's bakery in Cuba. There was a time, she remembered, when she would spend entire mornings beside her father's workers, fascinated, then bored, by all the processes that the baking profession entailed: the transformations of flour, shortening, salt, and water into the ever tasty biscuits that pleased so many people seeming so magical to her. . . . The thought was fleeting.

She said, "How delicious," thanked the doctor for her thoughtfulness, and returned to her chores.

Later, that night, at around three in the morning, Lydia, sleeping in an odd position, awakened because her legs had gone numb underneath her, and for one fleeting moment she imagined that a spell had been cast on her: then her circulation returned and she became aware that she was in her bedroom in New York, as a grown woman, not a young girl in Cuba having a bad dream; that her mother and father were not asleep in their room down the tile hall from her door, nor her sisters in the rooms next to hers. She realized, quite simply, that she was a cleaning woman leading a more or less humble, largely uneventful life in New York City.

With Dear Miss Jenkins

By this time Lydia had climbed certain stairways in the New York City subway system thousands of times, had paused by the same kiosks nearly every morning of the week to buy from a blind woman her *El Diario* and *Daily News*, if she were in the mood to read English. She nearly vomited, one morning, when sick with the flu, the crush of bodies and their smells of perfume, Sen-Sen, body odor, and heavy breath in the car almost too much to bear, and she stopped before the clouded windows of a subway car endless times to make sure that her hair and lipstick looked fine, something wearying beyond her own broken reflection, each time she looked, in the funerary processionals of subway girders, the darkness going on, it seemed, forever.

She put up with a lot. With calluses, sore joints, the discovery of *arrugas* around her eyes. With hot trains and bad-breath people, some guys in excited states, *cochinos*, rubbing up against her even on the steamiest, most uncomfortable rides home—she once turned around to see a man who'd been fondling the girls, just as he tilted back his head, grimacing with orgasm. And there was more that she had endured, or not understood, things that were simply ugly, like the time she saw a man with his two young children on the downtown number 1, the man nodding tranquilly and smiling, as his children, up on their knees on the subway seats, licked the filthy car windows like candy, or like when she had been riding back down from the Bronx with Raul after a birthday party for a friend and watched one man exhibiting his skills in oral love with another, so that Lydia hurriedly led the family out of that car. There were other things that did not seem "regular" or "normal" that she saw nearly daily as she went about her cleaning lady's life in New York.

In the name of the family, the future, and the holiness of bucks, she used to say.

As bad as she felt sometimes, dealing with the trash and nonsense of life, she was not in a hopeless situation like Miss Jenkins, that pretty actress in the wheelchair. Now there was someone with real troubles. She'd injured her spinal column as a girl and yet had managed to dream about a career on stage. She lived in a studio apartment on Columbus Avenue, when it was a hoody street, and the chaos of her lodgings, with make-up mirrors, and cosmetic trays, and lotions and creams and tranquilizers everywhere, broke Lydia's heart. She had become an actress because as a young girl she wanted to be like Marilyn Monroe. On her wall there was a poster of Marlon Brando from his film *The Wild One*, and whenever Lydia came to the apartment, Miss Jenkins, in the open way of *los jóvenes de hoy*, would tell her, "I would love to have a thing with him."

Lydia laughing would say, "And who wouldn't. He's a good actor, and a friend of mine once told me, Marlon Brando really knows how to mambo."

Miss Jenkins was always telling Lydia about her acting prospects. She made it out to her auditions, and the producers and directors were tolerant and compassionate enough to give her the time of day, but she never got any jobs. How could she? Lydia marveled at her good nature: the reliance on bed-pans alone would have made Lydia crazy. But the young woman somehow retained, or seemed to retain, a childlike optimism. Truly a brave-seeming soul, Miss Jenkins. Lydia almost felt guilty about collecting her pay. This young woman, without any romantic prospects in her life, left even Lydia with the feeling that money did not solve everything, for Miss Jenkins was from a wealthy family.

Most painful were their "hopeful" conversations, for Miss Jenkins, daydreaming, in the way that Lydia daydreamed herself, would say, "It's never too late to become a movie star: there's a saying in my business that if you hang in there long enough you'll eventually get your break." Lydia nodded and said, "I am sure that you will get whatever you want," and this always made the young woman happy. But one day, she was so sad that she blurted out, "Mrs. España, could you just give me a hug for a minute?" And Lydia did so, holding the young woman and feeling as awkward as she did when she held her own children. . . .

The Coffee Shop (1967)

Priests and theological students, walking about in all their righteousness, were to be seen on Broadway coming out of their seminaries. The smell of stagnant Hudson River water mixed with animal blood from the meat packing plants on 125th Street, and garbage trucks pulled up in front of tenements at four in the morning; packs of forlorn dogs roamed the streets, poking through the garbage. Sometimes, on those nights, some jazz musicians climbed up to the rooftops to practice their scales or to beat on drums, by moonlight. Out of one of the dark basement entranceways, on Saturday afternoons, one heard the musicians of a mambo band rehearsing; the musicians, friendly fellows, sometimes worked with Mario and could be seen walking up the street at three in the morning, weary after a late job. There was a gospel group that rehearsed in a first floor apartment around the corner, in a building reputedly known for its prostitutes and music students.

Over on Amsterdam Avenue, on the same block as the Cuban beauty salon there was a basement coffee shop with brick floors, curlicue iron tables, and uncomfortable thin-legged chairs, a toilet bowl filled with peanuts in their shells set out in the middle of

139

the floor, a source of fascination for the cleaning woman's children, who were barely teenagers when this shop first appeared in 1964; jazz albums—by Cal Tjader, Herbie Mann, John Coltrane—hanging taped to the walls alongside framed Marxist homilies, which they read as taboo and therefore enchanting. There was also a signed photograph from a local celebrity, George Carlin, who grew up on 121st. The brighter kids of the neighborhood, like Rico, were attracted to this place—being desperate to experience something different—for the coffee shop was known for the voracity of its discussions, held mainly by leftist college students. And even though it would have killed many a recently arrived Cuban just to walk into that place, and would have deeply offended his own mother and father, Rico, liking the atmosphere, gravitated toward the owner, a charismatic and knowledgeable half-Puerto Rican, half-Italian man named Eliseo, who lectured the kids and anyone else who came into his shop, saying that modern capitalistic society, circa 1967, was just a form of feudalism in disguise.

A handsome, stringy fellow of about forty, he wore a Lenin-style beard; his main wardrobe seemed to consist of a beret, an oversized woolen turtleneck, blue jeans, and, if the weather was warm, sandals. He was, for all his fiery convictions, an easy-going man with intelligence and nobility in his light green eyes, and a quality of sweetness that female passersby found particularly intriguing.

Much like his father in his shyness and quietude, Rico would spend the little free time he had taking in the ambience of that place—the jazz, the passionate stances on politics, right or wrong, the sense of mission and seediness of the people who gathered there. Every so often, if something was bothering him, Rico would find Eliseo, to talk things over in a way that he could not with his own father and mother. He had confessed, among other things, that he had been attracted to "a rich chick," Osprey's daughter ("Why do you want to be with people like that, when they'll fuck up your values?") and his brief flirtation with drugs. When Rico told him about the heroin, Eliseo's eyes grew wide and fiery, like a preacher's, and he said: "You know the government wants that shit in neighborhoods like this. You know that?"

"No."

"They use it to keep people stupid." Then: "If you ever take it again, I'll break your neck, okay?"

Mainly, Rico hung around Eliseo because he liked the intellectual stimulation; because there was a musty bookish smell about the place, and because, regardless of his politics, he enjoyed Eliseo's friendship.

Alicia had gone there for the first time when Lydia told her to go look for Rico at "the communist's," as she called the coffee shop. Indeed when Alicia showed up, Eliseo was holding forth with diatribes against the system before a group of young people, among them Rico. Perhaps it was his ferocity, the passion in his eyes, the virility of his stance, but Alicia, then sixteen, was instantly taken by him.

"If the limb is putrefying, then it must be chopped off," he was saying—and somehow the contents of that phrase especially spoke to her; she beamed a smile at him and he, noticing the voluptuous schoolgirl (for she was in her Sacred Heart of Mary uniform), winked. He shouted, "To move forward and to throw off the oppressors, that's what it's all about, my friends." And even though he was talking about politics, Alicia trembled, as if he had intended the comment for a young girl in the midst of mounting familial troubles.

It was a fact that even though Lydia was the picture of civility when she was working for the Ospreys, at home she had become, in terms of temperament, much like her father when it came to dealing with problems of discipline. She was particularly vigilant about Alicia, who, as time passed, began to show more and more impatience with what she regarded as the provinciality of her family's life. She shuddered when she heard the "rinky-tink" of Latin music and aggravated her mother no end by playing her beloved Beatles as loudly as possible. Lydia threatened to smash every one of those recordings and to hide the phonograph.

Coming home from school one afternoon, Alicia found her Beatles fanzine posters taken down from the wall, and Alicia reacted by "running away." She took a subway to the Village, to Washington Square Park, where she listened to some musicians who were performing by a fountain, and there she had met someone who knew somebody at the door of the Cafe Wha, where she went to have a hamburger platter and a Coke, while a band played. The fellow who had taken her offered to give her LSD, but she refused, and when he became too pushy, she slipped out of the club and made her way to the East Village, spending the night in the doorway of an abandoned Yiddish theater on Second Avenue, awaiting the dawn.

In that time, three men offered her money to go to bed with them. But there she remained until seven in the morning, when a police officer, making his rounds, found her hiding behind a piling of boxes: by eleven-thirty she was back home. "Did you know that your father nearly died of another heart attack because you were gone?" "Do you know what people are going to think?" "Are you thanking God that something horrible did not happen to you?" "If you don't like it here, then maybe we should send you to Cuba, where the people really have it bad, then you'll see."

There was, as well, the usual punishment.

Smitten by Eliseo's worldly demeanor, Alicia got into the habit of talking with him nearly every afternoon. He would let her smoke one of his pungent French cigarettes on the sly and she could put on whatever records she liked. Every time she walked home with Rico she spoke of Eliseo as a "real friend" and as someone "who really knows about life." She took to wearing a beret (which Lydia promptly threw out) and even managed to smuggle one of his books, Fanon's *The Wretched of the Earth*, into the apartment without reading it. To impress him, she memorized communist aphorisms and wrote, at one point, on the inside back cover of one of her notebooks, "*Workers of the World Unite for You Have Nothing to Lose But Your Chains!*"

Watching all this from a perturbed distance was Lydia, who decided to go to the coffee shop herself after work one late afternoon. Irritable with fatigue, she wanted to slap Eliseo in the face, for the first things she saw when she peeked into his window were photographs of Che Guevara and Ho Chi Minh. She found him downstairs behind a counter writing in a ledger. With venom in her eyes, she told him bluntly, "I understand my son and daughter have been coming here. I want you to know, *señor*, that I do not care for them to be consorting with someone of your character and," looking around at the revolutionary posters on the wall, "beliefs, *me entiendes?*"

He invited her to sit.

"*Señora* España. The truth is, and ask anyone, I am not in the habit of encouraging children to come into my shop. But this is a free country and when people come in here, I don't care how old they are, they can participate in the discussions we have here; and they're welcome to the books." Then: "You know that you have intelligent children?"

"So?"

"Naturally they are going to be attracted to ideas. Both of them are very intrigued by certain progressive ideals, particularly your daughter."

"She's too young for this nonsense."

"Politics is not nonsense."

"But communism is," and Lydia, her voice more strident added, "and it is a poison."

Their conversation might have ended right then and there, but then Eliseo told her, "Mrs. España, I promise you, when it comes to your kids, all I want for them is to know the truth. My belief is that everybody is lying to everybody else through the teeth. The truth of something is what is important." Then: "But that's not all I discuss with them; if they're having questions about life, I try to steer them right. Mainly, I counsel them to love and respect their family . . . your family."

"You counsel them?"

"I can't help it. I was in a Benedictine seminary in upstate New York for three years before I went into social work, which I have practiced at adult education centers in the Bronx and in Manhattan. But this—these books and records and, yes, if the truth be told, politics, are all I really care about. That is my dedication: to be a part of the changes taking place in the world."

"Don't tell me you were a priest?"

"A monk," he told her.

"*Ay*, but you're a communist. . . . What shit are you talking?"

"I am a progressive man with a belief in helping others, that is all. If I am not a monk living in a cave it's because I could not find *God* in my heart." Then he poured each of them a beer and raised his glass in a toast: "Whatever else you think of me, I feel honored to meet you."

Suddenly she found herself so taken in by the guilelessness and oddball charm of his manner that she forgot why she had gone there. After another beer she found herself getting a little drunk and telling him, "You know, *Señor* Eliseo, some things have been hard . . ."

"On us all."

And she did not mind at all when he leaned forward to whisper a confidence—"I've tried everything, the seminary,

144

even marriage, but that was not for me ..."—and gently touched her on the wrist, the warmth of his heart and soul calming her.

They must have talked for an hour, before Lydia realized she had to get home to Raul—run a warm bath for him, cook his dinner, attend to the kids, and then, after finishing the dishes, she'd finally have some time to herself. But oddly, she didn't feel like going home—a kind of elation having come over her, because of the strangeness of the atmosphere, the music of Thelonious Monk, the openness of Eliseo's manner, and, steering away from the Cuban revolution, the woman's liberation movement, an idea that startled her. After a short time with him, she could see why Alicia kept going back: there was something so supremely reassuring about Eliseo, and he seemed to know exactly what to say: "I don't know what your biggest problems are in life but I am confident that you will solve them." And as she left him, he told her: "Please come back, *Señora* España, and think of Eliseo Fernandez as your friend."

She imagined that being charmed by Eliseo was equivalent to what happened with the Cuban people whenever they listened to a speech, often hours and hours long, by Fidel Castro. "We hear him on the radio and for the duration of the speech we feel fine: afterwards his effect upon us turns into air." Each time Lydia received a letter from her family, with their reports of difficult conditions, she always expected her mother and sisters to request that she act as a sponsor to bring them over to the United States. For the past eight years, like so many others, Lydia had it in mind that Castro would soon fall, one way or the other, or that her family would leave Cuba, that they would be reunited. But her mother and sisters were the types of Cubans for whom Cuba would be—or could be—their only home: their attachment, above hunger, above the grievances, and the losses of personal freedoms they endured. . . .

Even though she did not like Castro she used to think about what she would read from time to time in the commie pamphlets that radical college students handed out on Broadway to members of what they considered the oppressed class. In a just society everyone would work for the common benefit, the elitist ruling class would be eliminated, and the common man would have his share of the bounty. This idea made sense to her, except when she thought about her earlier life in Cuba and what had happened there with Castro since, the way that world had turned upside down. She had Cuban friends, recent arrivals in the neighborhood and in cities like Newark and Union City and Miami and Ft. Lauderdale, who were hooked into welfare, food stamps, and other forms of government assistance, slowly gathering their wits and succeeding in business and construction and many other jobs. Hustling with crazed dedication and energy, to prove that they—not the system—were what had made Cuba great. And certainly to show the left-wing Fulbright Americans that they could advance without the benefits of socialism, even if, as she believed, all the governmental help they were getting was kind of socialistic in the first place.

The exiles' sense of outrage and betrayal, however, was something that she experienced with detachment: her own debacle had taken place back in the 1940s and, gradually, her cleaning woman's life had become her destiny. So while remembering that there had been nothing in place to help her when she first came to the States and worked in that dingy factory for ten dollars a week with few real hopes for the future, part of her could not especially care about the plight of the new Cubans, especially those distant members of their family they had never heard from before who came out of the woodwork asking for help. Still another part of her, while remembering how lonely she had been when she arrived and how long it took her to even begin to feel right with the world, *that part of her* felt great sympathy for the new Cubans. From time to time she would say to Raul: "I wish none of this *miseria* had ever happened."

From all reports, the violation of old society had grown worse over time. Now she envisioned the mansions of Havana, depopulated of the rich and open to the poor—a story she heard over and over again—the lowest *campesinos* coming in from the countryside to replace the rich. Pigs and naked children running around in the colonnaded courtyards; laundry hanging in the ballrooms; animals roasted over spits on marble floors. . . .

Her friend, sweet Mireya, told her: "Trust in God and he will fix the situation in Cuba." And: "If He doesn't, then He must have a reason: it was meant to be."

Many of her friends prayed and nothing changed.

Although she did not agree with Eliseo's politics and she had ordered her daughter to avoid him, Lydia found herself debating, on many an afternoon, whether she should visit her new, if different, friend, again. Really, even if he was one of "them," she found his thoughtfulness and his interest in ideas reminiscent of the qualities she admired in the other men of her life: her own husband (at times), Mr. Osprey (with his massive library and intelligence), Mr. Fuentes, the butcher (in his poetic vision), Dr. Merton of her building (with his professorial studies of history), and, once again, her own father, the late *Don* Antonio, who knew many many things about the world. She found herself often thinking about Eliseo. If Lydia happened down Amsterdam Avenue to visit a friend, or to get her hair cut at the Cuban beauty salon, she would often pass his shop, and, for all her doubts and feelings of foolishness, softened at the sight of him. His manner was so friendly that after having walked by his shop a half-dozen times in one day she gave in and sat to drink with him again.

In addition to a coffee bar, he had something of a library in a corner, a wall of bookcases filled with the writings of Marx, Engels, Lenin, and the sacrilegious *History Will Absolve Me* by Fidel Castro (the title of which, anti-Castroists had pointed out to Lydia, came from a speech once given by Mussolini during Italy's fascist era). He also kept a rack of out-of-date foreign language newspapers and radical-style magazines, mainly mimeographed publications put out by groups like the Students for a Democratic Society, issues of *The Worker*, and, among others, Paul Krassner's *Realist*, which certain neighborhood children, like Rico, loved to read for its often ribald and irreverent contents. Taped to the wall was a Gus Hall for President poster. Sitting at a corner table, sipping coffee, she was under the distinct impression, from the very start, that Eliseo had wanted to pick her up, something that, in those days, much appealed to her vanity and her sense of waning allure.

Having decided that politics was not a good subject for him to broach with Lydia, Eliseo spoke of how hard it was for him to make ends meet when most of his clientele were students with little money. His best business occurred on Wednesday nights when, in the tradition of the Village cafés, he would hold poetry readings, the room filled to capacity. ("*Ay,* I have a friend who is a poet," she said happily referring to Fuentes, the butcher. "He belongs here.") And on Saturdays he held a folk-music night that proved popular with the students. A gentleman, with a Quixotic air of gallantry, he once exhaled a great cloud of foul smoke, sighed—as if the loneliness of his hours was weighing on him—and asked, "And you, *señora?* What is it that you do?"

148

"What do I do?" she blushed, finding it somehow difficult to admit that she cleaned other peoples' houses for a living, that she in fact felt proud, her life happily "enhanced," working for Mr. Osprey.

"I'm studying ... studying to be a schoolteacher," she reported falsely.

"At this university?"

"No, another one, the public one."

He looked at her, nodding. "It's good for people to pursue their ambitions regardless of their age," he said. "And that you are *latina* is beautiful, because in this society, who the hell cares for us, if we don't ourselves." Then: "Well, if you like to read," Eliseo told her, "by all means, help yourself to any of my books, for as long as you like, free of charge."

Out of courtesy she stood up to look at the books, but they reeked of sinister intellectualism. She could barely stand to touch them—Marx having been indirectly responsible for the monthly pound of meat rations that her family in Cuba had to live with, for the Russian soldiers there, for the existence of the Committee for the Defense of the Revolution, for the fact that the packages she sent to Cuba often arrived at her family's house emptied of their contents. Still she opened one of the books, something densely written by a writer she had never heard of, Sartre, pretending to read, to show an interest, knowing that Eliseo was watching her. Then as he moved directly behind her, she could smell the nicotine of his sweater and skin, and for a moment, enjoyed the notion that he might put his arms around her. "Take any of the books you want," he told her.

He was standing so close to Lydia that she began to think of what most virile men would have done in that moment: press against her until the small of her back sweated, a hand reaching around to slip a few fingers under her wire-rim bra. . . . But she told herself, "No, this man is the devil." And it was a good thing, because just then her son and daughter came into the shop. Rico had said, "Hey Ma, whatchew doing here?" but Alicia, put off and embarrassed, turned red and looked at her mother as if she could kill her.

Later that night, Alicia said not a single word through dinner, and afterwards, when Lydia challenged her solemnity, her beautiful daughter told her: "Can't you leave anything alone? Can't we even go over to Eliseo's in peace, without you interfering?"

"With what?"

"Just with whatever the hell we want to do, that's all 'with what.'"

"You mean that you don't want me to be with your friend Eliseo? Why he's old enough to be your father." Then: "And for another thing, what is he but a confused lost soul, skinny and pale, reeking of tobacco and beer. Go with him if you want, but you may as well be going with an old man."

And her daughter left the living room and a week passed before she spoke to Lydia again.

The Great Wait

Now and then, when she and Raul were invited out, into the then changing precincts of Union City, New Jersey, and Astoria, Queens, Lydia would catch glimpses, but in a different guise, of individuals much like her own father. She'd see them sitting in front of the barbershops and bodegas—on folding chairs or metal milk crates—playing their games, dominoes usually, and, more frequently, the game of watching the street and passersby, a certain wishfulness—and ambition—in their expressions that had to do with what might be called "the great wait." Certain enterprises to topple *El Líder* led to endless discussions of what would be done to restore Cuba to its former grace. A continuing influx of refugees was strengthening the cause in the United

States: hence the gentlemen, in their *guayaberas* and linen trousers and white leather shoes, watched the street with the kind of square-faced intensity that was nearly military, *for their moment to act could come at any time.*

When she saw these men, Lydia began to think more and more about her father. While he had never given benefits like retirement money or health plans or large salaries to the many people he employed in his bakery and bodega and in his household and, in fact, probably looked down on them, he never let anyone go hungry. If someone needed a doctor or money for a funeral—her father offering a bereaved widow a roll of bills, to see her through the hard times ahead—or some *largesse* for a wedding, he always gave. (Here, with this kind of memory, she particularly regretted her insolence toward him: there was that time when they would get dressed up and go to church together, when they were like a force of vitality and class, visions in white moving as one, with their parasols and elegant manners down the cobblestone streets, when they always sat in the first row of the church.)

Cubans like her father had the attitude that the poor who worked for them, and who lived in their vicinity, were to be looked after, in a benevolent, and, she thought, heartfelt and familial manner. Her maids were treated like members of the family. Who would have supposed that there were so many poor and suffering souls in Cuba, too many for people like her father to take care of? And that was the problem; so many of the Cubans who had been displaced and alienated by the *Fidelistas,* and by what the pamphlets called the "Noble Experiment in Cuba," had been, for the most part, decent and compassionate in their dealings with the poor: giving food and alms and exercising, in their own way, a kind of communal support for the less fortunate. An old family friend, Dahlia Gomez, had told her how, after the changes when *El Líder* had announced his new policies, she had remained living with her husband, an engineer, in their old house in Holguín, trying to fit in with the new system, and watching "everything go upside down." In her case the betrayal began when her "best" maid became a vigilante, a spy for the revolution, a party regular, keeping track of the family's movements for signs of counterrevolutionary activity—

"Even though we had loved her like one of our own."

The stories coming out of Cuba were many—sad stories about imprisonments, unjust harassment, food shortages, the suppression of free press and unions—calamities she and Raul heard a million times. Every now and then some recent arrivals took up the sofa bed in the living room for several weeks, these persons moving, feeling, thinking, acting differently from what Lydia herself, in the States for nearly twenty years, and certainly the children, had grown accustomed to.

Batista's Cleaning Lady

A Cuban woman she knew from church, Florencia, had, once upon a time before the revolution, worked in the presidential palace in Havana for Batista himself, cleaning his halls, his toilets and laundering his clothes. She used to clean up after the president's parties, when he hosted great soirees and dances for the richest of the rich, gangsters and industrialists alike (or "capitalist slavers and pimps" to use the leftist jargon), afterwards collecting little keepsakes—programs, menu cards, ashtrays, party favors, cigars, table-sized Cuban flags, autographs, and much more, which she hoarded thinking, as if presciently, they might become valuable. Back in the 1950s she would send them off to a cousin in Hialeah who kept them in her attic, later donating a few of these items to a Dade County University archive. Sweeping up his floor after Batista (a dapper and elegant man of an intense expression) had received his weekly haircut, she had kept locks of his jet-black hair. (These never made it out of Cuba.) She did not, incidentally, have a great amount of sympathy for her former employer, for, as she put it, "If he fell it was because he was surrounded by dummies and cowards. How could he not have foreseen what was coming?"

Her husband had been a police officer, who minded his own business, one of the "honest ones, I swear to you," but in Cuba, because of their lack of support for the revolution, they were both treated like criminals. They, like so many others, had come over on a freedom flight in '61; he ran a dry cleaners on 182nd Street, off Bennett Avenue, and she, cleaning apartments like Lydia, made hating Castro her life's passion (and that of her young children).

As with many of the newer Cubans, Florencia and her husband moved steadily toward their goals—find a job, a home, put some clothes on the kids' backs, buy the patient wife a piece of jewelry for a change, maybe start a business, move up and up, and suffer and work until the goal is achieved—that's called the work ethic baby, right?

Like Florencia, Lydia was proud of being Cuban. In her happy moments she basked in the kind of serenity that comes from knowing, in no uncertain terms, who and what you are— the serenity of belonging without a doubt to something greater than yourself—like the most devout priests, die-hard military men, musicians, and the very rich. And certain immigrants— those Irish whose clothes somehow smell like the mists of Dingle Bay, or those Sicilians on Mott Street who speak an Italian that confounds the university professors, the Jewish folk of Hasidic faith who would never, in their lifetimes, read a single English-language newspaper. Or those Ukrainians of the Lower East Side who still trundled the streets in peasant garb, in babushkas and heavy skirts in the summertime, as if walking up a hill in the Caucasus. Or those Chinese restaurateurs whose

establishments one found at the end of a twisting passageway—
as twisting as any search for identity—and down stairways, and
into yet more passageways until one passed through beaded
curtains into low-ceilinged rooms with dark scarlet walls,
where the steam smelled like bamboo and one would not hear a
single word of English spoken—like those Chinese, and those
others who precisely knew just who and how and what they
were, even if life wasn't always easy—that kind of serenity.

Despite her loathing of Eliseo's politics, Lydia enjoyed his
attentions and this somehow made her feel nervous. He had
become one of the people she talked about derisively with
Mireya and her other friends—for she told them about his
"serpent's eyes" and "stupid mouth." But it was self-deception,
for she often thought about him in a romantic way. Though
she did not confide this to anyone, she often thought she
would have enjoyed the intimate company of a man like Eliseo
for, lately, Raul was not what he used to be in terms of love and
their amatory relations. She took comfort in hearing that this
falling off of enthusiasm sometimes happened in a marriage
(Dr. Joyce Brothers, WMCA radio in the mornings) and that
there were ways to resuscitate waning passions. But who had
the time or inclination, at the end of the day, to get dolled up
for bed? And what was wrong with her in the first place?

In those days, she longed for the renewing exhilaration of
love. When she took her baths she judged herself to be in
decent enough shape, her self-appraisal reminding her of how
she had first noticed her maturity when she was just barely
thirteen. Bathing with a glass of beer nearby, a transistor radio
playing, she tried to envision Eliseo without his Lenin goatee,
what he might look like if he went through the trouble of

dressing in the way that Mario did. She went to work at Mr. Osprey's and could not look around without hearing Eliseo's voice: "You know that life is only about the acquisition of money for some people, the rest of the world be damned!" She found herself going by his café at least once a day on the pretext of making sure that her daughter was not there. People talked. Twice she was seen on the street outside his café with him, sending the beauty salon ladies into a frenzy of gossip— "Nothing goes on," she would tell them. "What would I do with a man who needs a haircut and a shave, anyway?" She found herself peering into his window, even if she did not go inside, ever annoyed if she saw him holding forth with the young college women, who always seemed enraptured by him. What was it about him that so appealed to her? Was it, she wondered, that he seemed above the ordinary struggles of life, nearly priestly, his religion—socialism—having imbued him with the strength and purity of the righteous? "What's happening to you?" she would ask herself.

Once he surprised her by actually saying something sympathetic about her point of view: "A lot of people are too rough on the *gusanos;* I can't imagine that it's easy for many of the Cubans who have come here." And she liked him for it.

As they were talking one afternoon outside his café, he asked her, "Now how is it, Lydia, that you are a student and I never see you with schoolbooks. I think it's that you've not been telling me the truth." Then: "In fact, I know this from your son."

"Eliseo," she told him. "I go to the school that is in my heart and my head. The other schools mean nothing to me."

But because her face had flushed he did not bring up the subject of her schooling again. He surprised her with a stack of old Cuban movie magazines, issues of *Carteles* and such, because she was always talking about how she liked the movies. They became friends, and he always said that he would go after her if she were single. "If I could, I would take you to the movies every week, and dancing." He played mambo records for her, and gave her a recording of the "melodies of Ernesto Lecuona" played on the piano. He invited her to one of the poetry sessions, and that same night she turned up with Fuentes, the butcher, who sat at a corner table, listening to a pleasant-looking young man read something called "William Blake's Flea, I am Not," and debating about whether he should get up and recite one of his poems. He was too modest, too stout, too Puerto Rican, too old. ("One day, I will have my time," Fuentes would tell her for the rest of his life.)

Despite her reservations about Eliseo and the impossibility of a love between them (as impossible as a love with Osprey), Lydia found herself diverted and in some ways comforted by his presence. For all her dissatisfactions and her trepidations and concerns about her family in Cuba and her own family's standing and future in that glorious world, for all her *quejando,* or griping, about the way many people did not respect her, she was almost happy in those days.

Thank God
for
Mr. Osprey

One afternoon in the spring of 1968, during the time of the famous university riots, a college girl, wandering lost in the cavernous and winding recesses of a many-stairwelled building at the edge of the campus "occupied"—*liberated*—by rebellious students, had nearly been raped, or so she had claimed, by three local youths.

In the gloomy recesses of the 126th Street precinct house, two officers and a detective sat with her in a room, gave her tepid coffee, and listened to her complaint. She was a pretty curly-haired blond, a blue-blood hippie (who the fuck else, the cops thought, went to fancy schools?) in tight, bottom-worn jeans, a denim jacket, a nearly transparent Indian cotton blouse, turquoise earrings, a silver peace symbol hanging off her neck. Her shapeliness made a favorable impression on the officers: her dark nipples, visible through the fabric of her blouse, were as flat and wide as winter coat buttons. They listened, barely hearing her, so jammed up were their heads with their own resentments and hatreds and numbness; emotions they nursed nightly, for half the cops in the precinct spent their evenings in a bar on 125th Street, under the highway overpass, cursing the rich, spoiled kids of this country and drinking until dawn, when they would shuffle (stagger) out and head to work.

The riots had brought more and more police around, especially by the university campus, these policemen stopping people for no particular reason, like Raul, on his way to visit Martinez, an old friend who lived over on Amsterdam on the other side of the school. They were Tactical Police Force officers, who at that point had endured weeks of tension, standing in at-the-ready formation in riot gear and with Roman-looking shields poised before them, along certain points on upper Broadway and in various places around the campus.

Irritable and vindictive, they couldn't really give a damn about the complaints of one of *them*, for they (rightly) lumped her in with the bourgeois kids who'd started the trouble over a deserted piece of shit, glass-strewn university property in Morningside Park in west Harlem. The university's plan to clear away several acres of granite and shale and thickets of poison oak to build an athletic field (it is there now, just off 110th Street and Manhattan Avenue) had outraged the radical students, though few of these kids, in the ordinary course of their life at the university, would have been caught dead in that place, or anywhere else in the park, unless by accident. (In fact, it happened from time to time that a student would catch the wrong uptown train at the West 96th Street station and end up, terrified and wary, on East 116th Street and Lexington Avenue, the center of Harlem, a victim of the occasional caprice or misfortune.)

The "community" itself—that is, the working people of Harlem and the West Side—were not really involved, nor was their opinion solicited; rather, in the manner of the upper class, the radicals declared that the project would be exploitative of the people, that it was yet another example of racism, as the university leadership was white and much of the community black and Hispanic. Assuming the righteousness of their cause, the radicals sought agreement with what they had already decided upon. Street protests against the Vietnam War, ROTC on campus, and university ownership of armament company stocks melded with the cause of community rights. In the name of liberation, students went on strike, closing down the school and occupying many of the campus buildings.

The people in Lydia's neighborhood were against the war and for civil rights, but beyond that they were not really a part of the glory and heroism of the movement. Pamphlets were handed out on every street corner, public high-school kids were bussed in to protest (without knowing quite what they were protesting), condemnations of the university and the government were shouted through megaphones; a multitude of reporters roamed looking for interesting radicals to interview, while folks like Lydia and Raul, walking home, tired from work, went ignored.

Exhausted from long shifts and sick of being insulted by the crowds and pelted with garbage and eggs, the cops were nevertheless obligated to find the youths who had "almost" raped the young woman—three Hispanic kids, one of them "very tall and dark" with a slash down the right side of his face, a tattoo on his right hand, and apparently, as she explained with a trembling voice, a large sexual appendage; the second youth, well-groomed and dressed (freshly pressed slacks and creaseless cotton shirt) and of a modest handsomeness who, she pointed out, had not really seemed to want trouble; and a third, the leader, very thin, in glasses with Scotch tape holding one of the lenses in place, and a black raincoat. The tall one was wearing a pair of Converse sneakers, blue jeans with a thick garrison belt and tiger-in-a-roar buckle, a polo shirt, a pack of Kools rolled up inside the sleeve of his shirt. The tattoo, she said, could have been of a scimitar or a knife with drops of blood dripping from its tip, or of a rose on a long curving stem, but she had been so frightened and the light was so dim, it was hard for her to be sure.

Soon enough, around six-thirty in the evening, two cops and this young woman were in an unmarked car driving along the streets of different Hispanic neighborhoods; over to Columbus and Amsterdam Avenues in the West 70s and 80s (before they became chic and expensive) and all the way north to Tiemann Place and La Salle, the car circling each block slowly and then backtracking down Broadway, past the lights set up by the gates of the university, where crowds had gathered, as if to watch a movie premiere, then back toward 125th again—the cops going through the motions while the girl sat sobbing in the back of the car.

They had been driving along Broadway past the corner of 123rd Street where a group of local kids were gathered in front of a bodega—drinking beers and goofing around—when the young woman told the cops to stop the car. The officers, their revolvers drawn, approached the group and ordered them to stand in a line against the wall, hands held over their heads. It was then that she singled out two of them: Rudy Santos, indeed tall and dark with a scar down the right side of his face—and the other, Rico España, the cleaning woman's quietly demeanored fifteen-year-old son.

Not My Boy

The solemnity of Raul's expression when he walked into the living room, two policemen behind him, as mother and daughter were watching TV, had made Lydia feel as if something was unraveling inside of her.

First Raul turned on the living room light. "Lydia, Rico's gotten himself into some kind of trouble. I have to go to the police station."

He with his ailing heart?

"What has he done?"

"*Algo muy grave,* I'm afraid. They say that he and that Santos boy were up to no good over at the university . . . but I can't believe a word of it." To the officer: "And someone there will explain what's going on, yes?"

The Irish cop, a little wearily, looked at his watch: "Yes, sir."

Her heart, agitated by her sudden awareness of the police lights flashing in through the window, had started to beat wildly, too.

"Something happened with the university? Even when we'd told him to keep away from there?"

"Yes, something with a girl."

"*Y qué? Y qué?*"

Then as the possibilities of what that something might have been occurred to her, Lydia found herself repeating to the officers, "Not my boy, not my son, no, *señor*, not that decent boy."

In her wishfulness to undo the harmfulness of that moment, she crossed herself—and as a gesture to communicate to the officers and whomever else might be observing that she was "good."

"Do me a favor and call Mario," Raul said to her. "He knows a good lawyer." He took a deep breath as if standing by the edge of a rooftop in the dark. "And ask him to come to the station."

"I'll go with you."

"No, you stay here with the *niña.*"

The "*niña,*" Alicia, had passed the time on the couch swigging a Coca-Cola and eating Mallomars, absorbed in an episode of *Lost in Space.* Raul touched her shock of thick black hair (which she liked but would not admit it) and, with his blood pressure shooting ever upwards, asked his daughter for a kiss. Then he took a package of Lucky Strikes out of a cigar box on a hallway table, lit one, felt the elating and comforting smoke, its dense blue antiquity, in his mouth and lungs. And in a moment, following the cops, he left Lydia and Alicia.

By the window, Lydia saw him shuffle down their front steps, a man in a slightly baggy but well-made suit (he was always gaining and then losing weight), head cast low, into the oblivion of what awaited him that night. And as she stood there, surprised by her husband's composure in the face of what had happened, Raul sat in the back of the police car, fiddling with the thin crucifix that hung from a chain around his neck, his head tipped toward the window to catch some air. A train rushed into the station, a Mr. Softee truck pulled over to the curb playing its sing-song tune, squads of little kids congregating by the vendor's window; a few stars rose over the projects; great shouts of a crowd, as if from a sporting event, could be heard from the center of the campus, some eight blocks away; life was going on.

To Alicia, the child who should have been the one to go wrong, Lydia said: "What do you think?"

"About what?"

"*Chica*, about what's happening with your brother?"

"I don't know. He'll be all right, I guess."

She seemed passive and indifferent.

"Alicia, where are your feelings for him?"

"Look, Mommy, I don't know what's going to happen, okay? I can't tell the future."

Her voice was gruff in a moment when Lydia, despite the steeliness of her spirit, could well have used a little comfort. And when she stared imploringly at her daughter, so many visions and hopes for the future suddenly threatened, her eyes agonized, Alicia, feeling badly, told her: "*Ay,* Mommee, let's wait and see, okay? You're going to drive yourself crazy."

And her daughter got up and gave her a little comforting hug, in a manner, if truth be told, as detached as her mother had been in her expressions of affection when she had raised them. Then she turned to the television again.

In the next few hours, Lydia made telephone calls: to Mario, Mireya, to Concha and her friend Mrs. Esposito, a way to pass the time and to give her strength. She went down to the street to talk with some of the neighborhood kids, who had been there when the police had taken Santos and her son into custody, some of the very same kids she had always tried to keep Rico away from. As she stood there she found herself regretting many things, among them the fact that she and Raul lived where they lived: she daydreamed about that other world—

over on the East Side, Osprey's world. About ten o'clock, Rudy Santos's older brother rang the bell and, by her doorway, humbly offered an apology for "whatever might have happened." He was a large fellow like his brother, but well dressed; he had put on a checkered jacket and shirt and tie, and held a small bouquet of carnations. His knotted hair was slicked down and parted to the side, and somehow, because his eyes were so sincere, he seemed the type of young man to go door to door selling Bibles or issues of *Awake!*, the Seventh Day Adventists' publication.

Remembering this young man, Mikey, as having always been one of the better-behaved boys of the neighborhood—he sang in choir, worked all kinds of odd jobs, kept out of trouble—Lydia tried to be nice, but found herself lecturing him: "If there has been trouble," she told him, "I know that it's because of Rudolfo and nobody else; because the lowest people of this world, *la gente baja,* are the ones who make the trouble, and not people of refinement, do you hear me?"

He bowed his head.

"I know you're trying to be nice, Miguel, but if your parents had been better people, what happened with my boy and your brother would never have happened."

He tried to interject: "But we don't know—"

"And I'll tell you something else, when all this is cleared up, if, by God's will, justice is done, I don't want your brother anywhere near my son. *Me entiendes?*"

Then she started carrying on about how hard she had worked for so many years, *and for what?* "Do you know how this makes me feel and what it's like to come from a good family that never breaks the law, to see this kind of thing happen, do you know?" Rudy's brother, whose only intention had been to relieve her distress and to commiserate, trembled as Lydia held him there by his arm. And she would have gone on and on, but then Alicia came to the door, telling her, "Mommee, let it rest, it's not worth it. Mikey's our friend. Leave him alone." Then to Mikey: "Just go home."

Once he'd left, Alicia, now distressed herself, sat with her mother in the kitchen and poured her a glass of beer, waiting impatiently while she drank it. Afterwards she hurried off to her room, where she smoked a cigarette by the opened courtyard window and played British pop records on her pink phonograph, the one which Raul had given her as an eighth grade graduation present, some years before.

Lydia tried to sleep, having heard only once from Raul who, waiting with Mario for an attorney, had said that he would be home sometime around midnight. But there she was at two in the morning, watching television in the living room, the sound turned so low she could not hear it. Not yet knowing what had happened with her son and that Santos boy, she feared the worst—kids in that neighborhood were known to abruptly go wrong. It happened easily, as in the instance of that nice lady up the street whose son died of a heroin overdose in a men's room in some lousy bar, the grandmother, spared those details, told that he died of a heart attack while lifting a box, even though he was only twenty-two; or the kid from 120th Street doing three years' time for armed robbery in Brooklyn; another kid, the good-looking one who everybody said was probably going to be a movie star, punched in the face with a beer mug one night, losing an eye and whatever dim hopes he had of pursuing that particular fantasy. There was the married Dominican woman sleeping with a young boy home from a stint in the Far East with the army and (the rumors ran) with sexual techniques so advanced that her screams of ecstasy alarmed everyone in the building (the kind of gossip funny enough to make Lydia, even on her bad days, laugh). A neighborhood love triangle involving an Irish girl, her Irish boyfriend, and a Puerto Rican boy ended when he was found bleeding half to death in a basement with stab wounds to the belly, his mother, Virginia, a dear friend and a cleaning lady herself (the boy lived).

But Lydia's son? The boy she had tried to raise in a genteel manner? Her son to whom she had consistently pointed out the failings of others? Her son for whom she had so many hopes? How could it be, she spent the night asking herself, feelings of humiliation and despair tormenting her.

Worst of all was the feeling that came to her around four-thirty in the morning, when it seemed to Lydia that not much would ever change for them, no matter how hard they worked.

The Night Passed

In the holding cell, while college demonstrators, almost celebratory about their situation, were laughing and mocking the police, Rico spent the night, head low, staring at the floor. Outside, Raul and Uncle Mario waited to see the boy, but the chaos and clamor in the station house had put the police in an uncooperative frame of mind. One sympathetic police officer, Sergeant Ramírez, came by the holding cell several times to say, "I told your father that you're doing all right." And: "He's gonna iron everything out for you fellows, okay?" But another cop paced by, wracking his palm with his nightstick and then rattling it against the iron bars. Another would come by and say, "Are you fellows comfortable?" then walk away no matter what anybody said. Each time Rico closed his eyes, he felt the floor beneath him parting open, as if he would fall through. And he would go over and over things again, until he was sick of his thoughts, because there was nothing they could do to get out, not walk—or run, as he wanted to.

The Afternoon of His Troubles

Earlier, in the midafternoon, he had gone down the street to buy his father beer at the corner bodega, where Rico had met

167

up with the slippery Johnny Castro. Having big eyes for any windows that were lit with color TV sets at night, Johnny was a break-in artist with pocked hepatital skin, a pleasant enough fellow, whose main preoccupation was to find the easiest ways to earn money to buy heroin in the projects. "Older" at seventeen, he was among the throng of neighborhood kids who just hung around on the stoops, playing street games, viewing, as did most of the others, the world from afar (and not just from afar but from within the confines of a box, the "neighborhood," from which nobody was supposed to escape), and who considered the university students' passion for upheaval phony. It was his idea to prowl around the recesses of the occupied campus buildings to see what they could "come up with."

Forever trying to change his image as a mama's boy, Rico had a difficult time saying no to people like Johnny Castro, and while he had never participated in any crimes directly, by the time the university riots happened, he had been on numerous shoplifting excursions (wearing a suit, clean shirt, and tie, his presence seemed to reassure the clerks) and, in the name of friendship, had "played chickie" during several store burglaries, further downtown. He never felt comfortable about doing so, but he was a loyal friend to the kids he had grown up with, and because half of them were junkies, Rico, looking out for them, often found himself in bad situations (as in a project basement to buy some skag).

In any event, during the strikes, which had lasted for most of the semester, it was the habit of local kids to invade the campus, attending radical rallies and dances. When the students began to occupy different buildings, shut off from the outside world, the locals found ways to get inside. Because the students had an easy enough time bringing food, money, booze, and whatever else they needed into the occupied buildings (hanging from cord out the windows were picnic baskets into which passersby on Amsterdam or Broadway could toss money or drugs or cigarettes for the cause), there was much to eat and drink; jugs of cheap wine and beer were everywhere. Some of the kids went for the young college girls, for this was the time of free love, others out of pure boredom, and some, like Johnny, went because fancy electric typewriters (IBM Selectrics being state of the art and not too heavy to carry) and the occasional radio and guitar were his lucre. Caring little about the politics of the situation, and suspending their prejudices, the poor neighborhood kids were thrilled to partake in the rich kids' world (the pussy). They would go there with the expectations and high hopes of children visiting a theme park.

Partyland

On the way over to the university, Johnny and Rico had run into "crazy" Rudy who had nothing better to do; by the early evening they had not only penetrated the police lines, past dense packs of reporters and onlookers, but had spent several hours at what seemed like a perpetual party, held in a large third-floor salon, with decrepit carpets and tarnished chandeliers, in one of the occupied buildings. A rock 'n' roll band had brought in equipment—amplifiers and a PA system—and was performing long psychedelic jams of Velvet Underground or Rolling Stones songs; there were couples off in corners making love or rolling on the floor in drug-induced ecstasy. Rico regarded this situation with an amused detachment. From time to time, he took a drag of a marijuana cigarette, or a sip of wine, to be congenial, but for the most part he watched the rock musicians, trying to figure out the chords and figures that they played on their bell-sounding guitars, a form of education, as it were (in those days he had the daydream of becoming either a schoolteacher or a guitarist in a band). An electric guitar lick, played on a Stratocaster out of a big

169

Fender Reverb amp, with the volume all the way up and a power booster or fuzz tone added as effects, imposed itself in his mind as a major symbol of virility and youth, notes rising like scimitars, aftertones aflutter like birds, the bending of a blues note like the rising arc of an erection.

He loved music, as performed by the popular artists of the day, and liked it when the college students hung around the park benches playing folk tunes, the purchase of a guitar something he was saving for, his favorite recording, not Dancemania *by Tito Puente, which was Mario's, or* The Collected Melodies of Ernesto Lecuona, *arranged for strings! which was Raul's, or* En Mi Viejo San Juan, *which was Mr. Fuentes', but the Bob Dylan record* Mr. Tambourine Man, *a 33⅓-rpm long-playing album that he had purchased near the university for $2.99, and that he played over and over and over, to the point where Lydia, home from work and bitten by a moment of humor, would harass Rico by singing—or nearly singing—with the nasal intonations and delivery of Mr. Dylan, his mangled, garbly voice sounding to her—and Raul's—ears like nonsense. ("What's the matter, kid, you don't like Benny Moré?")*

But it was Raul's beat-up nylon-string guitar that Rico sometimes coopted from the closet, taking it down to the basement or up to the roof, learning fingerings from a one-hundred-chords-for-guitar-made-easy book, until he gradually became comfortable with two or three corny folk songs. Raul, who liked to strum the instrument from time to time, showed his son a few tricks, and they'd spend the evening handing the guitar back and forth to one another: Raul would play "Guantanamera," Rico, "If I Had a Hammer," and so on.

They had watched the band, had nearly picked up a few girls (to whom they seemed not sophisticated or good enough), when Johnny had said, "Come on." Climbing a stairway to the fifth floor of that building, they came to a dark hallway and a suite of faculty offices that had been already ransacked. File cabinets had been turned over, papers and garbage and wine bottles were strewn about (like a backyard!). Johnny, ever enterprising, had prowled about finding a door that had not yet been forced open; as he broke the lock with a screwdriver, Rico waited beside him shining a flashlight into the room, while Rudy guarded the stairway door.

What they heard was this: "Shit and more shit," as Johnny yanked the heavy volumes of an encyclopedia off the wall, the shelf collapsing and Johnny kicking the books across the floor. Then he pulled out the desk drawers and smashed a goose-necked lamp against the wall, screaming, "Motherfucker." Finally, he came out with a portable Smith Corona typewriter in its case, a few literary textbooks, and a thick Merriam Webster's dictionary, which he gave to Rico, saying, "I know you like this kind of thing."

They descended by another stairway, a wide zigzagging battleship-gray fire escape situated in the back of the building, which also served as an exit route for an adjoining structure— fire doors to the left and right of each landing—and led into a cavernous basement where there were storage and boiler rooms and a maze of halls. As they came to the third floor, they heard someone walking toward them on the stairs, and they stepped back into the shadows. Shortly they saw a hippie-looking blond, with a fine body (their first observation) and, seeing them, a frightened expression on her face.

She began to run back down the stairs as they approached her. She ran because Johnny and Rudy, if not Rico, resembled "menacing youths." She ran, perhaps, because of the look in Rudy's eyes, or because she had spied his erection, nestled like a piece of thick piping inside his blue jeans, for he was often in a state of priapic excitement.

171

When Johnny called out to her, his flashlight illuminating a utility wall filled with electric meters, cables, switches, and, just beyond, a set of double doors that had been chain locked, they found her crouching in a corner. As his flashlight beam moved over her body, she covered her face with her hands and Johnny said, "Relax, we're not gonna hurt you. My name's Johnny, and these are my 'boys,' Rico and Rudy."

She almost seemed relieved by the tone of his voice, but then she turned away. Johnny looked at Rico and they both looked at Rudy: standing a few yards behind them, he had opened his trousers and was smiling with unmistakable grandeur and pride.

Be Cool

Oblivious to what Johnny and Rico were saying to him, Rudy stepped toward the girl asking, "Whatchew think?" And: "You want to touch it?"

"Go away," she cried. And: "Please." But he, with a goofy look on his face, as if they were on some kind of twisted date, said to her: "Come on, don't you want to make time with me?"

She tried to run away, but Rudy pushed the woman against a wall, pressing himself against her; then she started to scream so loud that fists began to pound against the chain-locked doors from the other side.

Rudy was so out of touch with reality that he could not see that the woman had begun to tremble and cry, that Johnny and Rico were punching him in the shoulders and trying to pull him away from her. . . . Just as Rudy, coming to his senses, began to relent, a dozen stocky college students, wielding sticks and fists, burst through the chained doors attacking them.

It was during this melee that the young woman fled.

What Happened

They got away because Rudy carried a .22-caliber starter's pistol, which he pulled out during the fight, firing off three shots and scattering the students. Johnny had gone to East Harlem, but Rico and Rudy headed back to the neighborhood, gravitating toward 123rd Street. As they hung out with their friends, Rico had the same feeling he did the time he and some pals were walking along the tracks in the dark New York Central tunnels under Riverside Park, and a train came suddenly upon them; a memory of hitting one of the track rails with his right foot and nearly tripping, making him cringe to that day. Rudy, in a boastful mood, kept talking, not about their encounter with the woman, but about firing off some shots at the college boys they'd hated all their lives. Through all this he kept referring to Rico as "My man here . . ." and Rico reacted quietly, with a shrug.

Oddly, he found himself feeling sad about the Merriam Webster's dictionary he left behind. He then thought that if he got home around eight he could have dinner with Raul, maybe watch some TV, and gradually forget the whole business. But then the unmarked police car had come; they were shaken down, the pistol found tucked inside the top of Rudy's tube stocking. Taking them into custody, a cop had said, "Hope you like confinement, boys."

Early the next morning, Lydia, beside herself, telephoned Mr. Osprey to tell him that she would not be coming in that day, and perhaps not until the next week. Her voice trembled, and although another employer, less nobly disposed, would have left it at that, Mr. Osprey, who took the call in the kitchen, asked, "Lydia, is something wrong?"

And she told him, as might a child, "*Señor* Osprey, the very worst thing has happened, my son has been arrested."

"What for?"

She read from a list that she had written down on a piece of paper: "attempted rape, attempted burglary, accomplice to a felony" (weapons possession), and "trespassing." As she explained what she knew, Mr. Osprey took out a yellow notepad and began asking her a number of questions: Who was the attorney? Did her son have bail? What court would he be arraigned in?—and many other questions that confused her and reduced her to tears. But he calmed her, saying: "Give me the attorney's number and I will speak to him." Then: "*No te preocupes, vamos a averiguar la verdad.*" Or, "Don't be worried, we'll find out the truth."

How the World Works

In all likelihood, if not for the caprice of Lydia's connection with Mr. Osprey, both Rico and Rudy would have ended badly. Otherwise the process would have (perhaps) gone this way: the Legal Aid lawyers accepting a plea and her son spending a couple of years in an upstate correctional institution, a poor augury for the future. Or, the boy released after two days in a downtown detention center to await trial, taking off and running away; or (as they sometimes heard) becoming so despondent as to take his own life, or to get into drugs, or to say, "Fuck it," and indeed become a real criminal, since the punishment provoked criminality, regardless of his innocence. However, it turned out that this young lady's father, Mr. Patrick Harrison, was an attorney himself and one who had been a schoolmate at Yale of one of Mr. Osprey's law partners, and Osprey, pulling the kinds of magical strings that do not exist for most people, arranged a meeting with both daughter and father in District Attorney Hogan's office: eventually, Osprey, on Rico's behalf, argued that what had happened did not warrant the destruction of three young lives (for Johnny had been arrested a day later), even if their behavior, two passively, one more aggressively, had been reprehensible. In the end, the weapons charge stuck and Rudy was sent to a reformatory for a year, while Johnny was remanded to the care of ARC, a drug rehabilitation center on 125th Street; but Rico fared better. In order to clear away any confusions about right and wrong and proper civil behavior (and, quite frankly, to spare the system the burden of supporting another delinquent) he was ordered into counseling. Once a week he would take the train downtown to Centre Street to speak with a probationary social worker who found it hard to believe that this quiet and pensive young man could have been up to anything like "public mischief."

Before this intercession, however, the three young men had to spend several days in detention and their release was beautiful: life never seemed sweeter. Rico nearly kissed the sidewalk in front of his apartment building, and wrapped his arms around his father and kissed his mother, who was not at all convinced of his innocence, the arrest itself proof enough of his guilt, no matter what he told her, or what she truly wanted to believe. And everybody in the neighborhood knew about her public humiliation. Rico had told her: "Mommy, I swear to you, I didn't do anything." And she nodded and sighed. And when she walked into the living room or encountered him sitting on a stoop, she muttered something to herself and would not smile at him. Or if she did smile, there was shame in her eyes. She walked around saying under her breath, "*Chibao,*" or "Fucked up," and would never, no matter what Rico said or did with himself in his life, have anything approaching real faith in him, again.

This took place years ago, and it was the beginning of the dissolution of their mutual trust.

Thank God for Mr. Osprey

Osprey, the "saint," had always believed Rico's story. He spent hours with the young man and had been impressed by

175

the boy's soft-spoken intelligence. Even though nothing was proven, the fact that he had been arrested was enough to get him kicked out of Catholic school. Although he was set to finish his junior and senior years at a public high school on the West Side (where the kids spit in the teachers' faces) Osprey proposed to sponsor Rico as a student at a rich kids' school; being on that school's board, he also pulled those strings. His generosity was spectacular: Rico could not refuse, for to his mind anything was better than public school, which he had attended for six months, even rich kids' school. Besides, he had been persuaded by Osprey that events, unpleasant as they were, might work to his advantage. In that school he would find the key to his future, perhaps, and go on, God willing, to become one of the few successes to come out of the neighborhood.

All Things Being Equal (1970)

It should be reported that Rico's tenure in the rich kids' school was not as unpleasant as he thought it might be. A blue school bus would pick Rico up at the corner of 123rd Street and Broadway for the excursion north into Westchester County where this school was situated. He always sat in the back, and for weeks said nothing to his fellow students, who either dozed or read their books, or fooled around, flicking spitballs at one another. The tenements of upper Broadway left behind, the bus eventually entered a wondrous woodland, a road that passed dairy farms and seemed to cut through an enchanted forest, reaching at last a great lawn and the high-gothic visage of his school. Without knowing it Rico experienced the same emotion as his mother had when she first stood before Mr. Osprey's building: a feeling of being overwhelmed.

His first days in that school were spent with a social worker and an academic counselor. He was outfitted with a blue blazer, its top pocket boasting a glorious embroidered badge, a cache of books and school supplies, provided for by a "special" fund. When he looked at the student lists he saw that he was one of two Hispanics in the school—the other named Xavier García, who, as it turned out, happened to be one of the porter's sons. At the end of his second week in school he asked around for Xavier and found him in a field behind the school smoking pot with some of the refined prep-school boys, and when he approached, in a friendly manner, extending his hand and saying, "Rico España," the group, including Xavier himself, seemed to think it was the funniest thing in the world. On a second occasion Rico sat by him during the lunch hour in a grand hall, and asked, "Anybody give you a hard time?"

"About what?"

"About what and who you are."

"What's that supposed to mean?" Xavier was offended. Rico could see in his genteel, controlled manners and his un-Hispanic bearing the story of Xavier's upbringing; and, in his homogenized demeanor, his own future.

"What I mean is, does anybody give you a hard time because you're Spanish."

Xavier said curtly, "No." Then: "It's none of your business anyway."

"Man, I was just asking you a question."

"Well, you're embarrassing me. I'm just a student here like everybody else."

With that Rico got up and said, "*Cuídate,* man," but the Hispanic kid he thought would turn out to be a friend did not even look at him or nod as Rico walked away.

In those days, some of the students and teachers patronized him. Bright and well read enough to get through the courses, he was treated as if he needed special help, or derided as if he were the recipient of special help, as if he were not equal to the tasks. The fact was that he used to read whatever he could get his hands on, having always struggled as a kid to get rid of the "noises" in his head. Hustling work, delivering morning newspapers and watching over a laundry service after school, he always studied hard and, generally speaking, tried to do some good in the world. By the time he'd made it into the prep school he had read over a wide range of subjects, his reading often contingent on what the college students left out in the garbage (*Wisconsin Agricultural Trends for 1961 & 1962, A History of Carolingian Thought, Morals and Manners in 16th Century Italy*) and those books sold for quarters out on the street by the black fellow with the two missing front teeth ("Check it out, check it out!"), or the books and magazines that Lydia brought home from Osprey's.

Despite the down feelings he had to shake off, and his initial apprehension about how difficult the courses would be, Rico found his way and grew accustomed to the coded diction and syntax of his instructors. (In Catholic school his teachers always talked about life and school as a communal experience, as in "We must pray," or, "We must study." In public school the teachers were more tentative about their relationship to the students: "Which of you can answer that question? Anyone? You there. . . . Anyone?" In this school the teachers spoke in a detached but certain manner: "One must be prepared. One must study. One must be resilient.") He worked hard, and not for one moment, for all his misgivings, did he forget that, among the sons of investment bankers, advertising executives, lawyers, doctors, psychologists, corporate presidents, he was the son of a waiter and a cleaning woman.

It took him a while to get used to that place. He had certain prejudices going into his new environs—what poor and working-class kids felt toward the rich—and for the most part, he found them reinforced. He sensed that, with some exceptions, his blessed colleagues had a kind of class-based narcissism; it wasn't that these kids (like Osprey's kids), marching with confidence through that world of blue crest embroidered blazers, tennis clubs, European vacations, stunning girlfriends, country retreats, primo drugs, and other amenities were not particularly nice, but they seemed, in his opinion, to act in tandem, like members of the same club, to which he did not belong. The great clouds of smugness floating through the halls were as unnerving as the violence and larceny of the public institutions. Despite his private manner, he had to deal with a new reputation that preceded him, that of the tough street kid; this created an aura of power about him, especially among the more passive students, who kept out of his way—without knowing that he would have been happy to befriend them. Then, too, his "reputation" provoked the school bullies into picking fights with him.

Nevertheless, he was blamed for these incidents, nearly suspended, and ordered to see the school psychologist, who gave him some multiple-choice forms to fill out, and then told him, "You have a lot of anger inside of you." It was then arranged, as a matter of course, that Rico come in at eleven-thirty every Wednesday to have a therapy session to discuss whatever problems he might have at home. Actually, if he had been asked in those moments whether he would ever consider the career of a psychotherapist (about which he'd always have mixed feelings) he would have laughed. Any of the adults he knew—his father, Mario of the MTA, Mr. Fuentes, Ortíz, or even Mr. Fernandez, the superintendent of his building, who whistled at any female walking along the street, seemed to have more depth of feelings for life than did the therapist. Unimpressed by the therapist (too cut and dried and seemingly bored) he felt intrigued enough by the therapeutic process to research the subject in the mammoth school library. He loved the stories about symbols and archetypes, and began to reflect upon the oddness of those dreams that seemed to involve a *screen memory* of his mother's flirtatiousness with him, when he was a child and she used to parade around the apartment in a slip and a brassiere, dreams that he, if truth be told, found enticing. . . . And intriguing enough that, in his readings, Rico, longing for insight, began to understand something about the workings of the human heart and soul, and from that early age—he was just seventeen at the time—began to develop that priestly and introspective demeanor that characterized him, in later years, as a professional psychotherapist.

The Story of Alicia and Eliseo (1969)

During that difficult period, sideswiped by bitterness, Lydia watched as her children began to drift further away from her. It was true that Rico, in his new life, was holding out a greater promise for the family good, but there was always a tension between them, as if he had somehow disappointed her in an irreversible way. When she looked at him, back from the prep school in the late afternoons, in his wonderful new outfits (like Osprey's boys wore) she could not think about the future but seemed only able to dwell on the humiliation that Rico had brought to the family name. Even though Rico's predicament had long ceased to be a topic of interest, Lydia was convinced that was what people thought about whenever she went walking down the street. Because of that, she treated him badly; or, if not badly, indifferently—her expression revealing betrayal, not hope. . . .

As for Alicia? The allure of the "outside world" and its myriad pleasantries left her pining away for a different life. When she had graduated from the Catholic high school she not only threw away her plaid skirts and chaste blouses (that however did nothing to hide her voluptuousness) but she aspired to a different kind of uniform—sporting, to her mother and father's chagrin, the accoutrements of the hippies and flower children—wire-rimmed glasses, "granny dresses," sandals; she went braless, her magnificent physicality made clear to all, railed against the swinish attitudes of the men of her neighborhood (even as she tortured them), having out-and-out arguments with the young *machos* of the street whose expletive-driven and sexist speech made her face flush—she especially hated the word *chick*—and, to everyone's shock, allowed her hair to grow out long and gnarled, her underarms bushy; aside from some oversized loop earrings, which Eliseo had given her, she had no use for the makeup or jewelry of her mother's generation. In fact, when the apartment filled with visitors, she shuddered at how much artificiality attended the appearance of women like Mario's charming wife (of the school that women should dress to boil men's blood) and became absolutely sullen and condescending toward such women, on whom she took pity.

It did not matter that "Uncle" Mario, despite all the disappointments of his life—he was childless and had not become a famous musician—seemed to exude happiness, or that his wife was content with her role—to cook, look after, put up with her man; it did not matter to Alicia that, in fact, outside of a few vague musings about women's rights, most of the women were simply too preoccupied with survival to give a damn about "liberation." Who had the time to think about such matters? And what counted more in the end? Love, family, a good man (even if he might sometimes wander). She heard this, during boozy conversations at the table, again and again, and grew further outraged—unable to understand how life could have brought these women to such a state of simple-minded acceptance. If someone said to her, "You have so much to look forward to, like having children," she would smile and leave the room. The words *brainwashed* and *repressed* often crossed her thoughts (and made it into the diary she kept) when it came to the women of her parents' world. Only Mireya, who had seemed to find her own way, really impressed her. On those occasions when visitors came to the apartment, Alicia always sat beside Mireya, and thought, "This is the kind of woman I want to be."

(Alicia not having an idea of the loneliness of Mireya's nights.)

Raul, unable to let go of the little girl in the white communion dress, whose photograph sat in a frame on their bedroom dresser, still treated Alicia as if she were a child, often bringing her candies when he came home from work and, during his occasional jaunts to the markets of the city, buying her small stuffed animals and imitation, Hong Kong–made Barbie dolls. He could not understand why she did not jump with joy at these gifts, and, slowly, it began to occur to him that his daughter had long outgrown an appreciation for such expressions of affection, the notion depressing him. He liked it when she (and Rico) stayed home to watch television with him, but once she hit eighteen, keeping her in the apartment became more and more difficult. Reluctantly they laid down this rule: "As long as we are paying the rent here, you are to do as we tell you." But he never had the heart to enforce that, so that it was Lydia who had the screaming arguments with their daughter.

"You don't know how dangerous it is out on the streets these days!"

"I know exactly what's going on!"

"Well, you can't go out!"

"I'll do what I have to do."

"If you do I'll come out after you."

And there were some rough evenings, with Lydia trying to physically restrain her daughter from leaving the apartment, often blocking the door, holding her by the wrists, this sturdy cleaning woman often prevailing; but one way or the other Alicia would find her way out, and Lydia would pass the long nights fitful with worry. Sometimes she sent Rico out to find his strong-willed sister (he knew that she would often spend the evenings with an old friend, Sheila MacDonald, smoking cigarettes, drinking beer, and listening to music) but he always left her alone. The pity of it all was that Lydia and Raul were entitled to feel concerned: it was a rough neighborhood, especially at night; people were held up, women raped, passersby shot. The pity of it was that Lydia could not, for the life of her, say in a calm, restrained manner, "Please, my darling, we don't want anything bad to happen to you."

Instead, agitated emotions, strained voices, hours of worry were the norm.

Lydia Going to Work

She was on her way to the Times Square shuttle when she saw the hippie, which she pronounced *heepee*—a long-haired, cowboy-looking man, in an eye patch and Daniel Boone jacket, sitting on the floor of a dingy stairwell, deliriously involved in playing a guitar—the body of the instrument around the sound hole raked with pick marks. Looking him over, she had asked herself, "Where is his pride? And what of his family?" Most of all, "Look at him, *qué cochino!*" She was thinking about how, at his age—twenty-two, twenty-three?—she had been working long hours in a sewing factory, hating the dark, and feeling, for the most part, afraid about her own future. She was thinking that she made two dollars an hour scrubbing floors, that this young man was the opposite of everything she'd aspired to for herself and the family, and that she wanted to give him a little lecture about the virtues of work and responsibility.

She found it unbearable that this *"joven de hoy"* was *willingly* sitting in the drabness of that corridor, on filthy, urine-smelling floors. Where was his common sense, his dignity? As she passed by, the young man looked up at her and said, "I love you, sister." And then he stopped playing his improvisations in the key of A minor and launched into a rendition of *"La Bamba."* She was fascinated by his singing: that he, with so weak a voice, could go out in public without any self-doubt amazed her. So young, with worn denim shorts, his teeth nicotine stained and slowly going out on him, he seemed a lost soul. How sad his parents must be. She felt like telling him, "Please, young man, don't delude yourself."

But on an impulse Lydia had fished twenty-seven cents, mainly pennies, from her purse and dropped the coins into his tin can. She did so with pleasure, saying, "This is for you, poor thing . . ."

She almost felt triumphant about this small act of largesse when his girlfriend came out of a corridor to join him: she was a pretty, hairy-legged blond, in sandals and a tie-dyed dress, tenaciously childlike as she blew bubbles out through a spoon-hoop; her feet were dirty and there was something else about her, she was pregnant. As she leaned over him, he, kissing her, said, "I love you." She sat on the floor beside him, taking up a small tambourine, which she shook and banged as he began to strum the chords to another song. Then the young man cheerfully flashed a peace sign at Lydia; she climbed some stairs, and shortly caught the train over to the Lexington Avenue line, despairing greatly about Alicia.

"Carajo," she found herself repeating.

One afternoon, on her way home from work, Lydia made a detour over to Eliseo's shop on Amsterdam. She was not one for seeking counsel, but with Alicia becoming more miserable with each passing day, Lydia was at a loss over what to do. Up to that point, her few attempts at making things up to her daughter had not worked. She had bought Alicia two record albums, from a bin on 14th Street, one by a group pretending to be the Beatles, and another by a group pretending to be the Dave Clark Five; Alicia was not impressed. Twice she had offered to take Alicia to the movies, without success, and had, in her own way, attempted to give Alicia more room, arranging for a ten o'clock curfew, which Lydia considered extraordinarily lenient.

She had only seen Eliseo a few times after Rico had gotten into trouble—she did not care for the rumors that flew just because she had spoken with him in a friendly manner (and look how God rewarded her)—and his presence in the neighborhood had almost slipped her mind. But lately, feeling so tense, she had begun to look back at their pleasant conversations with a tremendous nostalgia. Certainly, with so many young people gathering in his coffee shop, he would know best how to advise her. . . .

Getting to his shop, she peered into his front window and saw Alicia sitting by a corner table in the back, smoking a cigarette; Eliseo standing behind her, rubbing her neck. Lydia's expression nearly peeled the gold-leaf lettering off his window. Rapping on the glass, Lydia shouted, "I see you," and "*Cabrón!*" There then ensued a scene that everybody in the neighborhood heard about, which went thusly reported:

The stuck-up Cuban lady found out that her daughter was banging the communist café owner; beside herself with fury she charged into the shop and attacked the owner with her purse—and grabbing her daughter by her long hair pulled her out into the street, where she publicly denounced her as a whore—without proof. A crowd gathered, amused by the domestic squabble; somebody called the police, but before they arrived, the daughter, a beautiful Cuban piece of ass, muy latina, *but dressed like a hippie, broke from the cleaning woman's grip and ran away. . . .*

Seeking Paradise

This daughter of Cubans made things even worse for her cleaning lady mother by not just disobeying her, but going off with the kinds of young kids who would have made her maternal grandfather in Cuba, *Don* Antonio, turn an ashen white—what of it? Staying in different apartments, she went off to chaotic all-night parties in the Village and hung around joints like the Electric Circus on St. Marks Place, where Sly and the Family Stone, the house band, performed weekly. And in that time, while Raul and Lydia spent many a late night huddled in the kitchen, terrified with worry, she fell in love with one boy after the other, and became very interested in the new hippie drugs, like pot and LSD, which the kids on the streets of Harlem and elsewhere took like candy.

Queen of the Forest

Disciplined, threatened with punishments, Alicia ran off to live with some hippies in Connecticut. Woozy with chemicals, she spent her days in a remote spot off the Connecticut River, half naked in the woods, learning to play an oak flute like a Native American and communing with the godliness of nature, with every spore, molecule, and radiant spray of light that glowed and ebbed out of the most ordinary things. The leaf of a common plant seemed rife with mysterious messages and she imagined certain angelic beings who were everywhere but could not be seen. Spending an immeasurable amount of time staring at a spotted butterfly she swore that she and that creature, sharing a common great intelligence, understood the very key to the existence of all things. Her mind brimming with a superclarity, she contrived the idea that everything in her life was something she had invented, even the family legacy of Cuba.

One afternoon, she stood naked in the river, the shadows of willow trees lapping against the froth of her pubic hair. As she reveled in the sunshine through the treetops, and in the plumes and diamonds of light that filled the world, the river suddenly began to boil and it seemed as if the sunlight itself was making love to her. She found herself falling to pieces during a daydream in which a god like Apollo came down from the sun and devoured her with his flaming tongue. . . . A young man was sitting on some rocks playing the flute— another downstream was strumming a guitar. She saw a smallish man, a Vietnam veteran, frolicking in the water and he waved to her and beamed with a happy smile and she jumped in and waded toward him where she was startled to find two rows of crescent-shaped scars crisscrossing his chest, as if he had been hacked by a sickle, the wounds from shrapnel, his face so sad. . . . Forgetting herself Alicia moved toward him and playfully splashed his wound and then cupped his testicles in her hands and fondled him until his state was such that she found herself on the shore with this man, fornicating, and his expression, the release of his pain, had made her very happy. . . .

For a long time, as they rested side by side, and as a chill breeze blew, fragments of her consciousness shredded like leaves in the water, somehow lilting toward the past—to all the conventions of dignity and religion she'd heard from her mother and father. As the man beside her watched the sky, Alicia listened to the wind as it whipped through the treetops, producing, she swore, a sweeping sound like a straw broom over a floor. "Can you hear that?" she asked. Suddenly ashamed of her nakedness she sat up and put on a dress, moving toward a cluster of oak trees where she found a freshly brushed trail leading into the denseness of the woods, a sea of pine needles scattered around her. . . . Looking about, it seemed as if someone had made their way through the woods, putting everything in order; stones and mushrooms bristled clean, even the trunks of rotted trees glowed. . . . And she heard the sweeping again and found herself turning in circles to find the source; each time the sweeping seemed more imminent, and somehow *more eternal,* and connected, in some way, to the powerful influences of her mother—"Mommy," the queen of the forest—whom Alicia imagined lurking behind every tree but never saw.

Later, bored, when the drugs were wearing off, she began to think about her friends at home and the amenities—her stack of glossy plastic-covered diaries, a chain made of chewing gum wrappers (stitched like knitting), her collection of 45 rpms, her own telephone (they'd pleaded and begged for a phone in the apartment), and the kind of simple comfort she derived from falling asleep at the end of a long day and hearing, from the alleyway, the din of television, low voices, a record player, utensils moving, the flush of toilets, the slamming of doors, the movement of feet upon the stairways, and so much more. In the midst of this, she realized that she was feeling nostalgic for the comforts (and even the tribulations) of home.

But she was as stubborn as her own mother had been, and refused to go home. She wrote to Rico apprising him of her situation and called her friend Eliseo, for whom she nursed a distant affection.

More of the Glorious Life
As for her brother, a couple of years later, after graduation, during the beginning of his tenure as a "spy" among the ranks of the

wealthy, Rico found himself as a sophomore, on scholarship, at a prominent Rhode Island university (with which Osprey also had an affiliation) and by that time, for all his skepticism, he had begun to adopt a certain kind of respectability. He was a polished-looking, cleanly groomed college kid, with intense eyes, an alert face, his thick sideburns his main compliance with popular fashion. He wore button-down shirts, chinos, and penny loafers and carried a soft leather wallet in his back pocket. Walking through the neighborhoods of Providence, along its tree-lined streets, appraising the architecture, the Norman Rockwell facades and porches, he saw the grandmothers in their aprons who peeked out from their windows whenever he went by, the dads and sons raking leaves on their lawns, happy dogs barking, and thought that this was America.

It was a world that seemed to open up, literally, at night when he would spend many an evening on Observatory Hill in the pursuit of his newest interest, astronomy; under the instruction of an elderly professor, he climbed a ladder, fidgeted with measurements, and hunted down star clusters and nebulae, the process of looking out, above all the shit of the world, taking him out of himself. He even reveled in the slums of that city, hitting ramshackle neighborhoods, and walking along certain streets, and finding bars where musicians gathered. . . .

His professors were taken by his serious demeanor; his fellow students could not figure him out, for he was private in his habits. Once a week, for several months, he attended meetings of something called the Latin-American Study Group, which mainly dedicated itself to Marxist ideologies. He heard rich kids planning excursions to Cuba, to chop sugarcane, in Che Guevara Brigades, named after the late revolutionary leader. Here and there he made friendships with exchange students, who, he observed, were from the highest strata of their society in Latin America; aside from certain cultural familiarities, he found that he did not have very much in common with them. Pressures to conform—whether coming from the hippies, the leftists, the Latin-Americanists, the studious, the athletes, the fraternity brothers—all left him cold. Love and peace, the working-class call to revolution, the study of banking and macroeconomics, the literatures of South America and Spain, the basketball games and auditorium rallies, the fraternity dances and ROTC clubs were all distractions from his quiet pursuit of the self.

Every morning he woke up and said, "My name is Rico España and I am the son of a waiter and a cleaning woman," a sentence that he could never shake out of his head, no matter how slick or together he felt on a given day.

Pursuing his studies, he had the occasional girlfriend, a job in the library, and played country and western and bluegrass songs with fellow students in a folk club two nights a week, missing his friends in the city and, yes, even his family. Odd surprises came his way. The fact that Mr. Osprey telephoned him every so often to make sure that he was all right both touched and bothered him, because as much as the world had seemed to open up before him, nearly *miraculously*, as much as it seemed that he would escape certain fates—"You do not want to spend your life waiting tables and smelling like meat and grease like me, son,"—behind all of that he heard a voice that said, "Who are you fooling?"

His ever-vigilant mother, Lydia, grand dame of *la escoba y los trapos*—the broom and rags—was nearly impossible to satisfy. Working hard and having to overcome numerous deficits (namely in terms of self-confidence, for he did not feel yet like an "inheritor of this earth") he had managed to maintain a high enough, if not perfect average, his grades nevertheless striking Lydia as a disappointment ("What is this B, when my friend's daughter at the City College gets only the highest, all A's?").

Once a week he called home from a pay phone in the hallway of his dormitory. First he spoke with his soft-voiced father who then handed the telephone over to his mother. And each time, she resurrected his memory of the university incident, and how she had maintained her faith in him even if he had disgraced the family. Whenever she mentioned Osprey it annoyed him: she spoke of the goodness of Osprey and thanked God for that man's presence in the world, and encouraged him to write Osprey letters of gratitude.

"You must understand, that without me *Señor* Osprey would not have interceded in your life and things would be very different: you would be paying for your stupidity now instead of fulfilling your life's dreams."

"My life's dreams?"

"You must thank Mr. Osprey. . . ."

But as much as he felt gratitude to Mr. Osprey, he also resented the idea of being indebted to anyone. Looking around, his vision colored by prejudices, he believed that the other students had it much easier than he did, that opportunities and advantages had been handed to them. Were they expected to be grateful? Did they not seem to take their lot in life for granted? A funny thing began to happen to Rico in his sophomore year: disinterest and torpor overwhelmed him. On some days he could care less about the future, avoiding classes, neglecting to study, or, like father like son, holing up to study for an exam with a bottle of whiskey or vodka, and sometimes smoking pot, too. . . . Given his erratic performances, for he went from high marks to nearly failing grades in several courses ("What the fuck is Tennyson to me?"), professors often called him into their office to speak about his "potential," and he listened, feeling as if only he knew the truth about things.

(*His truth? You're born into the world and the next thing you know you've got a couple of kids and two jobs: maybe*

191

you're chain smoking, coño, *and drinking a little too much; people are bugging the shit out of you but you keep at it because it's the decent thing to do, until the day comes along when you feel a punch to your chest and darkness comes over you; and there you are lying on a floor with all these people staring at you, the edges of that world dimming, and either you die and your dream dissolves into mystery, or you survive and, in a state of physical and spiritual disrepair, you have to start all over, most of your savings, if you have any, gone because the union benefits, if you are lucky enough to get them, are never enough, and in any event it's impossible to take another step in this life without thinking that the next might be your last. . . . And it gets harder, never easier, and the distant illusions you once held, your ambitions and hope for a few years of earthly happiness before you die, are crushed, crushed, crushed. . . .)*

He floated along but was not stupid. Certainly not stupid enough to fall in with a certain contingent of minority students, a group of black and Hispanic kids recruited from the country's slums, who occupied their own house off-campus and were at odds with the rest of the student population. Taking what they wanted, doing as they pleased, they terrorized most of the students. Even Rico, in his moodiness, saw the situation for what it was worth: short-term gains, long-term stupidity.

Mainly he kept to himself, and drifted, gradually, into the study of psychology, which "saved" him.

Lydia Working for Mr. Soto (1972)

She did not enjoy cleaning the undertaker's apartment above the funeral parlor on Amsterdam. One of the owners was a genteel Puerto Rican, Mr. Soto, in partnership with an Irish family who'd been running the business since the Depression. Though there had been a time of occasional friction between the local Irish and Hispanic populations—mainly back in the late 1950s—their partnership made absolute sense from a business point of view: over the years many Hispanics, moving into the neighborhood, would eventually die there. As the business prospered, it was especially crowded on the weekends, when most wakes were held, its many rooms and chapels attracting large contingents of Hispanic and Irish people.

This mortician, Mr. Soto, sometimes played cards with Raul and had a propensity for the cheerful greeting: "Have a wonderful day," he'd say to Lydia happily, as if he would sing to the corpses. "You always do a wonderful job, *Señora* España," he used to tell her. "If you ever want anything full time as a receptionist you let me know."

Smelling of cologne, he had the most perfectly manicured hands she had ever seen on a man. Nearing sixty, he'd been hoping to pass his trade on to his sons, Ernesto and Carlos. They had wanted to go to college to earn business degrees but because of hard economic times had settled for mortician's school. Often dressed in chemist's frocks and smelling vaguely (she thought) of lime disinfectant, his sons were big baseball fans, and became ecstatically happy in 1969, when the New York Mets went to the World Series—pennants hanging on the wall of their embalming room, beside a poster advertising a concert by the Doors. The apartment itself was always filled with vases of flowers (left over from funeral wreaths? she wondered) and Mrs. Soto, who did the firm's accounting, had a real liking for Danish modern furniture, the result of a European trip in their recent past. Framed letters from the parish priests hung among the local bric-a-brac, for sometimes the undertakers made preparations for the very poor at cost or less, and oddly, alongside them, there were two prints from *Paradise Lost* by Milton as illustrated by Gustave Doré (souls in great pits of fire, souls climbing a pathway to the celestial kingdom).

193

Lots of pictures of Jesus and His mother, Maria, with blazing hearts, glowing tongues of fire, transcendent doves. On a flower-patterned couch in the living room, with the lights off, was the mortician's portly mother, *Doña* Isabel, who spent much of her days watching soap operas on two different television sets, fanning herself, enjoying cold-cut sandwiches, and attending to her incredibly intelligent Chihuahua, Maurice. This little animal reflected in its glossy ball-bearing eyes the knowledge of the universe, and whiffed and snorted, wagging its tail as if it could read minds, particularly Lydia's, whom this dog constantly followed around.

"Yes, yes," said she who never liked animals, petting his firm quivering hide, "I wish I could take you home, too."

Now there were bottles of chemicals in the closets and, because of the age of the building, the smell of water-damaged walls and rotting wood; then, too, there were the odd scents of Freon from the huge refrigerators they kept in a back room in the parlor below, refrigerators as ornate as Osprey's—and the acrid let-me-out-of-here smell of formaldehyde and other bodily preservatives, the scent of flowers—lilacs and lavender in particular—and the indescribable scent of death. Sometimes Lydia found herself in the bathroom wetting her face or standing by an open window, just above the funeral home awning, trying to overcome her feelings of discomfort.

She was always amazed at just what some people, like Mrs. Stitch, the makeup lady, and Mr. Pappas, the corpse dresser, would do for money.

Whenever she cleaned in their apartment, her superstitious side got to her: she could not imagine how the Sotos lived in a place where there were so many ghosts. (Mr. Soto: "You get used to anything I guess.") Now and then she had to go downstairs to get her pay from Mrs. Soto, and she wondered if she arranged it that way because she knew Lydia did not like the parlor. Possessing the laconic manner of a hotel clerk at two in the morning, Mrs. Soto was a petite woman without much of a smile for anyone. She may have noticed the way that Mr. Soto beamed at the sight of Lydia, and, out of jealousy, or because the atmosphere and darkness below had gotten to her over the years, liked to treat Lydia as she would a servant. Making a big deal out of paying her, she'd have Lydia sign a log and a receipt, before slowly opening a trick drawer in her desk with a foot pedal. She'd bring out a metal cash box, unlocking that with a key from a heavy loop of keys, and then, finally, counting out the bills, not once, not twice, but three times, her bifocals low on her nose. (On the other hand, Mr. Soto just pulled the money out of his wallet.)

There had been an afternoon when Lydia had gone to collect her pay and happened by the opened door of a room where one of the morticians, a dapper white-haired Irishman named Johnny, was wiping down with a sponge and solution of alcohol and water the corpse of a young red-haired girl, naked on the table. The poor girl had the palest white skin she had ever seen, and in repose seemed both heartbreakingly beautiful and helpless: like a fairy tale princess, Lydia thought, on the verge of suddenly awakening. Having lingered just long enough for the mortician to notice her, she flinched when he looked at her, as he, with the calmest expression, reached forward and closed the door.

On her way home, she could not get the image of the young girl on the table out of her mind. In the early morning hours, as she rested in bed, still as a corpse, she had reflected, as Raul snored, turning beside her, how the world had fallen away from that young teenager. It made her question the value of everything—to put so many hours into life and labor and love for what? For what?

The
Passing Years
of Lydia's
Employment

Over the dense repetitiousness of her days, certain things had happened, some sad, some good, to those ladies who had been Lydia's fleeting acquaintances and friends over the years. One of the ladies she knew from the "profession," Elenita Perez, whom she often ran into on the downtown number 1 train, used to call her on Sunday nights, a weekly ritual that was observed in the hours after dinner, when each of these ladies, having cleared their family's plates, did the dishes over full sinks of soap and water, the time passing pleasantly enough. (If Raul left her alone.) It had been a habit the ladies maintained for many years.

On one Sunday night Elenita called Lydia to tell her that she was finally leaving the profession. After twenty-seven years of six-day weeks she and her husband had saved enough money to buy a little bungalow in the Catskills with a pool, a bird bath, and, among the luxuries of her newly anticipated life, a Sony Triniton color TV. The neighbors were nice and they had a sun porch with a view of the distant mountains. Once they were settled in, she promised Lydia, they were going to have a picnic for all the cleaning ladies she had known over the years. Lydia was very pleased for her because she had seen her on some days when the woman had worked so much she was too exhausted to talk.

But, as it happened, the very week that Elenita and her husband had moved out of the South Bronx and were happily installed in their new home, and she could look forward to the good life, or the relatively good life, just as she sat watching the dapper Univision news commentator, Rafael Piñeda, on whom she had a mad crush, Elenita doubled over in pain and was taken by ambulance to a hospital in Albany where the doctors found the interior of her body riddled with cancerous tumors.

She lived only another few months.

Hearing the sad news, Lydia spent one night seated in front of the television weeping hysterically over a mildly sentimental RKO film from the 1940s, rubbing her eyes raw; she was in such a state that Raul, shuffling along in his fluffy evening slippers, went over to plant a kiss upon her damp face, as a kind of reassurance that, despite all the awfulness of life, love still awaited.

You are cast adrift, she had thought over and over again, the shore that was your youth, with all the promise of the future, becoming fainter and fainter, until you are completely alone without illusion. And there is death waiting for you, at the edge of the endless-seeming sea.

At a party, after Elenita's funeral in the Bronx, Lydia and a few friends got drunk and passed the evening praising the will and strength (or stupidity) of women like Elenita who sacrificed so much, working so many hours for the benefit of her family that she hardly ever had the time to take care of herself. And besides, even if she had the inclination to go to the doctor's if something bothered her, who wanted to wait an entire morning in the clinic without pay, and who had the money to spend on private visits, for those noble doctors who used to charge five and ten dollars a visit had been replaced by a whole new generation of debt-ridden physicians, who did not always care to open their offices in certain neighborhoods, like Elenita's.

Home in a taxi by ten-thirty that night ("Lordy, I'm sick of trains") she was so saddened by the unfairness of it all that she felt like spitting at the face of the moon. Raul, who had not attended the funeral, was sleeping in the bedroom and so she decided to stay in the living room, as she wanted to be alone; while sitting on the couch and removing her shoes and pantyhose in the light of a street lamp out their window, and while thinking about the passage of those years, it dawned on her that life, no matter how hard one tried, never went well for some people.

"Bah," she told herself. The word *Bah,* and others, *Ay,* and *Dios,* she uttered with more and more frequency as the years passed and she found that certain aches, instead of going away like they used to, became more pronounced . . .

She had other friends whose lives of hard work ended badly—Amelia of Salvador, pushed in front of a number 4 express train by some crazed junkie who'd grabbed her purse; Anita Díaz from untreated diabetes; another, Francesca Ponce, from a stroke. She also heard about tragic things happening to their kids or husbands. She knew a cleaning lady named Berta Santiago, whose pride and joy was her son, a sterling pupil at the Mount St. Michael High School. Leading the secret life of a young drunk at seventeen years of age, he came home after a night out drinking Gypsy Rose and Thunderbird with pals in an alley, and climbing the tenement stairs, slipped, fell backwards, and snapped his spinal column on the floor landing. She saw a headline on the front page of the *Daily News* about another cleaning lady whose son became one of those hero cops shot by drug dealers, and saw a news item about another cleaning woman, whose daughter, hanging around with the wrong dance hall people in the Bronx, ended her brief life bound and gagged in a closet on Third Avenue and 173rd Street. . . . And there was the very decent husband of Miriam Alonso, shot dead in a bar for interceding in an argument. . . .

(On the other hand, some of her friends retired peacefully, like Maria Torres, who left the Bronx to live by the beautiful sea in Puerto Rico, near Mayagüez in the far west of the island; and there was the Mexican cleaning lady Rosalita Reyes, sunlight of those often drab mornings on the train, speaking brightly of her daughters, each of whom, she would happily

report, had gotten married to a nice man and good provider—
the cleaning woman's aspiration—and moved out to a safe
place, Staten Island or Jersey or Ohio. A sweet-natured
woman, who seemed to have never aged a day in the years
they'd known each other, she worked until she had saved
enough to return home and live in a house overflowing with
bougainvillea, a blossom pressed between two pieces of paper
scenting her cheerful letters. And there was Juanita Cruz, who
raised her four sons alone and watched each go to law school
despite the perilous climate and education-hating atmosphere
of her neighborhood—128th off Amsterdam. She also heard
the occasional but rare tale of a pretty cleaning lady's romance
with a well-off man, love precipitated by the unexpected death
of a wife, or old age, a tale of Cinderella, the poor woman, des-
tined for a long life of unpromising and unfulfilling labor, suddenly swept into the upper middle class . . .)

*Scrubbing clean the white enamel of the refrigerator door,
she often thought about something that a friend, Tita, had once
said to her, "Soy una esclava," or, "I'm a slave," and that had
remained with Lydia, coming back to her on those days when
things were not going well.*

*Tita had found work in Macy's as a janitorial assistant, her
job to clean the bathrooms, elevators, and displays of that
department store by night. Their paths often crossed in the
mornings when Lydia was on her way to work. She had wanted
to be a ballet dancer, having been enchanted by a performance
of Swan Lake she had seen on television in Puerto Rico. But no
one in her little town was a professional ballet dancer and no
one knew about ballet schools, just that they were something
far away, beyond the mountains. One afternoon, thanks to an
usher friend, she took Lydia to see a performance of the New
York City Ballet. In the midst of a ballet by someone called*

Delibes, poor Tita, living a reimagined existence, had started to weep and was still weeping when they parted company at the 59th Street Station, where she caught the Flushing train home.

One of the great revelations of Lydia's life? That she was never going to be rich, even though she played the lottery, like so many millions of others, hoping for that "pie in the sky" to come down, rarely hitting a single number, much less winning. (Now if you prayed more to God, Mireya and Raul would tell her. . . .) Sometimes she went to church for its basement bingo games and once, after attending the parish bazaar, she came home with a plastic piggy bank, which she left out in the kitchen, where it filled with pennies and roach eggs. She was elegant, as always, rarely venturing out of the apartment without being well dressed, though with the passage of time some of these efforts, day after day, took their toll. Losing patience with others, on some days she could not bear to live on the same street as those ladies in curlers with the flabby arms who were still dressed in their slips at three in the afternoon and passed their time looking out their windows. A few lines of unhappiness began to cut through the lovely angularity of her face, and she got into the habit of looking at herself with even greater scrutiny in the mornings, feeling obsessed with her changing loveliness while riding the subways or busses or scrubbing the floor (there she was polishing the lion legs of a nineteenth-century *armario* in Osprey's home, and as she was getting up, she watched her face in the reflections of the cabinet glass, asking herself, "*Dios,* who is that aging woman?")

She smiled in acknowledgment but did not believe it when Mr. Fuentes, from his butcher shop doorway, called out, "Hey, beauty of the springtime!" Heavier on the makeup than ever before and haunting the cosmetic counters of the more famous department stores to search for bargains and free samples, she sometimes wandered about both envying and feeling sorry for those fancy ladies who could afford face-lifts (sorry for the poor ones whose original faces were stretched so tightly that you could see all the veins on their forehead and temples, and their eyeballs seemed on the verge of popping out of their sockets; envying the more fortunate ladies, like Mrs. Osprey, who went to bed one night aged fifty-five and awakened on another morning looking a youthful thirty-five).

Mrs. Osprey's Observations about Beauty (1979–1980)
Fifteen years had passed since Lydia had first started working for the Ospreys; by then Mrs. Osprey was in her early fifties and yet she still possessed that neat and prim society-lady beauty, lovely blond hair and lovely manicured nails and lovely jewelry; her nicest attribute, it seemed to Lydia, was her pure and smooth skin—on her vanity Lydia found beautifying moisturizers with names like Peaches and Cream and Touch of Venus—and it continued to amaze Lydia how well she had kept her figure over the years.

The occasional eye tuck had scattered many an emerging wrinkle to the winds. Reappearing one autumn afternoon from the Vineyard, where she had hidden herself away for a month under a big sun hat and pair of dark glasses, Mrs. Osprey looked so well that Lydia, greeting her in the hallway, had gasped, touched her hand to her breast, and said, "My God, señora, you look so good, for a second I thought you was your daughter."

Incidentally, it should be noted that this kind of flattery was a well-intended and useful tool of cleaning women everywhere. And although it can be said that Lydia was prone to praise (to be followed by an attack) or scorn (usually tied to envy) in this instance she seemed genuinely pleased by the state of Mrs. Osprey's glowing, if partially artificial, youthfulness. On many another day, Lydia, arriving at work sullen, judgmental with others, quickly brightened at the sight of the rich lady's face, asking, "How is it that you always look so good?" And, "You are looking better every time I see you, *señora*."

Because Lydia seemed so sincere in her compliments, Mrs. Osprey let her in on her regimens of exercise and diet: the occasional Elizabeth Arden makeover was an absolute must (costing a week's wages), she had said, not to mention all kinds of helpful "youth revivifying" creams, as per those advertised in the rich ladies' fashion magazines. There was also, Mrs. Osprey explained, the need to have the proper "attitude" in connection with one's looks.

Standing in the hallway ready to plug in the chubby-corded vacuum cleaner, Lydia listened with fascination.

"I don't tell many people about my theories of the body-world connection, but Lydia, this is what I think," Mrs. Osprey began. "What you expose yourself to exerts a powerful influence on the way you are: ugly things breed ugly thoughts and these in turn affect the way a person feels and looks—I think ugliness in life can do harm to the body while you sleep. . . . On the other hand, the beauty you surround yourself with will help you to be beautiful. . . . And that is true with personal habits and hobbies." She brightened, adding, "Did you know that the prettiest and most well-preserved women I know are members of the New York Horticultural Society? It's exposure to blossoms that does it. I know of a woman, she's around ninety and spends her life devoted to roses, and these roses, I swear to you, Lydia, have given her skin a pinkish, rosy glint of health. Can you believe it?"

"Yes, my husband, Raul, loves flowers."

"And it's helped him, hasn't it?"

"Oh, when he is happy, I think so, yes," Lydia told her.

"Of course they do; they exert a power." And she took Lydia into the living room where that very morning fresh flowers had been delivered and set out on the coffee table.

Lydia was about to excuse herself when Mrs. Osprey added, "It's like people with their dogs. When I see squat short owners with their squat short dogs, or tiny little men with Pekinese or Chihuahuas, or bushy-haired curly-topped women with French poodles, or willowy types with collies . . . it seems clear to me that we as human beings are formed by all kinds of forces; that's why I am personally careful about where and how and when and with whom I consort: I would choose a museum like the Metropolitan any day over a movie house, a night of opera over television anytime . . . because they make you, well, more substantial and attractive, overall, don't you think?" Then: "Surely, you must have an interest that helps you?"

"When I was younger, in Cuba," Lydia began, "I loved to dance. Now, I like to go to the movies with my husband—how beautiful they can be sometimes—and to a club or a dance hall with friends, especially when my son's godfather, a *músico*, is performing with his band. Most nights we stay at home—we are tired after the day's work—resting, talking with friends, but not too much more than that." Then: "What else you gonna do? Wait for the children to call, when they feel like calling, yes?"

"You've got that one right."

From a slender package Mrs. Osprey tapped out a cigarette, which she inserted into a holder, lit, and then inhaled, offering one to Lydia.

"No thank you, *señora*."

Shortly Mrs. Osprey left the apartment to see some friends, and Lydia continued with her work. A melody, locked up for a long long time came back to Lydia, slipping into her thoughts as she dusted about the room: there had been a dance long ago in her town where the band had performed a moving version of Ernesto Lecuona's "*Comparsita*" and she had gone spinning across the floor, smiling at her admirers, the violins and horns of the orchestra sounding gloriously, as if from some kind of heaven—in retrospect the heaven of her youth. She began to hum that melody with a kind of joyfulness, but soon a melancholy descended upon her, the melancholy of one who knows that not too many things from that day on, or any other, will change.

Solitude

Over the years, she had begun to enjoy those moments of solitude when she was left alone at work, amusing herself in multiple ways: She would turn on the radio to the easy listening station, dance waltzes or simply sing to herself. She was not above the diversions of daytime soap operas—like *As the World Turns* and *Days of Our Lives*—which she would put on while she dusted and polished in a room. If she had the time she might sit by the window with a short-nubbed pencil in hand studying one of the books that Mireya had passed on to her, about English for the foreign speaker usually, filling a note pad with new words. To do so had been her occasional habit from the days when her poor son (thank God for Mr. Osprey) had gotten into trouble and she had been intimidated by the legalese of court documents, which, to her mind, were as complicated as Mr. Chang's dialects.

From that time on she had determined to improve herself, but learned that it was not becoming any easier with age. The meanings of words like *elucidate, trepidation, status,* or *abstemious* still escaped her. A newspaper like the *Daily News* was readable enough; the *New York Times*, however, was beyond her reach, though she got into the habit of looking through Mr. and Mrs. Osprey's copy. In any event, she was on a path of self-improvement, even if she laughed at Mireya's suggestions: "If you get a high-school equivalency diploma, maybe you could enroll in a night school for college."

Go to college?

"*Chica, eres cucka!*" she'd say. "I'm too old—what are they going to do with a woman like me? I'm old enough to be a grandmother!" And yet, there was something about having a son smart enough to go to college that made her feel a deep sense of accomplishment, even if she had not gotten the knack of the language herself. Maybe if she had the words, her relationship with her son would be better . . . and the oddness of feelings they had toward one another would change. (Once he had graduated from college, a grand event in the family history, and begun postgraduate work, he became more remote from the family. He wrote letters that had an impersonal tone, never divulging much information about himself, which Raul read over and over again and sometimes took with him to work to show to his fellow waiters.) That he would not misunderstand her protective, overly proud nature and confuse it with selfishness, that she would be able to make herself clear that, for all her moodiness, she did love him, that, in her way, she was proud of him, that *with her English improved their love would flow more easily.*

Rico's graduation (in 1975) had been a crowning moment in the history of the (peasant) family, something to brag about to her friends on the street, for her son had risen, through caprice and luck, in the ranks of the world. To her mind college was a mysterious place that turned young boys into men and these men into accomplished and newly aloof creatures, like her son, who never particularly liked to talk about what he was studying: for college, especially to Raul, seemed a magical place, beyond their reach and comprehension, best to be left alone. Besides, it did not matter what Rico studied as long as it kept him off the street and away from his hoody friends. Because they did not have to pay for as much as a single book on Rico's behalf, his education seemed a true Godsend (or Ospreysend) not to be tampered with or contested. Yet to hear her talking about this to her friends, one could swear that she had been totally responsible for the progress of his life: "Yes, we've always believed in the boy even if he didn't always believe in himself." And: "Of course, he did well, he has my blood and had our help!"

During his tenure in Rhode Island, she would take a few moments out of her workday to try calling him, though he lived in a dormitory and no one could ever seem to find her son, who was always "in the library" or "out." Even when they connected, he seemed to have no time or patience for her; after all she had done for him, he was ungrateful. Still, through a general persistence and dogged family loyalty, the kind one saw in their neighborhood, as in *"I don't care if I fucking shoot you in the head, I do it out of love,"* she believed in the bonds that linked them and persisted until she eventually reached him on the telephone.

"My boy, it's your mother speaking."

"Hola, mamá."

"How are things?"

". . . It's raining."

"Here too, *pero* the rain is good for the plants."

"So, what's going on?"

"Oh nothing, things are the same, your Poppy and me just working like always. Nobody's getting rich."

"How's he doing?"

"He's not doing so bad lately. *Está muy guapito,* buying some nice clothes at that place on 96th Street and Broadway, *esa tiendacita* run by the Egyptians, they have good bargains even if they have no manners. He's looking good, but you never know, my son, he could go like that—any of us could. Like Mrs. Delgado from the projects, she just died of a stroke last week, and . . ."

"*Mira,* Mommy, I'm trying to study now . . ."

"And what is it that you're studying? My friends always are asking me."

"You really want to know?"

"Of course. I'm your mother, like it or not."

"I'm studying a kind of psychology, what they call a humanist approach. *El profesor aquí es muy famoso, muy conocido. ...* My professor's a very well-known man in his field." Then: "You know what psychology is, right, Ma?"

"Oh yes, a study of the crazy people."

"It's not that simple."

"Then tell me."

"Look, I don't have time for that. I have to prepare some interviews."

For some reason that made her laugh.

"*Entrevistas?* You are going to speak to somebody about their problems?"

"Yes, some children from the poor part of Boston. And maybe a lady who tried to kill herself, a few months ago, but they—" and the concept of *they,* as if it implied the larger and greater world beyond, impressed her "—it's nothing really."

"No, but I'm interested, son."

"Yes, yes, but I really don't have time to talk about it now, okay?"

"Okay, but do me a favor and let me know how to spell that *seekology? Díme, por favor.*"

"Okay. It's *p . . .* "

"*Peh.*"

"*S . . .*"

"*Ese . . .*"

"*Y . . .*"

"*Igriega.*"

"*E . . .*"

"*Eh o i?*"

"*Eh.*"

"Okay, *eh.*"

"*C* ..."

"*C.*"

"*H* ..."

"*Hache o jota?*"

"*Hache.... H, H, H* ..."

"Okay."

"Now: *o* ..."

"*O.*"

"*L* ..."

"*Ele.*"

"*O* ..."

"*Otra vez un o?*"

"Yes ... *o.*"

"*O.*"

"*G* ..."

"*Ge.*"

"*Y.*"

"*Igriega.*"

"That's it."

"Okay, let me see. *Peh-ese-ese—*"

"No, only one *s.*"

"I know. *Peh-ese-igriega-*"

"Okay ..."

"*Ce ... jota—*"

"No, not *j* but *h* ... *hache.*"

"Okay, but you don't have to raise your voice." Then: "*Mira aquí. Peh ... ese ... igriega ... hache ... y qué más?*"

"*O.*"

"*Si, o pues ele.*"

"Right."

"*Entonces otro o* ..."

"Yes . . ."

"*Ge, igriega.*"

"Correct."

"Let me see again."

"Come on, I gotta go."

"Just one moment—"

"I don't have the time, right now. I gotta go. Okay?"

"You never have the time."

"I have my studies and things I do—you just don't know—and if I don't do it for myself no one else will. Understand?"

"Okay, okay. Good-bye."

Lydia hung up and sat in the Ospreys' hall by the telephone table with the word *psychology* written out on a pad, hurt by her son's briskness. "Gotta go." Is that what her efforts came down to? But what could she expect? For modern youth with very few exceptions—like Osprey's children—had lost respect for their elders; life as she had known it was shredding apart; *you worked hard and people still drifted away.*

Lydia would never admit it, for in the tradition of dear Cuban families much was made of their closeness and love, and yet, she worried that, for all her good intentions and all her efforts to see their lives go well, she had passed on to her children, without knowingly doing so, a certain temperament, one that made for distances, for solitude, even when what they sought was its opposite.

She sat for a moment and watched the sun lengthening in the hallway. (The light speaking to her: "*Gotta go.*")

The Quiet Existence

Some things never changed: each day she wondered about the "future" she was to share with Raul. When he looked to the future he daydreamed about retiring to a beautiful place like Puerto Rico, his idea to find a small town by the western ocean, near Mayaguez, like Lydia's friend Maria Torres. They'd lead a quiet existence—Raul could play cards, watch baseball, drink until his liver rotted with pals in a social club and awake in the mornings, his heart fluttering like a wounded bird, to a brand new world. (This would be a reverse immigration, as it were, back to the Caribbean, many years after he had left.) At dinner he'd carry on about such and such a *fulano*, some fellow who had not only managed to survive in the city but did so while saving enough money to go back to the country he had once sought to escape ... his eyes welling with tears (from beer, from rising cigarette smoke, from hope) and Lydia ready at any moment to explode: why on earth would she leave New York for a small hick town when New York was still the place to prove herself and command the gentlemanly and respectful love of others: that's what she wanted. (Well, that and so many other things: a young body and a virile young man to satisfy her, and beauty to draw the attention of every man in a room, and enough money to be driven through the city in a carriage—in her dreams a white carriage decorated with flowers—or a white limousine. In that circumstance, she and her family would become the royalty of the neighborhood, received with warmth and kindness instead of with the caution and detachment she saw in people's expressions; the way her family had been treated back in Cuba before the fall. . . .)

Eternal Life

Much as she loved Raul, she sometimes lost patience with him. Self-effacing and humble as ever, he was becoming somewhat mad, especially with regard to religion. During one of his attacks, a minor stroke, he had a religiously significant vision; *"This is where the Truth is told"* was the phrase uttered to him in his dream or vision, and over the years, while reflecting upon what had happened to him, he concluded that in each man's troubled and fragile body there did reside a soul, the true repository of all joy, wisdom, and love of God in the world, a fragment, as it were, of *His endless presence.*

Fortified by this simple bit of knowledge, he became more dedicated to the religion he knew best, his Catholicism. Feeling that he had awakened from a long-lasting sleep, he became a deacon at the local Catholic church and, as well, liked to spend his Sundays walking around the neighborhood in a sharp-looking blue suit, with a Bible in hand, and a large crucifix around his neck, rendering through the kindness of his voice and the dewy faith in his eyes (almost on the verge of tears over his discovery) a *reassurance that something beautiful was happening spiritually in this world and that finding the source of that beauty was worth every hardship and aspiration. . . .*

Over time he began to bring more religious items into the apartment—a wooden crucifix with a vial of extreme unction oil inside, a plaster bust of the Virgin Mary, a Virgin Mary savings bank that he'd found downtown, and tall candles, which gave his dresser top the appearance of an altar.

He also got into the habit of blessing old friends like Mario when he saw them, and strangers as well, raising his hand in an apostolic gesture, murmuring in his tender, smoke-choked voice, "God bless you, my friend."

She put up with his readings from the Bible at night and his wishful speculations about death and the afterlife.

"After many long hours of thought, I am convinced that I know what will happen when we die." He mentioned this one night when they were in bed. "Do you want me to tell you about it?"

"Yes, my love."

"Here is what I think, Lydia. You die. You close your eyes. The light around you fades. And it's a lonely kind of feeling, because you are being pulled away into a kind of peaceful sleep, that is, if you are lucky enough. Yet, at the same time, we are turned into a kind of light that is in unity with our Creator; or what I would call the principle of Love, which is knowing that you belong to something that is warm and good—and that is a truth—for what else are we without the love of others?"

"Who can say, Raul. . . . "

"Your death—that point of exit, when you walk through the sacred door—takes only an instant, like a camera flashing, but in that one moment you are drawn into this glorious unity, which exists out of time . . . and because of that, the beautiful moment lasts forever. Or it may as well last forever, because that is all we will ever know again; that is our new life, if I can call it that, from beginning to end, a world of pleasant meadows and light and memories, in a flash." Then after a moment, he asked her: "What do you think, my dear? Does it make sense to you?"

"Yes, it makes perfect sense. Now go to sleep, my love."

Through Liquor the Love of God

Lydia did not so much mind his religious participation in the church or even his increasingly fanciful thoughts, but what troubled her deeply was how dear Raul had come to worship the effect of liquor upon his soul. Most of the time Lydia did not want to believe there was anything particularly excessive about what Raul did. To get a bit tipsy—and this was a truism from the poorest to the richest—was a kind of instantaneous vacation from life's woes, albeit temporarily. He always had that proclivity and she put up with it for years, because it had seemed only a matter of time before he would die. Except for passing out now and then, or slumping to the floor while sitting in the kitchen, he had been careful enough: but whenever poor Raul had a bad night, when something terrible took place, when he threatened to leave the family or to kick in the television set, or turned over the table, with shouts and protestations of hatred and bitterness about life in this country and what hard work got you (which wasn't much)—acts contrary to the image of Raul as a completely good man—when he'd put the family through that kind of nonsense, becoming just like the people she had always looked down on, when he, in his humble and uncertain way, raised his fist against Lydia, he would regret all of that the next morning, swearing that he had gone against his own true nature, and the beloved Raul, of the quiet manner, returned.

Yet with the kids out of the apartment, off in their own lives, he fell back in love with this vice, and through the liquor he found his love of God, his belief in the soul reinforced. He bought some religious music from a shop down at St. Francis's on 12th Street one day and played the hymns again and again. He prayed and wept over the sad condition of mankind, held conversations with certain highly esteemed individuals like Jesus Christ Himself, Whom he, in certain states, heard and felt in the radiator buzz of the kitchen, the El trains thundering beyond the windows. Moved by the music, alcohol, and hope, he trembled. Was he happy? Was he ecstatic? Lydia did not know, only that he was talking to himself, and sometimes came out with some crazy ideas, as when, one evening, he felt his pulse and declared, "I feel the Holy Spirit flying through my veins." And when she told him, "Come to bed, you've been drinking too much," he answered, "You know who drank too much, Jesus Christ, otherwise he wouldn't have died for everybody!"

These episodes would pass—for he was not always like that—and, in a normal frame of mind, the notion of moving away to some small *pueblo* in a beautiful place stayed alive in Raul. Loving him, Lydia worried about his health and general well-being—*you know those latin men like to have a lady to take care of them when they're old*—and she had a vision of the

216

future that bothered her: of Raul as a very old man, enfeebled, demented, carrying on, tormenting her, even if lovingly so, until his very last days.

The Grandchildren from Upstate (1980)

If it was her destiny to have Raul as a husband, she could at least take comfort in the way her children had turned out. Even if they resided at great emotional distances from their parents, no great tragedies had befallen them. While Rico made his way through school, Alicia had not only weathered the difficulties of her youth, but had found herself a nice husband—a building contractor—whom she met while attending a jobs conference in upstate New York in 1973. Once the confusions of youth had abated, after a directionless tenure, she had gone to live in Troy, New York, where she worked in a health food store and shared a house with other young people her own age; she had never really returned home, except sporadically, for she did love her mother and father, but she had been determined to strike out for herself. Hard to believe but now the Cuban cleaning lady had two grandchildren by Alicia, two boys, Doug and Brad, a source of muted joy and satisfaction to Lydia for she and Raul only saw them once or twice a year, at Christmas and sometimes in the summer; they rarely had time to get up to Brewster, the small town where Alicia now lived.

There was nothing, nothing, nothing to do there during the day except hang around the porch or take the toddlers for walks, Lydia staring into the windows of each and every house (the people inside staring back at her) as she pushed the carriage along. Raul, shaking a rattle, having a smoke, looked for a beatific vision in the sky, that beloved sky hanging lush and blue over the houses and oaks and pines and traffic-whipped roads and malls. They didn't particularly like the in-laws either, who were always raising their voices like impertinent

217

restaurant customers, speaking to Lydia and Raul as if they could not understand their English. Alicia was happy enough (she breast-fed her babies!) living a post-hippy existence on a property with a rambling turn-of-the-century farmhouse and a brook running through their backyard. Pleading the encumbrances of children and disliking the tense atmosphere of uptown New York neighborhoods—the old neighborhood frightened her spouse—she did not make many trips home. To compensate her parents she bombarded them with photographs of the children, "Little Doug" and Brad Johnson (yes, *el marido*'s name was Douglas Johnson, can you believe that?), living out the life that Lydia had fantasized about for her children. Her daughter sent them snapshots of the children playing on a healthy green lawn, with a *swing* and a *dog* and a *bicycle* beside them, snippets of rolling countryside in the distance; the kids on their porch, *America half-prosperous, half-withered everywhere around them*—the kids selling lemonade in front of their house, or posed by a neighbor's Model-T—all fragments of a serene slice of small-town life. Those views of their life in Brewster would be their legacy, the place these children, of half Cuban/Spanish ancestry, would one day look back upon with sadness, in the same way their grandmother and grandfather regarded old photographs of Cuba, with longing for the beauty and possibilities of youth. . . .

And nearly every night, after seven, Alicia being a good (if not perfect) daughter, *much enamored of her own way of being*, would call so that they could speak to their grandmother, if only to say hello. That, with the holidays, was their life together. . . .

Raul's Little Secret
In time Lydia began to notice a change in Raul's behavior. Where before he had liked to stay at home, *tranquilito*, to do as

he pleased, she found that he seemed to be contriving ways to leave the apartment, particularly on the weekends. That is to say that Raul, with his health condition and self-preoccupations, was perfectly content to bide his time in this world before the television set, particularly on a cold winter's afternoon, when the boiler was working and the landlord none too stingy, often falling asleep, satiated, if not delighted by the progress and amenities, humble as they were, of his life. His only variations from routine had to do with his duties at church, collecting donations, serving as an usher, lending a hand at bazaars and clothing sales, and with his springtime forays to the flower shows and botanical gardens, where this gaunt presence would stand (slightly drunk) among the rhododendrons, daydreaming as happily as a caliph in his gardens in Andalusia.

In the latter years of his life, there was little beyond these outings—even fishing trips—that would lure him out of the apartment, and yet Lydia had begun to become aware of something in his behavior, an intimation, let us say, of someone scheming. *Furtivo*—sneaky—was a word that came to mind. It may well have been the cast of his eyes, the way he looked down or off to the side, never able to make eye contact with his wife, when, in the middle of a drab Saturday afternoon, he would get dressed, put on a tie and jacket, carefully primp before a mirror, and, scented of Old Spice, slip out of the apartment for a "walk."

When she would ask him where he was going, he would tell her, "To see an old waiter friend of mine." Yet, if this were true, he certainly would have invited his old friend over to the apartment, where he could carry on until late without worrying about having to take the subway and getting mugged in the middle of the night, as nearly happened to him on several occasions. Or he would tell her that the boss had rescheduled him at work or that he had forgotten to get his pay or that he needed to "look into something."

But more than Raul's fastidiousness about his appearance when he went out—for that was the manner of his generation—what made Lydia suspicious was his solemnity, his nervousness, and the quickness of his temper if she so much as mentioned going with him. The very idea would bring Raul to the brink of anger—shaking, he would shout, "What am I, your slave?"

Standing by the window she would watch him on the street below, lighting a cigarette and straightening his coat and collar, heading off to wherever "out" may have been.

Of course she speculated: if dear Raul were having a love affair, certainly it would be with a younger woman, for what else could so entice the interest of a man whose best years were behind him? She could see how it happened, saw it happening all the time. (As Lydia had observed, young women become more and more beautiful to men as they age—in fact Lydia had once heard their dear friend Mario say, "Even the plain-looking ones . . ." The aura of youth, the textures of the skin, the purely ravishing anticipation of the life to come—the future—that was in young women's eyes.) Despite her own fantasies about Mr. Osprey, whose warm presence lingered in some part of her mind as a powerful attraction, her true love was Raul, and the idea of his philandering, at once unbelievable and unacceptable, was a surprise to her. Sometimes she wanted to cry; sometimes she wanted to slap him across the face, or push him onto the floor.

Still she often asked herself what Raul had to offer a young woman.

Bienvenida

Cleaning out Mrs. Osprey's refrigerator one afternoon Lydia made a mental list of the lies Raul must have told a young woman to gain her affections: That he was rich? She might have believed him if she were a young immigrant from Salvador or Equador, for Lydia heard those stories all the time, girls coming to the States with nothing and doing anything to make ends meet. But he had no money—*they* had no money; the small amounts they had saved over the years seemed to dissipate in the course of paying for minor emergencies, such as when Raul lost several of his teeth. Aside from a "few" thousand she'd put away in a retirement fund that he didn't really know about, what did they have?

He was sweet with babies, doting on his grandchildren and on Mario's kids. He was the kind of fellow to approach a baby carriage on tiptoes in the park and go *click-click-click* with his teeth and mouth like a squirrel. He sometimes woke in the middle of the night and declared, "I hear the baby crying," even though Rico and Alicia were well into their thirties and lived far from home. He was the kind of fellow to give a poor kid looking furtively into a candy store window a dollar or two 'cause he couldn't take the sadness and longing in the kid's expression (sucker!). Children, especially the tiny ones, always seemed to like him—whereas in Lydia's presence, it must be added, they often cried.

But it was in Raul's very affinity with children that Lydia saw a clue to his whereabouts: for there was a young mother of two in the neighborhood, a husbandless Guatamalan woman in her late twenties named Bienvenida who labored in the factories on 26th Street and barely scraped by no matter how much she tried or how many hours she worked. She and her children shared an apartment with an elderly Spanish couple on 123rd Street, in a walk-up across the street from the Manhattan Gardens co-ops. She was pretty and morose and confided to women like Lydia that she hated her work and would do anything to find a man to take care of her. Hadn't Lydia seen this woman making eyes at the married bodega men or giving the young college boys (who could care less) a worn smile? Hadn't Lydia seen Bienvenida and Raul on the corner talking? And hadn't he gone to her apartment on several occasions with some tools to help her with minor repairs—visits about which he remained mysterious—Raul who was loathe to fix anything in their own apartment ("Call Martinez")? Hadn't he gone to the store to buy her a couple of freshly defeathered chickens and her kids a box of Entenmann's cupcakes? And perhaps given her money on several occasions?

Could not a young woman like Bienvenida, grateful for such generosity, put her friendships and common sense aside and seduce Raul? But Raul? . . . Squeamish about even Lydia catching him undressing—for in recent years his thin body had turned into a sack of bones—her own husband, when they made love, had to do so in the dark, and even then she heard his very bones nearly rattling from his movements: with all that, could he participate in an act of love with a much younger woman?

The Mystery of His First Marriage

Finding herself more and more distracted, Lydia decided to spy upon her husband. Not in any overt way, no more overtly than, say, when she used to look through Rico's dresser and the boxes he kept stashed in his closet and under his bed, searching for drugs and girlie magazines, and schoolboy love letters. Knowing Raul like a brother, a son, a father and lover—for these roles were concentrated in the single title of husband—she nevertheless searched for proof of his infidelity in certain hidden places, deep in the military surplus ammunition cases that he kept in his closet and used for storing his most private documents. While she found nothing pertinent (as he probably kept his most secret materials in his locker at work or with friends) she did come across some old letters

222

from his ex-wife that had been written years ago when things were good between them; a few sentences alone of these letters, doused with perfume, in faded light-blue ink and a surprisingly delicate script, were enough to double Lydia over with jealousy and wonderment over what seemed to have been a quite passionate courtship and early marriage, phrases like *"I burn with cravings for you . . ."* and *"I miss your kisses tender on my breasts . . ."*

The mystery of his first marriage was something Raul had never spoken about directly, but over the years, during certain evenings when he was in a particularly talkative way, she began to piece together what had happened between them. For a long time Raul had only explained his marriage in terms of "an early mistake," with a shrug and a sadness about the son he had left behind, but gradually the story emerged: they had found each other in a small town near Havana, along the coast, when he and some friends had gathered one night in a plaza strumming guitars and singing—the very guitar that sat gathering dust in his closet—and she, Olivia Díaz, looking for a husband, had been taken by his earnestness and reasonable ambitions. In those days, all he had wanted to do was to own a small business in Cuba, a bar or a restaurant, even a juice and beer stand where one could buy sandwiches and have a drink and talk and talk, his idea to live simply but well in the tranquillity—or seeming tranquillity (that which one reads in the eyes of any Cuban reminiscing about that epoch, whether they are speaking about Cienfuegos or Camagüey, or Holguín or Jiguaní)—of the Cuba of that time. It should be added that she, bedding him down quickly, soon became pregnant with their son, who was born in 1946. It was a hopeless marriage, for her personality was not suited to the routines of domesticity; or to put it bluntly, she turned out to be, and this was a word that did not fall easily from his lips, a whore.

223

For a time he had remained with her because she was quite spectacular in bed, her body a kind of addiction that poor Raul had, upon occasion in later years, alluded to, as in, *"There are women who are really women and know how to satisfy a man, the kind of woman I once knew myself,"* but after a few years this respectable and decent man could not take her cuckolding ways any longer; that's when he left her, *abandonada*, and headed for the States, which he had visited on different occasions, to salvage his dignity and lose himself in a new life.

Along the way he had fallen in love with Lydia, or seemed to fall in love with her, she sometimes thought, when he so lamented the past.

Olivia must have had some kind of hold on him, for over the years, however fleeting their contacts, when evil flowed from the telephone into the room, he would become quiet and particularly nervous—jumpy and moody—for days afterwards, and seemingly removed from his domestic circumstances— from sadness or regret or consternation, she never knew. Without any proof whatsoever, she became convinced that she would come home from work one afternoon and find Olivia Díaz in bed with Raul, or that she would be lurking in the hallway with a knife; or that, while she and Raul prepared for a quiet night of television, Olivia, having moved north from Miami to New Jersey, would knock on the door, ready to reclaim, in her old age—for she had never remarried—her exhusband's favors. It was this kind of thinking that made Lydia an uneasy presence in the household.

Waiting for Raul (1985)
One day when Raul announced, "I'm going to get some *cigarillos* and go over to Mario's," Lydia decided to follow him. Across the street in the bodega run by his friend Charlie, the

Puerto Rican, he bought some cake and beer, and then, as she had feared, walked over to 123rd Street and entered Bienvenida's building. Fretting, Lydia waited outside for about half an hour and prowled about, coming across a broomstick amid the trash cans; in the spirit of the scorned and angry ladies of that neighborhood, who sometimes beat, stabbed, and pushed husbands out of windows, her idea was to knock on Bienvenida's door, flail at her with a broomstick, and drag her (screaming) out to the sidewalk. Public denunciations and hell for her and Raul—whom she would find sprawled out on the living room couch, drink and cigarette in hand—his shirt half undone, arousal or its promise in his eyes; their marriage ended. But just as she was about to storm into the building, a few friends from "around" happened by: Mrs. Ortíz, the barber's wife, and Mrs. Esposito, who asked Lydia why she seemed so nervous.

"It's nothing," she said, trying to smile. "I'm just waiting for Raul."

"Are you okay?" asked Mrs. Esposito. "Your hands are shaking, Lydia."

"I have to go somewhere now."

And that "somewhere" was Bienvenida's building: of course the entranceway door-lock gave way easily, so many times had it been forced open, the light was dim, the narrow hallway to the concrete stairs strewn with rubbish. Through a landing window she could look into a courtyard, not so different from their own; for a moment the grayness of it, the grime and grit of the inner courtyard, weighed heavily upon her. Had she been living in a building like this for the last twenty years of her life? Then she heard Raul's voice from the third-floor landing: "You take care of yourself, Bienvenida." And there was the sound of a kiss and Raul added, "Oh Bienvenida, you are too nice to this old man." Then: "Bye-bye, little one," in a sing-songy way, as Raul bid her son farewell. "Be good to your mother, and I'll bring you some nice treats next time, kid." Then: "God bless you both. *Qué Dios les bendigan.*"

As Raul descended the stairs Lydia slipped into the shadows of the hallway: from there she saw him, cigarette in hand, his expression contemplative, his posture slightly bent; out of breath, he exhaled smoke and paused in front of the building. That's when she approached him.

"Raul, what were you doing?"

"Lydia?"

"Fooling around?"

"Lydia, please—"

"You were visiting Bienvenida, weren't you?"

"If you must know, Lydia, I just like to help the woman and her kid sometimes. She doesn't have anybody to look after her, and they're on welfare . . . and . . . it makes me feel good."

She laughed: "I have a half a mind to go upstairs right now: she has no business interfering with people's marriages."

"You're imagining things." Then: "Look, like I said, I'm going over to Mario's." And he took a ten dollar bill out of his pocket and gave it to her. "Why don't we get some pizza for tonight, huh?" Hugging her, he added: "You're too high-strung sometimes, Lydia. I promise you, as God is my witness . . . there's nothing between me and that young woman. I'll see you later, okay?"

With that he made his way down the street to the subway and she did not see him again until later that night.

What Then Happened with Raul

Continuing on his way, the cleaning lady's husband climbed yet another set of stairs; on the platform of the 125th Street station he caught a train downtown to 96th Street where he switched for an express to Brooklyn; within a half hour he was walking along Flatbush Avenue. On the corner of Flatbush and Church he came to a restaurant whose windows were decorated with Christmas tinsels even on that damp October day; it was a Dominican joint with a shapely waitress, a jaded chain-smoking owner, a jukebox blaring festive salsa, a progression of crowded booths, a smell of grease and beer and delicious fried foods in the air—and in one of those booths in the back, a strongly built Hispanic man with thinning hair, intense eyes, and a baffled expression: he was a nervous fellow, wringing his hands and tapping the counter as he waited for Raul; on his right hand he wore three rings and around his thick neck (for he looked as if he could lift a truck) there was a St. Christopher medal.

When Raul walked in, the man got to his feet and they embraced.

Raul said, "*Hijo.*"

His name was Wilfredo, and he was Raul's boy by Olivia. He was forty now and he had first gotten in touch with his father because of an emergency; he did so after many years of silence, for the legend of Raul in *his* household, the story of the marriage as per Olivia, was that Raul, long ago, had betrayed and abandoned his family to have a good time in the United States, that he was not to be loved or trusted despite the money he had sent them over the years. He had called Raul out of the blue because his mother had undergone a scare involving her health, and Wilfredo had thought that Raul should know; and he had called out of a natural longing and curiosity and because, after hearing so many negative things about his father, he had grown tired of the animosity and wanted to find out about the character of Raul himself.

Now these meetings were kept from Lydia, who detested Olivia. It turned out that Wilfredo had left Miami for New Jersey, where he had started a moving business, but this had not flourished, and he had gotten work driving delivery vans

227

for the biggest hardware store on Flatbush. He had his own family, a wife and three teenage sons, and when he and Raul got together, they would spend their time discussing a possible reunion, wherein Wilfredo would have the freedom to come to his father's home for the holidays, for dinners, to meet and become friendly with Rico and Alicia and all their relations. It surprised Raul to discover how much he liked Wilfredo—he was definitely more Cuban or Miami-Cuban than his own children—and, it should be added, he bore an amazing resemblance to Raul, down to a receding hairline and those dark, pained, soulful eyes.

Raul's own father had been a tobacco worker in Cuba, one of those fellows who spent his days rolling cigars for the Upmann Company; and his mother had worked as a seamstress in their small town. They did not have "much" and Raul had few expectations about his life. Raul's older sister and brother had died in the 1950s. His own children knew nothing of their father's side of the family, that Cuban legacy as remote from them as the moon, for Raul never spoke much about his past or "family."

That Rico had gone to school and seemed to be on the road of advancement and prosperity was a subject that made him go mad with pride. "I could die tomorrow, in peace" is what he used to think. But he'd always regretted the fact that he had never gotten to know his other son and, over the years, the fact that he had not been much of a father troubled his conscience and soul. He'd wished to God that Lydia and Olivia had not hated each other so, for their differences and their Cuban resoluteness had made reconciliation unthinkable (that Cuban stubbornness as adamant about family and love as it is about politics).

After those meetings with his "other" son, Raul would ride the subway into Manhattan resolved to talk everything over with Lydia, and, if necessary, to put his foot down about just who was the true authority of the household; but by the time he had climbed the stairs he would have a failure of courage or feel too much of a simple fatigue to follow through, for he always anticipated that Lydia would explode and that the evening would be long indeed; for as gentle as she could be with a feather duster, she was also fierce and quick to temper, especially when it came to matters of family and home.

An interval passed during which the air of suspicion and the tension that arose between Lydia and Raul began to exhaust him, and so he decided to finally tell her the truth. Of course, given her myriad suspicions, the revelation that the cleaning lady's husband had been traveling to Brooklyn to see his first-born son was almost a pleasant relief. With a trembling voice he confessed to his clandestine meetings with Wilfredo, saying: "Lydia I want our family to meet the boy and for you to open your arms to him as if he were one of your own."

She surprised him: "Yes," she said. "Invite the young man into our home and he will see just who we are."

A Visit

By the following spring, it was arranged that Wilfredo, his wife, Maria, and his three teenage sons would come to the apartment on 124th Street one weekend afternoon. Taking over the kitchen, Raul, who'd learned much about cooking in his years as a waiter, had made a large roast pig and all the fixings, rice and beans and yuca and fried plantains, both sweet and green; Lydia, who had left all the details to her husband, had spent the morning preening before a mirror, for the image she wanted to send to Olivia, through her son, was that Raul had an elegant and beautiful wife. The event was urgent enough for Rico to come down from Boston and for Alicia to drive down with her husband and two kids.

Alicia's husband, Douglas Johnson, always accompanied her out of a sense of duty and was affable and respectful enough, but Alicia's children, Brad and Doug, arrived with great excitement about visiting the wicked city and seeing their exotic Cuban grandparents, particularly Grandma, who struck them as someone fascinating, charming, even affectionate, but whom they really did not understand. When they came into the apartment they planted themselves in front of the television set. Seated before the glowing screen, they partook of that grand, particularly American pastime, *watching* life from a distance; the cartoons, advertisements, comedy shorts, and monster movies cut a swath through the familial Cuban drama that was to take place around them. They seemed vaguely aware of their grandmother's Cuban roots, and were always perplexed by Lydia's tendency to speak to them mainly in Spanish. *Tele-culturated, tele-saturated*, these children, with their Celtic and Spanish roots—beautiful boys—did not give a damn to know that their grandmother's father had been the mayor of a small town near the sea in Cuba or that their mother's maiden name was Colón; nor would they ever lose a moment of sleep about it, for these, Lydia and Raul saw, were the children of another world, another life altogether.

How the Afternoon Went

With his sons and diminutive wife by his side, Wilfredo had arrived in an emotional state; suspicious and wary and hopeful and nervous, he must have embraced Raul five times before finally taking off his raincoat. Then he sat at the edge of the couch, smoking, his fingers thick as wine corks around the fragile cigarettes that made him cough. Wilfredo's Cuban-looking sons, solemn teenage boys, also occupied the couch and stared obliquely at the "relatives" sitting opposite them. Despite the many handshakes and embraces and *Hola*'s and

230

Con mucho gusto's, they seemed altogether uncomfortable with the situation; they squirmed, for despite Raul's warmth with them, and the family's civility, and the apparent importance of this event to their father, they were there only because they had been told to come, for they had long ago gotten used to the notion that there was no "family" beyond their Grandmother Olivia's.

Despite the tensions, it would stand out as a special day in Raul's life. He had even made a small joke of introducing his son Rico to his son Wilfredo, cracking, because of a certain physical resemblance, "Rico España meet Rico España." They had smiled because there was something distinctly recognizable in their postures—shoulders slack, backs slightly bent—and in their eyes there was the same glint of intelligence and uncertainty; Wilfredo took the joke good-naturedly enough, but in that instant when he appraised the carefully put together and preenish exterior of Rico (who lately had been taking more and more after his mother), his dark eyes, while retaining wonderment, held contempt for the soft-seeming, very American relative. As for Rico? He knew about Wilfredo's disenchanted life and felt a nearly fraternal compassion for him: but at the same time, although he wanted to like his half-brother, the resentment he read in his manner held him back. (For he looked at him as if he were about to say, "You know, I wish I'd had it easy like you. ....") Nevertheless, Rico treated him with kindness; in a sense, Wilfredo was a version of Rico had he been born in Cuba and come to Miami as a boy with a single mother and absent father. Compared with what Wilfredo had endured as an exile in Miami, Rico saw that his own difficulties—the minor hassles, indignations, and self-doubts that came with growing up "poor" in New York City—were really nothing. On the other hand, Wilfredo may have had it worse than his half-brother, but at least he knew just where he stood in this world, for one of the things Wilfredo kept saying was "*We Cubans,*" and as Rico listened to him, he realized that it was a phrase that he, an American, would never think, in all honesty, to use.

But they'd all seemed to get along: even Lydia remained on her best behavior, keeping her darkest thoughts about Wilfredo's mother to herself. By the end of the evening Raul was so touched that he thanked God aloud for the blessings of family. He made promises, holding his first-born son tightly: "We will do this again and again." Then: "My God, this is enough to make this old soul cry."

Embraces, farewells. A sense of relief came over the parties as they left, save for Raul, who followed his first son to his car and said good-bye once again. Putting on a show, the family stood waving by the window, but once their relatives had departed the old family spirit—of disconnectedness, of solitude, of keeping barely afloat in the American seas of overload and loud happy TVs—returned, despite Raul's hope for a deepening of connections.

The Great All-American Day

A few weeks later Raul, true to his word, arranged an outing with his two sons, to watch a baseball game at Yankee Stadium. And with good seats, too! The Yankees vs. the Cleveland Indians. A cloudy day. As he and Wilfredo sat together, Rico, indifferent to sports, attempted to make conversation with his older half-brother, but Wilfredo's answers were always laconic, guarded. Mainly Wilfredo sipped foamy beer and looked at his watch, or at a curvaceous woman if she were walking by (and when this happened, Raul approvingly nodded at Rico as if to suggest, "You see the way men should behave").

. . . The clack of a bat hitting a pitched ball, the crowd cheering, people throwing cups, the aisles littered, clouds with their threat of rain. . . . Even though Rico, the American son of Cubans, was taking in the same events, drinking the same nearly rancid brew, even though his father's blood flowed through his veins, and his eyes could have doubled for those of his half-brother, he spent the afternoon drifting off into his own private, intellectually guarded space—as if he were, in fact, a stranger sitting between two Cuban men in the second mezzanine overlooking first base. . . .

He marveled at the rapport that seemed to exist between Wilfredo and Raul; they hardly said anything to each other, and yet an intense warmth existed between them, enough so that Rico felt pangs of jealousy: for there was Wilfredo, *reaping the benefits of his father's personality without having had to put up with the shit.* At one point, when Raul got up to relieve his "old bladder," Wilfredo leaned over and said, "Man, you must have had it pretty good, growing up with Raul." What could Rico do but agree? And, from time to time, Wilfredo would say something to Raul in a slangy Spanish, Rico catching parts of the meaning, but the language, baroque and whirling in circles around him, seemed to have created an unenterable field between them; that is to say, even in the company of his own father and half-brother, Rico, with all his studies and for the way he was striving to become something in the English-speaking world—to please his cleaning lady mother (and to survive)—felt as if he were on the outside looking in . . . at the very source of his own emotionality. . . .

So he drank more beer and enjoyed the congenialities of drink and sports and ogling women and smiled and whistled and nodded at a few off-color remarks, waiting for their outing to end. As it happened, the ball game was just the beginning, because as they were leaving the stadium around five in the afternoon, Raul suggested that they go to a place he knew over on Third Avenue. Wilfredo liked the idea, and when Rico hesitated, Raul told him, "Come on, don't be such a stiff, I could drop dead tomorrow!" And so shortly they drove over to Third and 169th Street in Wilfredo's Coupe de Ville (with the bobbing St. Christopher rubber-suctioned to the dashboard) and were sitting in a cheerful place called *El Palacio,* or The Palace, whose owner was a long-time Cuban friend of Raul's, a former waiter who had made good by working long hours waiting tables so that he could save enough money to work even longer hours running an inexpensive, somewhat popular restaurant near the subway, in an increasingly devastated neighborhood in the South Bronx.

In any event, the restaurant's owner, Marco, treated Raul and his sons with the utmost cordiality and respect, pitchers of sangria appearing promptly before them, the owner himself recommending the *lechón asado* (Sundays and Wednesdays only) and seeming genuinely pleased to see Raul. He was a heavyset, many-jowled man, with a massive head, a kindly expression, and somewhat spiritually exhausted eyes; he must have been a frugal fellow, for in his large hands he held the smallest nub of a pencil with which he jotted down their orders.

"These are my sons, Marco," Raul told him. "This is the older, Wilfredo. He's *muy muy cubano,* and in business, or going to be in business for himself, up from Miami for awhile, God bless his soul—a family man with kids of his own, a good man." And he continued, "And you must remember Rico?"

"Of course."

"Well, this one, he's so fucking smart, I don't know what the hell he's talking about half the time." And he rapped Rico and Wilfredo on the back. "I'll tell you something, Marco, when I look at my boys, I feel like I am the luckiest human being in the world, and I thank God for that."

Toasts were made, and even Rico, who was not a drinker, joined in, the men drinking until about two in the morning, when they made their way (stumbled) out to the car, their voices floating around him:

"You know what counts? The blood that flows in your veins!"

"And family—"

"And the love and fucking trust of your loved ones, right sons?"

"Yes, Poppy!"

"And another thing, never forget that without family this life is for shit . . ."

A flood of dense, slurred, capricious Spanish followed; distorted smiles; too loud laughter—Rico hearing, understanding, merely nodding at the voices.

Shortly, the Coupe de Ville was careening across a rainy slick of darkness, screeching over the Cross Bronx Expressway and southbound along the Henry Hudson Parkway, a serpentine version of the city, undulating with flaring lights around them—Wilfredo at the wheel, squinting for the exit, horns blaring, a flight of sparks shooting off the railing as they took the turn to 125th Street. . . .

When Wilfredo managed to get home to New Jersey at about five-thirty in the morning, his wife, beside herself with worry, nearly killed him and from that time on demanded that he avoid Raul's bad influence and have nothing further to do with his newly found "family." For another three months Raul continued to see his son in Brooklyn for Saturday lunches, until Wilfredo eventually relocated back to Miami, for a job had opened there. Just like that, Wilfredo, like so much that had to do with Cuba, dropped slowly away and, after a time, was hardly mentioned except in a sad reminiscence by Raul in passing conversation.

With the Great Susanah Morales

And in those later years, Lydia had the honor of working for one of Mario's acquaintances, Susanah Morales, one of the great torch singers of Cuba; that Susanah Morales who had left Cuba as a famous refugee in the mid-sixties and had since prospered so greatly—through the proliferation of numerous recordings and television commercials and countless concerts, both here and abroad—that she could now afford a two-bedroom Park Avenue apartment in the East 60s, not too far from where the Ospreys lived. She was an ageless star, a dark enchantress with vivid and piercing eyes, and such an air of warmth about her that she was beloved everywhere, by Cubans especially, for her personality as much as her famous voice. When Lydia, an old fan, had gotten word from Mario that Susanah's regular housekeeper was away on vacation she'd felt beside herself with excitement. Her apartment was decorated entirely in white and beige fabrics, great plumes, which Susanah had used in her act—for she appeared like a tropical Venus in a bejeweled turban and a long silken gown, a cape of Mallorcan blue draped over her lovely shoulders—hanging off the walls. There was a small aviary—white bird cages filled with her *pajaritos cantando* (and in one cage, a mechanical parakeet, which had been presented to her by the town council of Göteborg, Sweden, where she had once given a concert for the King)—and certain symbols of Afro-Cuban religious origin set out here and there in the room.

She had a wall covered with photographs that went way back, to the days when Lydia was a teenager in the 1930s and Susanah was singing on national Cuban radio; pictures of Susanah posing with Xavier Cugat and Tyrone Power, receiving the key to the city from Mayor Abraham Beame, and singing on television programs like *Sesame Street* and *The Tonight Show*. She must have been somewhere in her late sixties or early seventies, Lydia figured, but if you had seen the diva on the street you might have put her somewhere in her late forties. Renowned for performing energetically through exhausting schedules, an aura of magicality and divinity swirled about her; she was "one of those wonders that we'll never know about," as Concha would remark.

Such was her familiarity with the warmth of Susanah Morales that Lydia made herself at home. She played Susanah Morales recordings on an old RCA console phonograph as she cleaned, and the music made her hum and dance while tidying the place. On one of the walls, over the plump white couch, three gold records for her hits: "*Te Quiero Mucho USA*" — "I Love You Very Much, USA," "*No Te Puedo Olvidar Mi Cuba*" — "I Can't Forget You, My Cuba," and, Lydia's favorite, "*Soy la Reina de Amor*" — "I Am the Queen of Love."

Her life, as everyone knew, had been memorable, and her success and wealth were never begrudged by anyone. Her story was typical in that she had fled Cuba via a concert in Franco's Spain in '65, leaving everything behind, settling first in Miami, then in New Jersey, then Queens, then Park Avenue. It was the rare fund-raiser for exiled Cuban causes in which she did not appear. Glamorously larger than life, her wrists, ankles, neck, and ears percussive with jewelry, she was known as the Queen of Salsa. But she also gave free concerts to help out public schools, visited hospitals and orphanages, and went on radio talk shows to dispense information about immunizations and sound health practices. And she talked about love because that, after all, was what she sang about: love of men, of children, family, country, memory—the things that touched Lydia's (and Raul's) heart.

Lydia was marveling at how life had placed this woman, who'd come from the poorest of poor Havana neighborhoods, *Las Yaguas,* into a Park Avenue residence, and rearranging the dishware in Susanah's kitchen (tempted to take some keepsake, a fork or a spoon that *she had used*) when, to her amazement, she heard several voices by the door; that of a doorman with the grand diva's suitcases, the mellow baritone of Susanah's soft-spoken husband, Calixto, and then—a vision in white mink—Susanah Morales herself, fresh from a concert in Los Angeles, radiant and friendly.

In the way that Cubans are always friendly with other Cubans, the diva smiled and said, "You must be Lydia, Mario's friend, I'm Susanah Morales . . ." as if Lydia would not have known; and she extended her hand and, nearly jubilant with kindness, added, "That you're Cuban is beautiful, but even if you weren't I would be happy to meet you because I love my people"—"*mi gente*" (meaning all Latinos). With that Susanah went into the living room to relax, smoking a Tiparillo as her husband, Calixto, started to work in the kitchen, for they had been discussing what they would cook for dinner on their fancy stove.

Letting out a sigh she told Lydia, "I've been in this apartment for two years and I'm still not used to it."

"It's a nice apartment, beautiful," said Lydia.

"Oh very nice, but some of the people here can be difficult. *Algunos presumen mucho*—some of them are snobs." Then: "If you knew what me and poor Calixto had to put up with to get into here. . . . Now when I go back to Queens, where we still have our house, I love it! My children live there, and when the weather is nice, I sit out very comfortably in the backyard, like old times."

"But don't forget the writeoffs, my love. And that it was a good investment," a voice called out from the kitchen.

"Yes, that's what everyone says," Susanah conceded. "Anyway, Lydia, I leave you to your work."

With a drink of brandy in hand, Susanah seemed ready to fall asleep on her couch, and before she did, Lydia could not help herself from asking the grand dame for an autograph, "Just a little something on a piece of paper. My husband, Raul, has always loved you."

"Piece of paper? Nonsense," Susanah said. "I'm going to give you something better." And from a bureau drawer she removed a glossy 8x10 photograph of herself, which she signed, and gave Lydia a tape cassette of her latest recording, *Susanah Morales in San Juan*. Then, for the hell of it, she handed her a bottle of Chardonnay from the wine closet.

"You take a few sips of wine with your husband, close your eyes, and listen to my music: go back to Cuba in a song," she told Lydia.

Lydia blushed: "You know I was once known as the Queen of the Conga Line."

"I believe it!"

That night she and Raul listened to the tape, and feeling nostalgically inclined, danced to one of the more juicy boleros, their faces touching, warm. Raul affected the elegant stance he used to take in the ballrooms when he was courting his Empress, head erect, back straight, eyes focused only on hers, as if nobody else existed in the world. And that night Lydia, in the habit of worrying aloud about their future, maintained a happy mood, the evening passing like a holiday date. Because of a few moments of kindness, the two of them danced until past eleven, back in love, as if they were on the deck of a cruise ship way out in a lovely sea.

A Lady of Fancy Means

Had we mentioned what happened to Lydia on one of her jobs when her heart softened with compassion? She sometimes cleaned for a lady of fancy means, a contessa of fine European breeding and aristocratic demeanor who lived on Madison Avenue in a rambling overdecorated apartment. Admiring her old-world gentility, Lydia was fascinated by the evidence of this lady's travels, like the framed certificate that hung in the kitchen attesting to the fact that as a member of the Polar Bear

Society she had once journeyed to the North Pole. That anyone would go to so much trouble made Lydia laugh.

Somewhere in her seventies, after a life lived well and long in Europe, the contessa had an antiquated manner—the era of her youth, the 1930s; she wore embroidered dresses with tasseled hems and strings of pearls; she smoked cigarettes in a long ebony holder and had in one of her bedrooms a collection of cloche hats.

Altogether pleasant, the one thing that disturbed Lydia was the way she kept her two greyhounds locked in their cages; set out on a long oak table by the far wall of the living room under a medieval tapestry, they were the one note of anguish in an otherwise elegant setting. The poor animals whimpered and cried, scratching at the bottom of their cages, their sadness touching Lydia's heart, even if she did not particularly care for animals. The lady's admonition that Lydia never let the hounds out seemed unusually cruel, particularly on hot days when they howled with so much despair.

It happened that one July morning Lydia decided to let the hounds out of their cages. Happily they leapt onto the carpeted floor and, just like that, just as Lydia was feeling genuinely touched by her own kindness, the two hounds began to follow her about the apartment, their languid eyes swollen with gratitude and love, bumping the back of her legs with their wet cool noses, nudging her to pet and caress them: there was an interlude when she forgot about her prejudices against dogs, before the charm of their canine affection began to bore her, and she said, "Now that is enough, *perritos*." But when she tried to put them back in their cages, they resisted, circling around and away from her, and shortly their sweet whimpers became hostile growls, and their nudges became nips; defending herself with a broom, Lydia began to whack them on their snouts and hindquarters, this betrayal of their love driving the creatures into a frenzied charge through the apartment, their lithe bodies knocking over vases and chairs and glasses and books, things crashing everywhere.

After a while Lydia, defeated, slumped in a living room chair pondering her future with the contessa, and with that the greyhounds halted their frantic flight. One of them approached Lydia, ever so tentatively, as if to be petted, but as soon as the animal drew close, Lydia smacked its snout with a rolled-up newspaper and declared, "*Vete!*" or "Get the hell away from me!"

Later, when she left, after attempting to put that apartment back in order, she decided that she would not bother to ask the contessa about her pay or to inquire about further work.

Her Joyful Devotion to Mr. Osprey: Gifts

During the later years of her employment, when Lydia stood before a store window, say the College Shoppe on Broadway, wool jackets and cardigan sweaters and square-cut ties on display behind the stenciled glass, she always planned to buy Mr. Osprey something special. What she could afford, however, was another matter, so for his birthday (April 17) she usually bought him a Scottish wool scarf that a fellow sold out of the back of his car by the park, and one year, from *la marqueta,* she found Mr. Osprey a light-blue *guayabera,* from Mexico. Otherwise, going and coming to and from his apartment in the course of her week, she brought him bags of plantains and yuca so that Mr. Chang might cook his employer meals with a Latin-American lilt (Mr. Osprey much enjoying this). And she would sometimes leave a recording by Carlos Argentina or Susanah Morales on the hall table with a note for Mr. Osprey and the family. She liked to see the way he would react to her gifts; waiting for him to get home, she sometimes dallied past five, pulling books from the shelves in his study and wiping them with a felt cloth, one by one, until she heard him in the hallway.

241

Towering over her, Osprey always removed his hat, bowing
in a gentlemanly manner; handing him a book or Spanish language magazine, she would say something like, "*señor* Osprey,
to help you keep up your Spanish. . . ." Such gestures always
touched him, and he would say, "You know, Lydia, you help
keep my feet on the ground."

Whenever Mr. Osprey greeted Lydia, he would always grasp
her hands between his, the genteel skin of a man who worked
with papers and telephones, soft and nearly feminine, touching
the abrasions and calluses and strength of her hands—a kind of
consoling energy flowing between them. During these fleeting
moments, Lydia felt protected by Osprey, and Osprey seemed
to be enjoying the warmth of a woman who was not particularly warm with anyone else.

They were ever cordial, always friendly. She snooped
around his office, but ever so respectfully, wondering if
Osprey had secret loves. In her own fantasies about him, she
was about twenty again and they had met on Park Avenue, literally bumping into each other after taking a blind turn around
a corner, as in a madcap thirties Hollywood film. They had
taken cover in a doorway during a sudden rain; as the sun
quickly returned they decided to go for a walk in Central Park,
where they sat under a tree in one of the meadows behind the
grand Metropolitan Museum, holding hands, and talking quietly; and in the midst of this they embraced and fell upon one
another, a great heart looming in the sky above them and a
Godly radiance bursting out from under a roving bank of
clouds; a title floating across the horizon: "*Y vivían tranquilo y
feliz y rico para siempre*," or "They lived in peace and happiness and were rich for the rest of their days."

*An image that often crossed her mind: Lydia in flowing
robes, sitting regally on a throne. A queen, or empress, her sub-*

jects adoring her, transmitting love, that which was made for a most splendid season.

Okay, she sometimes got carried away, but such idylls made her feel young, and the truth was that she was getting older. If she had dreams of the future they usually involved her children. Except when it came to fantasies about love.

She was always saying to her friends, "I couldn't have a better boss." She said so thinking about some of the people she had worked for over the years. Like the ones who said, "You know, Lydia, there's a right and a wrong way to do things." And the ladies who had never lifted a finger in their lives, and yet scrutinized her work with a vengeance. Or employers who would let a cleaning woman work in the heat without thinking to offer her a glass of water; or those who could care less if a cleaning woman was hungry, or had been crying earlier that day. She did not enjoy smug or superior attitudes. She did not like being dependent upon the patronage of others, or having to defer to someone who was wrong. Nor did she like to hear certain stories: that such and such a couple had dismissed a cleaning woman because money was missing from a bedroom drawer *even when they did not have any proof and simply because she was Hispanic,* or that a woman was dismissed because she had accidentally dropped a French Biot glass dish. She knew about one cleaning woman who lost her job because after she finished up her work and left the apartment, one of her employer's kids had used the toilet and forgotten to flush it; and a cleaning woman who had been dismissed because a husband had liked her figure and the wife was jealous; and the frustrated wives who complained that Isabella or Conchita or *Cinderella*—whatever her name—did not *speaky-spicky* English so well and that's why she had the audacity to polish the Steinway parlor grand with furniture wax (dusting only,

243

please). She had come to know the attitude that implied that any amount of work performed within the eight and one-half hours spent in the houses of the rich was never enough. It was hardest on the cleaning ladies with children to support on their own, who dragged themselves out of bed early in the mornings and, leaving the kids with a neighbor, if they could, worked six days a week and still could never earn enough to make ends meet. She knew that to most people cleaning was the kind of labor that anyone could do, that she, in their eyes, whatever her virtues, was replaceable.

The Grundig

Once Osprey gave her a fine portable shortwave radio, a Grundig, several of which he had gotten from a company with whom he did business; it came in a fine leather case and with a note: "For my dear friend, Lydia. Thought your family might enjoy this." She kept this radio on top of their Frigidaire and she would often point it out to her friends, and say to Raul, "What a good sound." After dinner Lydia sometimes tuned in Spanish-speaking countries, Mexico, Argentina, even Spain. But once a haunted-sounding transmission came from Cuba, and perhaps, because it was very late, she had imagined hearing through all the wintry noises and static a voice saying, "Lydia, it's me, your papa."

Raul liked to take the radio to the park, where he would sit on a bench facing the river. Compulsively he turned the dial, to one country after the other, visions of countries he had never seen floating by him, like theme park barges on the Hudson.

The Wife of the Important and Generous Man

With the passing of the years it surprised Lydia how Mrs. Osprey, perhaps out of loneliness, became more friendly with her. With her children living away and Mr. Osprey often traveling—he had retired from full-time work with his firm and now did some kind of consulting for the United Nations in Latin America—Mrs. Osprey was often alone in that apartment, and on those occasions she would invite Lydia to sit with her in the living room and have "a bite" or in passing bid her not to work so hard. She flattered herself into thinking that Mrs. Osprey had at long last recognized her intrinsic classiness.

There had been a day when Mrs. Osprey surprised Lydia by offering to show her several photo albums. A particular and wistful sadness blossomed in her eyes when she came to photographs of herself and Mr. Osprey taken when they were "very, very young."

"That's us in front of the Ritz Hotel in Madrid, even though we were staying down the street in the Palace by the Prado."

"We had a Prado in Havana!" Then: "Were you speaking Spanish over there?"

"A little, not like my husband. He and my boys have always done so well with languages."

"I know he loves to speak Spanish with me—in a most *elegante* style."

Mrs. Osprey began to say something else, but then looked at Lydia in a frail kind of way, a way that said that for all her advantages something was missing in her life; perhaps Mrs. Osprey also felt the limitations of being a woman, for in Lydia's experience, most women had been denied much in this life (on the other hand, who wasn't?). That's when Lydia, wanting to be helpful, said, "If you like, *señora*, I could give you a few Spanish lessons."

So once a week, after Lydia was done with her work, they would sit in the living room for a few hours, repeating phrases that Lydia would write out in a neat script in a composition book bought especially for Mrs. Osprey. The Madame, as

Chang called her, tried hard, being one of those high society ladies who'd excelled in her French courses at finishing school, but in those days she was not the best of students, nor Lydia the best teacher. Still the lessons proceeded, and by and by Mrs. Osprey, after a few months, could effect a few rudimentary exchanges and this pleased her immensely.

"Last night I took my husband to this Spanish restaurant, the Havana-Madrid, have you heard of it?"

"Oh, yes."

"I did so well ordering that even the waiter complimented me. My husband was very impressed." Then: "Thank you, Lydia, *te agradezco todo*."

The Society of the Nevers

Of course Mrs. Osprey lived in quite a different world. You did not see her being watched ever so carefully by the security guards of even the cheapest discount stores, nor did you ever see her dallying before a shop window trying to explain to a son or daughter why they couldn't afford such and such an item, especially at Christmas, when, thanks to Mr. Dickens, the poor were supposed to be the spiritually rich of the earth and deserving of God's bounties. She did not have the look of middle-age failure in her eyes, or that of a forty-seven-year-old middle-management executive stuck in a nowhere job in the garment district and knowing it (the look that said not a year would pass when he didn't have to make that long commute from the north shore of Long Island and put up with shit and wear a jacket and a tie on even the most fatiguing, airless days of the summer), or that of a man out on the street, say the poor fellow selling ices on the corner of 108th Street and Amsterdam, gloomy in the heat and fearing the coming winter, or the fellow pushing clothing racks on 39th and

246

Seventh with a bleeding ulcer, or the bored postal worker drinking a quart of booze every night for thirty years, or the store clerk on his feet all day who would never have that dream house or dream vacation.

Truth was that she'd never have that look of the people who participate in the Society of the Nevers: Never go to Europe. Never buy a piece of property. Never own a firsthand car. Never sit by a late nineteenth-century French writing desk at the Armory Show, scribbling out checks without a single doubt. Never sigh with confusion over the abundance of travel brochures that the agency had sent over to you, when you'd simply inquired about an interesting place to go for a quick rest. Never receive a handwritten note of thanks from the maître d' of a major restaurant complimenting you for your generosity over the past year. Never eat in a fancy restaurant. Never get seen by a doctor immediately. Never go to a Broadway show. Never stay in a decent hotel. Never stop adding up the price of things. Never stop saving your pennies. Never dream of a retirement that brings more than the Social Security check. Never forget about betting the long shots at the race track; never stop buying the lottery tickets, or playing the numbers. Never sit for a single moment after work and breathe a sigh of relief that the bad day you just had, with the floor manager threatening to fire you because your coffee break was too long, or because you did not let him *take* you in his office, would never happen again. Never find that the everyday struggles of your life would fold over into some happy existence (outside of death). Never make the society pages. Or the newspapers unless you are murdered or rob a bank or become a famous baseball player or boxer. Never understand how all this happened to you.

And: even if things were to change, never lose the *bitterness of the poor.*

The Important
Dr. Rico España

Useful information was a kind of sunlight. To know that a young man like Rico could save his money instead of pissing it away in a bar, invest that money or take an airplane to Europe instead of going to Coney Island, with all the scam artists and beer-drunks on the train, was a kind of sunlight, too. That to give over one's youth to the tedium of school, one's first real job in life, to establish a work ethic and a certain useful bent of mind, with its plans and ambitions, and to keep with it despite the lameness of it all, and to put up with feelings of inadequacy and the seemingly pointless hours of study for the sake of getting "ahead," that was a kind of sunlight, too. Connections, self-confidence, and the general expectation that one would always have something or someone to fall back on in case of troubles; knowing that the names on a map of the world were not just fantastic abstractions but places that one could go to; that Europe was not just an oddly spelled, vaguely archaic-sounding name, but a great historic continent of beauty and possibilities; that one did not have to tremble with worry over how to pay a simple electric bill (cash only, Mr. Edison says) or about one's future if a job was lost; that there were ways of doing things that had nothing to do with blind rage, and anger; that, among many other things, was a kind of sunlight, too.

The Important Dr. Rico España (1985)

As for Dr. Rico España, Ph.D., he eventually made his way through a course of learning at an esteemed New England institution and ascended, alongside others of majestic caliber and drive, into the profession of psychology. He spent his days seated in a plush black leather chair in the half-light of a twenty-second floor office in the Lincoln Towers complex on West 70th Street, listening with as much compassion as was possible to a succession of more or less affluent clients, most of whom, it seemed, were suffering from loneliness and a need for intimacy or, as he saw it, a hunger for more depth of feeling and spirit.

He charged up to one hundred and fifty dollars for a forty-five minute session—what his Poppy Raul would have been lucky to earn for a forty-hour week and more than what his parents put together had ever made in a single day. In fact, on some days what he earned was what his mother used to get for two months of sweeping floors and cleaning toilets.

Anyone visiting him in his office would have taken Dr. Rico for an image of composure, completeness, self-confidence, self-knowledge, the kind of man for whom any mother or father would feel pride. *He had become the wondrous Hispanic who never offended anyone.* He never ventured anywhere without the proper attire, Lydia and Raul having instilled in him the sense that a man should be well dressed, that this was especially important in gaining people's respect, particularly if one was—or had been—"poor." (It was true that the best-dressed people Rico had known were the habitués of the dance halls and nightclubs where his godfather, Mario, used to play.) Long gone were the $3.49 wash-and-wear schoolboy shirts, five-for-a-dollar socks, one-dollar ties; now Rico wore Italian- and English-made suits, Italian- and French-made shoes, and all kinds of expensive accessories; his socks and undergarments, T-shirts and handkerchiefs freshly laundered weekly and wrapped in soft burgundy paper in boxes, like gifts.

He'd turned around to find that he, the son of a waiter and a cleaning lady, had not done badly in his life, but something about having watched the old man fucking himself every night for years and hearing the word *poor* and the phrase *somos pobres* too many times had detracted from his enjoyments. . . .

Truth was he never let on to his real feelings with people, even with long-time friends. Maintaining the calmest facade, losing himself in his work, he justified his labors as the fulfillment of certain of his parents' dreams.

Nevertheless, he came off, in his stiff, proper way, as if he'd attended finishing school. Hoods, like the fellows he knew from the neighborhood, fellows with slick sideburns who walked through life with toothpicks in their mouths and called everybody Chief or Ace, regarded him with the same kind of disenchantment and hatred he himself had once felt toward others of the "upper class."

He had become one of *them*.

No one speaking to him would have judged that he was a *first generation of anything*. He had no discernible Hispanic accent, for after years of assiduous effort, in college and graduate school, he had thrown off the streety end of his speech. People were surprised by the refinement (stuffiness) of his diction and intonations. No one would have guessed that Rico's head was filled with his mother and father's voices; no one heard his mother or father in the way he spoke—unless he'd had a few drinks. He knew a lot of professionals—Puerto Ricans, Dominicans, and Cubans, for that matter—whose roots, at every turn, were clearly evident, but somewhere along the way he had changed.

Once as a kid, when he had accompanied his mother to Osprey's, and was watching her as his mother was cleaning in the hall he overheard Mr. Osprey talking on the telephone in his study. He was home from his office with a flu and had a big stack of papers before him, and whoever he spoke with inspired him to look them over and say, "Okay" or "Of course," leaving a red pencil mark on the upper right-hand corner of each one. He said: "These people don't know a thing about economics, do they?" And: "What was the figure someone came up with? That if you broke the world's wealth down per person it would come out to about one hundred and fifty dollars each?" Then: "It's not fair, but true: more money in the hands of fewer people keeps the pendulum swinging, doesn't it?"

Later Rico, who'd been lingering by the doorway, asked, "Mommy, what's a pendulum?"

"It's like a monkey, un mono," she had answered him.

He rented an apartment near Central Park, traveled to Europe once or twice a year, gave money to charities (even sent money to distant relatives in Cuba), and dining out often (eating alone), still managed to save quite a bit, for he had never gotten married or had children, despite a few nearly passionate love affairs. "Over there" where he lived, all the "help" were black or Hispanic. Because of the years he had spent hanging around his mother when she went on jobs, he would find himself smiling and nodding at the cleaning ladies whenever he saw them leaving the lobbies of all those fancy buildings, trudging out with their plastic bags, making their way over to the subways for the long commute home.

Pan con Ojos

He had a cleaning woman, a Dominican lady named Amalia, who came to his apartment once a week, but he hardly ever talked to her, for their paths did not often cross, and, when they did, she read his reserved and polite manner as the kind of snobbery she was used to encountering in her other employers. She saw him as such even though he always took pains to make sure his apartment was not too dirty before she arrived, picking up after himself and performing as the cleaning person for his cleaning lady. Once when he happened to be at home

254

upon her arrival, he told her, "You know, my mother's a cleaning woman, too."

"Your mother?"

"Yes."

"I don't believe it. *Estás bromeando, no?*"

"No, I used to go around with her when I was a kid," he said in English. Then: "*Cuando yo era niño.*"

"Well, I can see you've done well." Then: "Is your mother still working?"

"Yes."

"And you don't take care of her?"

"In my way."

"Ah, 'in your way.'" Then: "Never forget how hard she has to work. You must always be respectful, and take care of her, yes? Because if you don't, one day you will deeply regret it. You understand me?"

"Yes."

"*Bueno,*" she told him.

As she got to work, Rico, feeling humbled, put on his coat and proceeded out the door, and to the importance of his life.

His clients were mainly businessmen—many network executives, corporation managers, a few artists and writers, too—and wives distressed by the perturbations of age. Some came because their spouses had begged them to. Some were sexually confused, married men confessing attractions to other men, and staring at Dr. Rico's dark eyes with a yearning for understanding and affection. Some were just neurotically inclined, from the burdens of finding their role in this world.

Many career women, in their forties, regretting the path they had taken, came to him in a panic when they abruptly decided to change their lives. Older recent divorcées had it the hardest. Usually the husbands had left them because they had lost their youthful luster, or because, with the children grown, they had outlived their usefulness. . . . He heard a lot of talk about suicide, as in the case of a certain woman who, on her way to work, had to fight to keep herself from jumping in front of an oncoming subway train. He tried to help them all as much as possible, to teach them to see that a semblance of happiness could be helped along after tremendous amounts of work. . . .

Mainly, many of his patients suffered from a failure of the imagination, especially in terms of religiosity—somehow they had gone tone-deaf to a certain inward music. It occurred to him that with the "poor and ignorant" a belief in God was a kind of manna from heaven, an emotional currency, the money of hope on which their futures in the other world were built; a kind of imaginative reconstruction of reality, for appeasing those who could not have otherwise looked to any satisfactions in this world.

(Contrary to the wondrous materialistic comforts of the modern age. What was it that Eliseo once said to him? "You can have a beautiful life if you fuck people over." Or Mario? "I would rather be able to play a single bar of music on the piano than have all the money in the world and not play anything.")

He had no answers, except the simple thought that to see the goodness in others and in yourself was a kind of redemption, as he had once written as a student; and it was this, in one form or another, that he tried to convey to his patients.

In his own experience, for all his success in this world, for all his efforts to understand what and where he had come from, he found that life, so far, was not what he had expected. Escaping the claustrophobic spaces of his own family's existence, he found himself traveling through a tunnel of light (knowledge and ambition)—like those life-after-death experiences that one always saw "dramatically recreated" on television—only to find himself in a much darker place, an icy world on the "outside," away from his past, his neighborhood, his family.

Often, between patients, when he was not making notes or filling out insurance forms or listening to his answering machine, he would stand by his big picture windows looking west over the Hudson. Sometimes he imagined glaciers taking over the skyline, glaciers moving slowly northward over the water. Sometimes he felt like screaming out his window.

She Often Called Her Son

At home, always thinking about her children—for were they not a reflection of herself?—Lydia often searched for pretenses to see Rico. A new bottle of vitamins, a book of Cuban idiomatic expressions that she had found in a store, a sweater she'd bought in the Egyptian's discount store on Broadway: any excuse to come by. On occasion when Lydia had a job down in his neighborhood, she would pass by his building and feel tempted to visit, but whenever she called him on the lobby intercom his voice was remote, his manner curt, his tone professional as he conveyed that he was busy—which was often the truth, for he did see one patient after another.

She'd sigh, make her way to her job, despairing over the distance between them, even if he on impulse sent her and Raul fancy boxes of chocolates, and telephoned usually every three or four days promising that he would come to see them, that they would all go out together.

Her *nene,* she still called him.

Even though he owed much to his parents, particularly his mother, who had always wanted the best for him, why was it that he always felt put out when she suddenly appeared in the lobby of his building? He kept a picture of her on the wall, Lydia España as a young woman posed somewhere in Central

Park in the early 1950s, her love, Raul, the photographer. She was wearing a sun hat and a prim 1950s sleeveless dress, and squinting into the light, that light which she religiously avoided. Her figure was comely, her expression sultry, her youth gratifying, a joyful thing to behold, her manner hopeful, and yet there already seemed a sense of disappointment in the cast of her pretty eyes. Who knows what she and his father were up to that sunny day, but that photo, which he had found in a tin biscuit box in the closet, with its air of hope and the promise of youth, somehow both cheered and saddened him in the course of those days when his patients, one after the other, came in to relate their troubles.

In one of the drawers of his important-seeming desk, a photo album, its acetate pages filled with family black-and-white photographs, from when things were black and white, he sometimes thought.

On one occasion, gloomy because he had felt a longing for an extremely beautiful female patient, and had comported himself in an unprofessional manner (that is to say, found himself fantasizing about her) he sat with the album of photographs and found it somehow reassuring, as if those old photographs were evidence of who and what he had come from; that from which he was floating further and further away.

He surrounded himself with books—among them a shelf of Spanish language novels he'd gotten on a trip to Spain, which he never had the time to read—psychological journals and magazines. A guitar, which he kept in a bare corner of his living room, reminded him of different days. He listened to classical music and jazz and had a subscription to the opera at Lincoln Center. He usually walked to his office, but when he took the subways, say down to the Village, his heart burst at the sight of the Mexican or Guatemalan flower vendors with their Aztec stolidity or at the workers in the subway cars, every Hispanic man, with his *Diario* tucked under his arm, a waiter like his father, every woman a cleaning lady like his mother.

The Strangeness of It All

If he had been born into his grandfather's generation, he often used to think, he might have been like a *vaquero,* in high leather boots and with a hat pulled low over the brow, riding the fields to make house calls on friends. He would have shielded his eyes from the sun; he might have been able to call five thousand acres of cane or grazing land his own. Or he might have been one of any number of bright young men from a small Cuban town, passing his youth as the manager of a sugar plantation or farm (or as a lowly field hand); he would have worn a linen suit on Sunday afternoons, might have become an important member of local society—the Gallego or Andalusian Club—and chances are he would have married the lovely and precious daughter of a prominent family and lived out his days with the comfort of certain routines and rituals, typical, he fantasized, of Cuban men, who knew, if they knew anything, just who and what they were. That he had a Cuban mother and father was a source of great pride to him; that Spanish blood flowed through his veins meant a link to a rich and beautiful past that was really no longer a part of his life, save for a week or two every couple of years or so when he might fly to Spain on a vacation and head down to Malaga where he would be treated indifferently by the jaded Spanish hoteliers.

A Priestly Vocation

Of course, back when he was a student, in the most idealistic and hopeful stage of his career, of what he had come to regard as an almost priestly vocation (*for did not one hear confessions*

259

and give counsel?) he was driven to succeed for his family, or most specifically, for his dear mother, or *la viejita* as Raul had taken to calling her, his dream to restore something vital that had been missing in the family dynamic: pride, importance, respect. And that desire kept him going through much that was tedious, this vague goal of restoration and rehabilitation, to bring to his mother and father a bounty of joy, to repent, if one liked, for the perceived misfortunes of his youth.

... And yet, what had changed inside of him? Did he know? It had taken him years to learn how to *seem* to live with the low humming anxiety and anger of the poor (and of immigrants, and the struggling working class). And even though he truly wanted to help others, and was serious about gaining a greater insight into the human condition, not a day went by that he could not keep himself from thinking that his professional life amounted to a scam.

Not trusting much of anybody or anything, he did not particularly believe in himself.

Most of his clients were second- or third-generation Americans, but once upon a time a Cuban fellow, Carlos, who'd been largely raised in Miami, came to see him. He was a gay man, a Cultural Studies professor, who was not physically well, and what he loved to talk about was the Cuba of his childhood, of the late 1950s, of Havana and his family's happy social life—his had been an affluent and cultured household brimming with bright children and pleasant adults—the memory of which would nearly bring him to tears. He was quite Americanized by then, to be sure, a Harvard man, but he, too, had become emotionally aloof from the world around him.

"Once you step away from the warmth of your past, there's no going back, is there?"

"Well, maybe you're idealizing it."

Politics in Cuba, the antigayness of Castro and Miami's Cubans, the small disaffections of modern life, and the fantasies that one had been born in the wrong time and place were what they often talked about.

Rico looked forward to seeing this Cuban fellow and thought their sessions special, for between them they had moments when the notion of Cuba grew dense in the very room, as if a certain kind of affection and consciousness could float like smoke with smell and weight. Dr. Rico saw him for about a year before he dropped out of New York and resettled in Miami to be near his family. Some time later, a relative wrote that when he passed away it was in a friend's sunny wicker- and plant-filled apartment in South Beach—decorated like a room in Cuba—with his family present, in a state of peace.

The experience with this Cuban had made Dr. Rico think to expand his clientele, maybe make an effort to see more *latino* clients, even if they couldn't pay those hefty fees; call friends at social agencies, maybe put an ad somewhere is what he often thought.

As if the *latinos* would be interested in the processes of therapy.

His Occasional Visits

As the years went by, Lydia felt great shame when her friends asked, "Why is it that we don't see your boy around here?"

She answered by singing his praises, telling her friends that if he didn't often come around it was because he was tremendously busy with important work. This was partially true—he was making a very good living off his troubled patients, one movie star, when in town, coming to see him three times a week, for example, to figure out that he was, in fact, a movie star and that was why people were staring at him. Pleading a busy schedule—his hours lasting from early in the morning to about nine at night, because of classes he sometimes taught on dreams down at NYU in the evenings—when Rico did visit Lydia and Raul, the evening became for Rico a ritual of politesse: the quaint hallway, with its black-and-white octagonal tiles, the stained walls, the crumbling pipes, that ever so slight smell of carbon and burned trash coming from the incinerator room, the building shaking from the trains, and, as his mother opened the door, the apartment dark and dark and dark and receding (into the past) forever, so many memories, coming back simultaneously.

They were always grateful enough to see him—happiest on the rare occasions when Alicia also came to visit with her dull husband and lively children—Rico arriving with flowers and gifts of chocolates from a fancy Broadway store.... There before him, Lydia and Raul, embraces, kisses, and then dinner in their kitchen, even when Rico wanted to take them out ("Getting old, kid, like to stay home," his father would say). Conversations centered on neighborhood events—so and so stabbed in the stomach walking along the street, the university's growing occupation of the neighborhood, tenant harassment, thugs kicking in people's doors, the abundance of new drugs, the poor getting poorer, gentle Dennis Malloy dying of kidney failure at age thirty-seven. Raul always offered Rico a drink, taking a drink himself, winking, and later, when his mother was out of the room, asking, "If something is disturbing you, my boy, have you considered going back to the church?"

On the other hand Raul, maybe missing the point of his son's prolonged silences—as if he were a chip off the old block—was always happy enough with their simple exchanges—about sports mainly, like the careers of boxers Roberto Duran or Muhammad Ali or Salvador Sanchez (killed in a driving accident)—safe, easygoing common ground; and yet the most essential truth about the old man and his son was that they did not need much to get along, his Poppy, when he was not drunk or preoccupied with death, a sturdy and calming influence. In fact, when his Poppy, smelling of restaurants and Vitalis, wrapped his bony arms around Rico, that act alone seemed to make those visits worthwhile.

The Ospreys, Again

He did not have much to say to his beloved mother, even loving her as he did. Certain subjects sustained them, when they did get around to talking: Cuba ("the horror . . ."), the deaths, marriages, and births in the neighborhood, and, of course, recent store sales, holistic health news (from Mr. Chang, thank you), the prognostications of television clairvoyant Walter Mercado, and finally, and most safely, the other events that defined her life (their lives) with that most splendid of families, the Ospreys.

. . . *The best family in the whole world,* living proof that disasters did not inevitably enter every family's life, not one of the children had turned out badly. The older, Thomas—or *Tomás*—headed off to Columbia Law School and the School of International Affairs and a fledgling career in the diplomatic corps; the other son, Bill—*Guillermo*—settled into a career in art history, his vocation involving sojourns to the great centers of study in Europe like Rome and London, from which Lydia received postcards ("Look how he thinks about me"). And the daughter? Engaged to a businessman, from Seattle, far far away in another part of the United States, she said, most happily.

In the recitation of so many details about that family, Lydia's devotedness bothered Rico, her endless prattling about how they, with so much money, were, on top of everything, *so nice.* Although he was grateful to Mr. Osprey and thought highly enough of the family to keep in touch—he sent them

Christmas presents and every year had a drink with Osprey at The Century Club—he only knew that whenever she talked about that family, and reminded Rico of how Mr. Osprey had interceded in his behalf—all those years before—he wanted to run out the door.

They'd spend a few hours watching television, until about eleven, when Raul usually fell asleep on his olive green recliner, which he'd saved and saved for (the petty comforts of the poor) and Lydia herself had begun to yawn; that's when Rico, having done his duty, would slip away, catching a gypsy cab on the street back to the comforts and solitude of his "other" life.

He was lonely, too, but could never admit it to himself; his trips back to the neighborhood filling him with nostalgia for the lovely day-to-day hopelessness that united everybody; even the loud, bigoted Irish drunks whom he never liked sort of touched him: quite simply, the passing of the years had somehow given even the more boring and enervating aspects of that life more value.

In that neighborhood, music was still in the air, some of it loudly blaring from the dickheads' boom-box cars, some of it the stuff he loved, like jazz and latin—sounding ever so sweetly out of certain windows; there had been a time, too, and this he missed, when the fellows gathered on the street corners or on the stoops to sing a cappella, and some of the younger musicians, now getting old like him, played their scales. How he wanted to hook up with them. When he did run into some of his old neighborhood friends, there was much talk about getting together, mainly in the bars, the offers to get high flying. The few occasions when he'd had some of his pals over to his apartment, like Rudy, the fellow with whom he had been busted those years before, his friend took in his elegant surroundings with stoic and perhaps envious appreciation, the question begging to be asked by most poor folks, what makes the difference in life? Luck? Brains? Drive?

It still broke Rico's heart to see poor families out for walks, the kids (thanks to television with its commercial overloads) with the "gimme" expressions on their faces. Or the mothers who had no business having so many kids dragging their children along, rage in their faces and the kind of anger that, to Rico's way of thinking, amounted to a craving to both *take and destroy* at the same time, like the kids he knew who started out breaking windows, gashing car finishes with broken beer bottles and knives, graduating to armed robbery and sometimes murder. . . .

He could never explain the discomforts he felt those days with the bourgeois life, or his uneasiness with most of his old friends, who seemed lost and oblivious to the depth and breadth of the world. And yet he had many a happy moment when he did return: there was Mr. Fuentes, the poet-butcher, happy in life, with a self-published book of poetry entitled *The Songs of Blood,* and his pretty wife; Mario, MTA *mambero,* whose slightest attentions—a rap on the back, a wink, an invitation for a drink—were a source of joy to Rico; and there was Mireya, whose elegance had always impressed him, touching his face with her soft hands, the Cortez sisters from the beauty parlor, Martinez, the super—and always his own Poppy, Raul, out on the stoop with a newspaper and a religious pamphlet, a cigarette burning between his fingers, boozy conviction in his eyes, smiling, always agreeably disposed to seeing his boy Rico.

Even when things went beautifully on one of his visits uptown, when he had gone to the apartment and spent the night in euphoric conversation and fun with his godfather, Mario, and other friends, and his mother and father were in good spirits, and a kind of peace had descended over the apartment, the kitchen table filled with the kind of foods that he loved but no longer ate, for they were unhealthful and cholesterol-rich—steaks and *chuletas* and platters of fried plantains and garlic-soaked *yuca*, and rice and black beans—much of this coming from Fuentes, who might intone, "*Is not the kitchen a remarkable place of worship?*"—when he'd left the apartment feeling one with his fellow man, there was always someone somewhere—a disenchanted Hispanic sales clerk, an angry factory worker on the train, a hood on the street—to break the spell. . . .

Such was the life of the cleaning lady's son.

An Irretrievable
Distance

The very day that Lydia began to first discover that not all was well in her employer's household she was already a little sad, for it was one of those mornings when she had woken up missing her parents. Even though the day was cheerful and full of promise—birds were chirping around the feeders on windowsills and fire escapes—spring was in the air—she had climbed the stairs to the El on her way to work visualizing her mother and fathers' spirits—or whatever remains with the living—among the crowd, and sank low, feeling that irretrievable distance. . . .

An afterlife? Her head filled with doubt, she wondered that day, again and again, if they, once dead, would ever rise again to be reunited in the comfort and grand beauty of Heaven, where they would put aside all pain forever. For a moment, as she made her way through the crowds in the Times Square station, everything, the memory of every bit of hard work and struggle, seemed pointless—like dishwater going down a drain. Where were the angels with the Borax and Comet, to wipe clean the world, and make every life valuable, every moment priceless? Even as she left the Lexington Avenue station, the sun did not glitter like a fresh-cleaned plate or a sparkling floor—it hung in the sky like a wrung-out mop (or the twisted rag of a bad heart) looking sad and defeated. Cars passed on the avenue like dirty shoes, and the expressions on some people's faces reminded her of hungry cockroaches.

She was tired: Raul had kept her up half the night with his gasping, gunfire had erupted at three in the morning, and her feet were still aching from the day before—she hadn't been too resilient as of late. As people pushed against her from two directions on the sidewalk, she thought, God help the person

269

in need of kindness, for civility has gone out the window! Her eyes were wet when she made her way into the Ospreys' servant's entrance, which caused Mr. Chang to furrow his brows and ask, "Mrs. Lydia, something wrong?"

She found herself snapping "No!" and made her way into the maid's room where she changed into her work dress.

An Outing

She didn't see Mrs. Osprey all morning, but around lunchtime Lydia saw her come in from a shopping trip with three of her joyous friends, one of whom was getting married for the third time; they had a brief exchange in the hallway and then Mr. Chang approached Lydia in the living room: "It's too nice a day to stay inside, why don't we go to the park for lunch?"

Feeling apologetic about having been rude earlier, Lydia agreed to accompany Mr. Chang though she preferred to stay in; shortly they went out, down through the majestic lobby and over to the Central Park Zoo in time to watch the Swiss clock, with its revolving dial of fairy tale animals, chime the midday hour; many children were out with their nannies, and the sight of the toddlers and their delight over the sounding of the clarion, as Chang and Lydia sat with sandwiches and sodas from a vending cart, were an enchantment, for both still remembered the joys of having children.

"Can you believe it, Mrs. Lydia, that in June I will have been with Mr. and Mrs. Osprey for nearly thirty years?"

"It all goes by so fast, doesn't it?"

"Yes, and now I'm feeling that it's time for me to rest. But you know I don't get a pension from them, and even though they say they will give me something, I can't count on anything. Only Social Security."

"But they are nice people."

"Yes, they are nice." Then: "How can I complain, when I've been able to raise a family. Of my three boys, two went to college, to Queens and Fairleigh Dickinson. Only one of them, my youngest, got into trouble—for trying to stick up a delicatessen in Astoria."

"No!"

"That happened last year—God, the lawyers cost me an arm and a leg—but he got off.... Now he's in the military, in Arizona."

"Do they know?" She meant the Ospreys.

"No, I would never tell them something like that."

And they sat a while longer, the sun beating down on them in a pleasant way. Later, they stood side by side amid a crowd watching as two park workers put on a big show of feeding the sea lions. Mr. Chang laughed and looked at Lydia sweetly, and put his arm around her ever so briefly. "You're very nice, Lydia," he said.

She blushed, thankfully, and, looking closely at Chang, was stricken, as if by a revelation, at how much her colleague had "suddenly" aged—his skin was pinched around his eyes, his cheeks were sallower than she had ever realized, and she told herself, "My God, I have known this stranger for nearly twenty years." And the thought nearly made her break out into tears again. Along Fifth Avenue and heading over to Park she wondered, "What is going on with me, this *mujer dura*— hard woman?"

A Discovery

Soon enough she was back in the Park Avenue apartment, cleaning Mrs. Osprey's bathroom. It was then, while replacing several jars of cream inside her cabinet, that Lydia happened to notice a new preponderance of medicine bottles—whether they were tranquilizers or poison, antibiotics or allergy pills she could not say—but they gave her the first intimation that things weren't what they had been with Mrs. Osprey.

Still, Lydia made nothing more of it. Later that same day, however, she saw something else she had never seen before; in passing Mrs. Osprey's bedroom, Lydia noticed the double French doors ajar, and upon her bed Mrs. Osprey, stretched out on her stomach in a silk gown, face jammed into her fancy French pillows, hands covering her head, in a state of great emotional duress.

Like a Maid from an Old Hollywood Film

In that moment she wanted to become one of those cleaning ladies from the 1930s Hollywood movies, confidante and friend, dispenser of wisdom and comforts, the kind of cleaning woman who would have said, "Nothing is worth such sorrow," or, "Madame, everything will be better, I promise you that." And yet, even though by now she was practically a member of the family, she hesitated about disturbing the Madame, for, in Lydia's opinion, Mrs. Osprey was the kind of person who would have felt offended. Besides, Mrs. Osprey was a strong woman, Lydia knew that. What did she need from somebody like her?

Even if her first impulse was to mind her own business, Lydia decided to rap on the door: yet as soon as she knocked, Mrs. Osprey suddenly regained her composure. Sitting on the side of the bed, Mrs. Osprey pressed a handkerchief to her eyes, blew her nose, lit a cigarette, and made her way to her dressing room vanity. There, her face a mask of self-control, she lingered before the glow of makeup lights, primping and rearranging her blond hair, as if what Lydia had just seen was a hallucination.

Though it was the kind of thing that most of the people from Lydia's neighborhood would have liked to think generally true—

that money and position smothered the soul and weakened the body and dissolved any possibility of true happiness (whatever that was)—from what Lydia had observed, most of Mrs. Osprey's life was happy. But as circumstances would have it, Mrs. Osprey, who'd never had a bad thing to say to Lydia, who had been as kind as someone of her detached ways could be, had come down with an illness. Its first manifestations were changes in mood: Lydia could hear her shouting at the efficient and very decent Mr. Chang where one had never heard such behavior before, and she was often gloomy, irritably so. She did not sleep well and this made her a weary sight in the morning. What she suffered from, Lydia was never told, but from her humble place in that home she observed how the medicine cabinets filled with more and more bottles. Cut flowers, sent by Mr. Osprey from his office or abroad (Lydia was convinced he was holed up with a lover in an apartment in Buenos Aires) came twice a week, so that the living room would glow sweetly in the morning light. And one day a spectacular piece of furniture arrived, an old French armoire "worth very much money" that Mrs. Osprey had picked out at an antiques show, a gift from Mr. Osprey to his wife.

The Restaurant with the Pink Tulips on the Tables

In the course of a year Mrs. Osprey aged dramatically; she went from looking like a well-preserved woman of forty or forty-five to somewhere in her wan early sixties. A cane did not help this impression. A Jamaican lady was hired to help her get around. One month she flew to California for two weeks, visiting a spa, returning with a fantastic tan, but with the malady nevertheless intact. The children visited more often. A nurse started to come and go.

Through this period a door to a kind of friendship between Lydia and her employer opened, a beautiful and lovely state of affairs that started when Mrs. Osprey asked her to come in one

273

day just so they could have lunch together. Lydia chose a Saturday and arrived at the apartment wearing her best clothes, looking as elegant and well put together as any of Mrs. Osprey's high society friends. The first of her pleasant sensations? Walking arm in arm past the doormen with Mrs. Osprey to the street. They did not have a lot to talk about. Despite the fact that they were around the same age, Lydia behaved as if she were escorting an older woman down the street. They went to the Metropolitan Museum of Art, but Mrs. Osprey faded by the steps, cluttered as they were with tourists. They went to a glamorous restaurant on Madison Avenue instead, the owner shaking their hands as they entered the pink dining room. Bright-faced ladies, half hidden behind tulip vases, waved hello, and then they sat, Lydia ever so impressed by the bird-shaped serviettes.

A dashing young waiter with a distinctly European air—not of a waiter but of a viscount!—took their drink orders, a gin martini for Mrs. Osprey and a gin and tonic for Lydia. She found herself staring at the handsome waiter. "He's so good-looking, what's he doing here?" she said. Then: "You know my husband, Raul, is a waiter, too, but his restaurant is nothing like this."

Shortly the drinks came. A toast, then the grand menus, whose prices made Lydia nervous, until the Madame told her: "Order anything you want and don't be worried."

Used to simple Cuban food, she explained to Mrs. Osprey how she and Raul rarely went out to eat—"He's sick of restaurants by the time he gets home after waiting tables all day"—and that became the basis of their conversation. A few of the things they talked about: Lydia's favorite restaurant in New York City was an Italian place on Mulberry Street called Santa Lucia where, she explained, she had gone with Raul in the early days of their marriage before the kids came along, and that they made their way down there once a year, as a kind of mutual Christmas present, the act of being waited on most pleasing to Raul, who could speak Italian with the owner, an affable man who brought them great dishes with a good-natured smile and wink, Lydia's favorite dish a kind of chicken *parmigiano,* which she smothered with grated cheese and pepper, and a side dish of pasta with artichokes. Mrs. Osprey, remembering better days, related how she had always liked French food, the best she mentioned coming from a place she and her husband used to frequent called the Marseille. And she loved ice cream, which took her back to her glorious childhood in Newport, Rhode Island, where her family kept a summer home on a street by the harbor (*"Dios mío,* we had a house by the water, too!"). And, since they were reminiscing, there was always the Oak Room in the Plaza Hotel: on a snowbound mid-December afternoon in 1949, after she and Mr. Osprey had gone to see *Miracle on 34th Street,* on a holiday-inspired lark and much in love, they had sat in that bar drinking martinis; Mr. Osprey had proposed and she had accepted.

A beautiful tale, which Lydia liked very much.

"For me it was a dance hall, my husband calling me an empress and opening his heart and soul, during a slow song that we call a bolero."

The waiter poured a delicious wine into their glasses and Lydia, feeling overwhelmed, and with tears in her eyes, made a toast, "To the best of the best," and laughed so loudly that everyone in the room looked over (or so she thought). Shortly the appetizers, then the main dishes, Mrs. Osprey picking at her food, so that while Lydia devoured her own (paper-baked scallion chicken) she began to eye Mrs. Osprey's succulent lamb, her heart breaking when the waiter later took her plate away, the food hardly touched: how Raul, she, somebody would have loved those tender filets.

Throughout the meal Mrs. Osprey spent much of her time staring fondly in Lydia's general direction; Lydia, drinking more wine, got somewhat drunk, but not in a bad way: the kind of drunk that makes people seem more and more beautiful and immortal, like gods, and that provoked Lydia to lean forward and say to Mrs. Osprey, "Really you don't look so bad," and, "God will see you through your worst trials." With that Lydia started to tell Mrs. Osprey how much she appreciated her, that she was a person of breeding, the kind of person her family would have known back in Cuba had things not gone so wrong: that they all would have been friends in another time and place, really good friends. . . . Then she went into Raul's situation, how some people never have anything while others have everything, it being good when someone like Mrs. Osprey got what she deserved in life. But, continued Lydia, delighting in some prof-iteroles, wasn't it sad that people like herself and her husband could work all their lives without ever once eating in a restaurant like that one? Like the way most people only ride limousines at funerals? Mrs. Osprey nodded, smiled, waved for the bill.

When they parted, Lydia went home, hardly able to contain her joy, and thinking that, after so many years, Mrs. Osprey finally saw her as the person she'd always known herself to be: elegant, aristocratic, a person to be respected and to be treated like the best. This left Lydia in such a bragging way that she was nearly intolerable for weeks afterward, recounting just about every detail of the meal to her friends and husband again and again, feeling an immense pride and thinking of Mrs. Osprey as her new friend.

Over time Mrs. Osprey became worse and, sadly, made the decision to abandon the Park Avenue apartment in favor of their home on Martha's Vineyard. The move took place on a weekend, and when Lydia arrived at work on the following Tuesday she found many of Madame's things missing, the apartment suddenly seeming empty and much larger than before. That afternoon, Mr. Osprey, home early from the office, explained to Lydia in a strained voice that he would be spending more and more time away with his wife but that they should not worry: he would keep Lydia—and Mr. Chang—in his employ.

Even if their closeness had not gone any further, her employer's physical decline and the details of her appearance were not things that Lydia cared to ponder; and while Mrs. Osprey was not religious, Lydia found herself going to church and lighting candles for her just the same.

When the time came, Lydia prompted her family to attend the funeral. That is, she got Rico to stand beside his mother and father in one of the pews in the rear of the church, Lydia sobbing loudly as the processional went by, even if, at home, she had been heard to say, "*Y qué?*" or "What of it?" and "We all have to go sometime." Still it saddened Lydia, and the sight of her beautiful children in the front of the church, noble and fine Americans, and the others who filled the knave, rich-looking people—maybe Rockefellers—lawyers and doctors and business people, ladies in heavy fur coats—nearly brought her to tears. She was touched by the flowers and the eulogy in which the minister solemnly intoned, "We come into this world as dust and to dust we will return," and she sat promising herself to be a better person, a better mother, to control her temper, and not to give Raul a hard time. And then she thought about Mrs. Osprey, remembering her as perhaps she would want to be remembered in eternity: fantastic in a silk robe and soft oriental slippers, her lovely hair piled atop her head, her skin aglow. . . .

It may be recalled that in the days when Lydia was working in the sewing factory she had made a joke about a queen: *Chica, now I know how Marie Antoinette felt before going to the guillotine. The poor thing.* She had said that with the glint of memory in her eyes, for as a small girl in Cuba who had comported herself like a young princess, she found much enjoyment in imagining the last moments of the French queen. In a long silken gown, and pacing about their solemn prison chamber, the queen tried to cheer the sad king, reminiscing about the good times, how she and their entourage would travel the picturesque countryside, visiting chateaux and vineyards, toasted at parties, beloved by all. How she, in a hooped skirt, sun bonnet, and shepherd's staff, had loved to attend to her little lambs in the garden (how delicious they were, chopped up, with mint jelly). . . . And what of those May evenings when she and the king dallied in the royal swan-headed barges on their pond at Versailles, gilded oars rising and dropping into the honeyed waters?

And Marie Antoinette's last thoughts, as she stood before the executioner's block awaiting the end? Was she thinking about farewells to the loveliness and plenitude of this world, to its delicious breezes, sad evenings, and brilliant stars? *Or was she thinking, No more shit?* Contemplating the implications of the end of the world, *of everything*, during the course of Mrs. Osprey's funeral, Lydia decided what she would have thought were she the queen resting her tender neck upon the block: "*Carajo!*"

The Story of the Cleaning Lady and the Haunted Sable Coat

She had hoped that after poor Mrs. Osprey's death, "something" by way of an inheritance would come her way. Her prayers in church must have been heard because after many items had been removed in the comings and goings of friends and family in Osprey's apartment, Mr. Osprey offered Lydia a choice of what remained of his late wife's personal belongings: hand mirrors, compacts, scarves and shoes, combs and brushes, bottles of perfume and jars of cream, gloves, hats, and much costume jewelry; not the best of what had formerly belonged to her, the finest of her jewelry and clothing having either been sold or taken away for charities or by relatives.

Save for Mrs. Osprey's movie star sable coat that Lydia had always coveted. The coat that Mrs. Osprey had worn on her nights out to the opera, to all those high society events over at Lincoln Center, to the political fund-raisers in which Mr. and Mrs. Osprey were photographed shaking hands with the president, the coat in which she had posed for the newspapers, the coat she wore when she lunched with her cheery circle of friends. The coat that bristled like a field of wheat in the wind (or if you like, the high grass of a Cuban meadow), that shone like a ferret's eyes, that rustled like a peacock's feathers, that sent through any room a somehow wintry breath; a coat suitable for a queen, Lydia thought, like the ones she had gazed at in store windows, which cost thousands of dollars!

When the coat came out of cold storage every year and hung in one of Mrs. Osprey's walk-in closets, Lydia marveled at its magnificence and beauty. On a dreary November afternoon, when she thought herself alone and had been posing in the coat before a mirror, Mrs. Osprey had announced her presence by clearing her throat, and saying to Lydia in a perturbed and frosty voice, "I'm glad you like that so very much." Embarrassed and losing her cool, Lydia told her employer, in the way that men used to speak to her, "It was just so beautiful, I couldn't resist," which in fact had brought a kind of smile to Mrs. Osprey's lips.

"Yes, that was one of my husband's nicer gifts, for our tenth anniversary."

Trying the garment on again and again, over the years, when nobody was around, as sort of a *relajo* with herself, in those moments before the mirror she could have been one of those ladies in an advertisement, or just like Maria Callas in a diamond tiara about to climb into her limousine.

One thing was sure, she never thought she would own that coat, but about three months after Mrs. Osprey's death, Mr. Osprey approached Lydia as she worked in the kitchen.

"Come here, Lydia, there's something I want to give you."

And as in dreams coming true, Osprey led Lydia back into his late wife's bedroom and presented her with the coat: "Lydia, this is now yours, my wife asked me to give it to you."

Then: "*Buen provecho*"—"Enjoy it."

Like those poor contestants on the old *Queen for a Day* television show, Lydia was overcome, and could not help embracing the lordly Mr. Osprey. "I can't believe it," Lydia found herself saying. "I can't believe it." But what of the family, the daughter? Didn't she want it?

"She has her own, believe me."

And with that, Lydia wiped her hands clean on a rag and put on the coat and sighed.

"So you see," she told her friends, "as I said before, that man Mr. Osprey is a saint." And his wife?

"A wonderful lady who I will always miss."

"But just last week," her friend Concha said, "you told me how she was cheap, because you heard that she had left something for the cook, while you had gotten nothing."

"Well, *chica*," she had said, "you know how I can be sometimes." Then, looking around, as if indeed she were being watched by someone keeping score, "The truth is that she was a fine lady deserving all the rewards of Heaven." Then, sending a kiss into the sky, "She's a saint, too."

The coat itself, for all its glamorous allure and value—a friend who knew the furrier's trade said it was worth about five thousand dollars—presented certain practical problems. In that neighborhood where thieves, generally speaking, had their run of the apartment houses, taking everything from stereo sets to the very plumbing out of basements, if one were not careful, there arose the question of how to keep and protect this boon. In fact the day Lydia was given the coat she had been so nervous about taking public transportation that she wrapped it in a sheet and caught a taxi home, thinking, all the way, that something or someone would take this evidence of good fortune from her.

Coming back from work, Raul took one look at the coat and, while appreciating Osprey's generosity and touched by Lydia's emotionality, had said, "Sell it."

She didn't want to.

In fact, for the first time Lydia and Raul had something of real financial value in their apartment, although objects of personal and nostalgic worth abounded. Once her elation wore off they sat down to make certain decisions: they'd already been robbed once, someone breaking in through the fire escape (that nice Grundig short-wave radio and a small portable television set, which they'd sometimes watch in the bedroom, as well as a jar stuffed with change and tightly folded one-dollar bills) and they had dealt with this by installing several window gates in the living room, which Raul never liked because they did not allow as much sunlight in. Now there were the back windows to the courtyard to think about; in a few days, having looked into it, Raul found someone who could put in some more gates at fifty dollars a pop.

"How one lousy coat could complicate our lives, I don't know."

"But you have to admit, Raul, it is wonderful."

So they installed the gates. But wearing the coat in public, in that neighborhood, was another matter. The first few times she had gone out swathed in that sable coat, to eat at a church banquet, and to visit with some old Cuban friends on Broadway, she drew much underworld attention, all these felonious souls checking her out as she made her way along. Raul felt that wearing the coat was ostentatious and courting disaster; the criminal element knew just where they lived, and when they came and went.

Some of these fellows were blatant about their lack of good intentions, standing out on the sidewalk and looking toward their windows, "scoping" everything. Even a local cop, eating an Italian hero in his squad car, had told her, "It's none of my business, but if that coat is for real, I think you better be careful."

But she insisted on showing it off to her friends, and poor Raul walked ever cautiously beside her, cane in hand, hoping for the best.

When she did go downtown in that coat, visiting certain shops and walking haughtily along, sales clerks fell all over her—and rich people in general, she swore, gave her a knowing nod. The coat allowed her to feel that she belonged in the "club" and yet the "club" may as well have been on the moon. Nice to be on Park Avenue and then to come home and smell rot within the walls; nice to feel as if the coat would suddenly lift her off the pavement and carry her away to the heavens above, and smell the urine in the halls.

She began to feel more strongly all the things she and Raul did not have. Not even a credit card, or a store card, or an automobile, or a retirement account, or a summer home, or a vacation plan, or a box at the opera, or a membership on a board: things that went along with the coat. Yet she insisted on making a big deal about it, posing Mario, Raul, herself, and Rico in front of the stoop and having the superintendent snap a photograph of them—the same super whose wife offered Lydia two hundred dollars for the sable, insulting her, so that when Lydia passed the superintendent's wife on the street, coming home from work, she averted her eyes and stuck her nose in the air.

"Mama," Rico told her, "you get offended too easily."

"Yes? That's only because I'm tired of people not knowing who I really am."

Raul sighing, Rico smiling for the camera; the shot.

Oddly, when the photographs were developed there appeared to be a residue of blue light emanating from the sable, in all the five photographs taken: the same bluish aura she had seen in certain rich people, what Lydia had taken to be the evidence of great inward power. But was it supernatural?

There were some very nice Cuban ladies over on Columbus Avenue with whom Lydia had become acquainted, and these women, practitioners of *santería,* the Afro-Cuban religion, surmised that the coat contained the lingering residue of Mrs. Osprey's being—that mix of recollection and emotion that constitute identity in living beings and the afterlife for the dead.

Lydia, becoming more prone to this kind of thinking with age, nodded, asking, "You mean this color in the photograph is a ghost?"

"No, my dear, it's the coat's sadness now that she is gone." A little too far-fetched for Lydia to believe, but she nonetheless found herself standing before the closet saying, "You may as well get used to it, your *señora* has passed on." Then: "I am the new *señora.*"

She said this, hedging her bets, as if there might be spirits inhabiting the coat, an enjoyable throwback to the wonderfully superstitious days when she was a girl in Cuba. Who the hell knew what lingered of a person? In Cuba ghosts had indeed appeared to people. When she had been a small girl playing with her sisters, their world was dense with spirits: the African gods running with the Catholic saints and angels to resurrect the dead, their presences ever subtle; a mass of light shimmering against the walls of a windowless room.

On top of that, over the years she had met cleaning ladies set to the task of cleaning out the apartments of people who had recently died, and the consensus was that although one could not *always see* the spirits, something lingered, sweetly, sadly, undeniably dead and filled with longing. (And tales of hands light as air brushing against them, and most rarely, of actually seeing the apparitions wandering in the hall, confused and lonely and lost, for as Lydia often thought, *what could be lonelier than death?*) In any event, one night, when she and Raul were in bed, she heard the coat rustling on its hanger and she could swear that it moved from the closet for she heard it brushing against the walls; indeed when she got out of bed she felt as if there were a "presence" in the living room—and from that night on, for nearly a month, she lived more and more with the idea that Mrs. Osprey's gift was enough to try one's nerves. And again, they were living with the idea that someone would break into the apartment to steal that coat, which Raul responded to by coming home with a .22-caliber starter's pistol that he'd gotten from a friend. While they felt more secure, Raul, who'd never fired off a gun in his life, felt as though something in him was being changed, and this he did not like.

On a number of nights she awakened hearing people breaking into the apartment; on one occasion there were a dozen men roving the rooms. Of course it was a dream, but the lack of security was real.

In the end she had to make a choice about the coat, and as much as she had gone over her options—Raul advocated giving the coat either to their daughter or to the church—they decided simply to sell it. Their friend had offered to find a buyer. That decision did not come easily, because whenever she went over to Osprey's she was afraid he would find out and feel offended by her action. Nevertheless, she wore the coat one last time, on a night when Mario's band was playing uptown in one of the social clubs, but even there—nothing came easily—she would not leave the coat in the coat checkroom and sat wearing it the entire evening, sweating, holding forth as if she were a European contessa and such items, in her world, were perfectly safe to own.

Her Dear Companion Mireya

It's a pleasure to report that Lydia's dear companion Mireya had made it through the master's program in education at Teachers College and in this incarnation passed her days, unmarried and not particularly interested in love, teaching pedagogy and Spanish at John Jay and Manhattan Community College. For the life of her, Lydia could not figure out why her friend of such long standing had no interest in men, but now that she was in her fifties, a finely featured, vaguely aristocratic silver-haired lady, the subject of potential matrimony dropped out of their conversations. It had been their habit to eat Saturday lunches in a Chinese restaurant on Broadway, Lydia unable to resist rating the men who came along: "That fellow in the brown suit, with his hair combed down the middle, happens to work as an accountant for a very good company, but look he's always got dandruff on his collar and still lives with his mother, no good, my dear, sweet *querida*." "That one there owns two stores on Columbus but he has dead eyes and look at those testicles of his! My god, hanging like sacks of fruit in his trousers, you don't want that, do you?" "And that fellow, the superintendent, he does something they call the Tai-Chi, he's not good enough for you, Mireya, I mean you're much too refined for his kind . . . but you could do worse, if you were willing to compromise. Have you ever seen such beautiful eyes in a man?" "Now that one is the kind of fellow you could

285

wrap around your little finger, but what do you need with someone at your age anyway, just a man you will spend your last years looking after: with no children, who's going to look after you?"

Mireya, shrugging, always smiled, always said something like, "Oh Lydia, let's just have lunch and enjoy ourselves, okay?"

But as they watched their youth slip away, Lydia no longer bothered to talk with her friend about men because, even if Mireya never considered herself an old maid, Lydia's prodding made her think about it, and the very subject of marriage turned the even-mannered Mireya irritable—which was to say that Lydia, in the right mood, could make anyone angry. So after a while Lydia kept her comments to herself, admitting, if anything, that most men, in any case, were a waste of time; but once they had run out of that subject, and once Lydia's patience and energy for the grammar and spelling lessons that had kept them busy in earlier days had faded, there was not always much for them to talk about.

For her part Lydia had gotten into the habit of gossipy (and she thought amusing) conversation, and relished what tidbits of forbidden knowledge she heard about people in the neighborhood. Mireya seemed more intent on reading than anything else, carrying around the kinds of frayed books one found in the used book carts of university shops—*The Notebooks of Henry James*, *The Poetry of García Lorca*, *The Elements of Style*. She spent those lunches with Lydia trying to maintain a dignified and cultivated manner, and seemed, in her bookishness, somewhere else, even as Lydia went on and on about the local intrigues.

As Mireya got older, it seemed to Lydia, she showed more of her origins: in Cuba her father had been a schoolmaster in her small town and her mother, a transplanted Spaniard from a good Madrid family, had all the refined tastes and habits of class—that is, Mireya had been raised with books, ballet, a knowledge of music and art, and, in general ways, of the world. She had been content in Cuba, but the ambitions of an older sister, who had long ago married and moved to California (or some such distant place), had brought her to New York: finding herself a life as a perpetual student, a translator, a shopkeeper, a teacher of languages, she made her own way and was proud of that. Yet even Mireya experienced that form of malaise that comes to anyone appraising one's life in middle age, that which asked, "After so much work and effort, what on earth am I doing here?"

On those days when Lydia, feeling tense or anxious or hyperbolically disposed, went on for too long about the chicanery of certain sales clerks or, more usually, about those so-and-sos who had no class whatsoever, when all this got on Mireya's nerves, she would feel that, after so many years in this country, her life had come down to gossip and attitudes and a friend who would not have particularly cared to listen to her troubles had she ever wanted to express them.

But they were friends, and even though there were days when Lydia's inability to appreciate Mireya's reflective nature sometimes made the pedagogist short on patience herself—as in "I just remembered an appointment, my dear"—and even though they shared many moments in which they would find themselves staring at each other in a way to suggest, "*My goodness, after all these years I hardly know you,*" not a week went by when they did not get together at least once, for Mireya and Lydia were, in the end, family. Or a kind of family.

After the death of Mrs. Osprey, Lydia had become more acutely aware of mortality, and because of that she had a fright when Mireya, who never went to a doctor, was diagnosed as having something in her breasts. It turned out to be benign—but in the initial rush of apprehensions it amazed Lydia that even the self-contained and self-reliant Mireya could become unraveled. In those days, she gravitated to Lydia's side, coming regularly to the apartment to watch television with her cleaning lady friend, even if that was not what she would normally do at night; she did not want to be alone. For her part, Lydia took care of her, becoming, for that period of biopsies and doctors' visits, Mireya's mother, sister, and daughter, dropping jobs in order to accompany her friend around town, taking her to movies, to the libraries and dress shops.

Mireya had been deeply touched by her friend's compassion and concern. And her involvement with spiritual matters. As when, on an impulse, they'd been out shopping downtown one autumn afternoon and Lydia dragged Mireya into St. Patrick's Cathedral to look for the archbishop, his Eminence Cardinal Cooke, in the hope that he would give Mireya his personal blessing: instead of finding his Eminence they settled for a young priest, a pleasant "hispano," a transplanted Mexican fellow, who anointed Mireya (at Lydia's insistence) and gave her a small rosary and a church calendar as keepsakes. Mireya, head bowed, was deeply moved by the sweetness of it all.

Afterwards Lydia kneeled before the altar with her friend, and affected, with trembling hands and lips, the appearance of someone who may well have been extremely devout; and this gave Mireya a tremendous lift, even if she suspected that Lydia was exaggerating the depth of her conviction. In any event, Mireya's scare, as previously mentioned, passed, and although Lydia's involvement in so crucial a moment in her friend's life was a sure sign of friendship, Mireya would be reminded of this selfless act whenever Lydia wanted something, as in "Can you come with me to the market today?" She drafted Mireya into that circle of citizenry—her husband and her children, for example—who she felt "owed" her dearly for an act of kindness, the way a lord or lady, in more ancient times, may have favored a minor subject and expected lifelong devotion in return.

With Eliseo, Bookseller

With the passage of years the university had put up new and ghastly buildings in the neighborhood, a law school and a school of international affairs, among others, and modern sculptures so breathtakingly ugly that passersby and long-time residents of the neighborhood were immediately depressed; and they constructed all manner of blocky high-rise student housing, demolishing many a tenement (out with the past, upward and onward with the future!) and raising the rents so high that businesses like Eliseo's café were forced to close. Eliseo began to sell books on Broadway, and every so often Lydia, taking a walk, would stop by to see him.

Over the years Lydia's feelings of suspicion and resentment about him, for what *may* have once happened between Eliseo and Alicia, had softened, giving way to a superficial friendliness. Aging, he had never prospered. Despite his skinny frame, his rotten teeth and bloodshot eyes, he was never wanting for companionship—there always seemed to be a younger woman about, maybe down on her luck, or some former college students who had never gone anywhere in life, helping him out with the sales of his books. Six days a week he showed up with a shopping cart filled with books he had scavenged here and there in the neighborhood, spread two sheets on the sidewalk in front of a church on 113th Street and Broadway, and covered them with his merchandise. He also sold magazines and phonograph albums and in this manner, just got by. . . .

His greatest nemesis in those days? The cops who sometimes chased him off the sidewalk, even if an avenue over, a few blocks further downtown, street corner dealers were selling a new, instantly addicting drug, crack. And the rain: a heavy downpour could ruin his inventory, so that he was particularly worried on overcast days.

Seeing the hard times that had befallen him, as she passed by, Lydia would feel that justice had somehow been served, but in time she began to feel sorry for him, and got into the habit of buying his books.

"How much, for this one?"

"A dollar."

"A dollar? Is it good?"

"Yes, Stephen King writes very good novels. If you like to be frightened."

"And that one?"

"*The Interpretation of Dreams* by Freud."

"How much is that?"

"A dollar."

"I will buy this for my son." And she reached into her purse and pulled out a bill. "You know he's doing very well these days. And so is my daughter." Then: "You never had children, did you, Eliseo?"

"No, I never had enough money."

"Ah, who needs money? Why, I see people on relief all the time with five or six kids! It's just that you never found the right person."

"We each choose our own road."

"Yes, that's true." And then, because he seemed so forlorn, she told him, "We may not be rich but we have our health, don't we?"

When Mr. Chang Retired

What other events defined her life?

When Mr. Chang retired, leaving Mr. Osprey's employ, he presented Lydia with a postcard on which he had written the address where he would live in Florida: "Please, Mrs.

España—Lydia—make sure that you come to see us." But even though she promised that she would, she thought it unlikely—for where did she and Raul ever go? Polite and reserved as always, he'd given her a hug. "After today, I guess, I will have to say good-bye." And that was all. In the late afternoon, he became a disappearing figure, in a topcoat and hat, with a slightly bent back, at the end of the hall, making an exit from her life.

Just like that, after so many years, Mr. Chang was gone.

That evening she went home on the Madison Avenue bus feeling as sad as she did when somebody wonderful died, when it felt as if the world had become a lesser and lonelier place, even if Mr. Chang was, in fact, just moving to Boca Raton, a few miles north of Ft. Lauderdale, but in Lydia's frame of reference, endlessly far away.

Taking Care of Mr. Osprey

Now it seemed that with Chang's departure, with the apartment often empty, that her own tenure with Mr. Osprey would soon enough be over. And yet in a way it seemed unimaginable, like growing older, like death itself. Lydia continued to take a nearly custodial pride in looking after him. She went there mainly to dust, to rearrange the cushions on the L-shaped sofas into which Mr. Osprey sometimes plopped at the end of the day; she emptied his ashtrays and trash cans, washed his clothes from the hamper, and found herself standing, awestruck, in his study, for it seemed just a few days before that she had first walked into his apartment to interview for the "part-time" she thought she would never get. His legal books, a fortress of knowledge arranged across his shelves, the law firm paperweights, the framed certificates for outstanding civic deeds from the City of New York, the family photographs. . . .

A funny thing, it would sometimes occur to her that he was in his mid-sixties and yet when she thought about him, she only saw the early middle-aged man she had met those years before, tall and dignified, bald and lorldly. Her heart did reach out to him, even if her sexual fantasies (those of youth) had faded with the passing of time, replaced with some confounding wish that those who loved her and treated her well be happy in their lives, no matter what *happy* meant—which she did not know.

By and by, with the passing of the years, a soft heart and a near love for her fellow man had begun to grow within her. As she looked around and saw how easily people vanished from this existence—poor Raul, given his health, was bound to leave her soon—she did not want to be alone. On a day of tremendous sadness (melancholy) when she thought about how she herself would one day die (*to enter a frightening lifeless unknown—or an afterlife shared with a judgmental God and angels and saints?*) Lydia decided to stop in church, on her way home from work, to make a more sincere effort to communicate with her divine superiors, whoever, whatever they may be. Entering the nave of the church through the large red doors she knelt by the altar, said a prayer for the soul of Mrs. Osprey, and asked God to protect her husband and children from grief and illnesses.

Rich or Poor, It Didn't Matter, It Did Not Take Much for a Man to Fall

Lately, in the several years since Mrs. Osprey died, she noticed how Mr. Osprey, like her own husband, had taken more and more to drink. For in her weekly visits to clean, she found half-empty glasses of liquor here and there, even in the bathroom. Whiffing their residual vapors she determined that he was drinking cognac. In fact, a stack of cases of Courvoisier

VSOP had appeared in a hallway closet and upon the art deco bar, and tucked away in a far corner of the living room there were numerous opened and emptied airline cordials. She had noticed a flashing ruddiness to his face, a drinker's blush, and in fact, when he happened to speak to her he seemed more gushing, less reserved, just the declaration *"Estás trabajando bien, como siempre!"*—"You're doing a great job, as always!" coming out in an overly happy, nearly slurred flight of patter. On one occasion he told her, "You know, Lydia, I'm thinking about leaving here. This place feels like a tomb to me, but where to go is the question." Then: "What would you do if you had enough money to do whatever you wanted?"

He had looked off, the way people do, into an imaginary distance, adding, "You know I sometimes think about heading down to Mexico or Argentina. I have a lot of friends there." But he alluded to nothing further, made no mention of a *specific someone* who might have been there for him to see.

Excusing himself he went off to his bedroom to undress and shower and came out again to have another drink from the bar, leaving under the glass a C-shaped stain, like the sun in eclipse, on a mahogany tabletop (solution: linseed oil and furniture wax)—and she felt just as she always did when Raul did not pay her attention, a feeling that she would storm into Osprey's bedroom to slap some sense (*"Señor, don't you know that the drink is no good!"*) into him coming over—and leaving—her simultaneously.

It would be beautiful to report that Osprey saw the light and straightened himself out, but what happened was that he simply got used to his new way—or perhaps Mrs. Osprey's absence had given him a new freedom and he was just more open about what he had always done. He never became falling-down drunk or ever uttered a rude word to Lydia. And there were times when he seemed perfectly fine, when his son came in from Europe, or one of his other kids came to visit with their children, and he was the perfect gentleman. (Much like Raul.) Not that she saw him often, for her time in that apartment was kept to a minimum, as she worked only between nine and two in the afternoon, before going off to see a movie with Concha or Mireya. Mr. Osprey continued to travel, with seeming immunity to health problems, though she once spied him standing in the hall touching his right kidney as if to soothe some pain.

Often when Osprey saw her he would say, "One day I'm going to give you a very nice gift."

Not like the coat, but something more. (Please God, money.)

They were friends, and he was ever gentle with her, sometimes sweetly pecking her on the right cheek, something he would have never have done when his wife was alive.

A Fleeting Encounter (1987)

One day in the autumn of what would be remembered as one of the sadder years of their lives, Dr. Rico arrived in his office and checked his answering machine to find a call from a certain Mrs. Marie Merrill, or as she had put it, "You remember me, I'm Mr. Osprey's daughter." She needed to speak to someone about something, and because they went so far back, and were "kind of friends," she wondered if he would mind if she came to see him.

Surprised, delighted, befuddled, for it was all too late, as he was set in his solitary hardworking ways and she was married, he replayed the message to make sure he had heard everything right. Indeed it was the very same Marie Osprey for whom in the mythic recesses of his heart and mind he had once nursed a passing teenage infatuation. The last time he'd seen her, some four or five years before, at her mother's funeral, he had gotten the chance to briefly say hello to Marie and her family as the processional was leaving the church: her tall, vigorous husband, Barry, and their two small children, well dressed, healthy, physically pleasing, and polite. He even shook the husband's hand, finding his grip strong, his manner confident and friendly—a well-adjusted fellow. And that had been all; he had not really thought about Osprey's daughter: she was nothing more than a remote part of his memory, a little star in the farthest end of the night, and the daughter of the man who had given him a step up in this life.

When she came to the office at two the next afternoon, she cut a striking figure, still youthful and attractive. Having removed her scarf, a fur hat, and cashmere coat, she had stood pink-faced in his waiting room, and then, as he came out to see her, she turned around and gave Rico a heartfelt embrace.

"I'm really happy to see you," he told her, as he led her into his office.

In his earlier speculations he imagined that she had come to see him out of desperation, that her life was empty and bereft of meaning. He imagined that she would describe her businessman husband as cold and detached, too bent on work to devote himself emotionally to her or her children. But that was not the case: stretching out in a chair, she told him that her life, generally speaking, was "deliriously happy." Having made money in the technological industries of the northwest, her husband was a loving spouse, a good father: they had a mansion on Puget Sound, and the realization of their dream, which was to retire by fifty and travel the world with their children, was not so far away.

"Then what brings you here?"

She laughed, lowered her head, looking at her hands, then told him the following: "I've been having an affair with a married Hispanic man who lives in Seattle. He is a Mexican-

American doctor who I met when one of my kids dove off a boat in the Sound and conked his head. It was just one of those things. One day I went to see him in his office for lunch, and as soon as we were alone, there was this incredible attraction: I never wanted to have sex with someone so badly in my life, and I think it was the same for him."

She went on about how both she and this man, whose name was Frank, had been trying and trying to stop but could not help themselves—"like a couple of characters out of a James M. Cain novel"—and that she didn't want to hurt her husband and was looking for a way out.

"The hard part of it is that I've fallen in love with him—it's gone beyond sex, and yet I don't want to hurt my husband, because I love him, too."

Reeling from the surprise of hearing her talk in so open a manner, Rico told her, "You have to be practical; passion is fleeting; it's the more important things, like family, that last."

She looked at him in a shocked manner, as if she had been seeking permission to pursue this affair.

"God, I feel so embarrassed. It's just that I wish I'd met someone like him a long time ago."

She had turned briefly away—fidgeting uncomfortably—while Rico was surprised by two overlapping memories: of seeing her many years before, one day as she sat before her piano, and of looking for her in Central Park—his little dream that never came true, now sitting before him.

But shortly the session proceeded onto safer, more superficial ground. He made a few suggestions that this affair, coming as it did a few years after her mother's death, may have had a compensational purpose. He took an APA directory of counselors from the shelf and recommended someone in Seattle he knew from school, if she was interested.

"I'm here if you want to talk some more, Marie," he later told her. "Take care."

"Thank you again, Rico," she said.

After Marie left he remembered how he had once jerked off when he was seventeen years old thinking about what she would look like naked and how he had often fantasized about her sexually. But there had been something infinitely sobering and torturous about seeing her after so many years. He wished he had been spared the story of her love affair. Once upon a time, he would have cut his hand off for a chance to be with her, and now that desire struck him as some kind of adolescent folly. He remembered when every trip he made downtown, as a teenager, as a messenger or just accompanying his mother or friends, left him tense and tantalized at the prospect of crossing her path. Somehow he had believed that a girl like Marie was the key to a higher adventure—to a new and exciting existence—without the hard work.

If he had had a different kind of personality, he might have searched harder to find someone like her, but deep down, a part of him resented the way rich people made him feel, his sense of aspiration colliding with a sense of shame about his accomplishments. He did not find it easy to relate to *latina* women, mainly because he felt that he had stepped too far away from the culture, but when he dated other women he felt as if he were betraying his roots. And when it came to women with money, he felt the old prejudices. Speculating about what his life might have been like in the company of a certain kind of woman like Marie, he envisioned wealth without happiness. Nevertheless, he had slipped away from his past and the limitations of his background, thanks in part to Mr. Osprey, and for all his reservations, he had joined Marie's world, becoming the good and rational doctor.

Later, he was grateful to sit in the living room of his Central Park West apartment, with a Cal Tjader vibraphone recording on his CD player and a bottle of brandy before him, drinking, passing the night in solitary reflection, the city, its diversity, its teeming life, beyond his panoramic windows.

In the Realm Where Things Are Truly Different

It happened that Mario and his musicians were playing uptown, and because they had not been out for a time, and because it was Fuentes the butcher's birthday and he was hosting a table of friends, Lydia talked Raul into taking her to that social club on a Saturday night. Radiant scarlet party light, ringlets of light shooting from a spinning aluminum ceiling globe; an ecstatic night with Fuentes and his wife, the barber Ortiz and his wife, Raul and Lydia, seated around a table getting plastered, their pictures snapped by a a pretty young woman in a short gilded *minifalda* dress. Much goodwill everywhere, much good food, and rum-and-Cokes and beers and bottles of wine coolers, Fuentes making a toast, declaring, in his endearingly corny style, "*I am as a sea squirrel amongst the mermaids and serpents of love...,*" everybody laughing, including Raul, who presiding over the table for another toast, lifted his glass, and in a wobbly manner declaimed: "*You are part of what the good Lord has given me, and for that I thank the heavens. To my dear friends of many years...,*" and he led the second clicking of glasses.

Then Mario, at the helm of his ship—to run with Fuentes' line—led his band of suave caballeros into boleroland, and many a couple began to dance, including Raul and Lydia—Raul having arrived, the usual white carnation in his lapel, hands impeccably manicured, and Lydia, arm hooked into the crook of his elbow, in a knee-length blue sequined dress, a velvet belt tied about her waist, the string of Mallorcan pearls, which Raul had given her one March birthday, around her neck, pearl earrings lustrous and dangling, beautiful as her eyes. . . . A funny thing, in the dim light, Raul quite resembled the serious-minded and tender waiter she had met those years before; in fact, 1949 was in the air that night, and somewhere between the music and the rum, in the press of their sweet-scented faces and with Raul given over to romantic musings—"Who is this young and ravishing beauty I hold in my arms?"—time itself seemed suspended, that trumpet-dreamed bolero sweeping into the consciousness of the cleaning woman and her husband like incense (or the cheap smoke of cigarettes and Woolworth's candles, roses and lavender from the centerpieces) and rendering them, as Fuentes put it, "like fragrant herbs in a broth of late life," so that Raul, in good spirits and feeling affectionate, gave her many tender kisses. . . .

It was all so pleasant, even for the moody Lydia, who had lately been thinking about retiring. They'd been spending more and more time together, taking walks in the park when the weather was good. They had even gone to see some movies together at the Spanish-language cinemas. They were hopeful about things. Raul had been looking into a pensioner's rental in a tranquil small town on the west coast of Puerto Rico near Mayagüez, and he still liked to lose himself in flower shop windows, in dreams of speculation—for would it not be lovely to pass one's last years in a place resplendent with flowers?

They'd long since abandoned the idea of returning to Cuba, because Castro had never fallen. What they had settled into instead were the small comforts of their decent, genteel, low-key life—*the kind of life that nobody really notices*—adapting themselves to the roles of a "nice old couple." Even Lydia's occasional aloofness had, given the mellowing of age, emerged as the kind of confidence and self-assuredness that people genuinely appreciated in their elders. The snobbery and pride of her earlier life, once rankling people, now struck others as a kind of elderly dignity, like a saving grace, a person coming closer to death, but doing so in a manner of unperturbed serenity.

That night the social club was a place of ageless grace and wonders. Even Mario, who'd never become a star after so many years of plugging away, happily lost himself in the delusions of the microphone, crooning as if everything were beginning all over again, the ambitions of his life realized. ... Mario and his musicians went back with each other to the heyday of the mambo nightclubs and dance halls. In previous professional incarnations they had played with quite a number of famous musicians, from Don Aziapau to the dapper Johnny Colón, but what mainly counted was their popularity with Lydia and Raul and many of the others gathered there that night, "workers" like Dr. Cruz, Manny the dentist, José the accountant, Daniel the UPS driver, Salvador the construction worker, Vincent the truck driver, Alfonso the bodega owner, Miguel the porter, Felipe the Cuban flying instructor, and their wives and girlfriends—Maria-Luisa the bank clerk, Helena the secretary at Columbia University, Miriam the accountant's assistant, Graciela the lingerie salesgirl, Juanita the manicurist, Irene the schoolteacher, and many others, all getting older but for the most part contented enough—what else could they do? They were of a generation that worked hard and then went out dancing a couple of nights a week, to all late hours. And although some of them had gotten old, age did not keep them off the dance floor or from enjoying the sheer benevolence and amicability of that event. ...

In this circumstance, Raul, tie loose, collar open, a toothpick between his teeth, a cigarette (always a cigarette, the room dense with smoke) in his yellow fingers, had by evening's end felt a measure of contentment himself. Smiling as the more energetic and longer-lasting couples took to the floor in the waning hours of that night, he leaned over to Lydia and mentioned that he wanted to make a stew for dinner the next evening, and that he wanted to watch *The African Queen* with Humphrey Bogart, to whom he thought he bore a resemblance, on the television (*"un gran actor"*—Lydia). Holding her close, his heart welling with joy, he had added, "And maybe we should get ourselves a secondhand car, so that we can visit the grandkids more often."

No fairy tales here, however, for in that same happy moment he experienced a certain throbbing within the aching joints of his arms, and earlier, while making a quick turn on the dance floor, he had gotten so light-headed that he suddenly saw a halo of light—flashes bursting around him. Shortly, the dizziness had subsided, however, and he thought he would have another drink. Then he and Lydia sat down again, watching the dance floor, an inexplicable emotion coming over him, a pure love, as it were, for the goings on and people there that night.

Later on, in the company of Fuentes and the others and with Lydia by his side, Raul walked out of that club and took a long look at the sprawl of gated storefronts, check-cashing joints, tenements and the holiday-like lights of buildings going on and on; and at the traffic, the few sad stars in the sky, reveling in it all as if some magnificent invisible kingdom had been suddenly revealed to him; then he beheld with great reverence this wonder of affection, crankiness, strength, and gentility that was his wife, Lydia, and he felt a nearly unbearable gratitude.

"You okay, Raul?" asked Fuentes, because Raul's eyes had started to tear over with affection.

"May God rain down glories on us all," Raul said. Then: "I love you all very much."

"Come on, let's get a taxi," someone said.

And as they waited, Lydia helped Raul button his coat.

"What a nice dance that was," Raul said to Lydia, as he stood in the bathroom in his pajamas, looking himself over.

"*Sí, mi amorcito.*"

And he had yawned and stretched and patted her on the bottom when she passed him in the hall on her way to the bathroom. It was about three in the morning and he was thinking that perhaps in the afternoon, after Mass, they might have some fun in bed, though, on the other hand, at his age, he would be just as happy to take a walk with her.

Back in the bedroom, as Lydia dallied in the bathroom, he prepared for his late night prayers, a habit of recent years.

The Flowers

It had been such a lovely night that if all life were like that, even given the crush of crowds, the cigarette smoke, the tiredness of drinking itself—he'd thrown back another shot of the "working man's vacation" as soon as they got in the door—he, inspired by the booze, would have wanted to live forever. So he began his ritual, getting on his knees beside the bed to pray. He tried to be unobtrusive about this act, saying his prayers to himself, for he knew it was something that Lydia, in her heart of hearts, found embarrassing; in those modern times that style of prayer seemed old-fashioned, even to her. So he always began after she left the room, as he did that night, making the sign of the cross, putting his hands together, and saying the Lord's Prayer ("*el padrenuestro*") to himself, in whispers. He would follow this with several other prayers, make a few personal requests involving others, and then he would rise and turn in. Lydia had often seen him in this quietly meditative state, a dumb, nearly transcendent grin in his expression that made him seem almost saintly, on the verge of rapture. (Or drunk.)

That night, however, he had a special experience. On his knees, he could have sworn that the room began to fill with the scent of flowers—as if out of a wildflower field in Cuba—and suddenly, with that extravagant scent, God was vibrant in the air he breathed, flowing through the very floor on which he knelt, in the very light about him. That waiter with the sore feet and aching hips, with the receding gray hair, closed his eyes and in that moment felt himself in intimate communion with the object of his meditations, his every thought and emotion enjoined in realizing the concept of *un Dios*. Indeed *He* seemed to be everywhere, even in Raul's own body, and that notion, as he prayed, made him feel ecstatic. *Somewhere, inside of himself, he went for a walk, on a beautiful spring day, along a road in the* campo *of his youth, delighted that as far as he could see, in the fields around him, there were row upon row of blossoms* . . . In the midst of his prayers, he became, as often happened, acutely aware of his own pulse, but instead of hearing his heart beat, of sensing his bodily rhythm, he heard a certain phrase being uttered, and that phrase was "*Soy Dios,*" or "I am God." And this grew louder and louder so that in a short time the gentle and tired waiter could hear nothing else.

With that he began to feel faint-headed again. And when he opened his eyes, he found himself enveloped by a halo of atoms, that exploding light; then he trembled and felt as if the inside of his body was shimmering, every cell giving off a faint blush of itself— in short, his soul separating from him; that for every single atom of his body there was a direction and that these *cell-souls* were shooting out from him in every direction of the universe, in all the infinite directions, that in that particular moment, he had become a radiance.

"The flowers," he cried.

When Lydia came back from the bathroom, she found him there, in their quaint tenement bedroom, in his final posture: kneeling by their bed, expression humble, hands folded in prayer.

At one point during the wake, Alicia brought her two American sons up to the coffin and, within earshot of Rico and her mother, the inconsolable Lydia, she said, "Always remember that your grandfather was Cuban."

The mystery of that comment, coming as it did from his dear upstate ex-hippie sister Alicia, surprised Rico, who had not thought Alicia particularly aware of her "Cubanness," and yet he had to admit that, with the room crammed mainly with Cubans and other Latinos of their father's acquaintance, so many of them grief stricken, he had felt a great surge of pride (among many other emotions). He would recall many of his neighborhood friends coming to pay their respects; handshakes, pats on the back. But in general, a great sadness descended upon him; part of the world, a curtain of identity, as it were, had been torn away.

As for Lydia? Comforted by friends and family she had been amazingly quiet throughout the ordeal. She thought about the funerals of Cuba, when a coterie of women dressed in black, with mantillas and shawls, would sit in stiff high-backed chairs all through the night in mourning, saying prayers. Then she, for the life of her, could not refrain from a certain image—how handsome and respectable and *immortal* Raul had seemed, sweet with cologne, in his white waiter's outfit, as he plunked down a set of glasses and a bottle of rum on her table at the lonely hearts' dance, when they first met those years ago. Several times she said to Mireya, sitting near her, "It was not very long ago, was it?"

That stillness in the morning, that sense that Raul should have been in the bed beside her, that stubborn desire to believe that he was still around. There was that maddening sensation of standing by their window and realizing she would never see him walking into their building again, or before the mirror clipping his pesky nostril hairs; or see him chatting with Mr. Brown, their mailman. . . .

A Few Dreams

What was that nice dream she had? In a heaven, she dreamed, Raul was taking a walk along the main street of Paradise. She supposed the way it looked depended upon your context in life: so maybe his Main Street was composed of buildings from Manhattan circa 1957, or from his town in Cuba circa 1935. Or you took a turn and the streets changed continually into whatever you wanted them to be, the main *placita* dropping out of the sky. On the corner, that nice bodega in Havana that he used to talk about where you could have a good meal for a few *pesetas,* and where there were troubadours always singing; next door, Freddie's Bodega from 122nd Street. Who knew? She liked to think about Raul looking dapper in a tan or light-blue suit, a carnation in his lapel, in the years of his best health, say when he was in his mid-thirties. And at his happiest, when he and she and the kids would go strolling along Broadway on Sundays, to visit friends like Mario, to go window shopping. But how old would the children be? Raul had loved them the most when they were little and could not see his flaws (or so he had thought), when they used to go fishing with him, jump into his arms, when she, with all her demands, always came off as the "heavy." On the other hand, as the kids got older he seemed to be getting closer to their son, Dr. Rico, and he had loved having grandchildren. . . .

Happily she imagined Raul in his own florist's shop, and she found herself standing outside the window looking in: there she could see an elderly couple buying an arrangement of roses

305

from him, Raul ever so happy, dressed in a *guayabera* and linen *pantalones*—of course a florist shop in Havana circa 1942! And the elderly couple were her long-dead mother and father, Antonio and Maria Colón. And in the dream, she was young again, a fine and shapely twenty-two-year-old, Dorothy Lamour in Cuban flesh, in a tight dress, stepping into the crush of lovely aromas; flowers everywhere—chrysanthemums, hibiscus, lilacs, white Easter lilies, roses—and Raul bowing before her and saying, "My love, look what has been given to me." And suddenly the flower shop filled with music and, with her dead mother and father standing off to the side, she and Raul embraced and began to dance. The song combined the melodies of "Unforgettable" and "Smile," but was performed in the tropical stylings of the Ernesto Lecuona Orchestra, and as they danced he said to her as he had many years before,

> *Lydia, I am to you, as a sparrow adoring the sky;*
> *Lydia, you are as the moon reflecting upon the water,*
> *which is my soul;*
> *Lydia, you are the queen of queens of beauty,*
> *the Empress of my love,*
> *and you preside over the splendidness*
> *of my feelings for you,*
> *like the morning sun on the most glorious day*
> *of the most beautiful and splendid season,*
> *which is love . . .*

And then there had been the first intimations of physical ardor, a heat rising through her limbs, as he pressed tightly against her, and she found herself falling into a bed of roses, smooth as excited human skin. . . .

It would have been glorious, wouldn't it? But in the middle of the night she sometimes awakened, and opened her eyes to the truth of the stillness in that room.

The
Empress Says
Farewell

For all her sadness, she sometimes laughed. And one of the things that made her laugh was what happened to her friend, a fellow cleaning lady, Daniela Rivera, when, miracle of miracles, after playing the lottery every week for ten years, she actually hit seven out of seven numbers and won five million dollars, a dream coming true, becoming the recipient of several hundred thousand dollars a year for the next twenty years. Lydia first read about it in the newspaper—CUSTODIAN CLEANS UP!—and then she saw Daniela on the Channel 7 News at Six, filmed leaving her cleaning job at 9 West 57th Street, where she was part of the night crew, a look of great bewilderment upon her face. Over the years Lydia had seen her here and there and she had always thought of Daniela as a poor woman whose luck in life had never been particularly good, as when she lost her husband when her children were small. She had always seemed demure, painfully shy, the kind of woman who would listen to Lydia and nod solicitously. But when their paths finally crossed some months after this event, on the subway, Daniela, with a new hairdo, a nice dress, and fancy shoes, having accepted Lydia's congratulations (and expressing her sadness at Raul's passing), had cheerfully announced, "I'm going to see one of my old employers, this very cheap couple I've worked for, to tell them to go to hell!"

Lydia had to admit that, as she remarked to Concha, "not having to worry about money has done wonders for Daniela's looks." Like so many other hardworking women, there had been a dowdiness about her. Not that she had been a beauty in the first place. She was a small, somewhat plump woman of advancing years, who rarely bought anything nice for herself. Now, she was making up for lost time. Her two sons were to have money for college. And she would move from the Bronx to a better apartment in Astoria, Queens, spend more time in the beauty salon, buy pretty scarves and shoes and glamorous wigs. Maybe take her sons and their families (for they were married) down to Disneyworld, which had formerly been too expensive for them.

And all this was good, thought Lydia. Daniela had a wondrous new confidence. The word *poor* had fallen away from her vocabulary. A miracle in itself. A different air about her— of having access to the bounties of this world, of luck—and therefore being blessed by the gods.

About a year after her good fortune, Daniela invited Lydia and Mireya over to her new two-bedroom apartment in Astoria: plastic-covered couches, of course, a grand color TV set (on continuously), and several large wall hangings, purchased on 34th Street, of Jesus and his disciples (Last Supper, Resurrection). And she had also acquired several prissy poodles, their hair wonderfully coiffed, wearing pink bell collars. For all that, Daniela, who knew the hardships of the cleaning woman's life, seemed very much herself, speaking tenderly of others, and saying to Lydia, Mireya, and her other friends, "Every night I pray to God that something this wonderful will happen to you."

She had hired a full-time maid, a young Guatemalan woman of uncertain immigrant status, who lived in a small room and whose duties were many, among them the cooking and serving of meals. This woman, being kept busy in the kitchen, had not made an appearance until everybody gathered about the table. . . . There were settings of splendid Macy's plateware, heavy beveled drinking glasses, several bottles of chianti in baskets, and a flowery centerpiece. Then there was the delicate porcelain bell from Hong Kong with faint blue carnations decorating its sides, by Daniela's right hand.

312

So thrilled was she at having a maid to serve her, Daniela took every opportunity to reach over and to give the bell a shake. And each time she gave an order: "More rice, Maria." "Please would you bring my friend here another glass of water." "I think the bread is too dry," and so forth.

The poor girl must have heard that bell ring several dozen times, even if everyone there had prompted Daniela not to ring it so often. Lydia, having assumed in her widowhood an even greater air of authority about life, said, in front of everybody at the table, "You're going to wear yourself out with that bell. After all, you don't want to be like some of the people you've worked for, do you?"

"She has a place to sleep, and food to eat, and I pay her, so why not?"

"*Oye vieja*, in Cuba we had many servants, and I never remember my father making them run around the way you do with that bell. *Chica*, you have to watch it, because if you don't, who knows what will be awaiting you in the next life." Then: "Imagine, having to clean up after people for an eternity." And she laughed, taking hold of her friend's wrist. "So *tranquilo, tranquilo*, okay?"

"Okay."

The evening passed pleasantly enough; dinner, an hour of television, a call to a taxi. Even the Guatemalan maid seemed to have enjoyed herself, for the ladies had been laughing all night. After she cleared the table and had done the dishes, she asked *la señora* for permission to retire, and excusing herself, she went off to her room to watch television with a broad smile on her face, winking at Lydia, whose speech she had overheard. On their way out, this chattering, exuberant group of ladies embraced and kissed their hostess. To make sure that she had not left her friend Daniela with any bad feelings, Lydia told her, "I am so happy for you."

For her part, Daniela had given each of her friends a box of Schrafft's chocolate, and this Lydia began to eat in the backseat of the taxi on the way home.

A View from Her Window

She hadn't intended to spy upon her neighbor across the way, but it just happened that at about four, on an overcast autumn afternoon, as she was making her way down the hall to throw some garbage into the incinerator, she passed by her dirty kitchen window (because of the security gate its outer glass hadn't been washed for years), and through the crisscrossed metal saw one of the young college girls who'd recently moved into the apartment on the other side of the courtyard. This young woman had a great head of shoulder-length red hair, and she spoke, as Lydia had overheard her on the sidewalk, a foreign language that was neither Spanish or English. There she was, stretched out naked on her bed with her legs spread wide and touching herself with supreme concentration; she had a shock of red pubic hair and long red fingernails, which she worked into herself, her pale white body squirming under her touch. Lydia gasped. It seemed fascinating and outrageous at the same time. Turning on her side the young woman's legs doubled up so that her knees almost touched her pink breasts and her bottom was like a plump and lascivious third eye watching Lydia, who nearly blushed because it had been a long time since she could remember experiencing those same kinds of physical sensations. Saying "*Dios mío*" under her breath, she made her way out into the hallway, jammed her bag of *basura* down the incinerator, and came back into her living room where she was watching a Spanish language television show, *Cristina*. Even as the elegant Cristina questioned a young teenager about how her mother's new middle-aged boyfriend had made a pass at her and taken her to bed—who would have thought years ago that such shows in Spanish would exist?—Lydia could not help but be drawn back into the kitchen, ostensibly to get a glass of water but in truth to see what that college student was up to. Now when she peeked across the courtyard, she saw the young woman in the throes of intense pleasure, for her legs were trembling, her hips and pelvis rising, her head whipping from side to side as she reached a climax.

As Lydia made herself a peanut butter sandwich and washed it down with a glass of beer, she trembled remembering what it was like to be so young, not to feel shame over the lushness of her own sexuality, to look to the future and not to the past.

The girl across the way went to Barnard, and whenever Lydia came home from work and saw her in front of the building she frowned and felt like scolding her. Didn't she have any common sense—or shame—or know that in a neighborhood like that, where everybody knew everybody else's business, she was inviting trouble? Every time the young woman passed the building, Lydia gave her a sour look—in the way the old duennas sometimes looked at her when she was young. But one afternoon when Lydia was coming back from the supermarket, her shopping cart heavy with groceries, the redhead offered to help her up the front steps of her stoop. Lydia was touched by this gesture and took the young woman aside, asking her, "Young lady, what is your name?" And when she answered "Elizabeth," Lydia tightened her grip on her wrist and proceeded to ask her a dozen questions. "Where are you from?" "What do you study?" And because the young woman answered respectfully and had looked into Lydia's eyes with some kind of admiration, she decided that she liked her despite the young woman's indiscretions. From that time on, they would sometimes stop to chat on the sidewalk, Lydia making her way into the solitude of her apartment, the young woman heading into the glories of her life.

It's Always a Man

One of those late afternoons, when Lydia stopped to talk with Elizabeth she learned that the young woman had dropped out of the university. She had been studying art and hoping to one day teach drawing to children, a modest enough goal. Suddenly she was waiting tables, and her facial expression, of grand energy and focus, was replaced by one of resignation. (Lydia knew that look from her days in the sewing factory.) A certain man had been responsible for that, Lydia determined, a fellow who had come to live with Elizabeth from Europe. She sometimes spied them in bed together late at night, when Lydia could not sleep and had nothing better to do. Or to put it another way, sometimes when she could not sleep, when the empty space in bed beside her had expanded to the size of a meadow in Cuba, or if you like, in Central Park—for what could she remember of Cuba now after so many years in this country?—Lydia would get up and peek out across the courtyard into the woman's window. It happened that one night at two in the morning she saw them making love, a bedside lamp illuminating their contorted, writhing bodies. She was sometimes so lonely that she would stay up and look and look, then, feeling disturbed, pass the night twisting about in the sheets, sighing and remembering the good days when Raul was around. . . .

A dream of being touched again, his presence everywhere, the sad-eyed Raul vying with the handsome Raul of her hope and dreams. (Dios, please let me know that there is something, she pleaded.)

He was a tall thin man with a fox-shaped face, clear gray-blue eyes like a cat's, and a delicately formed mouth, a goatee, thick bangs hanging over his brow and ears. He wore dark clothing and leather *pantalones*, a black leather jacket stuck through with countless safety pins, and upon his hand he sported a German Luftwaffe ring (a skull and bones against a black field). He would be handsome, Lydia thought, if his beautiful eyes weren't so cold

316

and if he smiled more, instead of scowling at the world, which was what he seemed to be doing every time she saw him on the street (*"Ay, no me gusta,"* Lydia said to her friend Mireya). She thought him ridiculous. Rico, coming to visit Lydia, in his old New York manner had said, "Hey," when he happened to cross paths with this man, but the fellow, instead of greeting him, laughed in a mocking way. *"Un come-mierda"* was Lydia's judgment, hearing Rico's mention of this.

The man appeared to be about thirty-five or so, a few years younger than when Raul had suffered his first attack . . . her poor dear Raul. . . . Was it fair that so many hardworking people were afflicted with bad health, while this man seemed to float above it all?

Talking on the sidewalk with Elizabeth, holding her to the spot, she had learned that the man was some kind of German nobleman, that he had come from an old and distinguished family in Bavaria, and that he had been raised in a sixteenth-century castle. "Oh yes, he has his ways," the girl told Lydia, "but he's actually quite an interesting and nice man." Then: "We met five years ago in Budapest—you know, in Hungary?"

He sometimes left the building with a briefcase—who knows what was in it, but he would seem extremely careful as he made his way along the street. Drugs? Money? Diamonds? He sometimes got his coffee at a new Cuban place around the corner, the customers regarding him with tremendous suspicion. He bought beers and cigarettes at the corner bodega and was always running out without collecting his small change. The younger kids of the street, it should be added, seemed to like him, for he treated them well, doling out handfuls of coins and dollar bills to them, which some of the neighbors noticed, approvingly.

Lydia, coming home from jobs, avoided his gaze.

One night at three in the morning Lydia heard the young woman screaming "No!" and she stuck her head out the win-

317

dow and shouted, "Stop that or I will call the police, do you hear me, the police." With that she heard his answer, "No problem, no problem. Okay, okay." And the window was shut and she heard slapping and crying noises, but then everything calmed down and she listened to the *Nostalgia* radio show on the A.M. dial. The next day she saw the young woman sitting on her couch weeping, and Lydia leaned out the window and called out for her to come over for coffee . . .

. . . *and to lay her head on her lap, the way she sometimes wanted, in her older age, to lay her head upon the lap of her long-dead mother, to feel Raul beside her . . .*

(On the other hand, she sometimes enjoyed the luxury of not having to worry about and take care of another, no more fastidias.*)*

When Elizabeth came over to the apartment, Lydia told her, "Take it from an old lady who only wants what's good for you. Be very careful about what you do with your life."

To be sure, he had involvements with a certain criminal element; a black man, known as Kingpin, from 108th Street once pulled up to the curb in front of the apartment in his Cadillac, and his burly driver rang the redhead's bell. Lydia happened to be in front of the building chatting with the superintendent, Martinez, when the driver came over to them.

"You wouldn't happen to have seen a German fellow, named Max, who lives with a redhead in that building, would you?"

"No, not lately," was their answer.

Funny thing was this: One afternoon while Martinez was sweeping the hallway of the building across the way, he smelled a gas leak, and traced it to the young woman's door. He'd rapped softly, and when there was no answer, he banged with more strength; when nobody answered, he put a handkerchief to his mouth and opened the door from his loop of master keys. When he got inside he could barely move, the smell of gas was so dense, and he immediately tried to air out the apartment, but found one, two, then three windows sealed with duct tape. He began to shatter the glass; in the kitchen he found the beautiful redhead unconscious on the floor and the German duke slumped at the kitchen table, with a box of kitchen matches before him. So they were saved—*life was luck, wasn't it?* Martinez had happened by at just the right moment to turn off the gas, call the ambulance and the cops, and to awaken the beautiful redheaded girl (as far as he was concerned the man could die).

Lydia had been talking on the telephone with Rico, making an arrangement for a Sunday dinner, when she first became aware of the commotion on the street, the police and ambulance sirens punctuated by the El train's song; soon enough she was among the crowd of passersby, the curiously disposed watching as the redhead and the German were carried out.

The event caught Lydia on a day when, earlier, while walking in Riverside Park, she had been delighted by a profusion of wild daisies in a field, and the sight of a sparrow foraging for food, as she sat on a bench, seemed gloriously sad and wonderful at the same time. Then she had watched the sun drifting sanguinely through some clouds over the river, and for a moment, Lydia had lifted outside of herself; for a time she had talked to a five-year-old girl, giving her a quarter to buy a candy ("In Cuba we would call this a *peseta*"), and then, as she watched the girl running to play with friends, Lydia began to feel irretrievably old. By the time she had gotten home she was being followed by the ghost of her own youth, a melancholy coming over her—*for it rankled her that she would never be young or foolishly in love again.*

The Accident
Oddly, her concern over the young girl's condition (for she did like her) and relief to hear that she would be all right gave

319

Lydia a reason to celebrate. After the excitement had died down, when all the speculations and tales of stupid youth dispensed with, Lydia had decided to buy a few quarts of beer at the bodega—"*Oye,* Miguel!"

Afterwards she was climbing the stairs of her building for the fifty thousandth time of her life when she took a bad step on the second-floor landing, and fell backwards, breaking a hip; the pain nearly unbearable, Lydia passed out.

The Emergency Ward on 113th Street

That late afternoon Lydia was taken by ambulance to the emergency ward, the very ward where Elizabeth and her German were resting. Half awake on a narrow cot in the emergency ward hall, she had cried out for water several times, but the young interns seemed hardly concerned about her condition. Finally one of the young and busy doctors had called to an aide, "Get the lady something to goddamn drink!" and when the aide didn't come, he threw aside a clipboard and got her the water himself, barely acknowledging Lydia when she said, "You're a handsome man, did you know that?" All the doctors there seemed way too important for the work they had to do, or too busy for the likes of most of the poor people in that place: huffing and puffing and looking at their watches, rushing by her, they hardly noticed when, suddenly feeling all alone in the world, she had begun to cry; a junkie, of all people, there to collect some methadone, was the only person to offer a moment's kindness—"You all right?"

She slept that night, drowsy with drugs, in a corridor on a cot. Although someone had taken her purse, and she awakened to find that she had urinated all over herself, what disturbed her most was the impersonality and strangeness of it all. She could not see too clearly, although every so often she heard a voice, someone telling her, "Don't be worried, you'll be all right." And: "It's me." But she could not remember or make out just who that might be. Instead she drifted in and out of dreams. She had spent a very nice interlude dancing once again with a handsome farmhand from her town in Cuba during a carnival party: his name was Manuel Gomez, and just like that she was out on the floor of the Gallego Society, lifting her skirt during the conga, shoulders jostling, hips swaying, the handsome and virile men with their thick and wavy hair and their cleft chins and coal dark eyes, watching her with nothing less than pure unadulterated lust. . . .

Then she heard that voice again, whispering, "Lydia, it's me . . . it's me," and another voice, rambling on about medical charts and finding her a room in the morning. Even if she knew that things weren't right—what were those dreary zombies, half of them sick junkies—doing around her? And that woman rocking in a corner, weeping and crying out, "I am in hell!" Better to shut one's eyes, and to withdraw into the self: for when she did so Lydia could feel her mother's soft hands, washing her hair in the basin of the tiled courtyard in their house with its smell of lavender, the young princess, Lydia Colón, beside herself with joy over her mother's attentions. . . . It was wonderful being a child again, to see herself, in a wide sun hat and yellow dress, aged seven years, standing before the doorway, her sisters by her side, with a bouquet of flowers in hand, as they waited to make their way to church in Cuba. . . .

Her Loveliest Dream

That was the night she had the loveliest dream, about finding herself walking along a road in ancient Judea. She was dressed in a coarse tunic and sandals, a cord wrapped around her waist, and carrying an amphora. Her muscles ached, her hands were calloused, for it was the time of the Romans and she was a slave.

A centurion in a plumed helmet drinking from a well, a chariot drawn by four horses, an image of the sun-god Apollo painted on its side, the driver whipping his horses . . . she felt confounded: Suddenly she heard someone laughing—it was the centurion, who told her: "Where have you been? Pilate has been waiting for his wine."

"But where do I go?" she asked.

"To Jerusalem." And he pointed to a distant compound with massive high walls on the outskirts of a town. . . .

It took her a long time to walk to the villa, which stood at a point that *seemed close but grew farther away the more she walked.* Finally coming to a villa gate, she saw a procession: a half-dozen slaves were carrying a litter, its occupants a man with a languid expression and cruel eyes, Pilate, and a woman in a diaphanous gown, covered in jewels, his wife, Procula.

Hurrying into the palace, she made her way into an inner courtyard, bougainvillea falling in great clusters over the surrounding rooftops and walls. Hearing voices, she saw two female servants hurrying about an upper lodge. Her sisters! She called out to them and they fell into each other's arms at the foot of a stairway.

When the dawn came, crowing cocks roused the slaves from their beds: beyond a high-ceilinged room of cool marble walls where the Romans took the waters, with mosaics of Neptune and Aquarius set into the floors, there was a second room opening out to a backyard—from its windows she could see the temple of the city of Jerusalem. . . . Someone shouted an order, and with that, a contingent of slave girls carrying jugs of wine converged from all directions on Pilate's private quarters.

When she passed close to the governor she could not help staring at him, for he had removed his toga and was stretched out naked on the bed: his body was hairy, well muscled, and he was exhibiting himself with a sly smile. She managed to avert her eyes, but did notice that despite the smugness of his expression, Pilate had a terrible melancholy about him; up and down his arms were the thick scars of self-inflicted wounds. The slave girls whispered about how he jumped into the sea of Galilee and drowned; that when his body washed up on shore a holy man brought him back from the dead.

"Why would he want to die?"

"Because even though he is the most powerful man in Judea, he is miserable and unhappy . . ."

". . . he has orgies every night because he is covetous of the flesh and cannot have enough . . ."

". . . he gorges on food . . . and paces in his chambers because he is terrified at the prospect of death . . ."

". . . so terrified that he wants to get it over with, because he suffers with it every waking day . . ."

Then someone else said: "Be careful with him. If he takes you to bed it will be the end of you. For after making love all night to a woman he then strangles her in the morning . . ."

"Yes, his nickname is Pilate the Cruel."

At that moment, Pilate called over to her: "You there! The beautiful one. Come over here. Now!"

But she hurried out and fled the palace.

Walking along a stony road, in a destitute area of Judea, she came across a crowd and the crowd was gathered around a man. The man was Jesus, unmistakably so; people were kneeling before him and trembling and weeping. He was addressing them in a gentle voice, and she had to move closer so she could hear his words: "This life is nothing more than a veil of tears," he said. "Blessed be the suffering for they will be welcomed to paradise at the end of this world." And: "For those who are evil, their moment of death will be terrifying. And those who covet the properties of this world will suffer the greatest loss of all. They will die in the torture of solitude."

His manner and tone changing, he began to kiss the children who were gathered there, to lay hands upon the ill. One by one the people moved toward him, to receive his blessing, and as she moved closer he told her: "Follow me."

That's when she saw, among the crowd, her beloved husband back from the dead.

Kissing his feet, she said, "My God, Raul, I'm so happy."

Both young again, they wept and kissed until they heard the Master's voice, calling.

Wherever He walked, dark and foreboding skies departed; tombs, in burial places, burst open and the dead, in tattered gowns, came stumbling out to the world. Lepers and the crippled fell upon them, begging for a release from their sufferings.

Holding hands in the spring's morning light, and in the freshness of a westerly breeze, Lydia and Raul began lifting, ever so slowly at first, off the ground, and up and up toward the beautiful sun.

On to eternal happiness . . .

The Presence

Suddenly she was back in the hospital. . . . For all the dreariness of that ward, that Lysol smell, the smell of hospital food and medicines, there loomed near her a benevolent presence. Occasionally it would reach over and touch her forehead and brush back her hair, dabbing her face ever so tenderly. And sometimes the presence would ask, "Are you okay?" Or, "*¿Quieres agua?*" Or: "Do you want me to get you something?"

For a long time this presence was a great mystery to her, even as she slipped in and out of her lovely dreams. Sometime in the early morning she began to look around her and saw that sitting not three feet from her, in a shiny metal hospital chair, was a man of soft and genteel disposition. A smile suddenly broke through his mask of concern, proffering, in that instant, a great wave of love, which she found instantly invigorating—*for even the Empress needed to be loved*—and she had cried out, as his kindly features came into focus:

"Rico?"

"Yes, *mamá*, I am here with you."

The Golden Light

In the days of her recovery it startled her to think that, at sixty-four, she was now older than her own father, *Don* Antonio, when he had passed away, and yet some part of her forever remained the trembling young woman he'd caught that morning, long ago, after a night of debauchery. She could hardly remember his face, just the exaggerated lines of anger in a flurry around his eyes and brow. She could not remember the timbre of his voice, and although there remained with her a general impression of his physicality, try as she might she could not envision him entirely. Old photographs helped, but gone were the times when she could look over her shoulder and imagine him standing there, with his air of authority, his strictness, his inability to be affectionate, ever disapproving. Her mother's face remained with her, however: sometimes when she was on the verge of sleep she would imagine her in the room, leaning over the bed. And all Lydia wanted to do was to reach out and touch her mother's cheek, to brush aside a lock of her hair, to pull her close and feel that breath of eternal life upon her, to look once again into her mother's kindly face, and those eyes burning with tenderness and compassion.

The face that she would never see again.
"*Ay, mamá.*"

Raul remained a vivid apparition. She found herself taking up certain of his habits, a way of keeping him around, and in so doing she, a sinner at her heart, found a measure of tranquility. In his honor she had erected something of a monument to him, a small glass cabinet in which she kept his picture, a few personal effects—a watch, a scapular, a religious medal, a comb, his union card—along with his corny statue of the Holy Mother and a bronze crucifix.

Church began to hold out a greater appeal to her. The sight of an angel blowing a golden trumpet, as one saw at the Church of the Ascension, with its suggestion that the King would come and bestow benefits and plenty on his believers, was an idea that she relished. Suddenly she found herself feeling the presence of a spirit-companion to help guide her through those days. One day while examining herself in her bedroom mirror, a mirror like all the thousands of mirrors she had cleaned and peered into, she noticed, ever so briefly, about her skin something of a radiance: let us call it a golden light, and it was this light, unseen by others but known to herself that accompanied Lydia, as she made her way through the rooms of her apartment and along Broadway, aided by a cane.

Mr. Osprey's Daydream

Mr. Osprey was, of course, informed of Lydia's accident. He responded with flowers and, although he did not visit her at the apartment (well-intentioned as he could be, he had no desire to venture so far uptown), he did call to see how she was feeling, and found himself reassured by the fact that she seemed always to have company: her friends Mireya or Concha and her son, Rico.

On a rainy Tuesday, a few months after Lydia had been discharged from the hospital, Osprey had come back from seeing his financial adviser, a statement indicating his net worth in hand. Including real estate holdings, stocks and bonds, trust funds, art, and cash, it came to approximately seven and a half million dollars. He had asked for this information in the context of making a will and also to gauge his life's progress: at twenty-one he had been given half a million dollars by his father, and over the years, despite living well and spending as he pleased, putting his children through college, setting them up with trust funds, and donating to charity, he had built his fortune instead of depleting it, as opposed to certain friends he had known in college. As he was approaching his late sixties, he planned to retire and spend the rest of his life traveling.

He was not lonely, even if he seemed so. It happened that over the years he'd had an on-and-off love affair—which began before his wife passed away—with an Englishwoman, someone he'd met through his travels. Every several months or so he would fly over to London and they would spend the weekend in a quiet hotel in South Kensington, take in a play, and then return to their normal lives. And yet when Mimsy had passed on, instead of running away with this lady, Mr. Osprey had found himself in a reflective and retiring frame of mind, keeping a careful distance, for he was now officially a wealthy widower. Discovering, in his wife's absence, just how much he had loved her, he maintained a strong loyalty to her memory and withdrew into himself. He had the occasional spirited, physically satisfactory liaison, but in general he found himself, as the days went by, most simply content with the more cerebral pursuits of his life—books and music and art.

A great joy of his recent years had been a trip he made to a resort in Mexico, where ensconced in a villa by the sea, he reread the Spanish language novels of his youth, even some newer works by the more prominent South American novelists, a felicitous two-week retreat into the culture he had loved very much from the time he had been a young man.

Back in New York, as a philanthropist, he devoted himself to cultural institutions that promoted the interchange between North American and Latin cultures, finding himself on a half-dozen boards and committees, becoming one of those WASPy types looking stiff in a tuxedo at a fund-raiser for a Spanish Harlem repertory theater, with champagne glass in hand, speaking fluent Spanish, nodding to the music—the kind of man that, given his reserved manner, one would never think was enamored of those things that seemed his opposite.

When by himself in his Park Avenue apartment, he did take a certain pleasure in his furnishings and objets d'art: his cabinet of British lead soldiers, which he sometimes considered frivolous, although they somehow helped him remember what it was like to be young again—these he took out and put on display on the mantle at Christmas, deriving enormous pleasure in making his living room a festive place, especially if his grandchildren were around. He got into the habit of leaning against the hall doorway and taking in the proceedings as if he would never see his family again, savoring each and every moment. . . .

Not religious, he sometimes felt depressed by the fact that sooner or later he would leave all of *that* behind. An unrealized intellectual with a fondness for the classical texts of his prep school and university, he enjoyed reading over Plutarch's *Parallel Lives*, finding something shockingly moving about the reduction of even the most spectacular (or foolish) lives to brief summations. He would have a drink—the pleasant and soothing effect of the alcohol on his brain pushing further away the prospect of his own eventual demise.

As he had gotten older, the *Satyricon*, by Petronius, in which Trimalchio the wealthy Roman stages his own funeral supper so that he can bask in the tributes and mourning produced by his death, made more and more sense to him: to take in what people really thought of you, to hear them singing your praises, to experience their love no matter how fleetingly was what counted, Osprey thought, with sadness.

Lydia

Even as world-weariness came over him, certain people, like Lydia, impressed him more and more. Her matter-of-fact approach to life had always amazed him. Sometimes she may have overreached by trying to be like the women of the upper class—why on earth would she want that?—but she had a very self-confident, no-nonsense manner that he truly appreciated: as in the tremendous strength she showed when her husband had passed away.

When Lydia called and left a message in a trembling voice that she would not be able to come in to clean that next Tuesday, Osprey's reaction had been to call back to offer help in any way possible. (He got only a busy signal.) He had gone to the wake and funeral, had sent flowers, and had handed Rico an envelope containing five hundred dollars as "a little something to help." "*Lo siento*," he had told her, holding her small hands between his. Aside from an understandable quietness of demeanor, sadness if you like, she hardly mentioned Raul's death afterwards, except when she thanked Mr. Osprey for the gifts he had sent to the family.

Then, with her accident, he did not see Lydia for three months, although they did speak every few weeks, Lydia calling from home to report that she was getting better, that the doctors at the clinic said she would be able to get back on her feet again soon. "Really, Lydia," Osprey told her, "you shouldn't feel that you have to rush back or be worried about your job."

But no matter how often he reassured her, Osprey had the impression that Lydia was pushing to come back, perhaps to her detriment, that she was worried about money, and this had gotten him to think about what he could do for her.

Having met with his attorney to draft a will, leaving most of what he had to his children and a few charities, he made a point of including Lydia. But the more he thought about it, given that he was in good health and was probably going to live for some time to come, the more Mr. Osprey thought it would be nice to do something for Lydia now.

And so that rainy Tuesday, having weighed this decision, Osprey called his banker and advised him that he was writing a check for the sum of ten thousand dollars to a certain Lydia España, that it was his intention to do so again in a year's time (to protect her from tax liabilities)—the sum of twenty thousand dollars somehow feeling right to him. Sitting at his desk before his open checkbook, he had a kind of daydream: he pictured Lydia in her humble apartment, gasping with surprise and delight, reading his note and examining the check over and over again, some measure of relief and (of course) gratitude coming over her. He felt gleeful because above all he considered it money well spent. What was ten thousand dollars to him, anyway—a year of business lunches, for which he was never really thanked?

Wealth

Indeed, the day that check arrived Lydia gasped, sat down, drank a beer, and instantly called Mr. Osprey, who was not at home. She swore to herself that the next time they met she would kiss the knuckles of his hands. She thought to call her very best friends to share the good news, but even then she realized that they would take her bit of good fortune as bragging, that she would have to play this down. (And in any case, never believing anything until she saw it, what if the check didn't clear?) Then she thought about what she might do with the money. Oddly, there was little she wanted. Travel was something she had once daydreamed about, and a part of her would love to have gone to Europe, to places like France and Spain, which Mireya had always talked about (once upon a time Mireya had led a few classes over there on summer tours, and nearly fell in love), but over the years Lydia had developed an aversion to flying, as it seemed that jet planes were being blown to bits every other day. Besides, she was feeling too old to go as a tourist except on a little-old-lady tour, and her vanity would not allow that. And what was there in Europe that she couldn't find in New York, or, for that matter, see in the movies?

(On the other hand, if Raul were still around she would have said, "Let's go to Puerto Rico to see if we can find that house to rent by the sea." And she would have bought him a pair of fancy two-tone shoes, fitted with those wedges that make you taller and are comfortable for the feet, and maybe a brand new easy chair and new cushions, so that he could relax all the more watching television.)

As for other amenities? Years of perseverance and fruitful, discreet scavenging had yielded her an elegant wardrobe. She had an inexpensive apartment, her television, her telephones, a phonograph console, pretty furniture, a wall full of family photographs, a mouthful of healthy teeth, her own good health, and, most of all, the love of her children, even if it did not always come so easily.

Besides, in the last five years before his passing, Raul had been relieved of his extrafamilial responsibilities and, living humbly, they had managed to put away six thousand seven hundred dollars. And his restaurant workers union not only paid for his funeral, but she received a thousand dollars from a widows' fund and the promise of a modest pension. And that came with the monthly Social Security! And her own kids, particularly the well-off Rico, promised to take care of her if she needed help. But ten thousand dollars? She felt absolutely rich.

What would she do with it?

By and by she made her own kind of decision. She gave two hundred dollars to both Mireya and Concha and a thousand dollars to the local church so that they could put up a commemorative plaque in Raul's name—in fact, it would be bolted to the pew where he liked to sit, toward the back of the church, near a statue of St. John the Baptist. And she bought herself a microwave oven, at a discount store on 14th Street, and a subscription to the *Readers Digest* magazine.

As for the rest of this godsend from Mr. Osprey, she put it into a separate money market account, promising herself never to touch it, to treat this money as if it never existed. For she wanted to have something to pass on to her children when she died, some reminder that through hard work, loyalty, and caprice, she had come to something after all.

A Farewell

A few years passed, and finally the day came when she no longer felt like making the trips downtown, not even to Osprey's. Her fractured hip had set in a way that caused her to walk with a slight arthritic limp; and on top of everything else, the doctors had begun to detect the beginning of something bad with her bones— *from all those years of bending and scrubbing and mopping*—and it was getting harder for her to get around. . . . But she kept going to Osprey's, even if her work was not what it once used to be;

even though she was doing her best to keep his place in order, dust gathered under the furniture, mold in the bathroom and kitchen.

Noticing this, Osprey never said a word. The sight of her coming to work with a cane had almost been too much for him to bear, and her own son argued with her repeatedly about taking it easy, but she persisted because of a vaguely penitential notion that to stop working would have been a sign of indolence or a resignation to aging. (Who wanted to be like those ladies in the rest home at 106th Street?) But over time, never able to abandon the cane, more and more mornings came when she really did not feel like going to work, when the prospect of the jostling subways and the bitter cold made her feel fatigued before even stepping out of her apartment building.

Still, when it came to informing this most benevolent of her employers, she had almost felt as if Mr. Osprey would regard her departure as a kind of betrayal. . . . She had her hair cut by one of the Cortez sisters and wore an ankle-length blue dress of a flowery pattern with a white leather belt for the occasion. Over on the East Side, that neighborhood with the beautiful islands of tulips in the spring, she made her way to his apartment and told Mr. Osprey of her decision.

"I'm not what I used to be," she said, and Osprey had laughed and gently told her, "If you say so, Lydia, but I think you have the constitution of a twenty-year-old."

That day there were many things she would like to have said to Mr. Osprey. About all her fantasies and how she had sometimes coveted the apparent ease of his life, but especially that, while vacuuming his Baghdad carpets, bored in the middle of the day, she dreamed he had fallen in love with her, as in those soap operas with which she so often amused herself, and that, if not for different circumstances or destiny, they might have, in some other life, been together. . . .

They drank a coffee in the kitchen, and she as usual thanked him for his kindness to the family. Beyond that there was not much else to be said.

Mr. Osprey, living with his own private emotions, wanted the parting to be a pleasant but brief affair. Several times he told Lydia, "You know, we're going to have to speak to each other at least once a week. I mean, I expect my telephone to ring and to hear your voice. *¿Me entiendes?*"

"Oh yes. And you must call me to let me know how everybody is doing."

And he smiled: "It's a deal."

Later, by the door, they hugged and he waved to her as she made her way to the fancy cherrywood elevator and stepped inside.

"Come and visit," he called after her. And: "If you need anything please call."

And Lydia had answered: "I will." Then: "*Y gracias por todo.*"

On the way home she had another daydream: that somewhere along Madison Avenue she would look out the bus window and, as if watching one of those enchanting television programs at two in the afternoon, see herself as a young woman of years ago, in a smart but respectable blue dress with black cinch belt, white cloth buttons, and pleated white polka-dotted skirt, and white low-heeled shoes, as she made her way toward a certain majestic building over on Park for the first time, the address written carefully out on a piece of brown paper bag. The young woman would have a good-hearted husband, a waiter, of strong work ethic and weakened heart, and two young children waiting for her to come home, the weight of so many responsibilities, worries, and doubts that asked, "How did this happen to me?" being dissipated, if only temporarily, by the onslaught of familial love. . . . How it all seemed difficult *and wonderful at the same time, Lydia found herself thinking. And with that she thought she might embarrass herself on the crowded bus—like the other cleaning ladies and, indeed, women of all kinds of professions she had seen as they, in the midafternoon, had suddenly looked off out the bus window, their faces in an agony of tender remembrances; that is to say, lost in some kind of sweet recollection of faded youth: the first time the kid saw the snow, or the beatific expression of a new baby, those fleeting moments of carnal pleasure, taken here and there on rainy Sunday afternoons; the boss in the factory having bought you a bottle of Coca-Cola when you were looking low, or that fellow who lost one of his fingers in a cloth-cutting machine bringing you those pasteles from the bodega; the Staten Island ferry circa 1954; a picnic with a group of dear friends who'd just arrived and could barely speak a word of English, in Central Park, memories sprouting like flowers in one of its meadows (Raul!), life itself as dense as the world, and yourself, in the thick of it, an insignificant dot, if you like, or as magnificent as a sunset—all depending, of course, on your mood. She tried to divert herself by reading one of bus cards, an advertisement for a hair electrolysis treatment, and the one next to that for Bufferin. And there was the amusement of reading the faces around her: some middle-class ladies looking huffy after having shopped, a fat fellow picking at a tin of cookies, a young beauty in riding togs on her way to a riding academy, a Jamaican nanny with a little girl, her face red with lollipop, and then, getting on somewhere around 86th Street, a young cleaning woman, a beautiful* chica, no more than twenty-two or twenty-three years old, her bag with a change of clothes and a pair of shoes beside her. This young lady sat across from Lydia and, looking over at the older cleaning woman, smiled, and left Lydia, in those moments, much moved by the simple kindness of that transcendent gesture.*

A
Postscript

A young lady suffering from loneliness was recounting her travails with men when Rico found himself drifting, unintentionally, into a remembrance of a certain afternoon when they had come across the actor James Mason. Rico was about ten years old, Alicia, twelve and they had gone downtown with Lydia, window-shopping (and to see how the rich people lived), their route taking them along the park. At 55th Street they had come upon the St. Regis Hotel, where, under the canopy, a man who strongly resembled the aforementioned actor stood waiting. That is, a handsome dark-featured man in a blue serge suit, who possessed certain deeply charismatic qualities, waiting for his limousine. The moment Lydia recognized him, or thought she'd recognized him, she ordered them to stop in their tracks; there he was, James Mason, a knightly figure, removing from his breast pocket a gold case from which he slipped a cigarette. This he lit, taking long drags. Then, as he looked at his watch, Lydia had said, "*Miren*, it's that famous actor! *¡Qué guapo!* How handsome!" and in that moment there was something ravenous in her expression—what, Rico could not tell then— perhaps a kind of *lust* or *envy*. . . . And when the man happened to glance their way, they were huddled against a wall, and she had said, "He is looking at us!"

Her dark eyes dilating with excitement, the same way they used to get at dinners when she'd talk about the time she was walking with her matronly aunt in Havana, back when, and encountered the actor Errol Flynn in a bar, and he, dressed in white from head to toe, was so good-looking that her conservative and religious and virginal aunt had fainted dead away. Lydia may as well have encountered Jesus, for she always

339

blushed in the telling, and that expression in her eyes, that glint of *erotic glamour*—what else could he call it?—had always confused him, as if talking about such an experience was in itself a way of making love. There was something so surrendering about her when she mentioned that kind of event, of seeing "the man who was Robin Hood," and for that matter, whenever she talked about the old Cuba, *her Cuba,* which was as much of a fantasy as the land of Oz, as far as the children were concerned.

Nodding sympathetically as the patient was saying, "He must have told me that he loved me a thousand times," Rico could not help but think about his mother and Errol Flynn and then James Mason, and his image of her, as witnessed or intuited somewhere, along with the rushing lights of the elevated train, and the slight trembling of the building. He had a memory of watching from some concealed distance, his mother, Lydia España, the Cuban cleaning lady, resting in bed in the late shadow-filled afternoon, an ecstatic expression on her face, like one of those saints, Teresa de Avila.

. . . And so she had been staring at the man she thought might be James Mason. . . .

What else was there? Working up the nerve, Lydia had decided to stride past him by the hotel entrance, pretending, along the way, to have no great interest in the movie actor. And although she seemed more preoccupied by the serrations of a rubber mat laid out by his feet and his shiny patent leather shoes (was he on this way to a ball?) her hands trembled: with a chivalrous sheen to his hair and with a winsome elegance of form, he seemed, indeed, almost a supernatural being.

For his part, Mason, his head perhaps filled with the lines of some important new Hollywood script, could not have comprehended the myriad fantasies that she amused herself with in that moment: that they would stop and chat—"You're not the first actor I've ever met," she would tell him. That she would just happen to overhear him saying that he needed someone to help look after him and that she would stop and offer her services; or that, in this fantasy, she was seventeen again and beautiful and that he would feel an instantaneous passion for her, inviting her to ride along with him in his limousine and they would fly off to his film location or to Paris, that he, with his dark good looks, would tremble while making love.

But just as she passed by him, luxuriating in his allure, the limousine had pulled up to the curb, and in a moment Mr. Mason, without as much as intimating that she was in the range of his vision, strode toward the vehicle, his driver, in white gloves, holding open the door; and just then, somehow, because he hadn't acknowledged her, as if she didn't exist—and in front of her children—she had actually felt offended, but just as Mr. Mason rolled down his window to give the doorman something, he had glanced over at Lydia, faintly smiling.

Then he drove off, dabbing a handkerchief to his brow, and their ordinary lives continued.

"Did you see that, the way he looked at me?" she asked Rico and Alicia. "*Ay,* but he knew that I was someone, all the best people do!" Then, because Rico and Alicia, instead of being excited for her, were looking so solemn, she had said: "Children, be happy and be proud, it's not every day that you get to see a movie star!"

What else did he remember? Either that night, or on a previous night a month or year later, after a bus ride in which Lydia had spoken to several passengers about the famous man she had once seen, they had gotten home to find poor Raul sitting by the kitchen table teary-eyed; and when one of them asked, "What's wrong?" he could not restrain himself from saying, "All this—and all of you!"

Wouldn't it have been nice, Rico used to think, even when his patients were relating certain intimacies to him, had someone like James Mason materialized at the door, waving his beautifully manicured hands about the room and changing everything; getting rid of the heartaches, the concerns about health, the bills, and the anxieties, and spreading before them the promise of a wondrous future, that piece of Heaven, like the ones they saw in the pretty magazines and television commercials; to let them forget themselves in the diversions of earthly pleasures. . . .

Then, just like that, Dr. Rico was back in his office with his lovely loveworn patient, preparing to dispense what he hoped would be good advice.